I0612966

Gothic
Revival

CARSON BUCKINGHAM

Sirens Call Publications

Gothic Revival

Copyright © 2014 Carson Buckingham
Licensed to and Distributed by Sirens Call Publications [2014]
www.sirenscallpublications.com

Print Edition; First Edition

All rights reserved

Edited by Gloria Bobrowicz

Cover Artwork © Bob Freeman

Wraparound Cover Design © Sirens Call Publications

All characters and events appearing in this work are fictitious. Any resemblance to real persons, living or dead, is purely coincidental.

ISBN-13: 978-0692219416 (Sirens Call Publications)
ISBN-10: 0692219412

Dedication

This book is dedicated to the two most important people in my life:

My wonderful husband, Phil St. James, for many reasons, one being that he gets the jokes.

My father, Earle William Munson. You were the best, kindest, most loving parent in the world, and I shall miss you until the day I die.

Gothic
Revival

Acknowledgments

I owe a big debt of gratitude to the following folks:

Julianne Snow, Nina D'Arcangela, Gloria Bobrowicz (Editor), and the gang over at Sirens Call Publications. Thanks for believing in me enough to take a flyer on this novel. You are a great group to deal with, learn from, and grow with. I am most indebted to you all.

Jonathan Maberry for taking the time from his demanding schedule to answer this writer's many questions with patience and grace.

Dwayne Shepard, for his invaluable technical advice on exotic hardwoods, as well as for being an all-around nice guy.

Larry Gerard, the Friar's Club WebMonk, for all his kind help with my membership questions.

Carol Lemmon, President of the Connecticut Botanical Society, for refreshing my memory about mid-state inland flora.

Al Lemire, Bruce Liddy, and Jordan F. Smith for being the extraordinary friends that they are. You are the Cadbury Eggs in the Easter basket of my life, guys.

Harvey R. Johnson, for giving me my first break in writing, long ago and far away, in the land of Coleco. You're not only the best boss I ever had, but a great friend, as well. I learned a ton from you, Harvo. Thanks.

And let's not forget you, my dear reader, for opening your wallet and spending your hard-earned on this book. I hope I can entertain you enough so that when you turn the final page, you will sigh and say, "It was worth the price of admission." I would love to hear from you, and if you should feel inclined to drop me a note, my email address is: carsonbuckingham@yahoo.com. I can also be reached on Facebook.

And last, but most assuredly not least, Phil St. James for

all his patience with my endless questions while picking his considerable brain for construction pointers, his fabulous proofreading skills, and his sharp eye for draggy pacing and breaches in story continuity. Thanks, babe!

Chapter One

"Happy Anniversary, honey!" Alex cried, throwing her arms around her husband, Leo, as he emerged from his Silverado.

"Happy Anniversary yourself," he replied, kissing the top of her head. He held her with one arm because the other was behind his back.

"What's back there?"

Leo looked defeated. "It's not much, and I'm sorry it's not. You deserve so much more than this," he said, revealing the huge bouquet of spring flowers.

"They're just beautiful! Where did you get them?"

"They were stolen with love, let's put it that way."

"You didn't."

"Oh, yes I did."

"The park in Southfield?"

"That flowerbed needed some thinning, anyhow."

Alex laughed out loud, picturing this giant of a man sneaking around the park, picking flowers. "These flowers mean more to me than anything you could buy from a store, Leo. Thank you."

"Let's go inside before the neighbors call the cops. I hear you get three-to-five for flower stealing," Leo said.

"Okay. I have something for you, too."

"Well, yeah, I was counting on that."

"I mean a present."

"So do I."

"One track mind."

"I like that track," he said, slapping her butt.

Once he was seated in the living room and the flowers

were in water and on the table, she handed him his present. "Hope you like it."

"Sweetie, we don't have the money for you to be buying me anything."

"I know. I made it while you were out looking for jobs."

His smile could light up the world. "You did? You really made something?"

"Yes, but I guess you could say it's sort of a self-serving gift," Alex said.

"It's almost too pretty to open." Leo fingered the delicate pale blue rice paper wrapping. "Almost." He tore off the paper and metallic silver bow. "Oh, this is great! You made us a sign."

"Yep. I used the router and it was easy. Before I met you, I hand-carved everything."

Leo flipped the sign over and laughed when he saw that Alex had burned a small "AR" into the lower right corner at the back of it. "Aha! Now you're learning," he exclaimed.

Leo made it a practice to put his initials somewhere on all the woodwork he did. They were unobtrusive and you'd have to be looking for them to see them, but they were always there somewhere. Alex thought it was a nice idea. Why should artists have a corner on signing their work?

"You're such a natural with wood, Alex. You're going to be a huge help once we get some work to do. 'October's End Remodeling, Inc. Leo & Alex Renfield,'" Leo read from the two-lined sign.

"Speaking of work, how did the estimate go?"

Leo sighed. "Oh, you know. It's a little old lady who thinks she wants her whole bathroom remodeled, and I spend forty-five minutes with her before she tells me that her son-in-law does 'this sort of thing' as a sideline, but just can't seem to find the time to do her job."

"Well, that doesn't sound bad, if she needs to get it done. Could be work for us."

Leo shook his head. "Maybe, but unlikely. I've seen this kind of thing a million times before. I spend my time going out to talk to her, I spend my time writing up an estimate, and she takes the estimate to her son-in-law, or whoever, and he looks at it and says, 'I'll do it for five hundred less,' and that's that as far as October's End goes. All she wanted was an estimate she can take somewhere else. Forget the fact that we use the best materials and have skills honed over most of my life and part of yours. And forget the fact that if sonny boy screws up the job, she has absolutely no recourse. All she'll see is that the job is going to cost her five hundred or three hundred to whatever amount less, and she'll go with that."

"Crap. It sounded so good, too," Alex sighed, punching the sofa cushion.

"Don't worry, sweetie. Something's bound to break soon. I've gone on a dozen estimates over the past couple of weeks. One of 'em's going to hit, I just know it. But for now, why don't you go put on that pretty purple silk dress I gave you for your birthday? We're going out to celebrate tonight."

"Oh, honey, that's a nice thought, but how can we? Dinners out are a bit extravagant right now, don't you think? I can whip something up here... really," Alex said.

"No way. I found a really chea... *inexpensive* place to get terrific Chinese food. All the area contractors go there. I heard about it from a fella at Home Depot."

"Then let's give it a try. However it is, tonight it will be fabulous."

"That's my girl." Leo was so pleased that he forgot all about how odd it was that there was only one person in the entire Home Depot store.

Chapter Two

"So where is this place?" Alex asked as they bumped along down the road made rough with winter frost heaves and DWP—Drinking While Plowing.

"It's on Main Street, just past the Town Hall. It's been there forever, from what I heard."

"I hope the menu has evolved some," Alex said.

"What do you mean?"

"Velociraptor with duck sauce somehow doesn't appeal to me."

Leo chuckled. "Your friends warned me about you."

"I never had friends. I was too poor."

"They said, 'That girl will always have an answer for everything. It may not make sense, but she'll always have an answer.'"

"Even if I had friends, they never would have understood me."

"Half the time, *I* don't understand you!"

"And there we have the reason I was working as a stand-up comic when I met you. Nobody has to understand you—they just have to laugh," Alex said.

"You were very funny."

"What's this? Past tense?"

Leo shook his head in mock resignation. "Not at all. You're still really funny—especially when you get up in the morning."

"Low blow there, hubby—but that was a good one."

"I know I've asked you this before, but how come you stopped? Stand-up, I mean. You never really explained that."

Alex gazed out the window and thought back over her three-year career as a stand-up on the Boston/New York circuit. Jerry Seinfeld, before he hit big, was the closer on her first open mike night and had been kind enough to give her a few pointers after she died so hideously onstage that actual death seemed to pale by comparison. After Jerry's pep talk, helpful hints, and the loan of a handkerchief in order to make her mascara look a little less Alice Cooper-ish, she gamely gave it another try, and was a bit more successful. As the weeks passed, she got better and better, the laughs got louder and longer, and before she knew it, she was getting paid. After a year, she quit her day job and spent two more wonderful years as the most popular new comic on the circuit. It had been great fun, and she got to rub elbows with the likes of George Carlin, Rich Little, and even Jonathan Winters once. Sid Caesar was in the audience the night she took the "Best New Comic" honors at *Catch a Rising Star* in New York, and he actually came backstage to congratulate her. When two comedians in the exclusive New York Friar's Club offered to sponsor her for membership, she was convinced she was looking at a career.

Then she met Paul Rottiger—a killer comic who lived for his craft. As she got to know Paul, she discovered that the reason he lived for comedy was because comedy was all he had.

But it hadn't always been that way.

Before he hit it big, Paul had a lovely wife and two great kids, a house in the suburbs, a dog, a station wagon—the whole bit. Once he was in demand, however, he was working more and home much less—and when he was home, he was usually sleeping. He was never around for weekends, holidays, or his kids' birthday parties; so to make the loneliness more bearable, he found himself a new best friend named Jack Daniels. Then when he needed to get bright for a show after more and more frequent evenings with his buddy, the inevitable cocaine habit followed.

After a while, his wife developed a habit, too. She began habitually seeing other men until she found one who wanted to stick around.

One night, Paul came home to the tired cliché of a cold, unoccupied house and an envelope bearing his hastily scrawled name propped on the table in the hall.

The story of Paul's meteoric rise and earth-shattering personal fall terrified Alex, and she realized that it wasn't going to be possible to have it all. It would be either be a life where comedy was king or one in which she worked a day job somewhere and a man she couldn't live without took priority one. After some soul searching, Alex had decided that she'd postpone the idea of marriage and just date casually, and concentrate on comedy for a few more years.

Then she came home one night and found Leo's email from Yahoo Personals and the rest was history. She never told him that she gave up comedy because she valued him more. He'd have felt utterly awful about it. He'd seen her show a year before they met and he praised it to the skies when, through the many emails they exchanged, he discovered that she was "the" Alex Bluestone. And she *was* good at her craft. She was very good. But she was also smart enough to know when she had someone worth keeping, and the comedy career was shelved without regret or ceremony.

"How come I stopped? I never stopped. I still have one hell of a sense of humor. I married you, didn't I?

"Where do I go to surrender?"

At that moment, they pulled up in front of the restaurant. Alex looked at the eatery, then at Leo.

"This is a joke, right?"

"Behave."

"On, c'mon, Leo! '*Harry Wang's*'?"

"It gets worse. His wife's name is 'Wing," Leo said.

That did it. Hilarity reigned in the truck, necessitating much eye wiping and nose blowing before adequate composure set in. When they could say, "Wing Wang" to each other without laughing, they left the Silverado and strolled through the front door.

"Goo' evening," said a small bespectacled woman behind the podium. "Reservation, preese?"

"No, no reservation. It's our anniversary, though. Could we possibly get a table?" Leo asked with a blinding smile.

"You bilda?"

"I'm sorry?"

"Bilda, bilda, hamma, nail bilda. You bilda?"

"Oh! Yes, we're both builders."

The small woman leaned forward and peered through her thick lenses at Alex. "*You* bilda?' she asked, her disbelief clear.

Alex grinned. "Yes, ma'am, I am."

"Porrite bilda, too! Goo' for you. Tayba righ' this way," she said, selecting four menus from the rack behind her in a single graceful movement.

She led them across a carpet thick enough to hide a Pekingese to a booth with a heavy antique rose linen tablecloth and matching napkins. The entire restaurant bespoke of the understated sophistication that many exclusive restaurants try for and fail to achieve. The utensils were sterling silver and polished to a mirror-like sheen. A single white taper in an elaborate cut glass holder lent the final touch to the overall harmony and richness of the unfortunately named *Harry Wang's*.

Alex and Leo slid into the booth and the tiny lady placed the menus in front of them. Next, with a nearly undetectable flip of a well-practiced wrist, she popped open their intricately folded napkins and placed them on their laps. How she managed to do this last elegantly was a mystery. She then produced a gold lighter and leaned toward the candle.

Leo stayed her hand. "Please don't light it."

"No canda?"

"No, thank you."

She gazed at Leo, clearly perplexed, but the lighter disappeared into a pocket of her chrysanthemum motif silk dress of burgundy and ivory. She shrugged her doll-like shoulders and smiled. "Be righ' back, then." She vanished into the kitchen.

Alex sighed. "It's too bad you don't like candlelight, Leo. It's so romantic."

"Just one of my little quirks, sweetness."

The accommodating woman reappeared at their booth

holding a Waterford crystal bud vase containing two perfect blood red roses. She reached across Alex and removed the candle, replacing it with the fresh flowers.

"There! Das one fo' each of you. You take when you go."

"How incredibly nice of you! Thank you very much," Alex cried, jumping up and giving their small hostess an impulsive hug.

"You wercome, Miss porrite bilda," she said into Alex's shoulder.

When Alex resumed her seat the woman said, "Now, we find ou' who we are. My name Wing Wang."

Alex grabbed her napkin and coughed into it.

"She okay?"

"Absolutely. Just a cold. I'm Leo Renfield, and this is my wife, Alex."

Alex composed herself enough to say, "Pleased to meet you, Mrs. Wang."

"Ah, so porrite! You cor' me 'Wing,' I cor' you 'Arrex'. What kind bilda you, Reo?"

Leo was having a little trouble with her accent, so Alex spoke up. "We're both interior remodelers, Wing. The name of our business is 'October's End Remodeling'." Alex withdrew the slim leather card holder she always kept with her. "As a matter of fact, here's our business card for you."

"Nah fo' me. Put up on board down hawhway. Jobs there, too. You need jobs?"

"Yes, we do," Leo said.

"You rook there, you find. You got bilda ricense?"

"Yes, ma'am," Leo replied.

"Ah, *you* porrite, too! Show ricense, preese."

Leo took his wallet size copy out and handed it to her. She studied it for some time, then handed it back to Leo, and smiling brightly, said, "Okay, you bildas. You get specia' menu. You order dlink now. Then boy come take food order. How many years you mallied?"

"It's our first anniversary," Alex answered, completely charmed by their diminutive hostess.

"Okay! Dlinks on house—bes' Baijiu fo' you." Wing patted both their hands, then swept silently across the lush burgundy carpet and was lost to sight around the corner.

Alex looked at Leo. "God, I feel so guilty about laughing. She's so adorable. What a welcome!" She surveyed her surroundings a bit more closely. The walls were adorned with ornately-framed original watercolor paintings, nature-themed and done, of course, in Chinese brushwork. The wallpaper was flocked in a subtle dark burgundy pattern, like the carpet, creating an atmosphere replete with good taste and opulence without being obnoxious or tacky about it. "Can we even afford half-price dinners here? This place looks really expensive."

"No worries, my dear. We'll eat for next to nothing—take a look at the menu."

Alex scanned the bill of fare. "But how can they do this? These prices are bargain basement. It certainly doesn't jibe with the way the place looks."

"They have two different menus. Didn't you notice that she picked up four menus, but only gave us two? The guy at Home Depot told me that five years ago an arsonist torched this place and burned it to the ground. It was a going concern, family owned and operated, and the family lived upstairs. They lost everything they had, but no one was killed, thank God. The Wangs are well liked in this town, so the lumberyard donated materials, and area contractors donated their time and rebuilt the place for them. They never forgot that kindness, so licensed contractors and the lumberyard people get to eat here for less than half-price as long as the Wangs are in business. Pretty wonderful all the way around, isn't it?"

"What a great story. I'm glad we moved to a town that takes care of its own like that. I thought that only happened on television. So what about the second menus?"

"Everybody else gets those—and the prices in those menus reflect every inch of this place."

The Baijiu arrived. The waiter, who looked about fifteen,

said nothing as he poured the clear liquid into rosebud-shaped shot glasses, then placed the small ceramic bottle on the table. With a shy smile, he bowed to the Renfields, then glided away.

"Baijiu. Do you suppose it's like Sake?" Alex asked.

"Haven't the slightest," Leo replied.

Alex lifted her glass. "Well, honey, a toast to the first of many wonderful years to come."

"I'll drink to that." Leo raised his glass, then took a small sip. "It's warm, but this stuff could knock Sake's block off."

Alex sipped. "Wow. You're right, it's really strong. Tastes familiar, though."

"I can't decide if it tastes more like rubbing alcohol or diesel fuel," Leo whispered.

"You rike Baijiu?" Wing asked, materializing tableside.

"It's very unusual. Thank you so much for it," Alex replied. "We've never heard of Baijiu before."

"Baijiu Chinese national dlink. This Maotai Baijiu, make from bean and wheat. Vely old formula. From Xia Dynasty."

"And how far back does that dynasty go?" Leo asked.

"Seven t'ousand year," Wing replied with a trace of low-key pride. "Rots of kinds of Baijiu, but you get best there is."

"Well, thank you for the good stuff," Leo said. "How about having a glass with us?"

"Ah, no, t'ank you, Reo. In my culture, women canna dlink Baijiu. Against tladition."

Alex looked stricken. "Is it all right for me to be drinking it?"

"You *Chinese*, too?" Wing asked, peering closely at Alex.

"No, I don't have that privilege," Alex replied

"Den is okie dokie," Wing said, patting Alex's arm.

"I'm sorry you can't join us, but thank you for honoring us with this special drink," Leo said.

"No probrem. You come eat here many times," Wing said.

"I think you'll be seeing a lot of us," Alex assured her.

"Good. I get waitah for you now."

There was only about fifteen minutes between the placing of their order and its arrival.

"General Tsao's Chicken," Alex said, shaking her head and rolling her eyes.

"I always get this when I go to a new Chinese place. This is my benchmark meal."

"Benchmark meal?"

"Sure. General Tsao's Chicken is my favorite, so I know what a good version of it should taste like. For me, it's a way of telling, right off, if the food here is any good," Leo explained. "Whereas you, on the other hand, always try something you've never had before. I don't think I've ever seen you order the same thing twice."

"Well, anyway, the price sure is right," Alex said, digging into her braised fish with shrimp sauce. She rolled her eyes. "Ambrosia!"

Leo chewed thoughtfully. "This is, without a doubt, the best General Tsao's I've ever had."

"Grad you rike!" Wing exclaimed, whispering into existence at Alex's left elbow, startling her so much that she almost upset her water glass. "Waitah bling specia' dish for you, cerebrate new customahs! Have specia' ingledients – orr have meanings. Here come now."

The waiter set the oblong dish down in the center of the table, and bowed once again. Wing smiled her approval, and then glanced at the just-delivered steaming platter.

Her almond eyes flew open and she reached over, grabbed the waiter by the back of the collar and frog marched him to the kitchen.

"What the hell just happened?"

"No idea. But this looks good, too," Alex said, indicating the plate. "Want some?"

"You bet," Leo said, holding out his plate.

Alex served them both, and they had hardly swallowed the first mouthful, when Wing reappeared, with the chef and the waiter in tow.

"I'm very sorry about the 'Good Fortune,'" the chef said sincerely and in perfect English, indicating the newly arrived food.

"I solly, too," echoed the waiter, just as sincerely, though not as perfectly.

"This nevah shou' happen! I take away now," Wing said, reaching for the dish.

"I don't understand," Leo said. "What's the matter?"

Wing glared at her two employees and dismissed them with a gesture more appropriate to shooing away flies. They both plodded back to the kitchen, heads hanging, looking like kicked puppies.

"This dish cor', 'Goo' Fortune.' Cor' that becau' food in it *mean* goo' fortune." She indicated each item as she continued, "Brack moss seaweed stand for rots of money, dly bean curd stand for happiness and money, too; bamboo shoot stand for evelything to be good in rife." Then she stopped her culinary tour, as a deeply troubled look clouded her broad, serene face.

After a beat, Alex asked, "And what about those little cubes there? What do they mean?"

"Ah... so. That what bad. Shou' never be in this dish. Bad meaning. Vely bad meaning."

"What does it mean, Wing?"

"White tofu," she said, shaking her head. "White, in China, stand for death. White tofu nevah put in this dish. A thousan' aporogies. I take now," she said, reaching for the platter. She looked as though she might cry.

Fearing that an order of mass hari-kari in the kitchen would shortly follow, Alex put her hand on Wing's outstretched arm and said, "Wing, it's fine. No offense taken. And look, we'll take the 'Good Fortune' that's on our plates and put it back into the one you're taking away. We haven't eaten any of it, so there's no harm done. Please don't worry and please tell our waiter and the chef that we aren't angry."

Wing looked at Alex with glistening eyes. "You goo' girl," she said as Alex and Leo scraped the 'Good Fortune' back onto its original charger. "Arex an' Reo mos' hono'ble." Wing took the plate and bowed low to them all the way back to the kitchen door.

"That was a nice lie you told," Leo said after Wing was out of earshot.

Alex chuckled. "They really take their symbols seriously, don't they? It's too bad, too, because the tofu was the best part of the mouthful I had."

"Yep. Oh, here comes Wing with a replacement 'Good Fortune.'"

From that point forward, the meal continued to be delicious and mercifully free of further drama.

Chapter Three

After the empty dishes were cleared, and replaced with a fragrant cinnamon ginger digestive tea, Alex and Leo settled back into the comfortable banquette, simultaneously heaving contented sighs.

"What a great anniversary celebration. Thank you, sweetie," Alex said.

"I wish I could do more. I'd give you the world, if I could, you know," Leo said.

"Who needs the world? I've got you and you're everything I need," she said, blowing him a kiss. "I'd hold your hands, but I'm too full to lean forward."

"Fortune cookie an' rychee nut!" Wing announced, stepping out of the ether just long enough to place the ornate little dish on the table. She smiled at them both, then evaporated once more.

"How does she move that quietly?"

"Ancient Chinese secret," Alex replied, as she cracked open her fortune cookie. "Oh, you're not going to like this one."

"Why? What does it say?"

"It says, 'THAT WASN'T CHICKEN'."

Leo looked blank for a second, and then laughter rumbled up like a sudden thunderstorm on a sunny day. When he could talk again, Leo said, "Seriously. What's your fortune?"

"Okay, okay, here it is: 'HELP, I'M A HOSTAGE IN A CHINESE BAKERY!'"

Leo chuckled.

"Okay, that one wasn't as good. Here's my real, honest and for-true fortune. Are you ready?"

"I'm starting to be sorry I asked in the first place."

"No, really. Here it is: 'AN EAGLE MAY SOAR BUT A WEASEL NEVER GETS SUCKED INTO A JET ENGINE'."

Leo rolled his eyes. "I give up. With that quick mind of yours, you could do this all night." He paused, looking down at the table. "You could have done a lot better than me, you know."

"I love you, Leo. Don't make me hurt you."

He looked up; grinning again, and Alex marveled at how, periodically, Leo still needed reassuring about his place in her life. Not really surprising, though, when she thought about his childhood. Growing up with seven brothers and sisters and two emotionally absent parents who were religious to the point of fanaticism was one tough road. *I'd need reassuring, too, she* thought.

"Hey, I was thinking…" he said.

"Did you enjoy it?" Alex interrupted.

"You're a riot, Alice. How about a trip to the moon?"

"Okay, but don't you want to hear my fortune first?" Alex asked.

"No."

"Too bad. So, what were you thinking?"

"I was thinking that maybe you should try writing," Leo suggested.

"Oh, man, now that's just super weird with extra nuts and a cherry." Alex's brow furrowed as she picked her paper fortune up off the tablecloth.

Leo immediately felt the fault was his. "I'm sorry, honey. Was that a bad idea?"

Alex came back to the present, shaking her head as if to clear her thoughts. "No, no, Leo. It was just what you said."

This cleared up absolutely nothing for him. "I don't understand."

In answer, she handed him the strip of paper from her fortune cookie. "Read it."

"'YOU ARE INTELLIGENT AND CURIOUS AND

17

WOULD MAKE AN EXCELLENT WRITER.' You're right, that is weird," he said, handing her back the fortune, looking vaguely troubled. Leo wasn't fond of coincidences or odd occurrences that lacked immediate conventional explanations; conversely, Alex lived for them.

"That's really something, isn't it? It's interesting that you should bring up writing; because I've been considering getting back into it for a while. I mean, that's why I got a degree in English, and I did write all my own stand-up material."

"I think you'd be great," Leo said.

"Is that by way of saying that you don't want me to work with you?" Alex asked.

"Of course not. I need your help and I think you'll enjoy woodworking. Plus, you meet a lot of different types of people in this business—good characters, you know? You could write some in your spare time, couldn't you? To get started and see if you'd want to do more of it?"

"This is all a plot for me to write a bestseller, make a bazillion dollars and support you in the style in which you would like to become accustomed, right?" she asked.

"Well, that sure would be nice, but I'm more concerned about your having an outlet just for yourself; that's just yours alone. You work for me and you'll always be 'Leo's helper.' This is the work that I do, that I love, and this is the way I'll leave my mark on the world. I have a feeling that you'll want to go down in the annals as something more than 'Leo's helper.' You have a gift. You shouldn't waste it," he explained.

"You are truly my life's treasure, Leo, to think of me like that. And what, may I ask, is wrong with being 'Leo's helper?'"

He smiled sadly. "Not a thing, but nobody will ever take you seriously or recognize your talent, no matter how good a woodworker you get to be; and you'll hate that after a while. Like it or not, my darling, the field of remodeling is still very much a man's world."

"Hey, nobody ever took me seriously onstage, either—as a matter of fact, everybody laughed at me."

"For a stand-up comic, that's respect."

"Rodney Dangerfield didn't get any."

"You know, sometimes I forget who I'm talking to."

Alex sipped her rapidly cooling tea, then said, "How about this? If I write in my spare time and look at that as my profession, then working with you becomes the hobby and that way, there's no ego invested in it."

"I think that's a great way to look at it."

"Good. Problem solved."

"But I do expect that you're still going to make that bazillion dollars."

Alex waved her fortune at Leo. "Hey, you can't fight the universe! By the way, what's *your* fortune?"

Leo cracked open his cookie and brushed the crumbs off the paper. "The unembellished, straight poop about my future reads thusly: 'SUMMER BRINGS CHANGE.'"

"That's it?" Alex asked.

"Yep." Leo leaned back with his teacup and heaved another great sigh. "Man, I hope things change before then, hon. If I don't find us some work soon we're really going to be in trouble. We have exactly twelve hundred dollars left in the bank, so after this month's rent is paid, we'll be flat broke."

"I could go back on the circuit for a while," Alex said, swirling the dregs of her tea.

"I don't want you to do that. I know you well enough to know that when you walk away from something, you have good reasons for it, whether anybody else knows them or not. Hell, I'll go to work at a hardware store or a lumberyard for a while if I have to. Remodeling isn't the only thing I can do. We'll find a way to manage," Leo said; but there was more wishful thinking than conviction in his voice.

"Excuse me; did I hear you say you're looking for work?" said a voice from the next booth.

"Now that's what I call a fast-acting fortune," Alex whispered. Leo grinned, crossed fingers on both hands, and slid out from behind the table.

"Yes, we are looking for work," he said to the occupant of

the adjoining booth. "Would you like to join us? We're just finishing our tea."

"If that's the case, why not join me, since I've only just ordered?" the female voice countered.

Alex thought it odd that she didn't see this woman arrive or notice a waiter at her booth. She would have had to walk right past her line of sight, and Alex would have seen her— wouldn't she?

"C'mon hon, and meet Mrs. Hamilton," Leo said, snapping Alex back to the present. Evidently, introductions had already been made.

"I'd appreciate it if you'd call me 'Theodora,'" the woman laughed as Alex joined Leo. "And please, sit."

They slid in opposite Theodora, and Alex quietly appraised their new prospect while Leo chatted with her. She was a large woman—the sort Alex's mother would have referred to as "horsey." Not overly obese yet; but hefty... big boned. She appeared to have hit the half-century mark a few years ago, and her tightly curled brown hair was cut so short it was mannish, which was most unflattering when paired with her heavy, moon face. Her eyebrows were shaved off completely and then drawn back in with an eyebrow pencil— an outdated look that had its heyday in the fifties. Her attire was obviously expensive, but looked frumpy on her due to her weight and lumpy proportions. Everything probably did. She had a lovely smile, however, and large brown eyes; but they were framed by glasses with lenses so thick that they were enlarged and distorted to the point of being rather disturbing. Alex judged that she might have been pretty, even beautiful once... thirty years and a hundred pounds ago.

"And what about you, Alex?" Theodora asked.

Upon hearing her name, Alex broke through her personal fog. "I'm so sorry, I was woolgathering. What was it you asked?"

"I asked if you had any family living nearby. Leo said you're both new to the area, and that can be difficult when you don't know anyone and family is far away."

"Actually, neither of us has any family left," Alex replied.

Leo glanced at her, eyebrows raised ever so slightly, but said nothing.

"No family. How sad. I have three children, one of whom still lives at home, a husband still living, a brother who makes his home in Atlanta with my niece and nephew, and a couple of grandchildren with my son and daughter-in-law in Napa Valley," Theodora said.

She positively glowed when she discussed her family. Alex studied her hands and guessed she was a wealthy man's housewife, who had a full-time maid and a gardener. Since her breeding days were clearly behind her, that would leave her time to do all the volunteer work that Alex was certain she filled her days with, while her husband was most probably off banging his secretary in an out-of-town no-tell motel. And the odd way she described him as "still living?" What did that mean? That she hasn't killed him yet? And, of course, there would be the entertaining and the lavish parties and the oh-so-pseudo-intellectual snobs driving in from the city, who could be helpful to the husband's climb up the corporate ladder… *God, I'm such a bitch sometimes!* Alex thought. *Leo's right, I should do some writing—I've got this poor woman's whole life mapped out and I've known her for exactly…* she glanced down at her wrist… *five minutes. Not only that, but I've hardly listened to a word she's said. What in the world is wrong with me?*

"Are either of you vegetarians?" Theodora asked.

"Is that important?" Alex asked.

"It is to me. Vegetarians have no stamina. I find people who don't eat red meat regularly to be weak, listless individuals who undoubtedly have iron-poor, tired blood," Theodora explained, sounding like a Geritol ad. "People without the energy meat provides are unable to work very hard."

Leo laughed. "You don't have to worry about that. We're hard-working, meat eating people. Now, what kind of work do you need done on your house?" Leo asked.

"All right; to business, then," Theodora said. "I need a good bit of painting done—the entire lower floor of my house. We have stained bead board ceilings that I don't want touched, so you'll just be painting the walls."

Leo deflated slightly, but it was only obvious to Alex. *Damn! It's not going to be a big money job. Painting never is, and he hates to paint anyway. Double Damn!* she thought.

"Well, painting, by itself, is not something we normally do, Theodora, unless it's part of a larger remodeling job," Leo said. "Now, if you have a kitchen or bathroom you want to redo or a hardwood floor you need put down, we can do that for you. Do you have any work like that?"

"Unfortunately, I do not," Theodora said. "But if you'd be willing to do this job for me, there will be other jobs in the future that would be more in keeping with what you enjoy doing."

Leo thought about her proposal for a moment. "Fair enough. When would be a good time for me to come out and take some measurements?" Leo asked.

On the other hand, money's money, Alex thought.

"What on earth for?" Theodora replied.

"Well, I can't very well give you an estimate if I don't know how many square feet we'll be painting," Leo explained, smiling.

"Oh, I see what you mean. It won't be necessary for you to do any measuring. I can give you that information right now," she said.

Leo looked confused. "You can?"

"Certainly. The downstairs wall space measures 10,584.32 square feet."

Leo sat back suddenly, regarding Theodora with surprise. "Well, I must say, I'm impressed. You must have had your first floor painted before to know those measurements off the top of your head."

"No. It's never been painted before. I simply make it my business to arrive prepared with appropriate information when I'm discussing work on the house." Theodora's tone had lost all of its previous cordiality.

Wait a minute, Alex thought. *She's making this sound like a scheduled business meeting. How did she know she was going to be discussing work on her house tonight?*

Leo realized he'd put a foot wrong and hastened to correct things. "I'm sorry. You just surprised me, that's all. Usually homeowners don't have a clue. It's great that you do. Will there be any preparation of the walls required?"

"Preparation?"

"Sure. We'll be washing them, of course; but will there be large areas that we'll have to scrape down?"

Theodora looked horrified. "Absolutely not! You will do no scraping of any kind! Do you understand?"

"Yes, I understand, but…"

"There will be no 'buts.' No scraping. Period. Are we clear on that?" Much like Connecticut weather, Theodora's face had jumped from warm and sunny to chilly pre-storm darkness at a distressing speed.

"Yes, ma'am—crystal," Leo replied.

The odd woman relaxed slightly. "You'll be painting a medium charcoal gray over white, so nothing should bleed through. In addition, I will have, on hand, all the materials necessary to complete this project." Theodora warmed up enough to smile again. "And I already have a price in mind that I think would make this worth your while."

Unhearing, Leo had already pulled the pad and pencil he always carried out of his shirt pocket. "I can tell you in just a second what we'd be willing to do the job for," he said, scribbling furiously.

"I will pay you thirty thousand dollars," Theodora said quietly.

Stop the music.

Leo's head snapped up like a bear trap. "What?"

"I said, 'I'll pay you thirty thousand dollars' to paint the first floor of my house."

"As wonderful as that figure sounds, I have to tell you, Theodora, that it's more than four times what you should pay for a job that size. We'd do it for… let's see… seven thousand nine hundred thirty-eight dollars and seventy-five cents; but since you're providing all the supplies, that will reduce it to, say, an even seventy-five hundred. That's what it's worth, and

CARSON BUCKINGHAM

that's what an honest painter would charge you."

"That's right," Alex agreed. The vibes on this proposition were getting worse by the minute.

Theodora laughed. "It pleases me to no end that the two of you aren't out to rob me."

"I couldn't look at myself in the mirror if we took that kind of money from you for a job like this," Alex said.

Theodora's manner became abruptly sober again. "And I couldn't look at my reflection if I didn't pay that kind of money for this job. It's thirty thousand dollars. I am completely aware, sane, and serious. Take it or leave it. I need an answer now. This offer expires as soon as I have to get up and walk across the room to that job board to locate another painter."

Leo and Alex looked at each other, full of unspoken questions. Finally, Alex shrugged, Leo nodded, and Alex said, "All right. As long as you fully understand that you're paying way too much for the job, we'd be delighted to do your painting."

Her smile lit the booth once more. "Marvelous! I'll have the contracts ready for your signatures."

"Actually, we're the ones who draw up the contract," Leo said.

Theodora ignored him and added, "And there are one or two other items I must mention…"

Here comes that other shoe now, Alex thought.

"And those are?" Leo asked.

"You must both have complete physicals before you step foot onto the premises. I will cover the cost of those, of course."

"You really don't have to worry about that, Theodora. We're both healthy as horses," Leo said.

"Nevertheless, that's a condition of employment. Are we agreed?"

"Sure," Alex said. "I'll make an appointment with Dr. Munson tomorrow morning, though I don't know how soon we'll be able to get in to see him."

"You're new to the area, healthy as horses, and you have a doctor already?" Theodora asked, her eyes narrowing.

"In this line of work, it's smart to have a doctor with a local hospital affiliation—in case of on-the-job injuries," Leo explained. "We saw him initially to get our tetanus boosters. No matter how careful you are, it's easy to step on a nail."

"Well, no matter. I'll make an appointment for you with our doctor. He's always available when we need his services. Please give me your card and I'll call you with the appointment information."

Alex dutifully handed over a card. "Is there anything else?"

"Yes. You won't be driving yourselves to the house. It's extremely difficult to find, so I'll be sending Cooper Black, my driver and the caretaker of the house and grounds, to pick you up and bring you home initially. Of course, once work commences, you'll be staying at the house…"

"What, you mean living there? For the whole summer?" Leo asked.

"Naturally. It will be far easier for you to get the work done if you are on the premises twenty-four seven. Wouldn't you agree? All food and amenities shall be provided for you, so all you need bring is clothing."

Leo looked at Alex for feedback, but she merely shrugged, a half-smile on her face.

"What's funny?" Leo asked.

Alex turned to Theodora. "Is 'Cooper Black' his real name?"

Theodora looked confused. "Yes, it is. Why?"

Alex chuckled. "I only ask because 'Cooper Black' is the name of a typeface. I was about to ask you if he had a cousin named 'Curtis Linen,'" Alex replied.

"As far as I know, he has no relatives at all. Who is 'Curtis Linen?'"

Alex sighed inwardly, thankful that this humorless female never sat up front at any of her stand-up shows. "'Curtis Linen' is a type of paper."

"How fascinating. To return to the subject, Cooper will pick you both up the day work commences and will deliver you back to your home when the project is completed," Theodora continued.

Uh oh, Alex thought.

Leo balked. "Hold the phone a minute. I need my truck. How am I going to get my tools out to the house? And what if I need to run out and pick something up at Home Depot? How will I do that?"

"I fail to see where you will need to leave the premises for any reason, since I am supplying you with everything the job requires. And as to needing other items, you'll just give Cooper a list, and he will drive out and locate them for you. Believe me, Leo, whatever luggage and incidentals you will be bringing to the house will fit nicely into the trunk of the car," Theodora said.

"And you're going to feed us all summer?"

"Indeed. And to address entertainment during your off hours I must tell you that we do not own a television or radio, due to poor reception at the house, but you will have nearly unlimited access to the books in my, if I do say so myself, rather extensive library, as well as any other areas of interest on the first floor. The second floor, however, is strictly off-limits to you both. While you are on the premises, Cooper will be your line to the outside world. Oh, and you must not leave the property or step off the well-established pathways under any circumstances. It can be next to impossible to find your way back if you stray too far."

Alex looked at Leo's darkening visage as the seconds and bizarre ground rules ticked by. *She should have skipped the bit about the truck—that's probably a deal-breaker. He doesn't go anywhere without his truck.*

But Leo surprised her. "All right, I don't pretend to understand these rules, but we'll abide by them."

"And one more thing..."

Oh, God.

"Your work day is going to be a trifle out of the ordinary,

too. You will begin work at midnight and continue until six A.M. No earlier, no later."

"I guess Home Depot isn't going to be an issue then. How is Mr. Black supposed to get things we need if we're working hours like that? Nothing's open," Leo said.

"Cooper is remarkably resourceful. He'll find whatever you need," Theodora replied. "We leave for Phoenix on the morning of May thirteenth, so you'll begin working on May fourteenth, and continue throughout the summer."

"And the completion date?" Alex asked.

"September first, but I'm sure you'll be finished long before then."

"With two coats, we'll probably just make it, only working six hours a day," Leo muttered.

"Oh, no. Only one coat is necessary," Theodora said. "A single coat will cover just fine."

"Why not let us be the judge of that?" Leo said with a smile. "After all, you're paying us for our expertise, aren't you?"

"Among other things," Theodora replied, wiggling her eyebrows like Groucho Marx. Alex was taken aback. How inappropriate was *that*?

Before any response could be made, Theodora's food arrived, looking like something Dante might order stopping off for a quick bite at an all-night diner in the third ring of Hell. It was a mad tangle of squid and octopus tentacles with black mushrooms in a dark, gelatinous sauce. "Ah, lovely," Theodora sighed. "Would you care for some?"

"Uh, no… no, thank you. We should be going," Leo said, unable to even look at the disgusting entrée.

"You'll be hearing from me tomorrow morning," Theodora said, never taking her eyes off her plate. A dribble of saliva trickled from the corner of her mouth and ran down her chin. "It was nice meeting you." She then chopsticked an entire baby octopus into her mouth and chewed hungrily.

Chapter Four

After Leo paid the check, and assured Wing that they would most definitely be frequent customers, the Renfields stepped out into the cloudy April evening.

"Leo, we're in the money! Talk about a fantastic stroke of luck," Alex cried, grabbing his arm and hugging it, making a mighty effort to ignore the flashing red warning lights and sirens going off in her head.

Leo tried gamely for a smile, got halfway there and sighed deeply. Searching his coat pocket for his keys, he said, "Yeah, it really sounds great."

Alex stopped in her tracks. "But…"

"Dunno."

"Sure you do. Think about it," Alex said.

They shuffled to the truck in silence. Once inside, Leo started the engine and let it run. It certainly wasn't necessary to warm it up this late in the spring, but Leo liked to baby his truck. He even called it "Babe," and could usually sweet talk her out of stalling or acting up. Alex thought it both comical and endearing.

"Maybe I'm being foolish, but I don't know if I want this job, after all."

"Bad feeling?"

"More like creeped out. Talk about freaky conditions," Leo said.

"I have an idea. Let's stop off at that little pub over on Washington Avenue. We can nurse a couple of beers and talk this over, okay?"

"Sounds like a great idea," Leo said, gently putting "Babe" in gear.

Ten minutes later, they were comfortably settled in one of the tall wooden booths lining the walls of *The Half Door*. Alex loved the atmosphere of the place.

It was how she imagined a pub in Ireland would look—and to enhance that impression, the owners of the pub hired only native Irishmen as waiters.

"Welcome to the Half Door. May I take your order?"

"Eventually," Alex laughed. "For now, you can just stand there and talk—I love your accent."

The waiter blushed to the roots of his auburn hair, and ducked his head shyly. "Thank you, m'um. I like your accent, too."

Alex, never one to hide her amusement, laughed, embarrassing the young man even further. Her husband shook his great leonine head, smiled at the poor guy and exercised his adept subject-changing ability. "What kind of beer do you recommend?"

"Harp, sir," he replied instantly. "Though Guinness is spot on if you want something heartier."

"Two Harps, then," Leo said, and the waiter hastened to the bar. "Guinness!" Leo muttered. "Who wants beer you can chew?"

"Oh, come on, Leo, it's not that bad."

"Not that bad? Damn, Alex, you can seal a driveway with that stuff."

"At any rate, why so glum, chum? Jesus, Leo, this is a godsend. We're so damned broke." She wanted to see if his forebodings matched hers.

"I know, honey, and you have no idea how sorry I am about it."

"Leo, please stop apologizing all the time. If you weren't doing anything to change our situation, then you'd have something to apologize for. You take way too much to heart. I'm not complaining about our finances. I can make whatever amount of money we have work," Alex said. All Alex's considerable pre-Leo savings were invested and they both agreed that it was a nest egg they wouldn't touch.

"Yes, I know. You remind me of something my mother used to say about people like you—you're 'good poor.'"

"Hey, I like that!"

"Well, I don't ever want you to be poor, but it seems like that's all we've been since we got married."

The waiter arrived, dropped off their beer, smiled at Alex, and departed for the next table.

"Sweetie, I love you no matter what our bank statement says. Now tell me what's bothering you about this job."

"Hard to put my finger on it. You're the one who's good with words, not me. I just have a hinky feeling, that's all. It's like watching night-flying birds."

"How so?"

"There's just something not right about birds that fly around at night, you know? It's like they're hiding something."

Alex laughed. "Leo, my darling, that is one of the most interesting and succinct explanations I've ever heard. Maybe you should try writing."

Leo chuckled. "Ray Bradbury I'm not."

Alex smiled and returned to the subject. "Is your gut warning you off because of all the conditions, or did it start before then?"

Leo thought for a moment. "I'm not sure."

Alex smiled. "Know what I think? I think that if she'd have let you drive your truck to the job, you'd be celebrating right now, all the other conditions aside. So she's two pins short of a strike, so what? It's not like she'll be around when we're painting the place."

"You're right," Leo laughed. "You're so damned smart, it scares me sometimes. So tell me, Miss Marple, what was your take on Theodora?"

"Well, let's see. She brags about her family, but doesn't show us any photos, because she doesn't care what we think, or we're not important enough to show them to; so I would conclude that her seeming friendliness is just that—phony. It could be that she's tough to work for, if she's paying that much for the job—but we've worked with difficult people before, and they've come away liking us."

"That all makes sense. I have another question, though," Leo said.

"Yeah. I think I know what it is."

"Why'd you lie to her about having no family?"

"That would be the one," Alex said.

"What about your brother?"

"I don't know, Leo, and that's the truth. I have no idea why I said that, but something told me I'd better—and I was right. Did you notice her subtle attitude shift?"

"You know I don't pick up on things like that," Leo replied. "So what was the change?"

"Like this was a major question in the interview, and we gave her the right answers."

"But why would she care if we have relatives?"

"Oh, I think there were much more disturbing issues than that," Alex said, drawing circles in the sweat that had dripped from her glass onto the table top. "For one thing, don't you think it was pretty odd how she had her square footage on the tip of her tongue, right down to the decimal point?"

"Yeah, that is sort of strange, considering that she hasn't had work done there before."

"So she says."

"It would explain why she has such an unrealistic idea of how long the job is going to take, though. What else?" Leo took a long swallow of his beer.

"Well, the physicals could be for insurance purposes, so I guess it's not all that strange. The hours she wants us to work are unusual, to say the least, but that could be because we'll be working in the heat of summer, and maybe the house doesn't have central air, so that would explain that. And if the house is surrounded by dense forest, it might be easy to get lost," Alex said.

"Okay, you've answered most of the questions—but that's only if your assumptions are right. Another thing that got me was their vacation choice," Leo said.

"What, you mean Phoenix?"

"Yeah. Ever been there?" Leo asked.

"No."

"In mid-May through October, it's melt-your-eyeballs hot down there. Triple digit temperatures on a daily basis. Jeez, it can reach 121 degrees! And when the monsoons come in July and August, you get those temperatures with humidity. Plus, summer is the only time it's really nice in New England. Why do they want to leave then?"

"Maybe they have family there?" Alex hazarded.

"According to her, she has family in Georgia and northern California. Now, I don't know about you, but if I were going to leave New England for the summer, I think I'd go to Napa Valley to see the grandkids before I'd head southwest to hellish temperatures. Summer is the shut-in season in Phoenix, just like winter is up here. It's way too hot to do anything outside— not that there's a whole lot to do down there, anyway. I don't get it."

"You're right, that is weird," Alex conceded.

"No possible explanation?" Leo asked.

It suddenly dawned on Alex that Leo, despite his voiced misgivings, wanted her to explain away the darkness; probably because the money was too good to walk away from— especially in their present financial straits. Well, if he wanted reassurance, she'd give it to him.

"Could be that going to Phoenix has something to do with the 'still living' husband's business. Or maybe one of the grandkids has been accepted at a school there and they're going down to help her get settled in. There could be a lot of reasons, hon."

"I didn't think of any of that," Leo said. "I'm glad I married you."

"Me, too. It's ten after twelve. Ready to head home?"

Leo paid the check and they left *The Half Door* arm in arm. Though Alex had successfully put a good face on his concerns, all the way home she wondered if she'd done the right thing. She also wondered what Theodora had in mind when she grinned at Leo and said, "Among other things..."

𝔠𝔥𝔞𝔭𝔱𝔢𝔯 𝔉𝔦𝔳𝔢

"Hello, you two. This is Theodora Hamilton calling to let you know that your appointment with Dr. Orbon is scheduled for twelve-thirty on Wednesday of this week. It's already paid for, so all you have to do is show up. Good luck."

Alex clicked off the answering machine. "Talk about fast. Orbon must not have much of a patient load."

Before Leo could comment, the phone rang.

He waited for the second ring, then picked it up. "Hello. Yes. Yes, we just got in. Sure, twelve-thirty is fine—it will give me the rest of the afternoon to finish up…"

He listened, looking confused.

"Uh, well, that's kind of unusual, isn't it? I mean, I've never heard of…"

He rolled his eyes at Alex.

"No, that's fine—if that's the way it is then we'll work with it. Can you give me directions to his office, please?"

Leo picked up a nearby pen and jotted down directions on the memo cube by the phone. "Uh huh. Right or left? Okay. Oh, yes, I think I know where that is. Could I get his phone number in case I need it? Really? All right, then, don't let me keep you. Good-bye."

Leo cradled the receiver softly. "That may not have been the strangest conversation I've ever had, but it rates right up there in the top two. You're not going to believe this shit!"

"Oh, come on—how bad can it be?"

"That twelve-thirty appointment? It's twelve-thirty in the morning! And I couldn't get Dr. Orbon's phone number because, according to her, he doesn't have a phone."

"*What?*" Alex italicized.

"You heard it."

She was stunned. "Okay, Leo, this is officially not funny anymore. What kind of a doctor has office visits after midnight? And no phone? That's a steaming load of crap—all doctors have phones. How else can you make an appointment or reschedule one if you need to?"

"I'm much more freaked out by the appointment time. Oh, and as if that's not enough, guess where his office is?"

"I'm afraid to," Alex said.

"Remember when we were house hunting? That little gray house we found down that gravel road off Church Street that we thought was charming until…"

"…until we saw the town cemetery in the back yard? Is that the house you mean?" Alex asked.

Leo nodded.

"But wasn't that house abandoned? When we saw it the wind was opening and closing the front door, and it was black as my first grade teacher's heart inside. It didn't look as if anyone had lived there for years. As a matter of fact, I just assumed it was an old caretaker's cottage."

"That's Dr. Orbon's office."

"Oh, swell. Well, at least we're not meeting him by a glowing gravestone under a full moon. That was going to be my second guess."

Leo sighed. "Want to back out, babe? Because I'm about ready to. I don't like being expected to go along with weird requests without a single word of explanation."

"I know. Things are pretty damned strange, that's for sure," Alex said, absently leafing through the mail that she had dropped on the counter yesterday morning. Yesterday morning. It seemed like three days ago already. She extracted a handwritten envelope from the pile and examined it. "This is for you, Leo," she said, handing it over. "Forwarded from New York."

"I'll look at it tomorrow—or rather, later today. I'm bushed. Let's go to bed," he yawned.

"Good idea. You still haven't gotten the second half of your anniversary present yet," Alex said, with a wink and a smile. "But, of course, if you're too tired…"

Leo snorted. "I'll never be that tired."

Chapter Six

Alex was awakened from a sound sleep by Leo shaking her shoulder and jumping up and down simultaneously.

"Holy Mackerel! You won't believe this! Wake up, Alex!"

"What timeezit? Wassa matter? Who's dead?"

Leo waved an envelope at her. "No—it's good news. Great news! It's from Joyce! That letter you gave me last night? When I opened it just now, a check fell out of it—for ten thousand dollars!" He grabbed Alex in a bear hug. "I never thought I'd ever get paid for that job. I wrote it off a long time ago."

"What job? Have a heart, honey—I just opened my eyes!"

Settling down slightly, Leo sat on the edge of the bed. "This was a job I did long before I ever met you."

"Do you mean to tell me that you actually had a life before you met me?" Alex yawned.

Leo grinned. "Not much of one, I grant you, but a life of sorts. Oh, there's a letter, too."

"Wait, wait! How much is the check for, again?"

"Ten thousand."

"Really? Ten *thousand*? Talk about fabulous! So what happened that made you write off this much money?"

"Let me give you some background first. Joyce and Art Randolph were a nice older couple who hired me to enlarge their kitchen and build a huge new deck off the back of the house, with a separate entertainment area, fire pit, and barbecue. It was a big bucks project and I was glad to get it. Then Art came home on the day I was wrapping things up and said he'd been let go—downsizing or something like that. The problem was, because I liked and trusted them, I let most of the payments slide until the final one, so there was quite a bit of money owed at that point. Anyhow, he asked me if he could make payments on his balance, and he did that for a while. Then I heard he was diagnosed with terminal cancer, so I called. Joyce was at her wit's end, because when he lost his job, he lost his health insurance and they had to pay all the medical bills out of pocket. I told her to forget about my bill and that if I could help in any way, to let me know. I ended up taking Art to a few chemo treatments when he got too weak to walk. Last I heard, he was in Hospice. I get a Christmas card from them every year."

"In that case, this letter is probably not good news, hon," Alex said, putting her hand gently on his shoulder.

"Depends on how you look at it. Here goes: 'Dear Leo, I hope this note finds you and your new wife happy and feeling well. I've some sad news to report. Arthur, my dear husband of fifty-four years, passed away one month ago from the cancer that he had been battling for the past three years. He's at peace now, and I'm glad—though I will miss him until my dying day.

"'Fortunately, Arthur had a large life insurance policy, so it is with the utmost pleasure that I am finally able to pay your greatly past due bill with the going rate of interest that would have accrued over the years. Do not even consider refusing this, Leo. Arthur would have wanted you to be paid, and I have plenty left to get by on. Whenever you find yourselves in the area, please stop by. I'd love to see you again and meet your new wife. Sincerely, Joyce Randolph'."

"Oh, how sad," Alex said.

"Well, I'm glad his suffering is over. The man was just a shadow the last time I saw him, and in miserable pain. We'll have to go see Joyce—you'll like her."

"I like anybody who sends us checks for ten thousand dollars," Alex said. "Seriously, though, anyone who is that honorable is somebody I'd like to meet."

"She's a real sweetheart. And you know what?"

"What?"

"I think if we get to the bank before it closes today, I'll be able to afford another cut-rate Chinese dinner. Whaddya say?"

"Two dinners out in two days? You spoil me, sir!"

Chapter Seven

Over another delicious meal, Alex and Leo chattered excitedly about their latest stroke of luck. When they shared their news with Wing, she smiled and said, "See? 'Goo' Fortune' work fo' you awready." She didn't seem at all surprised.

"Isn't it incredible, Leo? First a thirty thousand dollar paint job and now a check for ten grand. We're thousandaires!" Alex cried.

Leo smiled. "Sure looks that way." Then a cloud passed over his features and dropped a little rain on his enthusiasm. "What do you really think about working for Theodora? Still want to? We could keep going for quite a while on the check we got today if we watch our spending. If you want to back out, now's the time, because the opportunity just got deposited in the Southfield Savings Bank."

"Do you want to back out, Leo?"

"I'd like to have that cash, no doubt, but I get a tad suspicious about money that's that easy, don't you? I mean, thirty thou' for a simple paint job? It works out to two dollars and eighty-three cents per square foot. She's insisting on paying us nearly four times the usual rate. Doesn't that bother you?" Leo asked.

"Sure it does." Alex sipped her tea, savoring its rich, spicy notes.

"And what about all those conditions? And a physical in the middle of the night?"

"Maybe she's just rich and eccentric?" Alex ventured.

"I don't know, I just don't know," Leo muttered, winding down.

"Look, Leo, if you want to eighty-six this job, then do it. I'm fine with whatever you want to do. I certainly don't want you to spend the summer working for a client who makes you this uncomfortable," Alex said, easing her own conscience somewhat.

"I appreciate that, honey. Let me think about it some more."

***

By Tuesday night at eleven forty-five, he still hadn't decided.

Chapter Eight

"It should be right around here somewhere. Look for a gravel driveway on your side."

Alex peered through the fog. "Are you kidding? I couldn't spot the Chrysler Building on my side."

"Good thing we're not looking for it, then... ah, here we are," Leo said, swinging the wheel.

The gravel drive wasn't much more than a wide path, which the fog consumed after about three feet. As is usual with fog, the headlights only made it harder to see, so Leo turned them off, running with parking lights only. The tall pines drizzled their condensate onto the window like a slow bleed from a dying animal. Alex shivered as they crept along, her thoughts running to Freddy, Jason, and Michael—not to mention Bela, Boris, and Lon. By the time they pulled to a stop in the small parking lot at the side of the house that doubled as cemetery sentinel, Alex had imagined herself right into a George Romero movie.

"It seems we've arrived," Leo said.

"Hooray. Now all we have to do is make it to the door before the zombies get us," Alex said. "I trust you brought the zombie repellant." Though she made light of it, Alex was not looking forward to trading the cozy, safe truck that smelled like sawdust, leather and Armor-all for a walk in a fog so thick that to breathe it would be to choke on it. She used her sleeve to clear the window and locate Dr. Orbon's office.

"This is seriously strange, Leo."

"Why? I mean, aside from the obvious?"

"Do you see any lights on in there? Any real lights?"

"What do you mean 'real lights?'"

"Take a look. Tell me what *you* see."

He squinted into the gloom, and after a moment,

understood what Alex meant. His heart dropped to his knees.

The entire office was lit by candles.

"Holy crap—what *is* this?" Leo sat back in his seat, trying to think past his alarm. After a moment, he said, "You know what? He probably just lost power. Let's stick our heads in and see if he wants to wait to see us until it's back on again. We're just letting the weather and the time of night get to us, don't you think?"

"Don't forget location, location, location. I know how you feel about candlelight, hon. Is this going to be a problem for you?"

"I'll live," Leo said, as huge beads of sweat rolled down his back.

They walked through the murk looking like zombies themselves, with their arms outstretched and moving with stiff-legged slowness to avoid bouncing off a wall or tripping over, say, the carelessly tossed human skull.

"Hello? Who's out there, please?" a fog-muffled voice called from the doorway.

"Doctor Orbon? It's Leo and Alex Renfield. We have an appointment." At twelve-thirty in the morning, a statement like that sounded so ludicrous that Leo would have laughed out loud if he hadn't been so panic stricken.

"Oh yes? Well, come in and I'll check my appointment book."

"You'd think an after midnight appointment would be pretty damned memorable, wouldn't you?" Leo muttered.

"Please come quickly, I hate to let in the damp," the doctor's disembodied voice said.

They hurried over the threshold into a waiting room that looked like something out of *Beetlejuice*. Though only large enough to accommodate four folding chairs, it was packed with scores of lit tapers and was decorated, if one could call the state of the room 'decorated,' with a dusty assortment of animal trophies and a scattering of stuffed and posed fauna. There were candles, eyes, and bared teeth everywhere and not a magazine in sight—not that anyone would be comfortable enough to read in such a place.

While Dr. Orbon studied his appointment book, Alex studied him. He was a pleasant-looking man, about five-foot-six with sparkling blue eyes. His hands were no larger than Alex's and his feet were smaller. He was nearly bald, with what remained of his white hair kept short and neatly trimmed. His only off-putting feature was a large lumpy scar on his forehead. Alex put him at about sixty years old.

"Ah, yes, here it is. Who'd like to be first—Alex or Leo?" he asked.

"Er… what happened to your power, Doc? Don't you want us to come back when you have lights again?" Leo asked, edging toward the door. Beads of sweat now dotted his forehead and slicked his palms.

"These are all the lights I ever have, Leo," Dr. Orbon replied. "I live by candlelight.

"Additionally, in order for me to examine you, it is necessary for me to see you at night."

"Now I'm really confused."

"I do not venture out in daylight, nor do I use light bulbs."

"Okay, my turn," Alex said to Leo. She turned to the doctor. "Why is that?"

Dr. Orbon sighed. "Because it can burn my skin and eyes beyond repair. Now if one of you will step this way, I need to draw your blood."

Leo and Alex looked at each other.

"Oh, I'll bet you do," Alex said. "What is going on here? The next thing you're going to tell us is that you don't drink… wine."

"You're quite correct, I don't. Now if you'll…"

"Hold on a minute, Dracula…"

"*Dracula?*"

"An office full of candles, we're here for physicals at twelve-thirty in the morning, sunlight burns you, and let's not forget the waiting room of death," Alex said, indicating all the trophies with a single sweeping gesture. "Who's your decorator? Norman Bates?"

"Is she always like this?" the doctor asked Leo.

In spite of his acute anxiety, Leo managed a frayed smile. "Pretty much. An explanation would go a long way toward calming her down," Leo said. *Anything to move this along a little faster.*

"Of course." Dr. Orbon turned to Alex. "My dear young woman, I am afflicted with a disease called *xeroderma pigmentosum*, or XP, for short. To sum it up, I risk cancer if I expose my skin or eyes to ultraviolet rays even for a very short period of time and this includes not only sunshine but fluorescent light bulbs, as well. Though scientists say that light from incandescent bulbs is not harmful, I do not trust them, and so stick to candles. So, now you understand why I keep such unusual office hours. I don't drink… wine… as you so drolly put it, because it adversely affects me. I abstain from all alcohol. As to my 'waiting room of death;' my hobby is taxidermy. I don't apologize for it. It is how I pass the time. Satisfied?"

Alex was mortified. "Oh, please forgive me! I'm so terribly, terribly sorry, Dr. Orbon," she said. "I just didn't get it."

"Nonsense. My fault entirely. I'm so used to the way I live that I forget that others can't possibly understand without a bit of explanation," he said.

"I don't even have that excuse, I'm afraid," Alex said, unable to lift her gaze from the floor. "I just finished reading a book entitled…"

"*Fear Nothing* by Dean Koontz," the doctor finished for her. Alex's head shot up.

"How did…"

"It's the only book of fiction that I am aware of that discusses XP in detail. As a matter of fact, the protagonist is afflicted—but you already know all that. I assumed you were a fiction reader, due to your, shall we say, *vivid* imagination."

"Alex was telling me about that book a day or two ago. How accurate was it?" asked Leo, his heart racing and sweat pouring off him, but too polite to rush the doctor along.

"Oh, quite. Mr. Koontz is not only an excellent writer but a thorough researcher, as well." Dr. Orbon turned to Alex, who was thankful that her red face was much less obvious in the low light of the office. "You might want to read the sequel to *Fear Nothing*. It's called, I believe, *Seize the Night*."

"Thank you, I will. And, again, I apologize. I'm so embarrassed."

"Don't be, Alex. You have a wonderful imagination, though. Ever thought of giving Koontz a run for his money?"

"Yes, frequently," Alex said.

"Great, glad that's straightened out, but it's late, so let's get this show on the road. I've got an early day tomor... that is, today." Leo said. "I'll go first and you can pet the waiting room, hon."

Leo disappeared with Dr. Orbon through the door and into the back office.

Chapter Nine

Leo followed the doctor down an extremely narrow corridor illuminated by candle wall sconces.

"You must have one heck of a candle bill every month," Leo remarked in a shaky voice, staying as close to the center of the hallway as possible.

"It's not as bad as you might think—I have a special source. A fellow in town makes them for me at a very reasonable price. They smell odd, but they burn just fine."

They did smell odd. Leo hadn't noticed it until Dr. Orbon mentioned it, but there was a subtle odor lurking in the shadows that was impossible to identify. It wasn't exactly unpleasant. But it wasn't exactly pleasant, either. It made Leo more uneasy than he already was.

The doctor opened the door to the examining room, then stood aside for Leo to enter.

There were, easily, a hundred candles burning in the small room. Leo didn't move.

"Is there a problem, Leo?"

"Well, it's just that… well… I can't go in there, that's all. Sorry I wasted your time, Doc." Leo turned to leave.

"What's the trouble?"

"I don't do real well with fire, Doc."

"Oh, I *do* beg your pardon!" Dr. Orbon said, closing the door quickly. "Were you burned as a child?"

"No. My entire family died in a house fire. My dog and I were the only ones left—and that was because I was out walking him at the time."

"Dear me. How old were you?"

"Seventeen."

"I am very sorry for your loss."

45

"It was a long time ago," Leo said. "But I still can't go into that room. Just the waiting room nearly did me in. And that's only candles. A burning fireplace completely paralyzes me."

"Well, all I need to do is to draw your blood, and I can do that quickly right here in the hallway, if you can deal with these few candles for a short time."

"I suppose so. But will you be able to see what you're doing?"

"I've lived like this for an unexpected number of years now, Leo. My eyes are well suited to dimness. I must step into the examining room for just a moment to get a few things. Close your eyes, if it helps."

"Great. Let's get it done with, then I'll wait for Alex in the truck," Leo said as he rolled up his sleeve; but by this time, he was trembling so badly that it was impossible for Dr. Orbon to place the needle accurately. After several attempts, he suddenly snapped his fingers.

"I have a marvelous idea! Just a moment." The doctor dashed down the hall into a room at the end of the corridor. He returned with an alien-looking contraption on his head and snuffed all the hall candles until they were in complete darkness.

"Okay, Leo? A bit calmer now?"

"That's much better, Doc."

"Good. Let's get that blood drawn."

"How are you going to do that in the dark?"

"The apparatus covering my eyes is a set of night vision goggles. I can see you perfectly clearly."

"Well, I'll be. Draw away, Doc."

"Would I be correct in assuming that Lady Alex of the fevered imagination is unaware of the extent of your issue with fire?" He placed and tightened the tourniquet, felt for a vein, then placed the needle. Several empty vials clinked in his lab coat pocket, waiting to be filled.

"She's unaware of the *extent* entirely," Leo replied. "All she knows is that I don't like any kind of open flame, but she doesn't know why. She does know that there are fire extinguishers in every room of our house. She also knows that I'm not fond of dogs."

"One might think she might have figured things out, just based on the collection of fire extinguishers alone. And you *dis*like dogs? You told me that the reason you're alive is because you were out walking your dog, isn't that right?"

"Yes. The dog is the reason I'm alive. He's also the reason my family is dead," Leo said. "And we're in a rental, so that explains the extinguishers—it's not our house and we certainly don't want it burning down."

"Hmmmm. You may roll down your sleeve. All done."

"Thanks. And please, Doc, don't say anything to Alex about this. She thinks I'm this great big strong fearless protector type, and I don't want to disappoint."

"If you ever take a chance and tell her, she might surprise you, Leo."

"I never take chances and I don't like surprises, Doc," Leo said as the doctor stowed his goggles in a nearby closet and the two men returned to the waiting room.

Chapter Ten

After Leo and the doctor left the outer office, Alex sat down and surveyed her surroundings.

"He sure packs a lot into a ten by twenty room. Wonder where the Crypt Keeper is," Alex muttered. When alone, she talked to herself—an old childhood habit that she never conquered, or really cared to.

Since there were no magazines, and not enough light to read them by even if there were, she counted candles instead.

"Twenty. No wonder it's so dim in here. There's just one candle for every ten square feet of space."

The glass eyes of the trophies were about the only things that were well lit and every time the flames flickered, they seemed to move in their stiff, unyielding sockets.

In front of her was a desk with its right side pushed up tight to the wall. It was ornately carved, but it was too dark in the room to see the wood clearly. She glanced at the door that had closed behind her husband, then walked over and opened the top left drawer. Seeing that the interior was without a finish, she scratched the wood lightly, closed her eyes, lowered her head, and inhaled deeply. The faint but distinctive odor meant only one thing. Alex smiled.

The door to the inner office opened suddenly and she was caught in the act. She froze like a deer in headlights.

Leo stepped out first, and laughed when he saw what she was doing. Dr. Orbon followed, looking startled.

"What, may I ask…"

"Oh, don't worry, Doc. She's just smelling your desk."

"I beg your pardon?"

Alex, in her renewed mortification, suddenly developed the eloquence of a championship coffee drinker. "Well, you see, uh, I was just, that is, I mean…"

Leo intervened. "She wanted to know what kind of wood your desk was made of. There's not enough light in here to see it well, so she smelled it, instead."

"I still don't know how…"

"So, what is it?" Leo asked her.

"Hickory—and a lot of it dark, by the smell."

"Leo bent over and took a deep breath. "Yep. Hickory, all right. Can't miss that aroma. Here, Doc, take a sniff."

Looking doubtful, the doctor did as he was bid. "Ugh. I never realized that hickory smelled like this."

"All wood has a distinctive odor," Leo said. "And most other types are much more subtle than the dark part of a piece of hickory wood, which is even stronger when it's put through a saw, by the way—smells just like a cow manure. The odor is so authentic that it even attracts flies. Alex is getting to be a real pro at distinguishing wood by its odor. Anyhow, thanks, Doc. Hon, I'll be in the truck when you're through." With that, Leo opened the door and was immediately swallowed by the now welcome fog.

"Come this way, Alex," he said, withdrawing a box of matches to relight the hall candles.

"Dr. Orbon…"

"Oh, there's no need to be so formal—after all, you did just smell my desk. Please call me Beverly," he said, holding the door open for her.

"Excuse me?"

"I asked you to call me Beverly." He looked at her confused expression then said, "Oh, yes, I see. Let me explain. 'Beverly' is a man's name that's more common in England, I'm afraid."

"I wasn't aware of that."

"There may be one more thing you aren't aware of," he said, lighting the wall sconces as they moved down the hall.

"And what would that be?"

"The fact that one of the most masculine and macho movie stars on the American screen was named 'Marion.'"

"Who?" Alex asked as the doctor opened the inner door for her.

"John Wayne—born Marion Michael Morrison. He grew up in Iowa, and once appeared on a television show called *Laugh-In* in a pink bunny suit."

"I take it you enjoy reading biographies?"

"When you have this affliction, about the only things that are unfailingly good company are books."

"What about dogs?" Alex asked.

"Dogs cannot live healthy lives in the dark, unfortunately."

He opened the examining room door and Alex walked in. "I just love candles, though I don't understand how you're going to do a physical by them. You can't really see accurate color, so how would you know if a mole was a healthy brown or a cancerous black?"

"This isn't exactly that sort of physical," he said.

"Yes, I meant to ask. Leo was only in here for five minutes. What's up with that?"

"All I need to do is draw blood."

"That's not much of a physical, then, is it?"

"I would agree, but it is all I was asked to do. It's all I'm ever asked to do for those workers Mrs. Hamilton refers to me. She seems to believe that the worst diseases are blood borne and she's probably not wrong. So just have a seat at the blood-drawing desk here and you'll be on your way in no time."

"Does Theodora send you a lot of people?"

"Every summer there are people doing work up there while they're gone." Dr. Orbon held the syringe up to the candlelight.

Alex felt a little faint. "I have to tell you, Dr. Orbon... I mean, Beverly... I hate needles. I really hate them." She rolled up her sleeve.

"I'm painless, my dear."

"Well, of course you are—I'm the one getting stuck!"

Dr. Orbon chuckled and tightened the tourniquet. "Just look away, then. Make a fist, please. That's right. So, who is your regular physician?"

"Earle Munson, in the next town over."

"Ah, yes. Southfield. I've heard fine things about Dr. Munson."

"He came highly recommended. We both like him very much."

"Good, good. That's important."

"Let me ask you something, Beverly. Why wouldn't Theodora allow our own doctor to deal with this blood work?" Alex asked.

"As you trust Dr. Munson, Mrs. Hamilton trusts me. Okay, all finished."

"How could you be? I didn't feel anything."

"I told you I was painless." The doctor showed her the vials of blood he had drawn. "Now, as you are my last appointment of the night, I shall wish you a safe journey home and a good rest, and begin my nightly task of candle-snuffing before I retire to my rooms in the back."

"Would you like some help?"

"Why, if you would be so kind, then yes, thank you," he said, handing her one of the snuffers from his lab coat. "I usually do this with a snuffer in each hand, but it really isn't the safest way to extinguish so many candles."

An errant night breeze had come up that thinned the fog a bit and from his safe vantage point in the truck, Leo watched as, one by one, the candles in the office at the edge of the cemetery winked out.

Chapter Eleven

"I don't even pretend to know what to make of that," Leo said, pulling out of the gravel driveway and onto Church Street.

"I know what you mean. If you break the whole thing down to its individual parts, then each bit of strangeness has a reasonable explanation. But put it all together and..." Alex could only shake her head.

"Doesn't exactly spell 'mother,' does it?"

"I don't know what the hell it spells."

They rode on in silence for a bit, each lost in thought.

Alex wondered about what it must be like living with XP, and had a hard time imagining going through life without sunlight. It would mean no gardening, no pets, no color, really. But, if Dr. Orbon had never known anything else, perhaps the way the rest of humanity lives seems strange to him; living on the edge of the cemetery the way he does, with nothing but the fog and the damp and the never-ending silence of the moldering multitudes to keep him company while he reads biographies and becomes a spectator of normal life. What puzzled her most was his environment. He certainly didn't seem to care if it was cheerful or not. You'd think he'd want to make his surroundings as pleasant as possible. Can't do living plants? What about realistic silk ones? Anything would be better than a waiting room decorated with dead animals—and by candlelight, yet! Can't have a dog? What about a nocturnal pet? There are plenty of those around, weren't there? A small owl, maybe? What else is nocturnal? Bats, spiders... uh, yeah... back to cheery. A small owl would be a nice companion, though, wouldn't it? No pets and no gardening! The very idea was anathema to her.

Leo suddenly chuckled.

"Please tell me something's funny," Alex said.

"I was just thinking about your Dracula remark."

"Oh, don't remind me. That was the most embarrassing moment of my life. That poor man has a horrible disease to contend with, and I'm branding him 'evil undead bloodsucker.'"

Leo laughed. "It was still very funny, van Helsing."

"I guess," Alex smiled in spite of herself.

"Well, at the very least, you certainly impressed him with your 'fevered' imagination."

"Oh, God, did he really say that? 'Fevered?' You have no idea how much I wish I could take back that whole scene I made," Alex groaned.

"I don't think you offended him. He's probably used to remarks like that—he certainly leaves himself open for them with the candles, the Anthony Perkins ambiance, his crazy appointment hours, and no explanation for any of it unless someone asks. Christ, the only thing that was missing was a doorbell that played *Toccata en Fugue in D Minor.*" He pulled into their driveway and set the parking brake. "And did you notice? He thought you'd be a good writer, too. That's three votes."

"Three?"

"Sure. Dr. Orbon, me, and the fortune cookie."

"Right. I forgot about the fortune cookie."

"Oh, you should never forget about fortune cookies. He who forget fortune cookie wear underpants on outside of trousers."

"Sage advice. I'll have to remember that."

Just as they reached the front door, they heard their land line ringing.

"C'mon', c'mon, *c'mon!*" Alex muttered as she fumbled with the key.

"Relax, hon. It's probably a wrong number. Who'd be calling at this hour?" Leo asked.

The phone continued to jangle in the empty house. "Got it!" Alex cried, bursting across the threshold and grabbing the kitchen phone. "Hello!"

"Hello. Is this Leo's wife?"

"Yes it is. Who's calling, please?"

"This is Theodora Hamilton. You sound a bit out of breath."

Alex couldn't believe this. Theodora was having a conversation as if it wasn't—Alex looked at her watch—one thirty in the morning!

"Yes, well, it is pretty late."

"But you were up, were you not? As a matter of fact, you've just arrived home, isn't that right?"

Leo, looking irritated, was mouthing, *Who is it?*

Theodora! Alex mouthed back.

"Do you want me to take it?" Leo whispered.

"Are you still there?" Theodora asked.

"Yes, yes, I'm sorry. We just weren't expecting to hear from you tonight, or rather, this morning," Alex replied, trying to keep her tone light. She turned the earpiece of the phone so that Leo could listen, too.

"Well, I have your test results, and I thought I'd call and give them to you, since I knew you'd still be awake."

Leo and Alex stared at each other.

"You have the results? Already? How is that possible? We just left Dr. Orbon," Alex said.

"Isn't his office charming? Wonderful location. So scenic—I just love it there, don't you?" Theodora asked.

"Oh, does he have another office somewhere else?"

"No. You were at the only office he has. I find it truly lovely, wouldn't you agree?"

"Well, it's certainly peaceful…"

"Exactly."

"But how did you get the test results so quickly? I don't understand…"

"You don't need to understand, but I'll explain anyway. Dr. Orbon rushed them through for me. He does all the necessary testing on the premises, so there is no need to send the samples out to a laboratory and wait for weeks. He's terribly accommodating," Theodora said.

"Obviously. That's very nice," Alex said, shrugging her shoulders at Leo.

"At any rate, your blood tested fine—much better than other younger applicants I've had in the past. I like a mature couple without drug, alcohol, or smoking habits."

"I should tell you, Theodora, that though we don't smoke or take drugs, we do have a cocktail or two at the end of the workday," Alex said.

"How charming of you to want me to know all. As it happens, a moderate amount of alcohol is actually good for you—especially wine, so no worries there. Now, if you would be so kind, I will need your address," Theodora said. After Alex complied, she said, "I will send Cooper to pick you up at noon tomorrow... or rather, today, and we'll get the contracts signed and the deposit turned over to you."

"But Theodora, we haven't had time to draw up the contract and figure out the amount of the deposit and a payment schedule yet," Leo said, commandeering the phone.

"Ah, hello, Leo! Don't concern yourself. I've taken care of it all."

"Yes, you mentioned that before. This is not the way we prefer to do business, Theodora," Leo said.

He was talking to an empty line.

"Damn it!" Leo slammed down the receiver.

"What did she say, there, at the end?"

"Oh, we don't need to bother about the trivial little detail of drawing up a goddamned contract, because her highness has taken *that* out of our hands, too!" Leo was absolutely furious.

Alex had never heard Leo raise his voice since she'd known him, which admittedly wasn't all that long, since they only had a little over a year of history together. Naturally, there'd be a few surprises for both of them about each other, but they trusted the strength of their love to overcome them.

This was the first surprise for Alex. Leo was such a big man that when his deep voice boomed and anger contorted his face, he was a bit on the scary side. Well, more than a bit. *Lord, never let him be angry with me.*

"Sweetie, you need to calm down. Your face is bright red. Now have a seat and I'll fix us a nice cup tea, okay?"

"'A nice cup of tea' is not going to solve anything, Alex."

Surprise number two. Alex took a breath before speaking.

"Fine. How about a nice cup of cyanide, then? Or a contract killing? We can pay extra for torture."

"Would you be serious, just for once?" Leo shook his head, looking disgusted.

Hat trick.

"It would appear that the honeymoon is indeed over," Alex said. "In the space of thirty seconds you have shouted, mocked my tea, and resented my sense of humor. What*ever* will the next hour bring?"

Leo reacted like he'd been slapped, then hung his head. "I'm sorry. I don't know what's wrong with me, honey. Of course I'm not mad at you. I get so damned frustrated trying to deal with all this nonsense—these stupid rules—just to make a living. I want us to have a good life, without having to tiptoe through the Twilight Zone to get it!"

Gentler now, she said, "I'm sorry you're upset, Leo. The only advice I can offer you at this point is to try to keep in mind who it is you're mad at. I know it's not me. When last I checked, we were on the same side. I understand that the rules are bizarre, but if we're going to do this job, and I assume, since you haven't said otherwise, that we are, then we'll just have to try to roll with them. And if you don't think you're going to be able to do that without getting upset all the time, then I don't want to take this job. No amount of money is worth becoming a stress-widow over. Want that tea now?"

"Sure. Pour in a little whiskey, will you? Maybe it will help me sleep," Leo said.

By the time the tea and oatmeal cookies were on the table, Leo was in a better frame of mind. "Remember the first time you made oatmeal cookies for me?" he asked.

"Oh, don't remind me," Alex moaned. "I was trying so

hard to impress you with my cooking skills. And I still don't know what I did wrong. They just wouldn't set up properly. What a gooey mess they were."

"Oh, c'mon! They were good!"

"I can't believe, to this day, that you ate them anyway so my feelings wouldn't be hurt."

"They were fine. I like your 'cuppa-cookies.'"

"I've been afraid to make them ever since; but now that we're married and you're stuck with me anyway, I thought I'd give it another shot," Alex said. "Try one."

"What are you? Scared?"

"You betcha. If nothing happens to you, I'll have one," Alex said.

Leo sighed. "Okay, gimme a straw."

Alex laughed. Her Leo was back. As she sipped her cinnamon tea, she noticed the deposit slip at the front of the wire letter rack on the table. "Remember, Leo, we have Joyce's check. We don't have to take this job."

"I know. But the cash we could put away if we do take it is what keeps me from walking away. It could buy us both health insurance, which we desperately need. Our teeth could stand some attention on a regular basis, too."

"We both have good teeth. It's not like our teeth are even close to falling out, hon."

"No, but if we can get to a dentist regularly, they won't. Plus, there's another thing I'd like to do for you, too," he said.

"Really? Like what?"

"Down payment on a house."

"A house? Really, Leo?"

"Why not?"

Alex thought that all of Leo's reasons for taking Theodora's job made complete sense. The lack of health insurance that made doctor visits that weren't emergencies beyond affording—and they couldn't even think about dental work. Dentists were twice as expensive as doctors. And what she wouldn't do for a small house with some land for a huge vegetable garden and maybe some chickens, oh, and flowers and a hive or two of bees, and let's not forget the apple trees and berry bushes…

"What are you thinking about? You look so happy," Leo asked.

"Just dreaming about what I'd like to do if we had a house with a decent piece of land attached to it. I've never owned my own home before."

"I didn't know that." Now Leo was doubly resolved to give home ownership to Alex.

"You have, though, right? Owned a house?"

"I've owned three or four houses, but I've never had a home. Not 'til now, anyway. Now, home is wherever you are."

"Oh, Leo, that's so sweet—thank you. But I don't want us to take on a job, or any job, that you have misgivings about."

'Misgivings' was a pretty mild word for what he felt about Theodora Hamilton and her overpriced paint job; but the money was just too good to turn his back on and still be able to consider himself a responsible adult. Alex never complained about their tight finances, but he knew there were things she wanted that she had to pass up time after time. What killed him was that they weren't even big things, the stuff she wanted; but even when the stores had huge sales, there just wasn't the spare cash to take advantage of them, and so she did without yarn for her knitting and trips to the area nursery for flowers and bulbs to plant outside. She was going to contact their landlord to see if she could put in a small vegetable patch in the back yard, but until they'd deposited Joyce's check, even the price of the seeds for it would have been a financial stretch.

Thank God Alex wasn't a "shop 'til you drop" type of woman. He'd had enough of that with two previous wives and a pile of bills deep enough to stock with trout. By stark contrast, Alex did all her clothes shopping in Goodwill stores, and she claimed the secret was to find one in or near a wealthy area. That way, the clothes were of fantastic quality and barely worn half the time. It worked for her, because she always looked great and she delighted in telling him the ridiculously low price she paid for each of her outfits. It was a big game to her, finding new ways to squeeze a buck and not sacrifice quality, and it was a game she was good at.

But this job…

Leo's gut screamed, "Run away! Flee while you can!" In the past, he always wound up regretting it when he ignored such urgent internal warnings.

And he was very much afraid he was about to ignore this one.

He drank the dregs of his tea. "Let's not make a decision right this minute. I'm for sleeping on it. What about you?"

Alex nodded. "Probably a sensible idea."

But neither of them closed their eyes for too long, and what sleep they did get was crowded with threatening shadows of disquieting, vaguely remembered images that left them troubled upon waking.

Chapter Twelve

"Hurry up, Leo! I still have to shower yet," Alex called. "Breakfast in ten minutes!"

After a night of tossing and turning, they finally fell deeply asleep at dawn and didn't wake until nearly eleven. Being ready on time for their noon pick up was going to be a near thing.

Alex got the coffee going and started Leo's eggs, bacon and toast. She put a bowl of leftover soup into the microwave for herself. By the time everything was hot, Leo was bustling down the hall, still in his bathrobe, but showered and shaved, at least.

"Sorry, sorry, sorry. I'm running a little late. The damned raccoon or skunk, or whatever we've got marauding at night around here, got into the trash can again and I had to go out and play garbage collector. It was scattered all over the neighborhood—my grandmother would have said, 'from heck to breakfast'—speaking of which, that smells great!" he said as she filled his plate. "Where's yours?"

"I'm having borscht."

"I will never understand your eating habits."

"I could eat soup three meals a day," Alex said.

"Well, you do make great soup."

"And it's not just for breakfast anymore. Did you get everything picked up?"

"Yeah, it took forever, though."

"Why didn't you get me up earlier? I would have helped you," Alex said.

"I was going to, but you looked so comfortable, I didn't have the heart. We have to get some kind of locking top for that can, though. This is the fourth or fifth time I've had to pick up trash all over town before my first cup of coffee."

By the time they were both ready to go, it was twelve-thirty.

"Didn't Theodora say noon?" Leo asked.

"Yes. I'd call her if we had her number."

"Well, I, for one, am glad he's late. It gives me a chance to water the plants," Alex said, bending to fill the shallow crock beneath her huge Queensland Umbrella Tree.

Leo surveyed the plant-filled house. "Water your jungle, you mean. I've never known anyone with such a green thumb."

Alex shrugged. "Keeps me from stealing hubcaps, I guess. I just wish we had some south-facing windows. Without them, I can only grow shade- or partial shade- loving plants, and that pretty much rules out flowers."

"You'll plant flowers outside, then," Leo said.

"I already have our flower beds all planned out," Alex said. "We sure have to plant something out there in that dirt patch—starting with grass. It's like the Little House on the Prairie around here."

At that moment, a black land yacht of a Cadillac docked in their driveway.

"Guess that's our ride," Leo said. "Let the games begin."

"So, are we going to do this, or not? You wanted to sleep on it. What do you think?"

"I think the money's too good to turn down. How about you?"

"Keep your options open until we hear what she has to say today. We can walk away anytime before we sign whatever contract she has for us. But this is going to be a good day for us, I can feel it."

"Why?"

"I'm wearing my favorite shoes!"

Alex had on a pair of shiny red patent leather driving shoes that were bright enough to cause radio interference for miles around. Today, they stood out even more, considering that her jeans, blazer, and turtleneck were all black. Her feet positively glowed.

"I have no idea why you like those shoes so much. They

don't really go with anything," Leo said.

"They do so! They're a happy color and 'happy' goes with everything." She paused, peering out the window at the waiting limo. "I want you to know that I trust your judgment entirely as far as this job goes, Leo."

I wish I did, Leo thought.

The Caddy just sat there idling... waiting... like Liberty Valence at high noon. The darkly tinted windows rendered the interior invisible.

And maybe that was a good thing.

"C'mon. Let's get this over with," Leo muttered, staring at the car.

"I'm all for that," Alex said, less heartily than she would have liked. To be honest, leaving their house at that moment was the last thing she wanted to do. "Are you sure you wouldn't rather just be nibbled to death by ducks?" she asked, turning to lock the door behind her.

"I'm not sure at all," Leo said, taking her hand and approaching the black vehicle.

"There is one consolation, though. Today is April twenty-fourth, 2008. Numerologically speaking, that comes out to eleven, which is a master number," Alex said.

"And that's a good thing?" Leo asked, not taking his eyes off the car.

"A very good thing," Alex replied as they approached the limo.

It was quite the car. Despite tailfins that stretched into the next town, whitewall tires, and immaculate chrome, when looking at it, all Leo could think of was funerals.

At that moment, the driver's door swung open and Theodora Hamilton's general factotum emerged.

He was a dwarf.

Cooper Black was a dark-skinned little man who looked as if he called Calcutta home. He was a perfectly proportioned miniature with the exception of the overlarge head, characteristic of many forms of dwarfism. His hands were beautiful, though—delicate-looking, without the usual stubbiness more common in dwarfs. His longish hair was jet black and his enormous eyes were so dark that the irises and the pupils were indistinguishable. His nose, crooked and somewhat flattened, bespoke of a fight or two and the mouth nestled beneath it was tiny, with lips so thin they appeared absent. Also absent was even a trace of a smile or glint of welcome in his eyes.

He moved to the back door and heaved it open. This was accompanied by a drawn out metallic creak.

If cars could scream, that's what it would sound like, Alex thought.

Black then turned around and stood next to the yawning dark opening. Though he was not much more than three feet tall, his silence was immense. The black holes that were his eyes bored through them as he waited.

What was even worse was that Theodora had him decked out in a chauffeur's uniform, complete with a hat perched on his oversized head.

He looked frightening and ridiculous simultaneously.

"Well, let's make an attempt," Alex said. She wasn't sure if he would be insulted if she squatted down to speak to him at eye level; and she certainly didn't feel comfortable staring down at him like a buzzard. She opted not to take a chance and kept her upright position.

Leo, an antique car fanatic, strolled around to the look at the back of the Caddy. To its driver, Alex exclaimed, "Wow! What a great car! What year is it?"

Black stood ramrod stiff and stared straight ahead, pointedly ignoring her.

She tried again. "You must be Mr. Black."

Cooper Black gazed up at her, unblinking and expressionless, but Alex kept going.

"I'm Alex Renfield, and that's my husband, Leo. I guess we'll be seeing a lot of each other this summer."

Still nothing.

"Hello?" Alex said.

The driver continued to stare up at Alex just a beat too long, then, without taking his dead eyes off her, pointed to the back seat.

"Let it go, hon," Leo said, walking up and pulling her by the hand. Once they were seated, the heavy black door creak-chunked shut, plunging them into nearly total darkness. Black resumed his place behind the wheel; but before backing out of the driveway, he raised a dark partition separating him from his passengers and making their darkness complete.

Alex immediately began patting down the seat.

"What are you doing?" Leo asked.

"I'm looking for David Lynch."

"Now I know why she insisted we be driven to her house. I don't have the slightest idea how to get to OZ," Leo grumbled.

"He doesn't exactly look like he represents the Lollipop Guild, though, does he?"

"More like the Coroner," Leo said.

"Before he raised the damn partition, I was going to ask him how far away Theodora's house is. He probably wouldn't have answered me, anyway. I feel like a kidnap victim!"

"How's he driving this boat? He's too short to reach the pedals."

"I saw a show once about how Little People deal with living in a world that's not designed for them. To drive, they usually install pedal extensions for the gas and brake. Some of them have customized cars with just hand controls."

"'Little People?' It isn't PC anymore to call then 'dwarfs?' Has anyone sued Disney yet? I can just see the revised movie poster now: 'Snow Caucasian and the Seven Differently-Abled Little People' starring Snow Caucasian ('Snow Whitey' in theaters on 125th Street) with Allergic Rhinitis Little Person, Clinically Depressed with Anger Issues Little Person, Mentally Challenged Little Person, Narcoleptic Little Person, Little Person with Underdeveloped Social Skills, Little Person with an Advanced Degree, and let's not forget Extremely Agreeable Little Person Who Smokes Medically Prescribed Marijuana,'"

Leo snorted. "Political correctness will ruin us all!"

"I am *so* impressed, Leo," Alex said.

"Why?"

"You remembered all seven of the dwarfs. I always forget 'Bashful.'"

"Everybody always forgets 'Bashful.'"

"Why did you tell me to let it go when Black was being so rude before?"

"Because maybe there's more to it than we know. Maybe he was told not to speak to us. Or maybe he's deaf."

"Oh, gosh. Deaf. I never even thought of deafness, but I bet that's it—he didn't even say hello! Golly, the poor guy, a dwarf *and* a deaf mute. Holy crap! How unlucky can you get?"

"At the moment, I'd say our luck's not what it used to be, either, kiddo." Leo murmured.

"What? Why?"

"There are no handles on the insides of these doors—at least, none that I can feel, and I've checked the whole door."

"So?"

"So we couldn't get out if we wanted to. Unless somebody opens the door from the outside, it's here we stay. Just like in a police car."

"Really? I wonder what's up with that."

"I wish I knew."

"Well, since there's nothing we can do about it until we get to Theodora's, let's talk about something else. For instance, what year do you think this car is?" Alex asked, desperate to get her mind and Leo's off their present predicament.

It didn't work.

"I don't know what this car is, let alone what year it is," Leo said.

"What do you mean? It's a Cadillac from the sixties, isn't it? What other car had tailfins like that?"

"There's something weird with it."

"How so?"

"I'm not sure. It looks like someone's impression of a 1961 Cadillac limo. It's close, but not quite right. For one thing, the logo doesn't say 'Cadillac.' It says, 'Caddy'. Right script, wrong word. And this is a Fleetwood model, but the Fleetwood script is on the rear roof pillar. That's wrong. It should be on the rear quarter panel. The rear roof pillar was where they put the Coupe DeVille script on the Series Sixty-two models. It was exclusive to the DeVille—and it was a characteristic of a 1951 DeVille. Also did you see the eight vertical chrome louvers in the front edge of the rear fenders? Again, a 1951 feature, but in a Series Sixty Special Fleetwood. And did you notice the front bumper?"

"Yeah, I did. I thought it was pretty. I like all that heavy polished chrome and those two bumps," Alex replied.

"Those two bumps are called Dagmar bumper bullets. They were available on the 1953 Caddies, and were discontinued long before this body model. This car has a 1961 Series Seventy-five D body, but everything else is all over the place."

"What did you find at the rear? You looked awfully confused."

"There were side marker lights back there and they didn't come in until 1968 when the Feds started requiring them. But getting back to the front of the car—where's the wrapped windshield? In 1961, Cadillac eliminated wrapped windshields on *every model but this one*. And the grille, with the body-color horizontal divider bar is pure 1964, but the front fender cornering lights are from 1962 and the tall tail light backup lamps are 1963, as is the vinyl roof covering. And the auxiliary grilles underneath the tail lights were never, ever on any Caddy or, for that matter, on any car that I've ever heard of. Usually individual cars have one model year. This one has seven or eight with a touch of "completely fucked up" here and there."

"Anything else?" Alex asked, bemused.

"The door opened on the wrong side. Didn't you catch that? The hinges were on the right side of the opening, instead of the left."

"Why is it that you think you're not observant, Leo?" Alex

asked.

"I'm not observant like you. I just know cars, that's all," he said.

"Maybe it's made up of scavenged parts from all different models—like that Johnny Cash song—what was the name of it?"

"*One Piece at a Time*. And no, that's not it."

"Why not?"

"You'd never be able to integrate them so seamlessly. This car looks like it came off the assembly line this way... but it couldn't have. I just don't under..."

Before Leo could complete his thought, there was a loud bump and the car jerked to a stop.

"What was that? Did we hit something?" Alex asked.

"Who knows? All I know is if there's a flat, he's fixing it his own damned self—locking us up like this! I don't like this crap and Theodora's going to get an earful if we ever get there," Leo said.

"But Leo, he's deaf and so little..."

"Is the car my job or his job?"

"Leo!"

"Ah, shit! Yes, if he needs my help, I'll help, of course!"

As it turned out, Leo's help was neither required nor desired, and in ten minutes or so, they were on their way again. Alex cast about for a subject to pass the time.

"Did I ever tell you that I dated a dwarf once?" she asked.

"No. When?"

"It was before I met you. A Yahoo Personals lead. We hit it off really well through email, and we made plans to go out to dinner. I gave him my address, because he wanted to pick me up at my apartment, and..."

"Wait. You gave him your address before you even met him? What if he'd been a serial killer, Alex? Jesus!"

"Leo, my love, have you forgotten about that black belt I have in the closet? I'm better than a loaded gun because nobody suspects, when looking at little ol' me, that I could put them down with one shot from my little ol' fist."

"You drive me crazy sometimes, you know that? You're so cavalier about personal safety."

"Do you want to hear this story, or not?"

"Go ahead."

"So he was going to take me out to dinner at the Riviera—downstairs, if you please. Upstairs is Italian, downstairs is French and it's *tres* expensive."

"Yeah, yeah... so?"

"So when he rang the doorbell and I opened the door, ta dah! A dwarf," Alex said.

"So that's why you didn't get together?"

"Hardly. But when he walked into my apartment, he looked so terrified, Leo. I asked him to sit down and I got us both drinks. He took a huge gulp of scotch and then said that he'd understand if I didn't want to go out with him."

"Aw, that's really sad," Leo said.

"It gets worse."

"But how could you not have known ahead of time that he was a dwarf? When you fill in your vital statistics, there's a blank for height."

"He lied, Leo. In his stats he was six-two. When I asked him why, he said that he was afraid I wouldn't meet him if he told me the truth. I just wanted to cry. I said I'd be more than happy to have dinner out with him, or I could make dinner for us at the apartment—his choice."

"You're really terrific, you know."

"Oh, hold your applause, please. We had dinner at the apartment, because I didn't want him spending huge wads of cash on me. I knew how the evening was going to end, you see."

"Uh oh."

"When he asked to see me again, I said no. Not because I didn't like him—I did. And not because of his dwarfism—I didn't care. It was because he lied to me—for whatever the reason. And he lied about his *height*—a really stupid lie. I had to ask myself what else he'd lie to me about in the future. I explained all this to him and we parted with no hard feelings. He came over for dinner a couple more times after that, as a friend, and I noticed that he changed his Yahoo Personals stats to reflect his dwarfism. A week before I met you, he got married."

"To another dwarf?" Leo asked.

"Nope. To a gorgeous blonde fashion model who's five-ten. He looked really happy in the picture in the paper. For a wedding gift, I carved them a sign out of spalted maple for their wall."

"What did it say?"

"'SIZE IS NOT IMPORTANT.'"

"Did they like it?"

"Oh, yeah," Alex said, grinning at the memory of the phone call from the two of them. They had threatened to name their first child after her.

The darkness inside the passenger compartment of the limo was disorienting, since outside it was a bright, sunny afternoon. "Do you think these windows are tinted this way to keep us from finding the house on our own?" Alex asked.

"Who knows? I'm not directing this movie."

"I hate this. It's like riding in the trunk. I can hardly see you. Is there an overhead light anywhere?" Alex asked, feeling around.

"No overhead light," Leo said. "I already checked the ceiling."

"Swell. As screwed up as this car is, maybe it's on the floor."

The limo smelled strange, too. Instead of the rich leather aroma typical of luxury vehicles, this car had the stale, musty smell of disuse—as if it had been closed up in a garage for a year and hadn't been aired before being put back on the road.

"Aha!" Alex exclaimed, snapping her fingers. But before she could act on that "aha," she had a sneezing fit, breaking a previous personal record of twelve sneezes. She dug around in her handbag for a moment, and Leo assumed she was looking for tissues, but suddenly, there was light.

"Ah, good for you! I never think to put my Maglite in my pocket."

"Did you bring the comic books?" Alex asked, blowing her nose. She moved the small but powerful beam over their surroundings. There was actually a cobweb in the corner opposite the door. "You're right, Leo. No door handles. And just look at this!" Alex ran her finger across the windowsill and it came back deeply layered in what had to have been years of accumulated dust. "So much for the Good Housekeeping Seal of Approval and my dust allergy," she sniffed.

"If you find any dinosaur bones, I wonder if you get to keep them," Leo mused.

One thing there wasn't in the back seat was any sound from either the front seat or outside the car. Not only was the glass tinted black, but was also thick enough to be soundproof.

Alex yawned. "You know, I'm getting really sleepy all of a sudden, hon. I think I'll just close my eyes for a few minutes."

She was answered by a soft snore from Leo's direction.

Chapter Thirteen

"Hon," Alex said, shaking Leo by the shoulder. "Wake up. We've stopped again. I think we're there."

"Hnmph," Leo replied eloquently.

"Come *on*, Leo! Wake up!"

"I'm up, I'm up! What'd I miss?"

"Dunno. I was asleep, too. No idea how long," Alex said.

"It feels like hours," Leo said, stretching.

"Yeah, it does. I feel like I slept all afternoon. But we couldn't have been out that long. Theodora lives right in town somewhere, doesn't she?"

"We assumed that. Maybe she doesn't," Leo said.

"Curiouser and curiouser."

Further speculation was cut short by their release from the Caddy's dark backward.

"Leo, it's twilight," Alex whispered, following him out of the car. "We *have* been asleep for hours."

"Can't be," Leo said. But he wasn't talking about their naps. "It just can't be!" He was staring at the side of the Caddy with a horrified expression on his face. Cooper Black stood by the closed driver's door watching him with the intense interest usually accorded to lab rats navigating mazes.

"What's wrong, Leo?"

"The side marker lights are gone. So are the vertical louvers."

Before Alex could react, he dashed to the front of the Cadillac.

"The Dagmar bullets are gone, too. So's the horizontal body color divider bar on the grille." He looked up. "It has a wrap-around windshield now, and the vinyl roof covering is gone—it's a hard top now."

He ran to the rear of the vehicle.

"The tail light grilles are gone and the tail lights are right for a sixty-one. This car is a now 1961 Cadillac!"

"Well, maybe…"

"No 'maybe,' Alex. And look," he said as he came back around, "it says 'Fleetwood' on the rear quarter panel now. The logo's right, too." Leo looked as if he might cry.

"Honey, we've both been under a lot of stress lately. Maybe you just made a mistake," Alex said, and tried very hard to make herself believe it.

"You saw the front bumpers before. Have a look now."

Alex looked. "Well, I must have made a mistake, then. There was a lot of glare off all that chrome. It would be easy for the mind to fill in something that wasn't actually there when you can't see clearly."

"Okay, then look at the door you just stepped out of."

Alex glanced back at the door.

The hinges were on the left side.

"I don't feel so good, Leo."

Leo looked at Cooper Black, then said, "I think he probably feels worse."

The tiny driver was covered in what looked like dark rusty water and his right hand was wrapped in a dripping blood-soaked rag. His face betrayed no suffering, but his dark skin was ashen. He waited for them to collect themselves, then before Alex could ask if he needed help, he turned and tottered up the driveway.

"He looks bad, Leo."

Leo looked around, ignoring Alex's comment. "Where's the house?" he asked.

"Thataway, I guess," Alex replied, indicating Black's receding figure.

"Why didn't he drive all the way up?"

"Maybe the bridge over the moat full of alligators is out."

"Fun-nee."

"We better get a move on, Leo. Remember, Theodora said it's really easy to get totally lost around here, and it's getting dark."

"Honey, the driveway only goes one way and she said we could get lost if we left the grounds or stepped off the paths, remember?"

"Oh, right."

But still they stayed where they were, stalling.

"I feel like I'm losing my mind, Alex."

"Because of the car, you mean?"

"Yeah. I know what I saw before I got in."

"There are such things as shared hallucinations, aren't there? Couldn't that be an explanation? Between the glare, the stress, and the strangeness?"

"It could be, I guess," Leo said. "Crazy as it is, it's the only explanation that makes any sense."

Though Alex tried to explain things away, she knew damned well that Leo was not one for flights of fancy, since "imagination was discouraged in my house by the buckle of my father's belt" according to him. Evidently, old Mr. Renfield, throwing Dr. Spock to the wind, thought that a good imagination in a boy was an early sign of homosexuality, and he "wasn't gonna raise no faggots under his roof."

So the fact that Leo was not imagining things was what was so profoundly disturbing now. She didn't know enough about vintage Cadillacs to really pay much attention to what was where on the car and she thought she did see those bumps on the front bumper; but with the glare and without sunglasses, who could be sure? That would have been the story she'd have stuck to if it wasn't for the fact that Leo had seen them, too. And those door hinges. It was all so impossible! She was getting seriously – what? *Unnerved* was way too mild, as were *uneasy*, and *bothered*. What was the word she was looking for?

Ah, yes.

Scared. That's the one.

She was relieved that Leo seemed satisfied with her theory.

"What do you think happened to him, Leo?"

"Who? Black? He cut himself fixing whatever was wrong with this thing."

Alex turned back to the Caddy. "I think it's pretty serious cut, hon. That bandage of his was dripping like a faucet."

"Which reminds me—now that he's gone, I think I'll take a look at the engine," Leo said, raising the hood. "Oh, Jesus."

"What?"

Leo stepped aside to reveal the engine block.

It was completely covered with blood.

"Holy shit! Shut it, Leo! *Shutitshutitshutit!*" Alex cried. She turned and dashed thirty feet up the dirt road, away from the car.

Leo gently closed the hood, then trudged up to join Alex. He stared at the ground, silent.

"Leo, honey? You okay?"

"No, Alex, I am not okay."

"Let's just go, Leo. Let's just walk right out of here now."

"And go where? We don't even know where we are."

"Would you rather stay here? With the bloodmobile?" Alex asked.

"No. Come on, let's at least get a few answers before we leave."

On the way up the road, Alex asked, "Could Black really have cut himself that badly? I mean, bad enough to bleed all over the engine like that, and still be alive? He didn't look like he had that much blood in his whole body."

"Well, he didn't look too great when he left us. I wouldn't be surprised if we find him unconscious along the way somewhere," Leo said.

They pulled their jackets closer as a renegade lionesque March wind sprang up suddenly, long after it was supposed to have made way for the lamb and April showers. It whipped around them, shaking the silent woods with its roar and throttling the bare branches of the trees that closely hemmed in the roadway, giving them the macabre appearance, just for a second, of dancing skeletons shaking their heads. A crow darted past them, surfing down the wind to land on the edge of a nearby stump, where it paced about, sternly lecturing the area with raucous, jagged cries. It trained a gimlet eye on them, judging and obviously finding them unworthy as either food or adversaries. Just a couple of no-account strangers, trespassing on its turf.

Dry oak leaves, still clinging high above from the previous autumn, rattled their refusal to leave home at the breeze, and in response, several of their fallen brethren were scooped up in a small dervish, spun about in defiance, and relocated to resume their slow march to decay.

The crow punctuated its hostility by hopping forward and pointedly cawing in Alex and Leo's general direction.

"Xenophobe," Alex muttered at it.

The air, quite suddenly, became still.

The crow drew itself up with a great deal of dignity for a bird, and looked from Alex to Leo to Alex again, as if expecting some further, more interesting response. Receiving none, the rook stepped lightly into the air and flapped off to a shade-stunted, ancient gnarled apple tree to join two others of its kind. The three blue-black birds perched in silence, staring down at them. The forest continued to hold its breath.

After a moment, Alex asked, "Do you know what they say about three crows sitting in a tree?"

"Does this have something to do with K-I-S-S-I-N-G?" Leo spelled.

Alex snorted. "No. It's an omen. It's supposed to mean there's a storm coming."

"I'd have to agree that that's pretty accurate," Leo said. "I think it's going to hit just about the minute we walk into that house—if we ever get there, that is. How long is this piece of crap road, anyhow?"

"It can't be much longer."

"The house must be at the top of this hill. Must be a bitch to drive up in the winter," he said.

"They probably have it plowed."

Leo squatted down and brushed aside the leaves. "Doesn't look like it. You'd see plow marks and there aren't any."

"Maybe they go away for the winter, too. They seem to like hot places. Maybe they check in at an active volcano somewhere," Alex said.

They continued their trek, on the lookout for the bleeding driver, for another twenty minutes. The hill became less steep and then fully leveled out just before the road began a series of sharp twists and turns.

"You'd think they'd have these switchbacks where the hill is the steepest—where they'd do some good in the snow—not on level ground," Leo grumbled.

"This is like walking on a path through an intestine. We'd better get there pretty soon. I sure as hell don't want to be traipsing around out here at night. Who knows what's in these woods? Maybe we should just go back to the car and wait. What do you think?"

"I think I see a roof just over those trees," Leo replied.

Chapter Fourteen

"Well would you look at that!" Leo said, previous anger forgotten. "It's an honest to goodness Carpenter Gothic. I've only seen pictures of them… old photographs. Nobody builds these anymore. Alex, you're looking at a genuine piece of architectural history."

"Granted, Leo, but why in *hell* would anyone paint their house black? I've never seen a black house in my life. I mean, it's not like it's a dark grey or anything. It's locked-in-the-closet-without-a-nightlight black. It's… eerie; though I must admit, it's also beautifully built," Alex said. *And it scares me to death.*

Leo continued to rave about the house, but in low, reverential tones more appropriate to the interior of a church than the exterior of an eccentrically painted building out in the middle of the woods.

The house was, to put it mildly, gigantic—extending outward in several places at the back of the main house where, through the years, other rooms had been added. When she studied the tightly grouped additions, Alex got the unappealing impression of a cluster of toadstools.

But the main, the original architecture of the house was fine beyond words, in spite of its unfortunate color.

"Incredible. Just incredible," Leo murmured.

Alex shook her head sadly. "I can't get by the black exterior. It looks like Grant Wood's nightmare. All it needs is the Frankenstein Monster in overalls holding a pitchfork.

Leo chuckled. "With his lovely bride by his side. It is spooky-looking, though, isn't it?"

"Spooky-looking! This place would make an altar boy out of Freddy Krueger."

"You know, there aren't that many authentic Carpenter Gothic houses left in this country. Oh, and that house behind that pre-Prozac couple in Wood's *American Gothic* painting is a real house. It's in Eldon, Iowa."

Alex grinned up at him. "Leo, you amaze me with the things you know."

He shrugged off the compliment. "Carpenter Gothic has always been my favorite architectural style—mainly, I guess, because carpenters created it."

"What defines a Carpenter Gothic house?" Alex asked.

"Usually the vertical board and batten siding that you see here, which steam-powered sawmills made possible; also the arched, pointed windows and doors. The steam powered scroll saw was invented around that period…"

"Which was when?" Alex interrupted.

"American Gothic Revival ran from 1830 to 1860, and American High Victorian Gothic from 1860 to 1890. Carpenter Gothic in the United States made it appearance in 1840 and reached its height of popularity in the 1880s, so you could say that it overlapped two architectural periods."

"Impressive. You were saying about the steam powered scroll saw?" Alex prompted.

"Oh, yeah. Carpenters used it to create all the ornate "gingerbread" woodwork you see on the eaves and gable edges on these sorts of houses. It was a way of mimicking gothic stonework in wood. Steeply pitched roofs gables, wall dormers, and oriel windows are other characteristics," Leo explained.

"What's an 'oriel window?'" Alex asked.

"It's just a bay window on an upper floor. There's one on the left side of this house, see?"

"Oh, yeah, there it is. You are just a walking encyclopedia, Leo, and the first moment I'm at the library, I'm taking out a book about architecture. I never realized it was so interesting," Alex said. "Would Mark Twain's house in Hartford be considered Carpenter Gothic?" She took Leo's hand and they made their way toward the front door.

"I think his house is more Steamboat Gothic. The Steamboat Gothic houses were mostly built in the Mississippi and Ohio River Valleys because they were designed to look like the steamboats that ran on those rivers."

"Makes perfect sense. Twain worked on a steamboat. That's how he chose his pseudonym," Alex said.

"And how was that?"

"From checking water depth and calling out the number of fathoms to the captain. You strand one of those steamboats on a sandbar, you've got big trouble, so they checked depth frequently. 'Mark one' was one fathom, or six feet. 'Mark twain' was twelve feet."

They had reached the foot of the porch steps when the massive arched front door slowly pulled inward.

"Ah, *there* you are!" Theodora exclaimed. "I hoped you hadn't gone wandering off the path. So very easy to get completely turned around. It even happens to me sometimes and I've lived here forever. Well, come in, come in."

Alex glanced at Leo. "Showtime," she said. Leo didn't hear her, having turned his attention back to the Carpenter Gothic before them, his quest for answers abandoned. Sighing, she looked at Theodora and froze. A torrent of blood and gore burst forth from the inside the open front door, whirled around Theodora's legs, and splashed down the steps like mountain rapids moving fast from a heavy spring thaw. Alex's gasp snapped Leo out of his reverie.

"Honey? What's wrong?" Leo asked.

"Oh, she'll be all right," Theodora said, with just a trace of a smile.

"Alex!" Leo stepped in front of her, cutting off her view of the front of the house.

She turned her wide eyes on him. "The blood! Leo, didn't you see all the blood?" she hissed.

"What blood? You mean the blood all over the car engine?"

"No! There! Right there!" Alex pushed him aside. "Pouring down th..."

A few fallen leaves skittered across the dry porch.

"I could swear I saw..."

"See? She's fine. Now come on in before the flies completely take over," Theodora urged from the open doorway.

They mounted the front steps. Alex had no choice but to chalk her strange vision up to still being overwrought about the blood-soaked Cadillac engine, and so made an effort to collect herself.

"It's good to see you both," Theodora said, pushing the huge front door closed, with Leo's help.

"It's good to be here," Leo said.

"At last," Alex muttered.

"What a fantastic house you have," Leo exclaimed. "I was just telling Alex that I've never seen a Carpenter Gothic in anything but photos before."

"Ah, I like a man who knows his architecture. It is wonderful, isn't it? And we got it for an absolute song," Theodora said, touching Leo's arm. "It was built by Stephen Prince, you know."

It was apparent to Alex that Stephen Prince had since ascended and was now writing horror novels in Maine. "Where, exactly, is this house?" Alex asked. "Still in Woodhaven?"

"Why do you ask?"

"It took an awfully long time to get here, and Woodhaven's not a large town. We left around noon and it's twilight now. We could have traveled across the entire state in that amount of time."

"Yes, well, it can fool you," Theodora said, sidestepping the question. "But I see that you both wear watches, so you tell me. How long did it take to get here?"

"No good," Alex said. "My watch stopped at twelve thirty-seven."

"Mine, too."

Theodora smiled, tilted her head slightly and raised her drawn-on eyebrows. "It happens here all the time. You'll notice that there are no clocks in this house, and no one wears a wristwatch. It has to do with interference in the magnetic field or some such thing. Whatever it is, it stops every timepiece anywhere on the property. Now, if you'll follow me through here, I'll give you a tour and then we'll get down to business."

Alex nudged Leo and whispered, "Twelve thirty-seven is right about the time we got into the back seat of that Cadillac." Then, turning to Theodora, she asked, "Is Mr. Black all right?"

"Oh, his little cut, you mean? Yes, he'll be just fine," she replied.

"It was more than just a 'little cut,' Theodora," Leo said.

Theodora took his arm in what Alex considered an inappropriately chummy manner, and piloted him through the foyer. "You are so sweet to be concerned."

"He lost an awful lot of blood. We expected to find him dead in the driveway," Alex said, trailing behind.

"'Dead in the driveway.' How amusing," she said, her attention still riveted on Leo. "Was he leaving a trail with all this blood?"

Leo looked a trifle embarrassed. "No, no trail. See, I'm an antique car buff, and after Mr. Black left us, I popped the hood to look at the engine and…"

"…*and* the entire engine was covered with blood," Alex finished. She couldn't get over the way Leo was behaving. Once he set eyes on the house, he forgot all about how upset he'd been. Leo could truly see angels in the architecture, though Alex thought he'd have to look damned hard to find them here.

Theodora sighed. "Well, not to worry. My husband, Ross, is taking care of him right now. A stitch or two, and he'll be just fine. Blood all over the engine, you say? I do hope he had a good reason for that."

Leo, clearly confused, stared back over his shoulder at Alex. "Would a gash not be considered a good reason for bleeding?" his look asked. Alex gave a barely perceptible shrug and turned her attention to the first stop on Theodora's tour. The huge room was just off the foyer, to the right, and did double duty as a gallery and a living room. Too much artwork crowded the walls, giving the room a cramped, closed-in feeling.

The arched bead board cathedral ceilings were as magnificent as the parquet flooring that they sheltered, as was the collection of artwork adorning the walls. The room was, easily, forty by forty, and there was artwork filling nearly every open space on the walls. Since, unlike Leo, she wasn't anchored to Theodora, she strolled in for a closer look, while their employer continued to boast about her possessions.

Alex could only get a really good look at the lower-hung pieces, and was astounded to discover that they were all originals. Wyeth, Matisse, and Breughel here. Chagall, Rockwell, and Modigliani there. Rothko, Warhol, Agam, and Pollack on the side wall, and in places of honor on the back wall were no less than Picasso, Monet, Bosch, Gauguin, Whistler, Hopper, and even a small Van Gogh. It was the most eclectic and valuable collection she'd ever seen outside of a museum. There was also a section of art by illustrators and cartoonists, again, all original, and containing Hirschfeld and Beardsley pieces, as well as those by Edward Gorey, Gahan Wilson, Peter Max, and Charles Addams; the *piece de resistance* being a complete set of Gustave Dore's illustrations of Dante's *Inferno*. It was a dizzying patchwork quilt of artistic excellence and looking at it all in one room was a visual roller coaster. She was so engrossed that she didn't realize that all conversation had ceased.

"I see you are an appreciator of fine art," Theodora observed.

"You have a fabulous collection, to be sure," Alex replied. "Which is your favorite?"

"I find I'm rather fond of architectural paintings, and so I'd have to say that my favorite would be the one to your left, of the church," Theodora said.

Alex looked at the painting, and was surprised to see that, though it was a nicely done rendering of a church, it certainly in no way stacked up to the other, truly great art in residence. She glanced at the lower right for the artist's name.

Alex gasped.

It was signed, "A. Hitler."

Gothic Revival

Theodora laughed. "It is startling, isn't it? You'd be amazed at how reasonably priced his work is. I have several more of his pieces in my bedroom upstairs, and I have bids in on six or seven of his other works. I have nearly a dozen of Gacy's clowns upstairs, as well. It's quite a display.

Alex was gray. Her grandfather had spent the last days of his life in Buchenwald, where he got his free tattoo and a one way trip to the Execution Room after months of starvation and beatings. Her father, being younger and stronger, was lucky enough to survive until liberated by the United States Third Army; but though relocated in America, he never really left the concentration camp, afflicted as he was with hideous night terrors until he died in 1993 at the age of seventy-eight. Alex's earliest memories involved being frightened out of her sleep each night as her father's screams echoed through their tiny house. And this person... this *unspeakable* woman... was a *fan*!

Leo, standing many feet away, was unaware of exactly what was going on. "Now, I know that Red Skelton was famous for painting clowns, but who is this Gacy you mentioned?" he asked, oblivious.

"He was a Chicago painter I came to like during his heyday from 1980 to 1994. Though he was prolific painter for those fourteen years, his paintings are rather hard to locate now. I was exceedingly lucky. I corresponded with him for quite a while and in 1992, he sent me a dozen of his best pieces."

"Wow, how nice. Doesn't he paint anymore?" Leo asked.

"Oh, my dear, no. He's been dead since 1994."

"Oh, I'm so sorry," Leo said.

"Don't be," Alex muttered under her breath.

"Let's finish up our tour and then we'll get to the contracts," Theodora said.

I can't possibly be awake. This has got to be a nightmare, Alex thought.

"I'll just finish showing you around the first floor. Since that's the only area of the house you'll be occupying, you won't require a tour of the upper floors, in which you already know to

83

not to trespass." Theodora glanced meaningfully at Alex as she said this.

"Oh, don't worry about that, Theodora. Who needs the upper floors when there's so much to see on the first one?" Alex said. Her voice roiled with barely suppressed rage, and it took every ounce of effort she could muster to keep from telling this wacko bitch exactly what she thought of her.

They left the living room/gallery and walked down the main hallway, where Theodora, with help from Leo, opened an enormous set of solid wood double doors on their right.

"What kind of wood is this, Theodora?" Leo asked. "It's beautiful."

Jesus. The next thing you know, he'll invite her over for dinner!

The exotic hardwood had a subtle yellow-orange base color with a grain streaked with red, purple, and black. Though smaller than the enormous front doors, they were obviously heavy in their own right.

"It's Canary wood and it comes from South America— Brazil or Bolivia I believe, though that's not where I got it. It's quite breathtaking, isn't it?"

I haven't gotten my breath back from that art gallery, Alex thought. She was still in shock, and she knew that Leo didn't know why, since he hadn't looked at the paintings as closely as she had.

Leo, ever interested in procuring exotic wood, asked, "May I ask where you *did* get it? I can always use new sources."

"Of course. I had it shipped up from Woodworkers Source in Phoenix. My taste in wood runs, as you can see, to the exotic, and they have a fine variety from everywhere in the world. And if you want the more ordinary, run of the mill hardwoods from this country," she sniffed, "they have them, too; but when you can get caviar, why choose peanut butter?" Theodora said, oozing her arm through Leo's again.

"Do you have their card, by any chance?" Leo asked.

"No doubt. I'll see that you have it before you leave today," she said, smiling up at Leo. "And be sure you ask for

Dwayne Shepard—he's the only one I deal with."

The only one who will deal with you, *you mean.* Alex felt sorry for Dwayne. *Wait until he hears that Theodora is on her way to Phoenix. They'll probably have to talk the poor guy down from the roof.* She shrugged and walked to the hinged side of the door, where the wood was unfinished, bent closer, and sniffed.

"What in the world is she doing?" Theodora demanded.

"Uh, she's smelling the wood, Theodora." Alex was taken aback to realize that, this time, Leo was embarrassed.

"Whatever for?"

"All wood has an identifying odor. I can smell many different types of wood and tell you what trees they came from," Alex explained, glaring at Leo.

"But I've just named the tree it came from." Theodora seemed irritated with what she evidently perceived was a lack of logic on Alex's part.

"Yes, that's true. But now I can add it to my olfactory library and be able to identify it by aroma alone the next time I come across it," Alex said.

"How very peculiar."

"Except this wood doesn't have a distinctive odor. It may be that it isn't noticeable until it's sawn. For example, when you saw dark hickory, it smells just like…"

"Cow manure," Leo cut in.

Alex couldn't believe it. Was he actually afraid that she was going to say 'cow shit'? *Not that there's not a lot of both being spread around here today.*

"How extraordinary. I shall cross hickory off my list forthwith," Theodora said. "Shall I show you the library?"

The library was the immense room behind the Canary wood doors, in which rested thousands of volumes, all leather bound. Both Alex and Leo loved books and had a small library of their own in the space that other tenants might have used as a dining room. Unlike their library, however, this one was so orderly that all books of the same size and color were shelved together, looking much like a *trompe d'oeil* mural of bookcases than the genuine article. It was about as inviting as a law office. The only winning thing about this library was the walk-in fieldstone fireplace that took up the entire side wall of the room.

But even though the books said, "hands off," Alex knew she would be exploring this library another day, and so would Leo.

"...have in the neighborhood of fifteen thousand volumes, I think," Theodora said. "Nearly all of them are quite valuable. Many are first editions and probably half of them are inscribed by the authors."

Alex studied this pretentious woman again as she gushed over her possessions to Leo, seeming to forget completely that there was even a third person in the room. She decided that Theodora must be fairly new to money to be so wrapped up in this unattractive ceaseless bragging; because people who come from money are far too poised to go around rubbing other people's noses in the fact. If they receive a compliment on something they own, they simply acknowledge it without going into ecstasies over, and the cost of, every item within view. Theodora had no class whatsoever. And Alex really didn't like the way the woman kept touching Leo to emphasize whatever silly point she was intent on making. The worst part of it was that Leo didn't seem even remotely uncomfortable with all Theodora's stomach-turning coquettishness.

She was old enough to be his goddamned mother!

It was just too creepy.

"...that's the library." Theodora opened a normal, house-sized six pane wooden door to the right of the fireplace. "These will be your accommodations for the summer. They're small, but adequate." She herded them through the darkened bedroom and into a large bathroom so quickly that Alex had only the vaguest impression of where they'd be sleeping for three months. "These are the facilities that you'll be using while you're here," Theodora said, flipping on the lights. The bathroom was larger than Alex's first apartment, and it was equipped with a cavernous travertine shower, a marble bath tub big enough for Shaquille O'Neil to stretch out in, a fifteen hundred gallon Jacuzzi, and an eight foot vanity with double sinks.

But the walls… oh, those were another matter entirely.

"We've stocked this for you, as well," Theodora continued. "There is a wide selection of all-natural shampoos, conditioners, soaps, bath oils, bath salts, and body lotions, and you are to use *only* these products. Oh, and before I forget, I must tell you that should a drain become clogged, under no circumstances are you to try to clear it yourselves. Just point it out to Cooper. He is the only one authorized to deal with any plumbing issues in this house, and I cannot emphasize that enough. Do you understand?

"Yes," Alex replied.

"But Theodora, I do plumbing work all the time. It would be very easy for me to…"

"I am not implying that you don't know how to clear a clogged drain, or that you don't do it often. You will just not do it *here*. Is that clearly understood?" Theodora demanded.

"Quite clearly," Leo said. *Great. One more crazy rule to remember.*

"Uh, Theodora? What's the deal with the walls?" Alex asked.

She turned to Alex, an expression of rapidly fraying patience suffusing her face. "How articulate," she said. "I'm afraid I don't understand what 'deal' it is to which you refer."

Alex took a breath and reminded herself that telling one's employer to eat shit and bark at the moon was not the most politic of moves. "All the faces. They're a bit hard to miss, and kind of an odd thing to have in a bathroom. Sort of takes away the feeling of privacy, if you know what I mean," she explained. The crowd of sculpted male faces lining the walls looked down on the master bathroom like Romans at the Coliseum.

"This white marble frieze that covers three of the four walls in this room was custom carved for me by a rather well-known Italian sculptor. Unfortunately this was one of the last few pieces that he completed, and I feel privileged to have it in my home. I don't understand your privacy issue. They are, after all, only stone."

"Whose faces are they?" Leo asked.

"I haven't the foggiest notion."

Theodora gestured toward the door, closing the subject. Alex and Leo led the way back through the darkened bedroom. "As you run low on bath supplies Cooper will replace them. Oh, and feel free to call him 'Cooper,' by the way. Everyone does. Now, if you'll follow me, we'll visit the Billiard Room."

"Isn't that where Colonel Mustard bought it with the lead pipe?" Alex asked.

In response, Theodora looked up at Leo, smiled sadly, shook her head, and walked him down the hall without looking back.

At the Billiard Room, they again encountered a unique custom door, held open with an elephant foot door stop. The wood was a rich strawberry red with golden yellow stripes in the grain.

"This is Blood wood. It, too, comes from Latin America. Nice, isn't it?"

"It's far beyond nice," Leo said.

Alex made a mental note to smell it later.

The Billiard Room, nearly as large as the living room/art gallery, had three regulation pool tables; one with traditional deep scarlet felt, one with royal purple felt, and one with, of course, black felt. There was a wet bar against the far wall, with a door next to it, adorned with a small gold plaque which they were too far away to read. The rest of the wall space contained an assortment of animal trophies, reminiscent of Dr. Orbon's waiting room. Alex, who had found the door stop disgusting enough, studied the carpet.

"Well, this certainly looks familiar," Leo said, staring at all the animal heads.

"Ah, yes. Dr. Orbon does lovely work, does he not?"

"So he's not only your doctor, but takes care of all your taxidermy needs, too?" Leo asked, a tone of wry amusement creeping into his voice. Theodora either didn't notice it or chose to ignore it.

"Yes, and we're grateful for his skill, since my husband enjoys hunting—especially for big game—and goes every chance he gets," Theodora said. "He does rather well for himself, I should say. I especially like that Gorilla."

"I thought that Gorillas were protected, Theodora," Alex said, knowing that they were.

Theodora smiled. "Not from my husband," she said. "And this concludes the tour. Now let's get to the kitchen and the contracts."

Another gargantuan room, the kitchen was a gourmet cook's dream, with rich, Brazilian cherry cabinets, moss green granite counters, every kitchen appliance and gadget known to man, and a Thermador cook top built into the center island next to a built-in stainless sink. There was also an electric range large enough to cook three turkeys side by side and two Dutch ovens built into the walls. The stainless steel fridge was commercial grade and size and the main country-style sink was large and deep. There was a walk-in freezer to the right of the refrigerator and a walk-in pantry to the left of it— all fully stocked.

"Do you cook, Leo?" Theodora asked.

"Leo is a top drawer gourmet cook," Alex said, causing Theodora to look around with an expression of surprise that she was still tagging along.

"Alex is a terrific cook, Theodora. Don't let her kid you," Leo said.

"How nice," Theodora said, favoring Alex with a tight-lipped smile.

"This is most generous of you," Leo said.

"Not at all. Can't have you starving, can I?"

"Theeeeo! Where are you?"

"We're in the kitchen, Ross," she called.

That's the 'still living husband,' I guess, Alex thought.

Enter Ross. Alex almost laughed. He was about five-ten, slim, wore Coke-bottle thick glasses, a Bozo the Clown hairstyle of mousy brown hair, and a walrus mustache that was so unkempt that it reminded Alex of a garden full of weeds. He wore a pale blue pima cotton dress shirt with a suit vest that didn't quite cover his middle-aged paunch, no tie, and matching suit pants in medium brown with a light blue pinstripe. The suit was obviously expensive, but was ill-fitting and stained with food. Ross's best feature was his smile and his weakest would have to be a toss-up between his allergy-affected blue eyes, his bulbous nose, and his nearly nonexistent chin. What a train wreck of a person. He was even wearing a pair of saddle shoes… with argyle socks, yet… and not a golf course in sight.

"And who do we have here?" he asked, his eyes glued to Alex. "Hello, pretty one. What's your name?"

"That's my *wife*, Alex, and I'm her husband, Leo."

"Oh, sorry there, friend," Ross said, still staring at Alex.

"Ross, may I have a word with you in the Library please?" Theodora asked. Her tone warned of velvet-wrapped broken glass.

"Excuse me, won't you?" he said to Alex with barely a nod at Leo.

The second they were out of earshot, Alex said, "Leo, I do not want to work for that truly insane woman!"

"What's the problem?"

"Oh, I don't know, Leo. How about being abducted in a shape-shifting Cadillac? Or the blood all over the engine? Maybe the nauseating way she flirts with you? Or the fact that she collects and admires paintings by Adolph Hitler? And she corresponded with John Wayne Gacy and she hangs his artwork in her fucking bedroom? Could any of *that* possibly be the problem?"

"Who's John Wayne Gacy?" Leo asked.

"I can't believe that's your only question." Alex took a breath and tried to calm down. "John Wayne Gacy was a murderer, Leo. He raped and murdered thirty-three men and buried them in a crawlspace in his basement. He has the dubious distinction of being in the Guinness Book of World

Records for the longest sentence ever imposed on a serial killer—twenty-one consecutive life sentences and twelve death sentences. He got a hot needle in 1994, and that was way too good for him."

"How do you know all this?" Leo asked.

"Just like you, Leo, I read. I just read different things than you do, that's all. What gets me is that Theodora talks about Gacy like he's a favorite uncle. Do you really want to work for somebody like that? And she collects paintings by Hitler. Jesus, Leo, my grandfather was murdered in Buchenwald, and my father just barely made it out alive. I about threw up when I saw that painting."

"There's really a Hitler painting here?"

"Yes, Leo. That architectural rendering of the church that she likes so damned much."

"*Hitler* did that?"

Alex sighed. "Yes, Leo. He wanted to be an artist before he decided to chuck that and compete for the title of *Most Evil Fucker on the Planet* instead. He won, by the way."

"It's just so unbelievable that anyone would want to own his artwork, much less display it proudly. I wasn't doubting what you said, Alex; I was just shocked."

"Let's go, Leo. Let's get out of here."

"Look, I grant you that she's a lunatic and her goofy husband isn't a whole hell of a lot better, but think a minute. They'll be gone the whole time we're working here and they want to pay us enough money for a down payment on a house—and that's something I want to get for you more than anything in the world, honey. I love you so much. I want to give you things—it's important to me. Can't we please overlook the lack of artistic taste and just grab the money and run? What do you say?"

And she thought that Leo was welcoming Theodora's previous attention.

He was just being polite and trying to make the best of things, as he always did. She felt terribly guilty for doubting him. "Okay, Leo. You're right; she won't be around while we're working, so I'll deal with it, for now." Alex shuddered. "That she could have Adolph Hitler hanging next to Andrew Wyeth makes me want to call a cop!"

"I know. I had no idea your family was Jewish, Alex," Leo said

"Is it a problem?"

"Lord, no! I love you. If you want me to get circumcised, I'll find myself a Mohel!"

"Wow, you even know what they're called."

"I read too, remember? The Catholic religion I was forced to grow up with means nothing to me. If Judaism means something to you, I'll be delighted to address it. But please, let's get a house first?"

"All right. But I can tell you one thing: I don't feel bad about taking their money anymore."

"*So* sorry to have kept you waiting," Theodora said, bustling back in with a chastened Ross shuffling behind. "Perhaps we can get to the contracts now?"

"We usually draw up the contract, since we are the ones providing the service, Theodora," Alex said, receiving a pleading look from Leo.

"You'll find we do things differently here," Theodora said.

"Obviously."

"Is there a problem with that, Mrs. Renfield? Because if there is, let's get it resolved, one way or the other, right now," Theodora snapped.

"No, Theodora, absolutely no problem at all," Leo cut in.

"I'm happy to hear it." She smiled at Leo, relegating Alex to her previous nonentity status once again.

"I'm sorry about that... back there," Ross said. Theodora and Leo had moved to the kitchen table to go over the contract.

"Forget it. I have," Alex said, making it obvious that she was trying to hear the discussion.

"Good. I'm Ross Hamilton. We weren't really properly introduced." He put out his hand tentatively.

Alex sighed, abandoning her listening post and trusting Leo to see to things. In putting together their business plan, one of the things they'd agreed upon was that if the client was more comfortable dealing with one or the other of them, then so be it—that's who they'd deal with, nothing personal.

"I'm Alex," she said, smiling. She gave Ross as firm a handshake as possible, but yet not so bone crushing that she looked as if she were trying to prove something. Not that it would have been hard to do. Between Ross's soft, almost womanish hands, and her hands made strong by martial arts, gardening and building, she could have had him on his knees in a second. One of the many reasons she didn't was because, for some reason, she was certain he would have enjoyed it.

"Have you had the nickel tour yet?"

"Oh, yes."

"Well, what do you think of the old pile?"

"Some of your artwork is quite wonderful," Alex said.

"Only some?"

"I'm not much of a fan of a couple of your artists," Alex replied guardedly.

Ross leaned in and whispered, "I know what you mean. I simply detest Agam and Hirschfeld, too—Jews, you know. But they were gifts, so what can you do?" he said, shrugging his shoulders.

"Do you like Chagall?"

"Oh, indeed yes. One of my favorites," Ross chirped.

"Are you aware that Marc Chagall was Jewish?"

"Oh, that can't possibly be true. He's far too great an artist."

It took all her willpower to keep from reaching over and choking this moron.

"I see you also own beautiful paintings by Modigliani and Rothko, as well as some pop art by Peter Max," Alex said.

"Ah, yes. Aren't they wonderful artists?" Ross asked.

"Indeed. They were also Jewish."

"No, they're not. Their names don't end in *stein*, *thal*, *berg*, *man*, *baum*, *feld*, or *ski*," Ross said, grinning. "Can't fool me there!"

Alex had to remind herself to breathe.

Ross continued, oblivious. "The house, itself, though, is our main artistic treasure—incredible construction. It's a Greek Revival, you know."

From some area of her autonomic nervous system that controlled politeness, Alex summoned a response. "Oh? Leo thought it was a Carpenter Gothic."

"Oh, no, no, no! Carpenter Gothic came after Greek Revival," Ross said.

"*No*, Daddy, that's *wrong*!"

Alex turned to see a thirty-something dark haired heavy-set young woman, about five-foot-four with a mouth to match, storm into the kitchen. She marched up to Ross with a look of exasperation on her broad, porcine face. "This house *is* a Carpenter Gothic, which is *part* of the Gothic Revival period. It did *not* come after Greek Revival. *Honestly!*"

Alex was horrified that a child, no matter how old, would speak to a parent in such a disrespectful manner, especially in front of strangers.

"Hello, dear," Theodora called from across the room. "Come here, please. I'd like you to meet someone."

The fat little bitch, as Alex mentally dubbed her, flounced off to her mother, without even a glance in Alex's direction.

"Let me ask you something, Ross. Am I invisible?"

"You look pretty solid to me."

"Good. I was just checking."

"That was my daughter, Jane," Ross said. "She takes after her mother."

"So I noticed," Alex said, dryly.

"Dad?" A new voice.

"Ah, here's my other daughter, Candace, the light of my life," he said, his face brightening. "In the kitchen, princess!" he called.

Dear Lord, what fresh hell is this? Alex thought. *And didn't she say she only had one of her children living at home?*

"Hi, Daddy!" Candace came bouncing into the room and threw herself into her father's open arms. She was Mutt to her sister's Jeff, being about five-nine, thin, and apparently a year or two older than Jane. She had wavy brown hair to her shoulders, unlike her sister's close cropped unruly black curls, and she would have been pretty if not for the fact that, in spinning the genetic prize wheel, she'd won a copy of her father's nose.

I guess there won't be any nose job for her—too Jewish, Alex thought, plastering a wooden smile onto her wooden face.

This father-daughter relationship was a world apart from his and Jane's, or from any father-daughter relationship that Alex had ever heard of. Instead of a bad-tempered lecture, or a quick hug and a peck on the cheek, this daughter stayed in Daddy's embrace far longer than any daughter should. It reached the point where Alex didn't know where to look, so she attempted to break it up herself.

"Hi, there. I'm Alex. You must be Candace," she said, extending her hand.

Candace looked at Alex, but stayed locked in Ross's arms. "That's me. Are you one of our summer workers?" Her supercilious tone made Alex want to slap her until her hand fell off.

"My husband and I are going to be painting the first floor of this house, yes. And we work for ourselves, by the way. If you'd like to meet my husband, I'd…"

"How charming," Candace replied, looking as if she smelled something bad. "Daddy, come and take a walk with me around the grounds, please? Please? Pretty please with sugar on top?"

"When someone this lovely calls, how can I disobey? See you later, I expect," Ross said.

Candace grabbed his hands and pulled away from him.

He had a huge erection.

And what was worse, they both knew she saw it.

They wanted her to see it.

Leo heard Alex's gasp from across the kitchen. He turned in time to see Ross and a young woman strolling away arm in arm.

"Alex?" Leo called.

"Coming," Alex said, rushing over and taking a seat at the table.

"Ah, I see you just met Candace. Isn't she marvelous?" Theodora asked.

"Peachy," Alex replied.

"Hon, I read through the contract and it covers everything we talked about in Wang's," Leo said. Then he paused, searching her face. "Are you all right?"

"Later," Alex muttered.

"Okay. Theodora, do you need both our signatures, or just mine?"

"Both?" Theodora looked mildly confused. "Oh, you mean your wife, of course. What was your name again, dear?"

Alex ground her teeth. "Alex."

Theodora turned back to Leo. "It will be necessary for both of you to sign. You don't mind, do you, Alice?"

"That's 'Alex,' and no, I don't. Anything to do with the business is always signed by both of us," she said, giving Leo a questioning look for even asking if she should sign.

"How sweet of Leo to keep you involved," Theodora gushed. "I'm so very impressed by you, Leo."

What the hell does this broad think I do all day—hold his ladder and hand him nails? Alex wondered. Though it was true that she didn't know anything about building until she met Leo. He had since taught her a great deal and she was nothing if not a quick study. She certainly knew enough that she could hold her own during a day's work. Not only could she handle demolition, but she could frame, lay tile and hardwood flooring, paint, run saws, and do fairly complex electrical work, too. Alex really liked working with electricity and it was fascinating enough for her to do some research about it on her own. It was fun surprising Leo with something new that she'd learned that he hadn't taught her. Leo was teaching her basic plumbing, too, but that didn't have the allure of electricity. It galled her that Theodora acted like Alex just hung out with Leo in between manicures and spa days, and she could now see what Leo meant when he said that no matter how expert a remodeler she became, no one would take her seriously.

As if reading her mind, Leo said, "Please let me explain something to you, Theodora. Alex is an equal part of everything this business does. When you're talking to her, you're talking to me, and vice versa. She works right alongside me and is a tremendous help, both from the standpoints of good ideas and of hard physical work."

"Ah, what a fine man you are, Leo, sticking up for her like that," Theodora beamed. She then produced a Mont Blanc pen and offered it to him.

"No need. I have a pen right here," Leo said. "During spring pneumonia season, we like to use our own pens. No offense."

Theodora's eyes narrowed. Offense, clearly, had been taken. "I'm afraid I must insist that you use this pen, Leo. Humor me, please. It's lucky."

"A lucky *pen*?" Alex asked.

Leo, ever the diplomat, said, "Well, since it's a lucky pen..." and accepted the heavy writing utensil, signed the contract, and then held out the pen to Alex.

Cobra-fast, Theodora snatched both the pen and the contract out of Leo's hand. "Oh, no. I have a separate pen for your wife to use, as well as a separate contract for her to sign," she explained, extracting an identical Mont Blanc from her skirt pocket.

"Two contracts? I don't under..." Leo began.

"Don't worry, Leo. It's exactly the same as the one you read and signed," Theodora reassured him.

Leo still looked doubtful.

"I know a quick way to be sure, hon," Alex said. "May I have the other contract, please, Theodora?"

Looking dubious, she handed it over and Alex took the first page of each and put one on top of the other. Then she held them up to the light and readjusted them so they were in perfect alignment.

"What in the world are you doing?" Theodora asked.

"Just a sec... there. I'm superimposing them. If anything has been changed from one to the other, the type won't line up. It's an old proofreader's trick," Alex said.

"And where did you learn it?" Theodora inquired.

"From an old proofreader," Alex replied.

Nobody laughed.

Tough room.

She checked the other two pages. "Exact match, Leo," she said, re-collating the contracts.

Theodora withdrew another Mont Blanc pen from her skirt pocket and handed it to Alex.

"*Two* lucky pens?"

"You have no idea," Theodora said.

Alex looked at Leo, who nodded, so she accepted the pen, signed where Theodora indicated, and was mildly surprised at what she saw.

"Purple ink?" Alex asked.

"Yes. Believe it or not, I blend it myself. It's sort of a hobby of mine." She picked up Alex's signed contract. "Lovely." She extracted a third sheaf of papers from the oak tag folder in front of her. "Here is your copy, which I have already executed. And now I'm sure you would prefer to be on your way. Just let me locate Cooper to drive you back. I won't be a moment."

The second she was out of sight, Alex hissed, "I don't believe this."

"Shhhhhh! She'll hear you. We'll talk about it in the car."

Theodora returned a few minutes later. "Cooper is feeling a bit unwell, I'm afraid, so Ross and Candace will drive you home."

"That would be great," Leo said. "Thank you very much, Theodora. We look forward to working for you."

"The car is just outside in the drive."

"Right. Thanks again."

"Oh, Leo? Aren't you forgetting something?" Theodora asked, batting her eyes at him.

Well, at least now we finally know what happened to Baby Jane, Alex thought. *I hope she doesn't expect him to kiss her good-bye.*

Leo met her question with a perplexed look.

"Your deposit, silly! Is five thousand dollars enough?" Theodora produced a thick envelope and handed it to him. "It's in cash. Is that acceptable?"

Leo blushed to the roots of his hair. "Oh my gosh, you must think I don't know what I'm doing. Yes, five thousand is perfect, and cash is just fine, too. Thank you, Theodora. Would you like a receipt?"

"If you would." Theodora held out a pre-printed receipt form that she had already filled in. Leo just had to sign it.

"Again, thank you," he said.

"You're more welcome than you know, Leo. And you, too, Alicia."

Alex didn't even bother correcting her this time. They stepped out into full darkness with only gibbous moonlight to find their way to the black limousine. As they approached, Ross exited the driver's seat to open the back door for them. Walking past, they noticed Candace sitting in the "date seat" on the front bench seat. She'd be snuggled up to Ross when he got back in.

"Guess we won't be doing much talking until we get home," Alex muttered as Ross closed the door after Leo gave him their address.

It hardly mattered. They were both asleep in minutes.

***

"Boy, are you two sound sleepers!" Ross said, shaking their shoulders. "You're home! Wakey, wakey!"

"Huh? Oh, thanks," Leo said, sitting up quickly. "Must have dozed off."

"Well, time to get up and go to bed, then," Ross laughed. He offered Leo a hand out of the car, and Alex the same. The second they were clear, Ross said, "See you," then jumped back into the driver's seat. While the limousine disappeared up Judson Avenue, Leo and Alex were left standing in their driveway still rubbing the sleep from their eyes.

"What time is it?" Leo asked.

"My watch says seven-thirty," Alex replied. "Hey! It's running again! But is it morning or evening?"

"Yeah, so's mine. But they can't be right; because they stopped running all the while we were gone. It must be morning, though. When we left Theodora's it was pitch black and the moon was up, remember?"

"So we traveled all night? How far away is this house?"

"What worries me more is how we're going to know when it's midnight or six A.M. if our watches won't keep time there," Leo said.

"After what we've been through in the last, oh, I don't know how many hours, the fact that our watches stopped is what worries you most? We bought these watches at the same time, Leo, remember? I don't buy that 'magnetic field' malarkey of hers. The batteries are probably just running down. We'll get them replaced tomorrow… or today… or whenever. At this point, I don't know about you, but I'm starving. And who knows? Maybe we took the long way home and it's evening, not morning. I don't know if I should make dinner or breakfast." Alex said.

"One way to find out. C'mon." He unlocked the door, and once inside, picked up the phone.

"Who're you calling?"

"Time and temperature."

"Brilliant!" She leaned in to hear the recording with Leo.

The line rang twice, then the robotic voice said, "Today is April twenty-fifth, the time is seven thirty-seven P.M. and the temperature is forty-eight degrees…" Leo hung up.

"I don't believe this, Alex. It's April twenty-fifth—the *evening* of April twenty-fifth. Since we went to Theodora's yesterday afternoon, April twenty-fourth, that means we've been gone more than twenty-four hours!"

"Guess I'll make dinner then," Alex said dully.

"Maybe this is why we have to stay there to work. It's one crazy commute, otherwise," Leo muttered.

Chapter Fifteen

Initially, not much discussion took place over their catch-up meal of leftover chicken, ham, baked potatoes, peas, and broccoli. All talk was limited to the "please pass" and "do you want more of" variety. They had never been so hungry in their lives and were making up for the missed lunch, dinner, breakfast, and lunch all in one go.

"Hey, do you want something to drink? We have a gallon of cheap red wine, Killian's Irish Red beer, and a bottle of Wild Turkey we were saving for a special occasion," Alex said, rattling off the inventory through a mouthful of chicken.

"If missing this many meals isn't a call for a special occasion drink to make us feel better, then I don't know what is," Leo said after swallowing what felt like a half a ham. "We deserve it. Break out the Turkey."

"Works for me. I don't know about you, but I really could stand to get a little buzzed tonight."

"I could stand to get more than a little," Leo said.

Alex gazed at him. He looked so very tired... like 'death warmed over' as her mother used to say. His eyes were ringed with dark circles and loose bags and his forehead was lined with the stresses of the day... and night... and day again. He resembled the Marlboro Man after a week-long cattle drive. She was afraid to look in the mirror herself and discover what the visit to the Hamilton House of Insanity, Incest and Fine Art had wrought upon her own features.

"You look fine, don't worry," Leo said, patting her hand.

"How did you know what I was thinking?"

"I just know sometimes."

Leo had a disconcerting way of peeking into her thoughts now and then, which told Alex that he knew her better than she knew him. If she ever had a line on what Leo was thinking, it was just a lucky guess, not true insight.

Alex stood, stretched and went to get the bottle of Wild Turkey stashed at the back of the pantry in their L-shaped kitchen. *It really ought to be in a wall-mounted case with an "In Emergency, Break Glass" legend on it,* she thought.

On the way back, amber elixir in hand, she happened to catch a glimpse of herself in the mirror on the wall opposite the pantry door.

It was much worse than she imagined.

Her hair was greasy and separating at the part, her skin had the oily sheen of the unwashed, and she couldn't tell if her mascara had smudged, she had joined a football team that she had forgotten about, or there really were such black circles under her sea blue eyes.

"Jesus, Leo, I look like a raccoon!"

"Yes, but you are *my* raccoon, and that's all that matters," he said. "Stop worrying so much. After this field trip you're entitled to look how you look, and so am I."

Alex's reflection smiled tiredly. "What would I ever do without you, Leo?" she whispered.

"You'd be lost," Leo called.

"Where did you get those ears—Batman?"

"I sent away for them. They work much better than the X-ray glasses did. Where's that good booze, woman?"

In seconds, she was back at the kitchen table with the bottle and two ice-filled rocks glasses. "Could you pour, Leo? I just ran out of steam."

"If it wasn't Wild Turkey, I wouldn't have the energy, either, trust me. But this'll cure what ails ya." Leo heaved himself up from his slouch and grabbed the bottle in a single, almost balletic motion.

"Say when," he said.

"April twenty-sixth," Alex replied.

"You're a woman after my own heart, Alica," Leo said, filling his own glass.

"Oh, don't *you* start!"

"Couldn't resist."

"She did that on purpose, you know," Alex said.

"Of course she did. But that's usually a power game that men play. I was surprised when she did it."

"I think its dangerous to be surprised by anything that woman does."

"Well, no matter, sweet pea, when next we show up there, they'll be gone and all we'll have to contend with will be a deaf dwarf," Leo said. "Shouldn't be tough."

Alex took a warming swallow of the top shelf bourbon and said, "We ought to compare notes, Leo, because I have many observations from the Lunatic Fringe for you."

"Me, too. You first."

After rehashing her outrage over the Hitler and Gacy artwork, she mentioned Jane.

"She really spoke to her father like that?" Leo was incredulous. "And she didn't get the back of his hand across her mouth? That would have been the least of what I would have gotten if I'd smarted off to my father like that."

"Same here," Alex said. "He just ignored it and she went to Theodora when she called.

"Well, let me tell you, that one is clearly Theodora's favorite," Leo said. She even looks like her, but you have to see them together to really get that. Anyway, Theodora introduces her to me and, get this, the kid looks at her and says, 'Mother, darling, why are you introducing me to the help? I don't care who they are, I just want them to take care of the house,' then she kisses Theodora on the cheek and leaves the room, without even looking at me."

"Yeah, she ignored me, too. What a piece of work. So what did Theodora say to you? Did she apologize?"

"Nope. She just looked after the fat little pig as she waddled away and said, "She's the best thing that ever happened to me," and she actually had tears in her eyes as she said it.

"So this means that she's either had a really shitty life or that she's proud of how the little sow turned out," Alex said.

"I think the latter is far more likely," Leo said.

"So do I."

"But you haven't heard anything yet." Alex recapped her meeting with Ross and their discussion about Jewish artists.

"Are you kidding? I didn't realize people like that still existed. He condemns their work because they're Jews?"

"Yes. Agam is Israel's national treasure, as far as contemporary art goes. One of his pieces is the entire Mediterranean Sea facing the side of a hotel in Tel Aviv—in stripes— and the colors are so well blended that you can't tell where one leaves off and the next starts. Al Hirschfeld is the premier caricature artist of Broadway—or was until he died. And this WASPY piss ant acts like these masterpieces are finger paintings done with feces."

"Okay. He's an asshole. Let it go. You won't see him again," Leo said.

She took several deep breaths. "I'm sorry, Leo. I've just never had to contend with someone like that before. On the surface, he seemed so mild-mannered and sort of nice—well, after Theodora had her little confab with him, anyway."

"So what was the other daughter like?" Leo asked.

"Candace? Daddy's little whore."

"Pardon?"

"They have, to put it diplomatically, an unusual relationship. While you were talking to Theodora and reading the contract, those two were getting up close and personal. When they finally did separate, Ross had a colossal hard-on, and Candace obviously liked it."

"That's the most disgusting thing I've ever heard."

"I don't know why, but I have the feeling that we've only just begun to scratch the surface of revolting where that group is concerned," Alex said. "I'm glad we won't be seeing them again."

"And we've got a vacation until May thirteenth, if we want to take it," Leo said.

"Good. That's three weeks that we can hang out together,

work on the lawn and putter around the house."

"How about if I build those raised garden beds you want?"

"Oh, Leo, that would be fabulous. But if we're going to be away all summer, is there really any point?"

"Sure there is. Just plant stuff that will mature late. I'll install drip lines in each bed and put it all on a timer so that everything will get enough water. By the time we get back, ta da, vegetables!"

"Oh, that's a great idea, honey. What shall we plant?"

"Let's talk about it tomorrow, sweetie. After being up for a day and a half, I'm beat."

"Good idea. Just leave this stuff," Alex said, indicating the dishes. "I'll clean it up tomorrow."

"Sure. Now I think I might have just enough oomph left for some exercise before sleeping. What do you think?"

Alex managed to tap into an inner reserve of energy she didn't know she had and afterward, they fell asleep in each other's arms.

Chapter Sixteen

The next day was a typical early spring morning in Connecticut. The sun cast a pale yellow tint over the back yard and the dew on the grassless lawn glittered like a miser's eye. The air was full of the freshness of winter's end but without the cold bite. Alex had on a light jacket, an old pair of jeans, her favorite James Cagney tee-shirt and a sturdy pair of work boots. She held a pad on which she was busily sketching a garden plan, and was so engrossed that it took a few minutes for her to notice the man standing at the edge of the property.

He was oddly attired in a top hat, black tie and tails, and Alex couldn't decide if he was on his way to a formal event or a funeral. The shadows surrounding his face were so deep that they hid his features almost completely. While Alex watched, the man raised his left arm to shoulder height. His hand appeared reptilian and his scaly index finger, with a deadly-looking claw at the end of it, pointed down the road. He did not look in the direction he was pointing, but continued to stare fixedly at Alex.

She tried to call out to him, but her voice had suddenly faltered, preventing all but an ineffectual croak. Alex couldn't see what he was pointing at because a ground fog was rising rapidly and the sun was obscured in moments, transforming her beautiful morning into bilious gloom.

Afraid now, she looked back at the house for Leo, but instead saw a large black dog sitting in front of the back door. It turned and howled at the open entrance, the mournful sound raising the small hairs on the back of Alex's neck.

From somewhere inside the house, a bell tolled, and when she turned back to the strange man, he was gone.

Her pretty day spoiled now, Alex continued to feel uneasy. She looked down and discovered a bright green leaf of such an unusual shape that she picked it up to show to Leo, but as she crossed the threshold, the leaf withered, turned brown, and curled up in her hand.

"There you are! Let me help you," Leo said, emerging from the darkened house. He bent down and picked up a rusty nail. "This'll do the trick," he said, hammering it into the lintel. "See? That's all it needed. Look. The sun's out again."

"Yes, but..." Alex began.

"No buts. We have to go to see the priest now. Come on, and don't say anything. Remember, it's a gift. What can you do?" Leo said, taking Alex's hand and drawing her into the house.

Theodora walked out of the kitchen and took Alex's other hand. "In here, dear," she said. "I have a present for you. It was just delivered. Come see."

"Oh, my God!" Alex cried, finding her voice.

In the center of the room was her father, naked, nailed to a cross, and quite dead, with Adolph Hitler dressed in clerical garb standing by smiling.

"It's his latest work of art," Theodora said. "Isn't it *marvelous*?"

Alex screamed.

"Hey! Alex! Wake up!" Leo cried.

But Alex continued to scream, unaware of anything but that last abomination she had witnessed.

Leo pinned her arms and turned her to face him. "Alex, honey!" he shouted. "It was just a bad dream! Wake up now!"

At last, Alex recognized Leo and their moonlit bedroom. She collapsed, sobbing, into his arms.

"Wow. That must have been a humdinger," he murmured, stroking her hair and rocking her gently.

"Oh, Leo, it was the worst ever."

"Want to tell me about it? That way, you won't step right back into it when you fall asleep again."

Alex reached for a tissue and blew her nose. "Is that really true?" she sniffed.

"I dunno. I'm just nosey. I've also heard that if you want to forget a dream by morning that you should stare out a window for a couple of minutes before you try to go back to sleep.

Alex wasn't taking any chances. She stared out the window while she told Leo about her nightmare.

When she was done, Leo said, "You know, most of that is explainable. There were a bunch of elements in it from our visit to Hell House today… or yesterday… or whenever that was."

"For instance?"

"Well, Theodora for one. And Hitler, and your father's death at his hands and Theodora thinking the death of a Jew was 'marvelous'."

"But my father got out of the camp. Hitler didn't kill him. He died here."

"And from what you told me, he woke up screaming every night for the rest of his life. Oh, Hitler killed him, all right."

"Point taken, but what about the rest of it?"

"You couldn't talk, right? Isn't that just the way you felt at the house?"

"Yes, it was. And you even told me not to say anything in the dream," Alex replied. "But where did the guy in tails come from?"

"You were working on your garden in the dream, right? Maybe he was your scarecrow."

Alex smiled, thinking about it. "Could be. Tell me more."

"Let's see. What haven't we explained yet?"

"The morning fog and the leaf."

"The fog is confusion and maybe the leaf is disappointment—that we thought things were going to be so great here, but green turned to brown, so maybe not so great?"

"How do you do that?" Alex asked.

"What? Interpret dreams?"

"Yeah. You're really good at it."

"Does that mean that I'm right about your thinking that

this place isn't so great after all?" Leo asked.

"No, I think you missed the mark there." Alex thought back to the day they stumbled upon the town of Woodhaven when they were out leaf-peeping last autumn. The town just drew them—the brilliant old trees awash with color, the quaintness of a small town with no big-box stores cluttering it up. Antique shops proliferated instead, and if you needed groceries, you bought them at the nearby A & P market. And they would even deliver them for you if you wanted—the sign in the window said so. There weren't a lot of people out and about, either, though there were plenty of folks in evidence. Cars in driveways, kids toys scattered about, the flickering blue of television lighting up rooms at night. But it clearly wasn't an "evening stroll" sort of place, and if you wanted to see other people, you had to go out to dinner or shopping in Southfield, the adjacent town. Woodhaven was truly a den of homebodies, and that suited Alex and Leo just fine, because they were, too.

Another interesting facet of Woodhaven was that there were no churches in the town; some ordinance or other was the way the guy at the Home Depot explained it. Didn't matter, anyhow, because neither Alex nor Leo was a believer.

They'd fallen in love with the Cape Cod on Judson Avenue the minute they saw the place and the FOR RENT sign on the lawn in front of it. The house itself was less than seventeen hundred square feet, but it was perfect for two people. The garage was nearly as large as the house and made a fine workshop for them. The landscaping or lack thereof, on the other hand, was atrocious. No grass, no shrubs, and one sad little maple tree. Both the front and back yards were uninterrupted dirt, but Alex and Leo could visualize the possibilities, and the landlord had finally written them with permission to develop the land however they liked. They were also considering the rent-to-own deal that the landlord had offered.

Not like it here?

"I love it here, Leo. The last couple of days have really taken it out of me, that's all. Outside of a big vegetable garden and lots of flowers, shrubs and a tree or two, preferably fruit or nut trees, the only thing we still need is a couple of neighbors.

Like Fred and Ethel Mertz. I can be friends with Ethel and you and Fred can pal around," Alex said. "However, there are some strict requirements, you understand. Ethel must bake perfect oatmeal-raisin cookies and must love gardening and cooking so we can swap recipes. Fred has to be a retired fine woodworker who can give you tips about woodworking if you need them and a hand if you guys decide to build us girls something for Christmas."

"That's a pretty hefty list of neighbor specs, kiddo."

"Only the best for us. Do you have anything to add?"

"Well, Fred has to be able to fix anything that I can't, and not be obsessed with sports."

"And they have to say stuff like 'for corn sake' and "bless your little heart,'" Alex said, then sighed, still staring out the window at the vacant house across the way. "It looks like it's been empty for a long time, doesn't it, Leo?"

"It also looks like it's about to fall down. Don't expect neighbors anytime soon, sweetheart. Ready to try for some sleep again?"

"Sure," she said, turning away from the night scene and snuggling back down into bed. "I think I'm all right now."

"Well, if you need me, just scream," Leo said.

"You're a riot, Alice!" Alex said.

"No, I'm not Alice—that's you, isn't it? Or is it Andrea? Or Adrian? I simply can*not* remember!"

"Think 'Bang! Zoom'!" Alex said. "Go to sleep, you clown."

"Yes, but one of Skelton's, not one of Gacy's."

"Amen to that," Alex said.

The rest of the night was disturbed by nothing more than Leo's snoring.

Chapter Seventeen

Alex and Leo were so tired that they slept through the morning and didn't get up until two o'clock, feeling completely refreshed and slightly guilty.

Alex was still in her bathrobe drinking her second cup of coffee and reading the paper when Leo bounded in, fully showered and dressed.

"Hi, sweet thang," he said, kissing the top of her head. I've got an errand to run. Be right back." He headed for the door, humming.

"Want me to go with?" Alex called.

"Nope. I won't be that long. Enjoy your coffee."

"Okay. Be safe, be careful," Alex said. That was her mantra of protection for Leo and she said it every time he went somewhere without her, which wasn't too often, but it didn't pay to gamble.

"I will. 'Bye." Door slam, truck starting up and truck pulling out.

Then, silence.

Alex was alone.

Contrary to Leo's assurances, she did not forget her traumatic dream of the night before. Being alone in the now quiet house brought it all rushing back. She stood, coffee mug in hand, and stepped outside the back door.

It was a beautiful day, nothing supernatural or odd about it—just the back yard dirt and the forlorn looking empty house next door, but her dream of the previous night was still very much with her. There was no man in formal attire, no strange leaves, and, thank heavens, no Theodora. Alex walked to the edge of the property, where the man in her dream had been standing, and looked to the left—the direction he'd been pointing She gazed down the narrow concrete-paved road that separated the Renfield's house from the ramshackle one next door. Alex hadn't walked to the end of this road yet, but she made a mental note to do so soon.

She never looked down.

If she did, she'd have seen the footprints.

But she didn't and now she chuckled. Carrying a bad dream with her on such a glorious day seemed a trifle silly now, and she relegated it to the back of her mind. When she turned to reenter the house, she was startled by an unexpected visitor.

"Hello there. Well, aren't you beautiful."

Near the open back door stood a box turtle, its wizened face bearing the signature look of world-weary bewilderment common to the creatures.

Alex approached the small reptile slowly and quietly, expecting it to pull in its head and feet and live up to its name, but it didn't. It continued to watch her with sleepy interest.

She squatted down to get a closer look at her uninvited, but most welcome guest. Beautiful, indeed, the small turtle was about five inches long with orange starbursts covering its brown shell. Its head was mottled in yellow and its legs had bright red spots. Its eyes, too, were bright red. "Are you hungry?" Alex asked. She extended her index finger to stroke the turtle's head and it didn't resist or show any fear at all. As a matter of fact, it closed its eyes, giving every indication that it was enjoying the attention. Alex carefully picked it up and ran her hand gently over the plastrons. "Aha! You're a little boy," she said, upon feeling the concavity by the tail. "Let's go inside, buddy. I think I have a strawberry with your name on it."

The small turtle turned out to be very hungry indeed, consuming a strawberry, a leaf of lettuce, and a chunk of tomato. "I have no worms for you, but if you want to stick around, once I dig out the garden bends, I'm bound to find some."

The turtle looked up at her quizzically, then lumbered over, walked up onto her fuzzy slipper and promptly fell asleep.

"I'll take that as a 'yes'." Alex murmured, honored that

the little animal was so at ease with her. Not wanting to disturb his sleep, she finished her coffee standing in the middle of the kitchen. This was how Leo found her when he came back.

"Hey, hon!" he shouted from the driveway.

"Shhhhhhh," Alex said as Leo stuck his head around the doorjamb.

"Why?"

She pointed at her slipper.

"Oh. Being held for ransom, is that it? He must be stronger than he looks," Leo whispered, grinning.

"He's asleep. I just fed him. Poor thing was starved."

"I see. I realize that this is a stupid question, but feel compelled to ask it, for some reason," Leo said. "Are we keeping him?"

"Yes, Harold has graciously agreed to join our family," Alex replied.

"Harold?"

"Yes. My high school advanced biology teacher looked just like a turtle, so I'm naming this little guy after him."

"Then 'Harold' it shall be. What do we feed him?"

"Fruit, vegetables, and high quality dog food are fine. They like earthworms best, but I couldn't find any in the fridge."

Leo snapped his fingers. "Damn! I ate the last ones with my eggs this morning, but there's a live bait place in Southfield. We could get some worms for him there. Let's take a ride later."

"That's great, Leo. Thanks."

"Where will he live? I mean, we do have a guest room, but I think the bed is going to be a way too high for him."

"We could always build him his own garden box. Eight by eight will give him plenty of room, and I can add hiding places and plants for shade. I'll even plant a lettuce patch in there for him."

Leo looked down at Harold. "It was a lucky day for you, buddy, when you wandered into her yard. You're set for life

114

now." Then a thought occurred to him. "What about when we leave for the summer?"

"What about it? We take him along."

"We can't do that, Alex!"

"Why not? He doesn't make any noise or take up much space. Black will never even know we have him."

"I suppose we could. There wasn't anything in the contract that prohibited pets."

Harold awoke yawned, and looked up at Leo sleepily. Alex picked him up. "He really is cute, isn't he?"

"Yep. He takes after you, obviously. Until we get the box made, he can stay on the porch. It's closed in, so he won't get out—not that I think he has the slightest intention of leaving *this* hotel."

***

Alex carried a large plastic potted plant saucer filled with water to the center of the porch. The moment she put it down in the sunny spot, Harold waddled right over and climbed into it. Though it was shallow enough for him to easily keep his head above water, he submerged it and stuck his snakelike neck straight out.

"What's he doing?" Leo asked.

"He's getting a drink. His neck has to be extended," Alex said. "Otherwise, it's hard for him to swallow."

"Guess he was thirsty too, then. What kind of box turtle is he?"

"I'm not sure. I'll have to hit the library in Southfield to find out."

"Ah, but that's where you're wrong," Leo said. "In honor of our cash windfall from Joyce, I got you a present."

"A book about turtles?"

"Better. Come help me with it."

"Help you with it? What did you buy?" Alex asked. She followed him out to the back of the truck, where he dropped the tailgate, revealing three large boxes with a familiar logo on them.

"A new computer? How wonderful!" Alex exclaimed. "But can we really afford it, Leo?"

"There was a huge sale at *Byte Me* in Southfield, and we really do need one. It was a lot cheaper than I expected. I got the whole bundle for about $500.00, laser printer included. We needed to replace that clunker we got rid of before we moved, anyhow. Now you'll have something to write your novels on. Plus, if we use it for the business I can write off most of the cost. Oh, and this is for you, too." Leo handed her a smaller gift wrapped box. Alex pulled off the paper and lid to reveal a journal with a dark green velveteen cover.

"It's for when you get a brilliant idea away from home."

Alex hugged him fiercely. "Thank you, my darling, for the encouragement, the support, and for this fabulous computer and journal, but most of all for being the man you are. I love you so much," she said.

Leo laughed. "Save the mushy stuff and help me get this sucker unloaded and hooked up."

When they returned to the porch, boxes in hand, they discovered that Harold had not only used his new pool for a drink and a bath, but for a toilet, as well. He was across the porch, asleep under a wicker chair, having distanced himself from the watery mess even farther by turning his back on it.

"I guess that the turtle version of a litter box," Leo said.

"He'll be easy to clean up after, anyhow. I'll just have to dump the water and scrub out the saucer more often. I'll clean it up after we get the computer into the house."

"I don't think there's a big rush. It looks like he'll be zonked out for a while," Leo said.

They unpacked the system like it was Christmas morning, read all the instructions, made the requisite phone calls, and by evening their new computer was up, running, and connected to the Internet.

Alex glanced at her watch. "Oh, jeez, I better start dinner, Leo. Why don't you play with this until it's ready?"

"Okay, hon. Oh, hey, don't forget about Harold's water."

"Oh, gosh, I meant to change that hours ago. Poor Harold." Alex hurried to the porch, fearful that the turtle would have consumed the soiled water looking for another drink. But no. He was still asleep in the same place they'd left him earlier. Alex picked up the plant saucer-*cum*-turtle spa, dumped the water outside, then took the container in for a good scrub and a refill.

When she returned, Harold was standing where the pool had been. He looked up at Alex, cocking his head slightly. She squatted down and placed the filled saucer on the floor next to him, thinking that he was waiting for it, but instead, Harold ran to the farthest corner of the porch.

Not walked. Not waddled. Not even strolled.

He ran.

Startled, Alex recoiled, overbalanced and landed squarely on her butt. She had never seen a turtle move that fast before.

She didn't think it was possible for a turtle to move that fast.

Meanwhile, Harold backed into the corner next to a pink geranium, stuck his head out of his shell, looked up at Alex and cocked his head again, as if to say, "Pretty good, huh?"

Alex got up and ran back into the house, chased by the fear that if she remained, he'd start tap dancing and singing, "Hello My Baby, Hello My Honey, Hello My Ragtime Gal," thereby obliging her to relinquish what was left of her sanity.

"Leo? There's something wrong with the turtle."

"He's not just 'a turtle' anymore, my dear. He is an Eastern Box Turtle. It says so right here," Leo said, indicating the computer screen with a flourish.

And there was Harold.

"Does it say how fast they can run?" Alex asked.

"Very funny."

"I'm serious. I just saw Harold run across the porch."

"You mean, 'walk fast?'"

"No, I mean run. Turtles aren't supposed to move that fast. Their defense is closing up their shells, not flight."

"How fast?" Leo asked.

"Running like… like… like a cockroach runs. Skittery. More like a bug than a turtle. It was really freaky."

"Sure your imagination isn't getting the better of you?"

"It could be, I guess. I know I couldn't have seen what I think I just saw."

"You're probably still tired. Let's eat, watch a little TV, and go to bed early. Then you can bring out all the mushy stuff I told you to save earlier."

Chapter Eighteen

That night, Alex moved in and out of sleep, dreaming about writing a bestseller on their new computer. She mulled over subjects for her first novel. No romance treacle for her. She wanted to be taken seriously, not just read by blue haired ladies at the beauty parlor and then traded in at the local senior center. She wanted pride of place on peoples' bookshelves. She wanted to write something that would stand up to re-reading. She wanted to write somebody's—a lot of somebodies'—favorite book. As she drifted off into a dream of audience applause, a sharp cold breeze brought her back to herself and she realized that the applause she was hearing in her dream was actually the sound of claws clicking on the hardwood floors.

"Back door must be open," she muttered, forgetting that she'd shut and locked it, as she did every night.

The rapid clicking continued down the hall, toward their bedroom. There were short pauses, as if their owner was looking into each room along the way.

Alex, wide awake now, remained still, mouth breathing to minimize noise.

click click click click

pause

click click click click

pause

click click

pause

Whatever it was had to be right at their bedroom door. Alex cursed herself for not closing it. Now they'd have to most likely deal with their garbage-strewing raccoon or skunk in the middle of the goddamned night. Not to mention the rabies possibilities. She was leaning over to quietly wake Leo when she felt a tug at the foot of the bedspread.

Whatever was in the house was climbing up onto the bed.

Alex went back to playing dead. You just didn't mess with rabies. She figured that once it got close enough, she could wrap it up in the bedspread and get it outside.

Raccoon or skunk, the animal had to be huge, as heavy as it felt pulling on the spread. She sighed inwardly, seeing rabies shots in their futures.

At the foot of the bed, now, the animal lumbered closer, up Alex's side of the bed. It put a paw on her ankle, then pulled it back, unsure of its footing. It paused. Alex was afraid to even move her head to look at it, and so remained lying on her back, staring at the ceiling. Beads of sweat grew on her forehead and upper lip as the intruder slightly altered its course to the unoccupied blanket furrow between Alex and Leo. The bed shook with each step the animal took. Alex was astounded that Leo didn't wake up.

Then, to her horror, the scavenger climbed slowly onto her chest and stopped there. She fought to control her breathing under its weight while she ever so slowly slipped her left arm out from beneath the thick layer of blankets and reached for the table lamp. She thought that if she could combine sudden light with a loud noise, she might at least be able to scare it off the bed.

The progress of freeing her hand was excruciatingly slow and by the time she managed it, she was a mass of sour sweat. She still had no idea whether her unwanted guest was a raccoon or a skunk, since she was afraid to move her head to look at it, but she fervently hoped it was a raccoon. She'd rather deal with rabies shots than de-skunking.

Here goes. Her ice cold fingers touched the switch.

The 40 watt bulb flashed on for a fraction of a second, then, with a muffled *pop*, burned out. Not long, but enough time for Alex to see the animal perched on her chest.

It was Harold.

Alex sat up, rolling the turtle off into the furrow next to her. She felt the blankets frantically, but couldn't locate him.

"No, no, *no*! No way! Where the hell are you?" Alex

shouted.

"I'm right here, honey," Leo said, half asleep. He switched on his night table lamp and watched Alex feeling around the bedspread.

She got up, flipped the overhead light on, and searched the room, checking under the bed especially carefully.

Nothing.

"Alex, what are you looking for at…" Leo checked the clock, "…two-fifteen in the morning?"

"You wouldn't believe me if I told you," she replied from behind the dresser.

"Well, try me anyway."

"I'm looking for Harold."

"Isn't he on the porch?"

"No, Leo. He was just here… on the bed, sitting on my chest."

Leo laughed. "Then I guess he has the right name, at that. Wasn't Houdini's first name 'Harold'?"

"Ha, ha. Are you trying to be funny?"

"Yes."

"Try again."

"You just had another weird dream, Alex." Leo got out of bed. "Come with me."

"Where?"

"Just come on—in the interest of getting back to sleep."

Leo took Alex's hand and walked her through the house to the back porch. He unlocked the door and turned on the light.

There, in the corner, snuggled into a pile of rags that Alex had put down for him earlier, was Harold, sound asleep.

"See? Just a tired little turtle who's happy to have a new home. No escape artists here. You had a dream, Alex, that's all."

"But it was so real. I'm sure I was awake, Leo."

"Ever heard of lucid dreaming?"

"No."

"You feel like you're awake when it's happening, but you're not."

"Really? I'll have to research that."

"You've got a brand new computer to do it on. Now let's go back to bed," Leo said.

When they were horizontal once more, Leo said, "You should write your dreams down, hon. They sure are interesting."

"Yeah, I've been thinking about that," she said. "Maybe I will."

Chapter Nineteen

JOURNAL ENTRY

April twenty-seventh, 2008 – Late morning

I've never kept a journal before, and I'm unsure as to how to go about it. Is it like a diary, where you record your personal, secret, innermost thoughts? Or is it a literary sketchbook where you jot short stories or pithy paragraphs? Or is it simply an idea book or a dream journal?

Or, worst of all, what if it's an affectation? Shall this be the first step toward the cliché of wearing nothing but black and hanging out in upscale hotel bars drinking Le Perroquets all day and chain smoking Gitanes while leading a life of quiet, but creative dissipation, working far into the night to turn out 5,000 good words per week, but being disdainful of actually selling them?

Or is that a poet?

No, it won't be an affectation. It won't be anything in particular at all. I'll write what I like in it. There won't be any self-imposed rules.

As a matter of fact, today I think I'll write about the garden we're putting in. I'm planning on planting the following: radishes, peppers, tomatoes, beans, eggplant, onions, garlic, lettuce, peas, potatoes, carrots, cabbage, broccoli, cauliflower, and spinach.

Leo is building raised beds for me, so after that's done, all we have to do is pick up soil and compost at the garden center and we'll be ready to go. I already have my seeds.

Harold, our Eastern Box Turtle, seems to be settling in just fine. Leo picked up some night crawlers for him and he's eating them like popcorn. I still can't believe I was afraid of him. I

Alex stopped writing. Who was she kidding? She was terrified of Harold. What was she thinking—that years from now, after she had enjoyed a bestselling career and was long dead, someone would read this drivel and think she was normal? Besides, this was too much like a diary, and she wanted it to be more important than that.

She drew a diagonal line through the page she'd just written and began again.

"Two A.M.! Dear God. I shouldn't have had so much tea. I'll be running to the bathroom all night," Sarah sighed, throwing off the blankets for the second time in as many hours.

The house felt odd since Mother died. It had an atmosphere of abandonment, even though Sarah continued to live there, though it might be more accurate to say that she still haunted the place—such were her lifelong feelings of insignificance that Mother had taken great pains to instill. She made damned sure that Sarah would never leave her by convincing her that she'd never survive out there in the real world. Additionally, Mother had been a real force of nature, and anywhere such a presence had been and gone would naturally feel like a black hole for a while.

Did Sarah miss her? It was a question she'd asked herself repeatedly over the past several months. She supposed she did, in her way; but it was more a feeling of not quite knowing what to do with herself, absent her mother's constant demands and controlling dictates.

"She was as strong as I am weak," Sarah mused, half asleep.

Dozing on the toilet, she heard her mother's voice, whether in her head or not, she couldn't tell.

"Don't forget," it said. "Don't forget."

Sarah snapped to. "Don't forget what?" she asked aloud.

"Don't forget to wash your hands, of course!"

Sarah shook her head and laughed mirthlessly. To be completely honest, she didn't miss her mother at all.

It was hard to miss someone who refused to go away.

Aghast, Alex put down her pen as if it burned her fingers and read over what she had just written.

"Where in wide, wide world of sports did *that* come from?" She closed the journal with a snap and pushed it away.

"Hello, sweetness," Leo said as he walked in from the shop. "Whatcha doin'?"

"Some journaling, that's all," Alex replied, her inner critic roundly reprimanding her for making a noun into a verb. She glanced uneasily at the closed book. "Want lunch?"

"That'd be great. Any chicken left?" Leo's favorite sandwich in the world was cold roast chicken on marble rye with avocado slices and blue cheese dressing.

"Sure. One 'Blue Chickado' coming up. Have a seat." Alex left the kitchen table, moved to her prep counter next to the refrigerator, and got busy on Leo's lunch. She was troubled by her journal entry—the emptiness of it, the despair. It didn't feel like it even came from Alex. It was as if…

"Hey, hon, what's this?" Leo called.

Alex arrived, sandwich and a mug of lemonade in hand.

"What's what? Oh, that."

Leo was reading her journal. "I liked the first part that you crossed out, but where did that second thing come from?"

"I don't know, Leo."

"That will teach me to look something over before I buy it. I'm sorry that some jerk defaced your journal, sweetie," Leo said. "After lunch, I'll get a razor blade and we'll cut that page right out of it."

"What are you talking about, honey?"

"I'm talking about this," he said, reading aloud the disturbing passage.

"But Leo, I wrote that ten minutes ago."

"You couldn't have. Not this part. Look at it."

Alex looked.

The passage wasn't in her handwriting.

"Leo, I swear to you that I wrote that—nobody else!" Alex cried.

"Then why disguise your handwriting? You have such beautiful penmanship."

"I don't know. I didn't do it consciously. I didn't even notice it until you pointed it out."

Leo looked at her, concern written all over his kind face. "But how could you not? It's small and crabbed and ugly. And the piece itself is so... so... I don't know. It sort of reminds me of the main character in *The Haunting of Hill House*. What was her name?"

"Eleanor."

"That's it."

Alex sighed with relief. "I finished rereading that one a couple of nights ago. It was probably my subconscious downloading onto the page, that's all."

"Must be it. That's one book that stays with you awhile, that's for sure."

"I think it's probably the creepiest book I ever read," Alex said.

Leo sat down and picked up his sandwich. "Why don't you try Donald Westlake tonight? I just picked up his new Dortmunder novel."

"You did? Wonderful. You can't get farther away from Hill House than East 19tth Street in Manhattan." Alex felt a whole world better. Leo was always good for that.

The weird handwriting was harder to dismiss, though... much harder.

Chapter Twenty

As the day progressed, Alex set aside the strangeness with the journal and concentrated on helping Leo place and anchor the nine four-by-four-by-one garden beds and the eight-by-eight-by-one enclosure that Leo had dubbed "Harold's Hotel, Resort, and Spa."

"Let's put Harold's place over here," Leo said.

"Right against the house?"

"Sure. He'll have some protection from the wind this way. If we face it south, like the back of the house here, he'll have sun all day. We'll just have to put in some shady areas so he can cool off if he wants to."

"That's good thinking, hon. I didn't know you knew so much about turtles," Alex said.

"Computers are marvelous things," Leo said, with a wink.

"You really like Harold, don't you?"

"What's not to like? He doesn't eat much, doesn't make any noise, doesn't chew up my slippers, and doesn't smoke."

Alex laughed. Harold had become more Leo's pet since the two scares she'd had with him, imagined or not. She was desperately trying to chalk her fears up to overtiredness and lucid dreaming, as Leo had suggested; but there was still a particle of anxiety that wouldn't let go and trust that Harold was nothing more sinister than a cute little box turtle.

More and more lately, Alex feared that she might be losing her grip. Though an imaginative person, she had never been prone to such wild, irrational figments before—at least, she didn't think so. What was happening to her?

Leo had Harold's Resort in place and anchored in a flash. "Wait'll you see the roof I made." He dashed back into the shop.

Alex smiled after him. When he got so excited about

simple things like this, she could see in him the boy he once was. She wondered what things enchanted him as a child. She'd ask him sometime.

"Close your eyes," he shouted from the porch doorway.

Alex complied, grinning. If he asked for closed eyes before an unveiling, you could just bet that he'd made something spectacular. But a turtle roof? How big a deal could that be?

"Okay. Open 'em."

A very big deal indeed.

Leo had built a Carpenter Gothic steeply pitched roof covered with cedar shingles the size of fingernails. With his scroll saw, he'd cut intricate bargeboards to decorate the two sides of the gable and he'd placed a finely turned finial at the peak. Attached to this striking creation were three vertical walls, done in miniature board and batten style with an arched doorway cut into them. The bargeboards were painted sage green and the rest of the structure was done in a medium marine blue. The roof shingles were left to weather to a natural gray.

"Oh, Leo, it's beautiful!" Alex was delighted.

"It only needed three sides because the fourth is the back of the raised bed, see?" Leo lowered the roof into place. It fit perfectly.

"You are such an artist, Leo. You go far beyond just run-of-the-mill carpentry. What you do is astounding."

Leo blushed. "Thank you, honey."

"What made you go to all this trouble for a turtle, though? I doubt he'll care."

"Oh, I know that," Leo laughed. "I had just forgotten how beautiful the Carpenter Gothic style is, so I thought I'd play with it."

"Is it going to be all right to leave it outside? What will the weather do to it?

"It's treated and sealed and painted with exterior paint, which has much more resin in it. It'll last a long, long time, believe me."

"You could make a fortune if you wanted to spend your time making doll houses for children of the rich and overprivileged."

"Maybe when I retire. Let's go get Harold."

Leo rescued Harold from his porch hostel and placed him gently in his new home. It took a moment or two, but he finally poked his wrinkled little head out of his shell and took a look around. Alex had put his food and water dishes in already, and planted a couple of dwarf boxwood shrubs to give him additional shade and hiding places. Harold immediately headed for the shelter of the ornate roof, and the moment he was safe inside it began to pour down rain.

Alex and Leo ran for the porch.

"Jeez, he's better than Al Roker," Leo said. "Maybe we can get him a job at NBC."

"He'd be cheaper than Al, too. Just pay him in worms."

They waited out the rain on the porch and it wasn't long before it stopped. Twenty minutes later, the sun was out again, and you'd never know it had rained at all.

"Mark Twain was right when he said, 'If you don't like the weather in New England, just wait a minute or two,'" Alex said.

"In that case, we'd better get back to work out there before it snows. Speaking of which, I meant to ask you—aren't you planning on planting the garden kind of early?"

"Normally, yes, but remember that big roll of plastic I bought just before we moved here? I'm going to stretch it over the top of the two-by-four frames that we'll build, then place it over the tops of the raised beds to make cold frames. They'll protect the seedlings and harden them off at the same time. By the time we leave for the summer, they'll all be up, so I can take the plastic off then."

"Okay." Leo said, still looking doubtful. "You're the expert. I'll go cut up the two-by-fours."

Now that Harold was established in his Donald Trump accommodations and Leo was in the shop cutting up the two-by-fours needed for the cold frame toppers, Alex concentrated on filling the boxes with her soil mixture. Each four-by-four-by-one box required one hundred eighty pounds of medium to fill it. That worked out to sixty pounds of peat moss, sixty pounds of vermiculite, and sixty pounds of compost per raised bed. Leo had put hardware cloth across the bottom of each in order to keep moles, woodchucks, and weeds out. Once each bed was filled, and her seeds planted, she'd give each bed a good drenching, then use the staple gun to fasten her heavy sheets of plastic over each topper frame and once these were put in place, voila—self-contained greenhouses.

Leo pulled all the cut lumber around to the back of the house with the pallet jack.

"You know how you want to assemble these beds?" he asked.

"Yep. Oh, you brought the anchoring spikes, too. Great."

"Okay. If you don't need me for a while, I have a few things to do in the shop."

"Oh? Like what?" Alex asked, smiling.

"Like a few things, that's all. Okay with you?" Leo snapped. He turned on his heel and stalked off.

Alex gaped at his retreating figure, open mouthed. What was eating him? They just didn't speak to each other that way. Not ever. But rather than go after him, Alex decided to give Leo some space. *He'll think about it and apologize later,* she thought. So, until 'later' came, she bent to her task and by dusk, the beds were all filled, planted, and watered; and when she finally looked up, she noticed all the cold frame tops stacked up against the back of the house. Surprised that Leo hadn't at least said hello when he brought them out, and equally, if not more surprised that she hadn't heard him stacking the toppers against the house, she fetched her roll of plastic.

Fortunately, it was in the basement rather than the workshop. She hauled it upstairs and outside, snagging a pair of scissors along the way.

Outside once more, Alex measured, cut, and stapled the plastic sheeting to the frames Leo had made, and then screwed the toppers into the raised beds to keep them in place. She wouldn't have to remove them until the seedlings were pretty far along.

As Alex cleaned her gardening tools, she thought again how strange it was that she hadn't seen Leo all afternoon; but after their earlier exchange, she felt that walking into their workshop would be an invasion of his privacy, so she dropped her gloves into her garden tool bag, shook out and folded the blue plastic tarp she'd been using to mix the soil components, and brushed off the knees of her jeans. Then she glanced up at the house.

It was getting seriously dark, yet there were no lights on in the shop.

Odd.

If Leo were going out, he'd have told her… wouldn't he?

Alex crept up to the nearest shop window and peeked in.

"What the…?"

Leo had boarded over all the workshop windows from the inside.

"Oh, this is just too much!" Alex cried. She sped across the porch to the shop door on the left, and wasn't surprised to find obstructions on this window, too. She turned the knob but nothing happened. The door was locked at the deadbolt.

"Leo? Honey? Why is the door locked?" she called, rattling the knob.

No answer.

Alex checked the driveway and saw that the truck was gone.

But why lock the shop?

Hold it! That door didn't even have *a deadbolt on it before today. He must have just installed it!*

She gave the knob another try; just to be sure it really was locked and not just stuck. No, it was well and truly locked. Her hand dropped from the brass knob and, in a daze, she sat down in the nearest wicker chair and set about removing her dirty work boots.

How could he? How could he shut her out this way? It was her shop, too; they were supposed to be partners. They were also supposed to be better friends than this. And for him to just take off without letting her know where he was going or when he'd be back? That wasn't like Leo. That wasn't like Leo at all.

Could it be that he was building something for her and wanted to surprise her with it? But her birthday wasn't until October and here it was, not even May. Alex couldn't imagine what he could be building. She hadn't hinted at anything. And anyway, he wouldn't be treating her like this if that was what he was up to.

The blocked windows and locked door were what really bothered her. Leo knew that if he asked her not to look in the shop that she wouldn't. Why all the extra safeguards?

And where was he?

Chapter Twenty-One

JOURNAL ENTRY
April twenty-eighth, 2008. Nine-thirty A.M.

Leo didn't come home last night until well after dark—and when he finally did, he went straight back to the shop.

So, of course, I marched straight out there to find out what the hell is going on, but the door was locked again. I put my ear to it, and between saw and drill noises, I heard another much more disturbing noise.

He was talking to someone.

Now why would he be locked in the shop with someone else?

I pressed my ear closer, but couldn't make out any words, just the sound of Leo's deep voice. I couldn't hear any replies from whoever was in there with him. Either his visitor had a very soft voice or he was having an animated conversation with himself.

I don't know which alternative frightens me more.

I didn't see him get out of his truck when he came back, so I have no idea if he had someone with him or not. I couldn't bear it if he was seeing someone else. It would absolutely kill me to lose Leo.

But who else could it be but a woman? I'd have heard a man's voice. And though I make no secret of talking to myself, it's more of a mumble, not an outright conversation.

So Leo's either losing it or seeing someone else.

Some fucking choice.

Finally, I rattled the knob hard and pounded on the door, calling him. All the shop noise stopped, but he didn't answer me. It was like he was holding his breath in there, waiting for me to go away.

After a while, I did.

I ended up eating dinner by myself, watching the news by myself, and at midnight, going to bed by myself.

He was still out in the shop doing who knows what with who knows who.

When I got up this morning, I knew he hadn't been to bed. That soft pillow of his always holds a dent from his head, and it was still as fluffy as it was when I went to sleep.

Surprisingly enough, I actually slept late. It's nine-thirty.

Will write more later.

Alex closed her journal and stowed it under some magazines on her nightstand. She dressed quickly and went the kitchen, glancing at the closed shop door as she passed the back door window.

"Well, howdy there, little missy!" Leo cried, nearly sending Alex through the ceiling.

'Little missy?'

"Leo! You just about gave me a heart attack," she said, hand on her chest.

He was leaning against the kitchen counter, drinking instant coffee. He had a smile on his face... a smile that looked wrong.

Of all the questions Alex wanted to ask him, the only ones she could come up with was, "Why are you drinking instant? Are we out of the real stuff?"

"Nope. I just can't ever remember how many scoops to put in and I didn't want to ruin a whole pot," he replied, still smiling.

Alex turned away on the pretext of getting the coffee filters and ground roast. He sort of sounded and acted like her Leo—except for that spooky smile. "For a full pot, you need one scoop for every two cups and one for the pot at the end," Alex said, filling the machine with water. "Oh, and by the way, Leo, what are you doing out in the shop?"

Leo set his cup down with exaggerated care. Then he looked up at Alex, his face white with fury. "I will not, repeat, *will not* be interrogated in my own home," he said, his voice deadly calm.

"I'd hardly call one question an interrogation." Alex was stunned. "Who are you and what have you done with my sweet, wonderful husband?"

Leo's face contorted with a mixture of fear and loathing, as if reflecting some horrific inner battle. Alex had never seen anything like it, and never wanted to again. Then, suddenly, Leo's features smoothed out again and that unnerving calm returned. His eyes, once so full of warmth now reminded her of Michael Corleone's with their snake-like deadness. "Right now, what you can do is fix me some eggs with bacon and two slices of toast. On a separate plate, I would like lettuce leaves with sliced tomato. Think you can manage that? Hmmm?"

"You never eat salad with your break…"

"*Just do it!*" he thundered. "Put it on a tray, leave it outside the shop door, knock once, and then leave me the hell alone!" Again, his face contorted, then relaxed.

For the first time, Alex was truly afraid of Leo. She didn't know who she was dealing with here, but it wasn't her husband. She half-wondered if there was a pod under the workbench as she watched him unlock the deadbolt and disappear into the darkness within.

Alex prepared his breakfast just as he ordered, knocked once, and walked back into the house. She watched from the back door window as he opened the door just enough to squeeze out, pick up the tray, then squeeze back in again. All Alex could see beyond the open door was darkness. After Leo shut the door, a bar of light suddenly appeared beneath it.

Well, at least he wasn't eating in the dark.

She scrubbed out the frying pan, her stomach in knots. Food was out of the question, so after cleaning up the kitchen, she decided to spend the morning gardening. Maybe it would help her calm down and clear her head.

She changed into her scruffy gardening clothes, picked up her tool bag and stepped out onto the porch. Before she continued outside, she put the bag down gently and crept up to the workshop door to listen.

Not a sound. He must still be eating.

Alex sighed and prepared herself for another lonely day.

Chapter Twenty-Two

Leo sat next to his workbench, staring moodily at his breakfast.

"Well, go on, eat it," his companion urged.

"Not hungry," he said, still staring at the tray. A tear ran down his cheek as he recalled the terrified look on Alex's face. His Alex was afraid of him.

"If you aren't going to eat, do you mind if I do?"

"No."

"Then pass that salad this way. And, for the love of Pete, quit your blubbering. It does a woman good to be afraid of her man now and then. Reminds her who's boss. I once bit the toe off a bitch I was screwing—not while I was screwing her, you understand—but later, when she least expected it."

"How can you be that way? I love Alex more than anything, but I'm treating her like garbage and I don't know why!" Leo exclaimed, slamming his fist down in the workbench hard enough to make the dishes rattle.

"Oh, you know why, all right."

"Why, then, if you're so smart?"

"Because you need my help to stand up to her, so I intervene. And right now, boyo, you'd better focus on more important things, and keep her out of our hair. You're working for me, remember?"

"How could I forget?"

"Leo, Leo, Leo. Do I detect a trace of discontent? Is the native getting restless?"

"I don't understand why all this has to be a big secret. She'll find out sooner or later, you know, when it's done," Leo grumbled.

"Oh no, she won't. Besides, I'll be relocating before then."

"Oh?" asked Leo. "Need help packing?"

"Sarcasm is unattractive, Leo, and I suggest you abandon it. If you are not going to eat, then you'd better get to work."

Leo sighed heavily, stood, and gathered the necessary tools.

"I'll be really happy when this is done," he said.

"Oh, so will I, dear Leo, so will I," his companion said, a trace of a smile on his face.

Chapter Twenty-Three

It was a beautiful day for gardening, or for doing almost anything outside, for that matter; but it could have been snowing for all the attention Alex paid to the weather. The only nod she gave to meteorology was to look up the date of the May full moon, so she'd know when to remove her plastic cold frames from her garden beds.

Growing up, she spent most of her time on her grandparents' farm, and she'd learned, the hard way, of the hazards of planting without a cold frame before the full moon in May.

"See, Sasha," her Gramma told her. "See how you plant too soon." They were standing outside five-by-five plot her grandparents gave her in which to plant what she wished. All the newly risen sprouts were dead. She had been misled by the early May warmth and had, contrary to Gramma and Grampa's gentle guidance, planted all her flower seeds. They had tried to tell her that there was always a cold snap right around the full moon, but she had been too headstrong to listen.

All Grampa said when she ignored their advice was, "Leave alone, Ma. She find out."

She sure had. A hard lesson, but at eight years old, she'd learned early, and Grampa had slipped her some cherry tomato seeds to plant at the appropriate time. "If you can't eat it, don't plant it" had been Grampa's motto and after her bumper crop of the small but sweet tomatoes came in, she found herself agreeing with him.

She never disregarded anything her grandparents said after that. She absorbed all they taught her like a sponge and, over the years, had read about a hundred books on gardening, too.

Alex sometimes questioned exactly how much good the books did, though. Gramma couldn't read, but she could grow *anything* on their farm. A soft smile of remembrance lit her face, thinking of the old folks, a decade dead now, and how Gramma used to say that she felt closest to God when she was milking the cow.

Grampa was a quiet, gentle man who worked as a janitor for the National Biscuit Company in Watertown during the week. On the weekends, he salvaged bricks and copper wire and helped Gramma with the livestock and garden. Alex remembered him sitting in his "brickyard" between the chicken coop and a mountain of old bricks. Grampa would spend hours painstakingly chipping off the old mortar so the bricks could be resold and reused. As he worked, wild birds would perch on his shoulders. Grampa always said that God sent them to inspect his work. "He's the foreman," is what he'd say about whatever bird was on his shoulder at the time. The funny thing was, the tiny creatures always looked very interested in what he was doing.

Alex got her way with animals from him. Wild birds wouldn't land on her shoulders, but they weren't afraid of her, either. No animal was. She had thought that Harold was another of the many wild pets that Grampa had sent her way. That was how she looked at it each time a new wild creature wandered into her life. Grampa was just sending animals in need to someone he knew would take good care of them.

"I don't know where Harold came from," she muttered as she dug a trench for the three copper colored rose plants Leo had bought for her a few days ago, "but it certainly wasn't from Grampa."

It was interesting that her Russian immigrant grandparents were not where the Jewish influence in her life came from. Gramma was from Vilnius, and she could speak Russian, Polish, and Lithuanian. She said it was because it changed hands so often that the citizens never knew who was going to be in charge from one day to the next. Grampa was from Minsk. The Jewishness came from her father's side, and it hailed from Germany, but she had spent so little time with those cold grandparents that she barely knew them. Whenever her father took Alex to visit, the first thing she was forced to do was to go say hello to Old Great Grandma Bluestone in her third floor room, high above the kitchen. This was always frightening for Alex, and not just because the woman was so terribly old that she no longer looked human, but more than that, senility had moved into her brain and brought furniture. Great Grandma used to think that Alex was her grandson (Alex's Uncle Izzy), and would address her by his name. Pretty scary stuff for a young child.

Though her German grandparents had never discussed it with her, her father had made her understand the seriousness of the Holocaust and Alex had strong opinions about that, even though she was about as far from being a practicing Jew as Al Sharpton was. As a child, she'd once asked, if being Jewish was something they were proud of, why had they changed their last name from 'Blaustein' to 'Bluestone?' Her father had explained about the importance of being safe from persecution and blending in to stay under the radar and out of trouble as much as possible. And besides, they didn't really *change* their name; they just translated it into English. To honor her father's memory, even though they had always celebrated Christmas in the house growing up, she now lit a menorah at Hanukah every year—this past year after Leo was sound asleep. In deference to his dislike of candles, she'd gotten up each night and lit the requisite number on a miniature Menorah she'd hidden at the back of a kitchen cupboard. Since it was so small, she used birthday cake candles, and watched them burn down and out each night.

Leo never knew about it, and it was the only time she'd lit candles since they met. Of course, he didn't like fires, either. No fireplaces, no gas stoves, no camp fires.

But that wasn't what bothered her.

What bothered her was that she didn't understand the reason for it. But there was a lot she didn't understand lately.

"I wish I had someone to talk to," Alex sighed. She never felt more isolated in her whole life. This tiff with Leo made her realize what life would be like for her if he were to die. She would be adrift and entirely alone. They loved each other so much that they felt they didn't really need anyone else in their lives. But now she wasn't so sure if that was such a good idea.

Alex stood and took off her gloves, clapping them together to get rid of lingering garden soil. She looked around and smiled with satisfaction. Not only was her garden all done and covered, but she'd put in a dozen sunflowers (Grampa's favorite) beneath the kitchen and several clumps of peonies (Gramma's favorite) beneath the rear workshop windows. She planted three rose plants and six purple lilacs (her favorite) along the south border of the property, a Japanese maple near Harold's digs for shade, and one peach, one plum, and one pear tree at the west side of the south facing yard. Next week she planned to stop at the nursery in Southfield to pick up some gooseberry and currant bushes and a cherry tree or two.

She'd get this place in shape yet.

The sun was nearly set. She'd have to get going on dinner pretty soon. But before she turned toward the house, she looked skyward and her eyes filled with tears.

"Thanks for spending the day with me, Gramma and Grampa. I miss you so much."

Chapter Twenty-Four

Alex was still smiling, her grandparents still on her mind, as she stood at the sink peeling potatoes. She was determined to straighten things out with Leo, and making him his favorite meal wouldn't be a half bad start.

"Roast chicken, oven roasted potatoes, stuffing, and corn. A symphony of starch," Alex chuckled, and popped the stuffed chicken into the rotisserie. Before ten minutes had elapsed the delightful ghostly aroma of chicken yet to come filled the kitchen, creating a warm, homey atmosphere. Food smells always did that, somehow. She quartered the potatoes, placed them in a baking dish and dotted them liberally with pats of butter. Then she slit the freezer bag and dumped the frozen corn into another pot. She'd jazz it up later with sesame seeds, garlic, and crushed red pepper flakes.

The chicken wouldn't be ready for another hour and a half, so she pulled out her journal. She was happy to have it, though she didn't think her writing showed much promise. So far, at least, it was just a place to mull things over.

Alex was about to put pen to paper when the first cramp hit.

"Jesus!" she exclaimed, doubling over. Instant sick sweat gathered and left damp tracks down her back as the pain continued. It felt like rotating knives were twirling through her insides, but even so, the pain was familiar. Unable to straighten up, she hobbled as fast as she was able to the bathroom.

"Must be gas or diarrhea," she muttered, fiddling with the zipper on her jeans.

She sat just in time. Alex felt something shift inside and then there was a heavy downward pressure that her abdominal muscles automatically assisted. Finally, a splash in the toilet signaled the subsidence of her pain.

She didn't even have to look to know that she'd just passed a huge blood clot. That was why the pain was so familiar. She had her period.

But how the hell could that be? I had a hysterectomy twelve years ago. I don't think that stuff grows back.

Alex could hear a liquid stream falling steadily into the toilet. She wasn't urinating, so it had to be blood. She wiped herself and the blood soaked right through the toilet tissue, even though she had a thick wad of it in her hand.

Okay, this has now gone from strange to scary. She reached into the linen cabinet and liberated a couple of washcloths. These she wrapped to create a makeshift sanitary pad, since she didn't have any in the house, set it in place, then pulled up her pants.

This can't be a period, so what the hell is going on? Alex did her best not to think of the C-word as she ran to the workshop and pounded out her anxiety on the workshop door.

No answer.

She banged again and called out.

Nothing.

At least the truck was in the driveway.

She ran back into the kitchen and grabbed the phone, dropped the receiver, caught it on the first bounce, then dialed.

"Dr. Munson's office."

"Hello. This is Alex Renfield. I'm a patient of Dr. Munson's and I think I have an emergency."

"I'm sorry, but this is the answering service. Dr. Munson is on vacation until April thirtieth. If it's an emergency, you'll want to go to Waterbury Hospital. Do you want me to send you an ambulance?"

Hysterical giggling bubbled up and threatened to spill over as Alex mentally rejoined, *No, no. Just flowers will do.*

"Are you there?"

"Yes, I'm here. And no, that's all right. There's another doctor in town I can get to. Thank you," Alex said, breaking the connection.

She could feel the blood soaking through the washcloths. *Think fast, girl!* she ordered. After a moment, she swept up a plastic freezer bag and ran back to the bathroom.

On the toilet once more, she extracted the blood soaked washcloths and deposited them in the sink to be rinsed later. Next, she took two more and placed them inside the freezer bag, then cut the zip lock off with manicure scissors. The folded washcloths went into the plastic bag and then she folded the open sides of the bag around the edges of her underwear, securing them with adhesive tape. She now had a waterproof barrier should the cloths become saturated.

When she was sure that everything was going to stay where she'd put it, she glanced up at the window.

"Good. It's dark now. Time to visit Dr. Orbon... er... Beverly," she said, zipping up and whisking her purse off the table as she rushed by.

While turning off the rotisserie, she thought of leaving Leo a note, but decided that he didn't deserve one. Her conscience sighed and hung its head, sending out electroshocks of guilt to get her back on track, but Alex ignored them and after a quick fumble, found her set of truck keys at the bottom (where else?) of her purse.

"Please be there, Beverly," Alex murmured as she backed out of the driveway.

Leo hadn't stirred from the workshop the whole time.

***

Leo sat, stricken.

"What's your problem now?" the client asked.

"Alex sounded like she was really in trouble."

"So?"

"So she needed me and I wasn't there for her!" Leo exclaimed, his eyes full of tears.

"Oh, can the waterworks, chum. She's a modern girl. She can take care of herself—you'll see. And, in a way, you are looking after her, because you know what will happen if you don't get this project finished on time."

"How many days do I have left?"

"Three."

"No problem there. As a matter of fact, I'm finishing it today, even if I have to work all night. I want you out of here. I want my life back!" Leo shouted.

The client was unfazed by his outburst. "Keep in mind, my dear Leo, that even if you complete it by tomorrow morning, I'll still be around until tomorrow night."

"Why?"

"Delivery. Remember?"

Chapter Twenty-Five

Alex sped down Dr. Orbon's half-hidden gravel drive, small stones flying behind her like a powerboat wake. The low hanging, overgrown tree branches tore at the windshield and doors as if restrain her, but they were no match for the Silverado. Alex came to rest in a cloud of dust as close to the building as possible.

Fortunately, the washcloth dam was still holding.

She jumped from the truck and another lightning bolt of pain doubled her over again. When she could catch her breath, she stumbled to the door of the odd little office by the cemetery, and rang.

Dr. Orbon must have been standing right behind the door, because it opened at once. He reached out, gathering Alex in to help her to the waiting room where, once inside the door, she collapsed.

"Wake up, my dear." A voice penetrated her muzziness. She took a breath to speak, and it was like snorting pins.

Alex came to abruptly. Dr. Orbon removed the smelling salts from under her nose with the help of Alex's two hands.

"Grnphmrprmph! What *is* that stuff?"

Dr. Orbon smiled slightly. "Mostly ammonia."

"Well it's so strong it ought to be wearing a cape," Alex said. "Thanks for rescuing me."

"Oh, it wasn't me. It was Ammonia Man. Dah dah dah *dah*!" Dr. Orbon laughed.

"And you talk about my imagination." Alex sat up, and as she did, she found herself in a puddle of blood. Her jerry-built waterproofing had finally given way.

"Perhaps you should stay put and I'll get some towels. We'll clean you up, and then see what's what," the doctor suggested. He locked the office door and pulled the blinds. "Be right back."

Alex was dizzy, weak, and terrified. The stuffed and mounted gazelle head above the door was the last thing she saw before losing consciousness a second time.

***

Leo did his best to put Alex out of his mind so he could concentrate fully on completing his project. He worked fast—faster than he'd ever worked before. Better than he'd ever worked before, too.

The client sat back and watched his every move with approval. After several hours, he said, "You might consider taking a break for some food, Leo."

"I just want to get this done."

"But you'll be no good to me if you lose fingers to that saw of yours. That would impede the project. Any delay, regardless of the reason, will result in, well, shall we say, *penalties* of a most unpleasant nature. You haven't forgotten, have you?"

"No," Leo replied, fingering the newly bandaged gash that extended from his left shoulder to his elbow. It was a good thing that the shop had running water and a first aid kit. He really didn't want Alex to know about his injury—at least, not yet.

"Go and make yourself a meal, and bring me a salad and a portion of chopped beef if you have it," said the client. "As a matter of fact, why not bring your food in here? I quite enjoy your company."

Chapter Twenty-Six

Alex came around this time to soft hands lightly clapping her cheeks.

"I didn't have the heart to singe your nostrils again."

She was lying on the examining table in a white johnny coat with a sanitary pad between her legs.

"I'm amazed. You must be a lot stronger than you look," Alex said.

"Hardly. It helps to have a scissoring gurney. I just rolled you onto it, raised it, wheeled you in here, and moved you over to the table – after cleaning you up, of course."

"What's wrong with me, Beverly?"

"I don't know. We both know it's nothing to do with women's troubles, since your reproductive system has been removed."

"It couldn't be hemophilia, could it?" Alex squeaked.

"Oh, my, no. Though it was originally thought that only men suffered with hemophilia, evidence now points to the fact that women can inherit it, as well. However, it's a much milder form and would not cause this sort of extreme bleeding in a female. You don't have hemophilia in your family, do you?"

"Well, that's good news, then. And, no, to answer your question. No hemophilia in my family."

"I'm sending you to Waterbury Hospital. They have diagnostic equipment that I do not. What I can tell you is that you'll need a transfusion immediately. I tested your hematocrit level while you were out."

"And?"

"Well, anything below thirty is considered dangerous."

"Okay. How do I stand?"

"As Henny Youngman would say, 'That's what puzzles

149

me.' Your hematocrit level is twelve."

"Twelve? But I just started bleeding today. How can it be twelve already?"

"You may have been anemic before you began bleeding, or you may be bleeding internally."

"But didn't you check me for anemia when you did my physical?"

"I didn't feel it was necessary. You weren't symptomatic at that time. In any case, you need to get to the hospital now. Have you a cellular telephone?" Beverly asked.

"Yes. In my bag."

"Fine. You'll need to dial this number," he said, handing her a pre-printed card. "Have them send an ambulance to get you—you're in no shape to drive. The address here is twenty-three River Road."

"But what about Leo?"

"Phone him from the hospital. You can pick up your vehicle whenever it's convenient. No harm will come to it here. For now, get dialing. Your life very much depends on it."

***

"I wish I knew where Alex went," Leo said, chewing moodily on his ham and swiss.

"I wouldn't worry about it. She's probably off shopping somewhere. Isn't that what women do when they get upset?"

"Not Alex. She'd go to an art museum, a library, or a garden center."

"Well, there you are."

"How's that? The library has been closed for hours, and so are the greenhouses around here. The nearest art museum is in Hartford and I doubt it's open at this hour either!"

"Perhaps she's visiting friends."

"We're new to the area, remember? Most of our friends are back in New York, and the nearest train station is Waterbury."

"Waterbury? Perhaps she's caught a train, then," the client

said.

Maybe, but somehow Leo doubted it.

He doubted it very much.

Chapter Twenty-Seven

The ambulance screamed up to the Emergency Room automatic double doors, where a doctor and two nurses were waiting with lactated Ringer's, glucose, and a unit of blood. Alex was swimming in and out of consciousness as the paramedics and the hospital staff went through their professional paces.

It was a day of lasts, it seemed. The last things she remembered this time were someone stuffing her hair into a shower cap, the smell of alcohol, and a pinch at the inside of her elbow.

***

At four thirty-six A.M., Leo put down his paintbrush. "It's done," he said, eyes on his creation. Hearing no reaction from the client, he looked up.

"Hey! Wake up! Your damned project is finished!" Leo shouted at the sleeping figure.

The client roused himself, yawned and gazed through bleary eyes at Leo's work. "Yes, so I see," he said. He got up and walked around the finished piece to see it from every angle. At last he said, "Yes, Leo, this will do."

"Gee, thanks," Leo grumbled.

"What were you expecting? A brass band? The heavens parting to the singing of seraphim?"

"A little appreciation would be nice, that's all. It's the best damned work I've ever done, and my marriage may be over because of it."

"If it's the best work you've ever done, then be proud of it. What does it matter what I think of it? What others think of you is really none of your business, anyway. If I find it acceptable, that should be good enough for you. But if you want to talk appreciation, then I will tell you that I have every intention of expressing it, but my mode of expression takes a rather different form that I imagine you are used to," the client said.

"Yeah? And what form would that be?"

"Not killing your wife, of course."

Leo sighed. "Appreciation enough, then."

Chapter Twenty-Eight

Alex awoke for the fourth time in twenty-four hours; this time tucked into a clean white hospital bed. It took a moment for her to remember how she got there, and when the fog cleared at last, she felt for a sanitary pad and was surprised to discover that there wasn't one. Evidently the bleeding had stopped, or they had found a way to stop it.

She closed her eyes, taking a pain inventory. In total, she felt like seven miles of bad road. She had multiple machines attached to her and a couple of IVs in her left arm, which was taped down to the bed rail so she wouldn't accidentally dislodge the drips of blood and glucose and whatever else they were pumping into her. She quickly looked away from the needles, suddenly feeling queasy.

Had she been operated on? Using her free hand, Alex gingerly felt her torso for a surgical bandage.

Nope.

She opened her eyes and sat up, which took some doing, between her weakness and only having one hand available to assist. Spying the call button, she pressed it, fearful about the time that had elapsed.

Leo must be beside himself!

Before long, a standard issue hospital nurse appeared. She was a nearing fifty, nondescript, matronly type, wearing the requisite red cardigan over her white uniform and the half spectacles on a chain dangling from her neck, just above the stethoscope.

"And how are we this evening?"

Oh, Jesus.

"I really have no idea," Alex replied, ignoring the irritating "we," and moving forward as directed so her pillows could be plumped.

"Open, please," the nurse said, inserting a digital thermometer beneath Alex's tongue. She then put two fingers on the inside of Alex's wrist to check her pulse, timing it with yet a third piece of neck hardware—a watch pendant. After the nurse removed her fingers and the thermometer, she scribbled some notes into the chart she was carrying.

"Well?"

"'Well' what, dear?"

"How's my temperature? How's my pulse? What's wrong with me? And what happened to my earring?" Alex replied, noticing that there was only one on the bedside table.

"I think it would be better if the doctor discussed the health issues with you, er…" quick look at the top of the chart "…Alexandrea. And as far as your earring goes, you were only wearing one when you arrived," the nurse said.

"I must have lost it in Dr. Orbon's office," Alex mused. "And what's your name"

"Florence."

"As in 'Nightingale?'"

"As in 'DiFazio,'" the nurse chuckled.

"Please call me 'Alex.' Is there any chance of speaking with a doctor at this hour, Florence? I'd like to know what happened to me and what I need to do to get well as fast as possible. I've got to be up and running in time for the Hamiltons' paint job."

"Hamilton? Would that be Theodora Hamilton?" the nurse asked.

"Yes. Do you know her?"

"Vaguely. Not to talk to."

"That's the only way to know her, in my opinion," Alex said

Florence smiled thinly. "I'll get you a doctor now. I'm not sure who's around, but I'll see what I can do." Florence said, turning to leave.

"Oh, and what time is it?"

"It's after three in the morning. You've been asleep for

quite a while."

Three in the morning!

"I need to call my husband. I came in with a handbag—do you know where it is? My phone is in it."

Florence nodded and stepped across the room to a locker, which she opened. Inside were Alex's belongings. The nurse took the purse off the hook it was hanging from and brought it over to the bed.

"Thank you so much. I'll make it short and keep my voice down."

"Oh, no need. You're lucky—you have the room to yourself," Florence said, pulling aside the dividing curtain. "Just as you came in, the patient who was in this bed was transferred. Now you call your hubby and I'll get a doctor for you," Florence said, patting Alex's hand. "Be right back. And if you order pizza, I like pepperoni."

Alex laughed and speed dialed the house phone. It rang and rang, with no answer.

"How can he not be there? I took the truck and the only time the answering machine is turned off is when we're home." She glanced at the phone display. "It's three fifteen for chrissake!"

She disconnected.

Could he still be locked in that damned workshop with who knew who? Ice cold fear constricted Alex's heart as she thought, again, that she might be losing her precious Leo to someone else. It was a thought that was beyond coping with. She couldn't imagine her life without Leo and even had trouble remembering it before Leo.

Propped up on pillows, and surrounded by the subtle miasma of hospital smells, she resolved, then and there, that she was not going to just let him go without a fight. Leo was her husband, goddamn it, and nobody was going to take him from her—nobody.

Alex put the phone aside. *I'll try again every half hour until he answers.*

Sleep was out of the question until she heard Leo's voice

again.

***

"Lock up and go to bed, Leo. I'll see you later on—say between ten and eleven? And when you come, please bring me a fruit salad for breakfast. We can discuss delivery then."

"Fine," Leo said, leaving the shop without a backward glance. "Lights on or off?"

"Off, please," said the client.

Leo clicked the switch, closed the door and locked it. He wondered if he'd catch hell from Alex for working so late. He hoped so. He smiled at the idea of something so normal until he saw the empty driveway.

She was still gone?

A wave of anxiety washed over him. Where would she go? Could she really have caught a train for New York after all? He looked everywhere for a note, but couldn't find one.

It's not like her to forget to leave a note. Then he remembered Alex pounding on the workshop door earlier (it seemed like days ago), and was ashamed of himself.

"Why the hell should she leave me a note, with the way I've been treating her lately? Damn it!" Leo punched the wall and missed the stud. He yanked his fist out of the neat hole he'd made in the sheet rock, disregarding the pain.

"Perfect." He was so tired he could hardly stand, but then a thought hit him like a snowball with a rock in it. *My God, what if she left me?* He thundered to the bedroom and tore open the closet door.

Her clothes were still there.

Leo's heart left his throat and went back home. His stomach returned from its trip to his knees. His breathing returned to normal.

The phone rang in the kitchen.

He got there on the third ring and snatched it up, nearly dropping it in the process. "Hello?"

"Leo?"

"Honey, where are you? I've been so worried!"

"I've been trying to get you for the last hour and a half. Where were *you*?"

"Uh, out in the shop finishing up a job," Leo said.

"What job? The job that has you locking me out of the place?"

"Never mind about the job. I'm finished with it. All done. Where are you?"

"I'm in Waterbury Hospital."

"Why? What happened?"

"Well, I know one thing for sure—you haven't been to the bathroom yet, or you'd have seen the bloody washcloths in the sink," Alex said.

"Bloody wash...? Jesus Christ, Alex, tell me what happened!"

Alex filled Leo in, from first blood through her second visit to Dr. Orbon to her ambulance ride to the hospital. "Sorry about the truck," she concluded. "It's still at Orbon's office."

"Forget the truck. I can get it later. What I'm going to do now is call a cab. I'll be there as fast as I can."

"Leo, that's silly. Don't. I'm not in any danger or anything. The doctor was in about a half hour ago and said they can't account for the bleeding episode. They can't find anything wrong with me. They did all those scan thingies, and I'm totally normal—at least as normal as *I* can be, anyhow."

Leo wasn't laughing.

"And anyway, I'm tired again. I think I'll just go back to sleep. They're going to discharge me at noon tomorrow, so if you haven't been to bed yet, go now. I'll see you tomorrow... er, later on today, now," she yawned.

"Sure, Alex. Like I could sleep."

"Well, take a pill and try. We have a few things to straighten out later and you'll need a clear head."

"That doesn't sound good," Leo said, alarmed.

"It doesn't feel good to have to say it, either. Good night,

Leo."

"Good night, honey. I love you."

But Alex had already hung up.

Leo cradled the receiver, and realized that he had no idea what time it was, since for safety reasons, he never wore a watch in the shop. He glanced up at the kitchen clock, and smiled sadly at the timepiece. It was ringed with ceramic vegetables, and on its face, a farmer on a tractor rode the sweep second hand. The hour hand was a trowel and the minute hand was a pitchfork. There was a barn was at twelve, a cow at three, a pig at six and a chicken at nine. They found it at a tag sale the weekend after they'd gone to the Town Hall and tied the knot. Alex loved that clock on sight. Shockingly overpriced at $10.00, Leo bought it for her "as a wedding present," and she was happier than if he'd showered her with precious gems.

"This will remind us every day of our goal to get a farm," she'd burbled as she hung it up over the sink in their New York apartment.

That was Alex for you. It sure didn't take much to make her happy.

And now, dammit, he might have screwed up the whole thing. And she wanted him to get some sleep?

As if.

He picked up the phone and dialed.

***

Sunlight poured into the hospital room, awakening Alex with its intrusion. Groggy from the pill Florence had given her, she peeked out through crusty lids and saw Leo asleep in the chair next to her bed.

Alex smiled as the medication gently pulled her back down into warm, soothing dreamlessness.

159

Chapter Twenty-Nine

Leo awoke to Florence lightly shaking his shoulder.

"Hrmmrph."

"And a smooth talker, too!" Florence exclaimed to a smiling Alex.

"Oh, uh, I'm sorry. Was I snoring?" Leo asked, rubbing his bloodshot eyes.

"Not anymore. Now the hospital staff can remove their earplugs and we can notify Bruce DePrest at Channel Three that what he felt was not a six-point-five on the Richter Scale," Florence replied, laughing.

Leo looked aghast.

"Just joking, Mr. Renfield, just joking. You were fine. Alex, you might as well get up and get dressed. Do you need any help?"

"If she needs help, I can help her," Leo said. "But thank you."

"De nada," Florence said as the door shut behind her.

"She's awfully odd to be so familiar with strangers," Leo commented.

"Oh, she's all right. She's from Woodhaven, too."

"She sends out some pretty weird vibes, I think. You don't feel that?"

"Leo, we need to talk about us."

"I know, and the first thing I want to say is that you have every right to be really, really, super mega pissed off at me. I deserve it. But you've got to trust me that it's almost over," Leo said.

"You told me on the phone that it was done."

"The job is done. I just have to deliver it."

"Deliver it where?"

"I don't know. The client hasn't told me yet and it's supposed to leave tonight."

"I have to say that this whole thing sounds pretty half-baked to me. I assume your client has a name, but you can't tell me what it is. I have no idea what you just built, because you can't discuss it or show it to me. You have to deliver it, but you don't know to where. I don't get it. Why all the secrecy?"

"I can't tell you anything more about it until everything is done."

"But why, Leo?"

"If I do, something unimaginable will happen," Leo replied.

"I doubt that. I have a pretty good imagination," Alex said.

"I know you do, but this beats it. Please trust me, Alex. Just a little longer. I'm begging you."

Alex looked away from Leo's pleading eyes and stared down at the sheet, instead. "It seems to me as if there's someone else in your life now, Leo. Some other woman. And I'll tell you something; I was going to fight for you, but I've decided that if you don't want me anymore, I'll step aside quietly, because all I want, all I've ever wanted, is for you to be happy, and if…"

Leo was giggling. Then the giggle built to a chuckle and the chuckle erupted into outright laughter.

"I don't believe this. Just what the hell is so damned amusing? I'm pouring my heart out here and all you can do is laugh?"

"It's just… heheh… just that… hahaha…" and he was off again. While waiting for Leo to get a grip, Alex idly wished she had gotten this kind of reaction at her first open mike night when she was *trying* for it.

It took a couple more minutes but finally Leo managed to rein in the hilarity. "I'm sorry, hon. You just took me by surprise. Another woman? Jesus," he said, wiping his eyes. "That is about the last thing that would ever happen."

Alex felt the weight around her heart lift.. She even

managed a half smile. "I heard you talking to someone in there, but couldn't hear another voice, so I assumed it was soft-voiced female."

"All I can tell you right now is that the client is male."

"Oh. Good. Did you take a picture of what you built?"

"I wanted to, but he wouldn't let me," Leo said.

"I hope he's at least compensating you well," Alex said, though it was really more of a question.

"Oh, he is, he is."

"Is everything really okay between us, Leo?"

"Of course it is. I'm really sorry about the way things have been the past few days. I was so completely preoccupied with getting this damned project done and getting my life with you back that I couldn't see or deal with anything else, and I almost ruined everything. I didn't mean to hurt you, Alex. Honest."

"Well, don't worry about it anymore. All is forgiven. I feel pretty ashamed for not having more faith in you, honey, and I'm sorry for that. I love you, Leo. I'll always love you. The thought of losing you scared me to death, that's all."

Past tense. Lucky you, Leo thought, checking his own fears as he answered her smile with his own.

Alex was all ready to go when Florence arrived with the wheelchair.

"Is that really necessary?" Alex asked. "I can walk just fine."

"Hospital regulations, dear. Hop in."

Alex did so, and they headed down the hall with Florence at the handles and Leo following behind, carrying the vase of roses he'd brought. Halfway to the elevator, Florence stopped.

"Before you leave, here are some sleeping pills you can take if you need to, and here are some iron pills that you must take to help rebuild your blood. Be sure you take them with food, because they can cause nausea if you don't." Florence pressed the two pill envelopes into Alex's hands, then turned around to face Leo. "I don't know if she told you, but she's been given four units of blood, so she's in good shape now," she told him, "but she was probably anemic long before this incident, so you make sure she takes those iron pills."

Alex made a good natured face at Florence behind her back.

"I saw that," the nurse said mildly.

Alex laughed. "How do you do that? With mirrors?

"No, just a clear understanding of human behavior when one person tells another person what to do," she replied. "Plus, I have eyes in the back of my head." She turned to Leo, her eyes too wide and an open-mouthed insane grin on her face. "Want to see?" she asked him.

"Uh, no, I don't think so," Leo said. "Thanks for everything."

Florence just continued to direct her pop-eyed glassy stare and that ghastly freak show grin at him. After a beat, she moved toward him, unnerving Leo even further. He ducked around her and propelled Alex down the corridor himself, calling "Hold the elevator, please!"

Alex looked back at Florence and waved. Leo was funny—he acted as if Florence might actually have something at the back of her head besides hair.

When they exited the elevator, Leo said, "You wait right here," He helped Alex out of the wheelchair and into a more comfortable lobby couch beside the window. "I'll just call us a cab."

"A cab? You mean you took a cab all the way here? You didn't just cab it to get the truck?"

"Nope. I just wanted to get here as fast as I could—no stops."

Inside of ten minutes, their cab arrived and they were *en route* to Woodhaven to pick up the truck.

"I don't imagine he answers the door during the day. I'd sure like to thank him for taking such good care of you," Leo sighed. "How come you went to him instead of Munson?"

"He's on vacation."

They rode on in silence, just happy to be happy again.

When they reached Woodhaven. Leo leaned forward. "We're going to twenty-three River Road."

"I dunno about no twenty-three. Only thing I know's on River Road is an old cemetery. Dunno why they even call it 'River Road.' It ain't near a river and it's more of a path than a road. Cemetery's laid out crazy, too—lotsa them little gravel roads to get to it— like wheel spokes all around it. Guard shacks at the end of ever' one of 'em. Strangest damn thing. That where you headed?" the cabbie asked.

"Yes."

"H'okay. But I don't drive fares to cemeteries. S'bad luck. S'very bad luck. I'll drop you at the toppa the street, if it's all the same. S'far as I go."

"Oh, have a heart. My wife just got out of the hospital," Leo said.

"If you're goin' t'where you're goin' you musta got some bad news."

Alex laughed. Leo sighed, "All right. Will you wait at the top of the street with my wife while I walk down there and get my truck?"

"Suit y'self—S'your nickel. I got no problem waitin'. It's cemeteries I got the problem with," the cabbie said.

"I know. Bad luck. All right, you can pull over here, then." Leo squeezed Alex's hand and left the cab. Before long, he'd disappeared beyond the scraggly overhanging tree branches and the riot of untrimmed shrubbery that lined the narrow gravel road.

The cabbie, whose first name, Alex noted from his hack license, was Ralph, rolled down his window and lit a cigarette with a lighter shaped like a woman's leg. The flame issued from the bottom of the foot. "If this bothers ya, I c'n put up the partition," Ralph said to the rearview mirror.

"No, it's fine. Interesting lighter you have there."

"S'my name," Ralph said.

"What do you mean?"

"M'last name's 'Lightfoot.' Get it?"

"Ah. Clever."

"Y'got someone in there?" the cabbie asked.

"I'm sorry?"

"Y'got someone in there? In the cemetery?"

"Oh, no. Our doctor has his office back there."

"You're pullin' my leg."

"No."

"Missus, I been drivin' this cab in this parta the state for more years n'I care t'think about, n'I ain't never heard a no doctorin' goin' on at the end of *that* road. S'just the cemetery, s'all. Just the cemetery."

"Well, perhaps he's new in town."

"Wossisname?"

"The doctor? Orbon. Beverly Orbon."

"Gosh, now why's that sound familiar? Dunno about the 'Beverly' part, but I heard that last name before. Just gimme a minute—I'll place it, right enough."

Alex sat quietly while the old cabbie searched his memory, and realized that Leo was taking an awfully long time getting the truck. He should have been back by now.

"Got it!" Ralph cawed, jolting Alex from her reverie. "That was the name a' the guy they caught, oh, must be twenny, thirty years ago now, shootin' up that big zoo in N'York – wossname…?"

"The Bronx Zoo?" Alex hazarded.

"Yep! Thass the one. Said he was big game huntin' or some such. Yeah, I 'member now. They caught him cuttin' the head offa some kinda Affican deer. When the cops surrounded'm he grabbed his gun and wouldn't put it down."

"Really? Did they arrest him?" Alex asked.

"Arrest'm! They shot'm."

"Did they kill him?"

"Y'don't take a bullet in the head n' live too long," replied the cabbie sagely. He paused for a hit of unfiltered nicotine and inhaled so deeply that his socks must have reeked. "And you say he's a doctor? My mem'ry must be goin'. Seems to me he was some kinda tradesman—electrical, buildin', or some such. Gettin' old, I guess. So, you folks live aroun' here or are you just viztin'?"

At last, Leo and 'Babe' came rattling down the driveway.

"Ah, there he is," Alex said. "How much to do we owe you?"

"Comes to fifty-two and a quarter, plus tip, a'course."

Alex fumbled in her purse and produced three twenties and a five. "Here you go. Keep it," she said, opening the door.

"Much obliged. S'was nice talkin' to ya. Here's m'card. Call me anytime you need a ride. F'I'm free, I'll be there to getcha."

Alex accepted the smudgy card. "Thanks, Ralph. Have a good day."

"It'll get better n' better the farther away I get from this boneyard," Ralph said, touching his cap.

The moment Alex shut the door and stepped away, Ralph was off like he'd just torched his house for the insurance money and discovered that there were witnesses.

Leo got out to help Alex up into the passenger seat, waving away the dust.

"What did you do, girl? Tell him you wanted to have his baby?"

Alex snorted. "Any baby fathered by that guy would look just like Marty Feldman, rest his soul," she said. "Not that the world couldn't use another Marty Feldman. Close proximity to vertically challenged subterranean people seems to put Ralph off a mite."

"Yeah, well."

At last, the dust settled to the point that Alex could recognize Leo by more than his voice.

"Honey, what's wrong? You're so white you'd glow in the dark!" Alex cried.

"You'd be white, too, if you saw what I just saw."

Alex chuckled. "What was it? Dr. Orbon capering about

all wrapped up like the Invisible Man?"

"Get in. I'll show you," Leo said, his lips set in a grim line.

"I'm sorry, sweetie. I didn't mean to make fun. I just had a conversation with Ralph that hit a nine point seven on my Weirdometer, that's all."

"Just get in. I'll show you mine, you tell me yours."

Alex couldn't help herself. "That hardly seems fair," she giggled.

Leo just stared straight ahead as the truck bounced back down the gravel path.

"See?"

"What the *hell*? Leo, this doesn't make any sense."

They were facing Dr. Orbon's office building. The door was hanging open, the windows were all boarded up and several were broken. As they watched, a feral cat oozed out the doorway clutching a mouse in its jaws. The shrubbery was all overgrown, adding its synergy to the general air of crumbling neglect.

"Did you go inside?" she asked softly, eyes glued to scene before her.

"Yeah. There's nothing in there, Alex. No waiting room, no trophies, no examining room, no Dr. Orbon, no nothing."

"I don't get it."

"There's an inch of dust and dirt over everything, and the whole place smells like mold—probably from all the rain that's blown through that doorway and the broken windows over the years," Leo said.

"What do you mean 'over the years' Leo? I was here last night and we were both here a couple of weeks ago. Could he have moved out, do you think?"

"Alex, nobody's occupied that place for a very long time. Want to go look?"

"Yeah, I think I do," she replied. When she left the hospital, all she could focus on was getting home to a nice hot bath and a bit of pampering. But that desire was now short circuited by the feeling she used to have in third grade when somebody threw a successful line drive into her stomach playing Dodge Ball.

"Maybe you shouldn't, hon," Leo said. "You just got out of the hospital, after all."

"No, I need to do this. There's something I have to look for," Alex said, opening the heavy door and carefully stepping down.

"Want me to come?"

Alex shook her head. "You've already seen it. I'll just be a minute." She shuffled through the tall weedy grass to the door, where she had to do battle with a barberry bush that had tree aspirations to secure passage into what the artist formerly known as Prince would have described as a hovel formerly known as a doctor's office.

When Alex's eyes adjusted to the half-light, what she saw made her doubt she was in the right place. No desk, no taxidermy, no candles; just a big, empty room smelling vaguely of rotting cabbages. The boards over the windows were bleached, warped, and checked from what could only have been years of exposure to both sunlight and foul weather.

The examining room was in the same state. The forlorn air of the structure nearly made her forget what she'd come in for in the first place.

Alex hastened back to the front room and extracted the MagLite from her purse. She shone it on the floor near the doorway, knelt and brushed away the dust.

Underneath, there was a large, rust-colored stain.

Somehow, Alex found her way back to the truck without passing out or throwing up.

"See what I mean?" Leo asked. He turned in his seat to look at her. "Jeez, honey, are you okay?"

"Not really. I'm about as removed from okay as I can be without painting myself bright green and riding naked down Main Street on a bicycle while declaring myself the Spirit of Spring."

Leo laughed. "That's pretty far from okay, all right."

Alex smiled wanly. "Glad to know I can still kill the

people—present location excepted."

"What I want to know is where did you see Orbon last night?"

"Right here."

"You couldn't have, Alex."

"I did, though. I can prove it."

"How?"

"When I got here, I was so weak I collapsed in the doorway. He must have dragged me inside because, when I woke up, I was in the office and the door was closed. He was standing over me with smelling salts, and I was sitting in a puddle of my own blood."

"So where's the proof, then?"

"There's a blood stain on the floor just inside the door, Leo."

"Show me." Leo opened his door and got out, with Alex close behind him.

Another quick joust with the barberry bush and they were inside once more. "It's right there," Alex said, directing the MagLite beam to the floor.

"Where?"

"Right there. Can't you see…"

The spot was gone.

"Oh no you don't! No, no, no, no!" Alex dropped to her knees, sweeping at the dusty floor with her sleeve.

"Honey, you were probably hallucinating last night. You lost so much blood, I'm amazed you even made it here," Leo said gently, putting his arm around her shoulders.

Alex shrugged off both the arm and the comforting babble. "But I was here, Leo, and so was Dr. Orbon." She felt the hairs rising on the back of her neck. "Jesus. Leo, what's going on?"

"That's what I'd like to know. Like you said, we saw the guy a couple of weeks ago. Why would he have cleared out so fast?"

"Leo, he didn't. He was here! Last night!" Alex shouted.

"I know you think so, sweetie, but how could he have been? Just look at this place," Leo said.

"I don't understand," Alex said in a small voice. "Am I losing my mind, Leo?"

"Of course not. You were just confused, that's all. Blood loss will do that to you." He gently pulled her into the comfort and safety of his arms.

"I think I want to go home now, please," Alex whispered into Leo's shoulder.

They left the building, walking faster this time. Alex was afraid to look back, afraid she might see someone standing in the doorway watching their retreat. Leo whistled softly through his teeth.

"Whistling past a graveyard? Don't tell me you aren't superstitious."

"I'm not. Whistling past a graveyard is done to remain cheerful in trying circumstances, or to keep one's courage up," Leo said.

"Good plan," Alex said. "Does it work?"

"Not hardly," Leo said, opening her door and helping her in again. He kept his eyes on his truck as he walked around and jumped in next to Alex. He executed a quick K-turn, put the pedal down and they were away.

"I really think Ralph has something there about avoiding these places," Alex muttered. "S'bad luck."

Chapter Thirty

On the way home, Alex told Leo about her bizarre conversation with Ralph.

"Must be a different Orbon. Maybe a relative," was Leo's only comment when she finished.

But the memory of the Gazelle trophy mounted over the waiting room door persisted like a bad taste in her mouth.

They rode on, lost in their own thoughts for a while, when suddenly Leo snapped his fingers. "I know why Orbon wasn't there. You just got the wrong gravel driveway. Didn't you tell me that our cabbie said that there were lots of ways to get to the cemetery, and that all the gravel roads have a guard shack at the ends of them? You got the wrong one, Alex, that's all. And with your blood loss, you probably just hallucinated the rest. That's got to be the answer, don't you think?" Leo asked.

Alex mulled it over. "Could be, I guess. Oh, but wait, Beverly gave me a card printed with the hospital ambulance number on it and I remember putting it in my bag. Hold on," Alex said, rummaging through.

"Find it?"

"Nope. No card. But I punched in a seven-digit number. Let me look it up on my cell phone call log." Alex grabbed her phone and called up her most recent calls. "Let's see, it would be the last call dialed before I started calling home every half hour." She scrolled down. When she found it, she just stared at the postage-stamp screen.

"Is it there?" Leo asked.

"Uh huh."

"So what was the number?"

Alex sighed and shook her head. "'911,'" she replied. "You must be right, Leo. I got the wrong place. But we came back there to get the truck. How do you explain that?"

"Today was the first time we've been there in daylight. Everything looks different from night to day. Put that together with plain old coincidence, and we ended up at the wrong place twice. Orbon's office is probably the next path to either side of the one we took," Leo explained, pulling into their driveway.

"Home at last," Alex sighed.

"What do you want for dinner? I'm cooking tonight."

Alex's hand flew to her open mouth. "Oh, no, Leo. I had your favorite dinner half made when I went running out of here yesterday. Oh, shit! It's probably all spoiled. The kitchen must stink."

They only had to take one breath of the prevailing atmosphere on walking into the house to realize both the truth and the understatement of those suppositions.

"Peeeeyew!" Leo exclaimed. "Let's get that chicken out of here." He grabbed a garbage bag from under the sink and Alex took the spit out of the Ronco and tipped the spoiled bird into its plastic shroud. "I'd say. 'May it rest in peace,' but it obviously isn't going without a fight." He knotted the top of the bag. "The corn and the potatoes are probably fine. What if I get out some ground turkey and make us a Shepherd's Pie?"

"That sounds great. I'm going to lie down for a while in front of the tube. If you need me, holler."

"I always need you. Go and rest now. I'll bring you some tea," Leo said. As soon as Alex was out of sight, he hastily put together a salad and some ground beef for the client and hoped he wouldn't be too angry about being forgotten that morning. As it turned out, he had slept right through, so Leo's timing with the food was perfect. Relieved, he relocked the door and returned to the kitchen.

Once Alex was comfortable, with her tea in hand and *All About Eve* on Turner Classic Movies, Leo set about making dinner. He loved to cook and Alex often said that he could make a Shepherd's Pie you'd shoot a small child's puppy for. He had just assembled all the herbs and spices he favored for the dish when the phone rang.

"Hello?"

"He*lo*, Leo. This is Theodora. I'm just calling to check in on our patient. How is she doing?"

"How did you kn...?"

Theodora laughed. "Oh, Florence DiFazio is a dear friend of mine. She kept me apprised."

"She's doing fine, thanks," Leo said, annoyed at her intrusion, but keeping it out of his voice.

"It's too bad she had to go all the way to Waterbury—so far away when one is hemorrhaging that badly. Tsk, tsk."

Leo was about to mention something called "patient confidentiality," but Theodora barreled on ahead. "Please tell Amy..."

"'Alex,'" Leo said.

"Yes, of course. Please tell her to take it easy. I'm sure she'll enjoy spending the time doing light gardening and visiting with the neighbors," Theodora said.

"Thank you for your concern, Theodora, but I have a big problem with that nurse discussing..."

Theodora either didn't hear Leo or chose to ignore him. "At any rate, you just tell Annie that we wish her the best, and remember that Cooper will be picking you both up on the afternoon of May thirteenth. Ta ta, for now."

Leo shook his head and placed the receiver back in its cradle.

"Who was it?" Alex called.

"Your favorite homeowner—Thelma."

"I thought her name was Theodora."

"Yeah, well she thinks your name is Amy or Annie now. Serves her right."

"Thelma it is, then. What'd the old bat want?"

"She wants you to rest and get well soon."

"Well, how did she...?"

"She says she just talked to that DiFazio woman a few minutes ago. Apparently, they're bosom buddies."

"Huh. That's not what Florence told me. Y'know, I keep

173

expecting a white rabbit wearing a vest and carrying a pocket watch to run through here. What else did she say?" Alex asked.

"That you'd probably like to spend time doing light gardening. Did you mention gardening to her?"

"I didn't mention anything personal to that Nazi-loving bitch."

"Oh, and she said something else that struck me odd, but I can't remember it now." Leo said.

"Maybe it will come back to you later. Just don't think about it and often it will pop right into your head," Alex said, yawning. "Right now, I don't think even the marvelous Margo Channing will keep me awake."

"I thought you watched that movie because you're secretly in love with George Sanders."

"That cad? Pul-leeze."

"Just snooze then. I'll wake you up when dinner's ready," Leo said, tucking the quilt in around her. "There. Anything else you want?"

"No, honey. I'm fine."

She closed her eyes and slept soundly and deeply for several hours.

Chapter Thirty-One

Alex awoke with a start to the eight o'clock news; well, more specifically, to the news bimbo's voice, which had the ability, she was sure, to defoliate entire forests in mere seconds. Leo was asleep in his recliner, but awoke the moment she moved to sit up.

"Hi," he said. "Hey, what time is it?"

"Must be eight. Mute that, will you?"

"Sure." Leo pressed the button, mercifully silencing the voice that could open clams at twenty paces. "I didn't have the heart to wake you up when dinner was ready earlier, but I'll heat some up for you now, then I have to go out for a while."

"Where?"

"It has to do with that nonsense in the workshop. I promise I'll tell you when I can." *When it's safe,* he thought.

Alex sighed. "All right. I'll just wait then. Oh, hey—have you fed Harold lately?"

"Yes. Harold's fine."

"Is his water clean?"

"Yep."

"When will you be back?"

"Just as soon as I can, believe me," Leo said, levering himself out of the recliner with a grunt.

Once he had Alex set up with her dinner on a TV tray and the remote and her cell phone within easy reach, he leaned down and kissed the top of her head. "I'll have my phone with me, so if you need me, call."

"Will you answer it if I do?" she asked softly.

It ripped Leo's heart out, remembering how he'd ignored her pounding on the workshop door yesterday. "Of course I will."

"Whatever this is about, please, be safe, be careful. I love you, Leo."

Leo nodded. "Love you, too. Back soon."

Alex was tempted to creep after him and peek out the back door window to see for herself what the big mystery was, but she didn't. Leo had asked her to trust him and she had agreed to, so trust him she would. She switched the channel to catch the new CSI: NY episode in the vain hope that perhaps this week Gary Sinise would actually smile for a change.

***

Leo looked back once before he unlocked the workshop door, taking in the flickering light of the television within and desperately wishing he was back there with Alex.

He sighed and turned the key.

"A bit early, aren't we?" the client asked.

"I just want to get this over with. You said that all it had to be was dark, and it is, so let's get moving," Leo growled.

"Temper, temper, my dear man. Do you have a hand truck?"

"Wouldn't be much of a builder if I didn't have a hand truck, now, would I? What do you want it for?"

"You will need it to make this delivery."

"Why? I can lift it out of the truck when we get there. It's awkward, but not that heavy," Leo said.

"We will not be traveling in your vehicle. We will be walking a half-mile or so. I'm assuming that your masterpiece here, though not heavy to remove from a truck, will nevertheless, be impractical to carry that far."

"All right. Whatever. I think I have some bubble wrap out here somewhere."

"My, my, you think of everything, Leo."

Leo secured his creation in two layers of protective wrapping, and then lifted the bundle off the workbench and onto the foot of the hand truck.

"I'd better bungee it on. The last thing I want to do is start all over again if it falls off and breaks."

"Yes. It would, most assuredly, be in your interest to see that that doesn't happen," said the client, as he stood. "Do you think you put enough weather seal on it?"

"I put six coats, just like you wanted," Leo sighed. "This will stand up to damp weather for years, though I don't understand why on earth you'd want to put this outside. You also never told me the reason for the little copper plate at the back of it."

"All in good time, Leo. For now, let's go."

Leo rolled his package across the lawn. The client led the way.

"Where are we going?"

"Just down that road there," the client said. He stood facing Leo, tall and still, and extended his left arm, pointing down the single lane concrete road that ran along the east side of the house.

Leo shrugged. "It's your show."

Even nature had turned away from the pair, as if expressing silent disapproval of their nighttime venture by refusing to light their way. Though the moon was in its last quarter, heavy clouds obscured its meager illumination.

"I can't see a damned thing out here. I don't know why you wouldn't let me bring a flashlight," Leo grumbled.

"I can see just fine, and that is all that matters. If there are obstacles in your way, I'll alert you, rest assured. But though we take this walk together, you'll have to find your own way back, I'm afraid."

"Suits me."

"I thought that it might."

For the next few minutes, they walked on in silence; then Leo asked, "So what is this for, anyway?"

"Beg pardon?"

"This project. Why did I build it? What is it for, exactly?"

"That information is given on a need to know basis."

"And?"

"And you don't need to know."

"I think I have a right to know."

The client stopped. Leo stopped. Without turning, the client said, "Right? The only 'right' you have is to remain silent. The question is, do you have the ability?" The client's tone threatened like a switchblade to the ribs.

"Sorry," Leo mumbled.

They resumed their pace in silence for several minutes. It seemed to Leo that they had walked a good deal farther than the half-mile that was originally mentioned, and was about to say so when they reached a crossroads and the client spoke.

"Ah, right here will be fine, Leo, just fine."

"Do you want me to unwrap it?"

"No. I would prefer that it remain protected until it reaches its final destination."

Leo shrugged and bent to remove the bungee cords holding the bundle to the hand truck. As he did, he heard a car approaching from the distance.

"And here comes the buyer now," the client said.

Great! Maybe I'll be able to see what I'm doing, he thought, as the engine noise drew closer.

As luck would have it, the car coasted slowly to a stop without the benefit of headlights, tail lights, or parking lights. The client moved to the back of the vehicle and opened the door. No ceiling light, either. He spoke to a passenger, though Leo couldn't make out what he said, after which he returned to Leo and took the bubble-wrapped package he held.

"Are we done?" Leo asked. "Can I go home now? You won't be bothering me again?"

"Dear me, one might think you didn't enjoy our adventure together. To answer your questions, yes, this ends our association. But one last point, if I may. I would strongly prefer that you didn't discuss this with your wife."

"Discuss what?"

"Our association… in detail. And tonight, as well."

"Why? She already knows I was making something for

somebody. What's the difference now? Besides, I promised her I'd explain everything when this was all over."

"In that case, your wife will have to learn to deal with disappointment. Our transaction shall remain between us and is not to be discussed with your wife or anyone else, for that matter. If you do, there will be consequences that you will be powerless to prevent. Do I make myself clear?"

"Perfectly."

"Good. How's the arm, by the way?" the client asked, handing Leo's work to an unseen passenger. He then followed the bubble wrapped bundle into the cavernous back seat and pulled the door shut before Leo could respond. Headlights still off, the car pulled away and slowly drove off down the road.

When the engine noise faded away completely, Leo turned and trudged home, empty hand truck rattling in front of him. He was worried. After he'd told… no, promised… Alex he'd be able to come clean, now he couldn't. What was he going to say to her?

Well, whatever. He'd straighten it out somehow. He was just glad that the job was done and the client was gone. And he was going to do everything he could to keep it that way. He looked up at the distant house, saw the warm, welcoming light spilling from the kitchen windows, and he stepped up his pace.

So absorbed was Leo in his thoughts that when he reached their back yard, he walked, unseeing, right past Alex's raised garden beds and clattered across the porch, intent on stowing the hand truck and getting back inside. He had no idea what time it was, and was half hoping Alex would already be asleep for the night. He hated the thought of having to go back on his word, but how could he not? The client meant what he said—of that Leo had no doubt. All he had to do was touch his bandages for a quick reminder.

"Leo?" Alex softly called from the back door.

"I'll be right in."

"That's okay, I'm right here," Alex said, suddenly next to him. It was the first time she'd been in the workshop in days and she cast her eyes about for clues as to what Leo had been working on. "Are you going to take the boards off the windows now?"

"First thing tomorrow. What time is it, anyway?"

"About eleven."

"That's funny. It didn't feel like I was gone that long."

"Well, come on in. I fixed us some sandwiches."

"Alex, you should be resting. As a matter of fact, you ought to be asleep in bed by now."

"Asleep? Are you kidding? I want to hear all about these last few days. Now that the job is over, you can tell me, right?"

"I can tell you some."

Alex's brow furrowed audibly. "How much?"

Leo sighed. "Not much."

"Leo! You promised."

"I know I did—but I promised before I should have, in this case."

"What do you mean?" A pout was rapidly setting in.

"Let's go in the house and sit down. I could use a sandwich," Leo said.

Alex nodded, turned and walked back into the house without another word. It was amazing how childlike she could be about some things. Whenever she showed her disappointment this way (which, truthfully, was not often), Leo caught a glimpse of the little girl she once was, and he adored her even more.

When he walked into the kitchen, Alex was sitting at the counter, staring down at the empty plate in front of her. Leo sat down across from her. "What kind of sandwiches?"

"Tuna or salami," Alex replied without looking up.

"Honey, please. The client warned me tonight about giving you or anyone else a lot of details about the job. I don't know why it's so hush-hush, but it is. If I don't abide by our agreement, he's threatened to hurt you."

"Me? Why me?"

"Because he knows that I'll agree to anything that will keep you safe."

"Good God, Leo, what did you get yourself into? Is he Mafia or something?"

"I don't know and I don't care. All I do know is that he's gone and won't be back as long as I keep quiet."

Alex sat back, eyes brimming. "And here I was getting all upset with you and thinking that... Oh, Leo, honey, I'm sorry."

"I'm the one who's sorry. You have nothing to be sorry about, Alex."

Yes I do. I doubted you. That's twice now.

Leo pulled his chair over to Alex and put his arm around her. She let her head drop onto his shoulder. It was good to be together, to have him back with her again.

"What can you tell me?" she asked.

"Not much more than you already know."

"Does this client have a name?" she asked.

"I suppose he does, but he chose not to share it with me."

"Why would you take a job from somebody like that? How did he convince you?" Alex asked.

"I guess I'll have to show you," he said, leaning back and unbuttoning his shirt. He stood and removed it.

And Alex saw the bandages.

The most recent one was around his left arm, but there was one on his right shoulder, one across his chest, and one down his back. All were stained with dried blood.

"He did this to you?"

Leo nodded. "He'd have done much worse if I'd continued to refuse. Now do you see why I had to leave you out of it?"

Alex saw, all right.

Alex saw red. "Where is this motherfucker? I'm going to get a baseball bat and..."

"I don't think so. I think you're just going to forget about it. These cuts will heal. You go after him and you won't be coming back, I guarantee it." Leo picked up his shirt to put it back on.

"No, don't put it on. Let's get those bandages off and see exactly how bad things are."

"Tomorrow. Let's have a sandwich now and then go to bed. I have a lot of lost time to make up for," Leo said, wiggling his eyebrows.

"In that condition? I think rest is in order for you, too, dear heart—and maybe a trip to the doctor."

"Just not Dr. Orbon."

"Wherever he may be. Munson's on vacation, though. Probably Pike fishing on Lake Champlain at that place in North Hero he told us about," Alex said.

"Then I'll wait for him to get back."

They addressed themselves to their sandwiches, then rinsed and stacked the dirty dishes and locked up.

Leo was already in bed by the time Alex came in after washing up. She doused the light and, on the way to bed, glanced out the bedroom window. What she saw stopped her in her tracks.

"What are you looking at, Alex?"

"You know that abandoned old wreck of a house next door?"

"Uh huh."

"There's a light on over there.

"What, you mean like a flashlight?"

"No, like a main overhead light. The whole first floor is all lit up. It looks like somebody's moving in."

"At this hour? Hard to believe somebody actually bought that shack," Leo mused.

"Guess so," Alex said. *By the pricking of my thumbs something wicked this way comes.* She should have been thrilled to have a neighbor, but instead, her mind quoted *MacBeth* at her and she felt like someone had just put flowers on her grave. Shivering without knowing why, she slid into bed and spooned up behind Leo.

"Hey, you'll have somebody to have coffee with,' Leo said, half asleep.

"I'm perfectly happy having coffee with you, cutes," Alex muttered into Leo's warm back.

"I mean for when I'm not here."

"You'll always be here, Leo, my love."

Leo was soon snoring lightly, but Alex didn't close her eyes. For a reason she couldn't explain, she now found the idea of anyone living in that house deeply disturbing. And who moves into a house at midnight, anyway?

At last, she did sleep, though, dreaming of Ray Bradbury's October People and a carousel that spun too fast for her to get off as the calliope played the Funeral March and the dark man in the top hat laughed and laughed and laughed.

Chapter Thirty-Two

Alex bounded out of bed at seven-thirty more energized than she'd been in a while. She knew she was supposed to be resting, but it just wasn't in her nature. Alex was a doer, not a malingerer, and there was plenty she wanted to do today.

Leo was already up so she went to the kitchen to put together some breakfast. So busy was she planning her day that she turned the corner and piled right into Leo's back.

"Ooof!" Alex staggered back. "And you didn't budge. I guess my football career is down the toilet, huh?"

Leo didn't move or respond.

"Say, why is it so dark in here? Storm on the way?" Alex asked.

"I wondered that, too," Leo replied softly, "until I looked out the window."

"Out the win…?" Alex slipped by him and went to the normally bright and sunny kitchen window… the view from which was obscured by a verdant screen of tall stalks and leaves.

Alex turned, perplexed. "They're sunflowers, Leo. But that's not possible. I only planted them two days ago."

"You didn't, by any chance, trade a cow for those seeds you planted, did you?" Leo asked, unsmiling.

Alex didn't hear him—she was already halfway to the back door. Leo tore his eyes from the sudden landscape and joined her in the back yard.

He hadn't wanted to go out there alone.

"Thank Christ you see it, too," Leo said, clearly relived.

Alex was turning in slow circles, taking in the wonder of all her raised beds. "Leo, it's all fully grown… in two days! Are we asleep? This can't be happening. Everything tore right through that heavy plastic sheeting. Look at these tomatoes.

They're absolutely enormous. They must weigh at least two pounds each. And the peas have climbed right up and into the maple tree—they're... they're everywhere."

"Take a look at the broccoli and cabbage." Leo said.

She cast her eyes upon prize-winning cabbage heads, larger than she had ever seen. "These have to be at least two feet in diameter. I had no idea they could even grow this big."

"This has to be a practical joke of some kind, Alex," Leo said, his pragmatism reasserting itself. "Someone must have come in here during the night and planted all these mature vegetables."

Alex bent down and tugged on the nearest cabbage head. It came out of the ground with next to no resistance. "Well, since I'm pretty sure the bags of compost we bought did not say. 'Food of the Gods' anywhere on the label, I think you're right, Leo—it's somebody's idea of a joke. If this cabbage had actually grown here, it would have well-established roots and would have been a whole lot harder to pull up. But who would do this? And more to the point, why?"

"Well, don't look at me to explain it. I'm as mystified as you are. How are you feeling, by the way?"

"Pretty good."

"Good, because I'd say you've got a week of canning and freezing ahead of you. At least you can sit down while you do it, and I'll help you. Harvest time in April. Jesus Christ on a tricycle."

"I'll get the wheelbarrow," Alex said.

"Can you manage all right?" Leo called. "Are you sure you're really up for this?"

"Sure, sweetie. I'm good."

"Good enough to be left alone awhile?"

"Uh huh. Why?"

"I have to go to Southfield to pick up a new saw blade."

"Why don't you get it at the Home Depot here in town?"

"I don't like that one."

Alex walked back to Leo. "Really? How come?"

"It sort of creeps me out, I guess. There's never anybody in there but this one guy."

"In Home Depot? Oh, come on—Home Depot is always packed."

"Not this one. And it doesn't matter what day of the week or what time of day I stop. It's just this one guy in the whole place—not even any customers. It's like a tomb in there."

"That is creepy."

"That's why I go to Southfield."

Alex smiled. "Fair enough. See you when you get back. Oh, hey! Don't you want any breakfast?"

"I had a bagel and coffee before it got light enough to see outside. After that, my appetite decided that if I was going to be watching a horror movie out my kitchen window, it was popcorn or nothing, and we don't have any."

"Make you something when you get back then, maybe?"

"Possibly. You pace yourself. Don't overdo," Leo replied. "And if a warty old lady comes by and gives you an apple, don't eat it, okay?"

"Gotcha," Alex said, blowing him a kiss. "Be safe, be careful." She went to the garage and, after a little wrestling and a lot of swearing, managed to pull the wheelbarrow down from the system of pegs Leo had installed to keep it up off the floor and out of the way. By the time she wheeled it out, Leo was gone and the silence that descended was so complete it put her instantly on edge, causing her to jump at shadows. There weren't even any "town" sounds—no doors slamming, cars starting or driving by, no kids yelling and screaming. The squeaky, clattering of the wheelbarrow was like a shriek in a morgue, so Alex left it beneath the pea-draped maple tree rather than push it any farther.

"Let's see. Pick the heaviest stuff first, I guess, while I still have some energy." She started with the cabbages. Normally (if any normal thoughts could possibly be processed today), she'd have left the cabbages in the ground until the first snowfall, covering them with plastic when frost threatened. Of course, that's if they had matured when they were supposed to—in

October. If she left them until then in their present state of maturity, they'd soon go to seed and become completely inedible.

"Right. Sixteen heads of cabbage. Cabbage soup, sauerkraut, and coleslaw, plus some for the root cellar." Alex had built a root cellar in the basement out of wooden bins containing dirt and sawdust. It was a good way to store root vegetables and cabbage that the refrigerator was too small to accommodate.

The cabbage harvest alone filled the wheelbarrow, so Alex moved it to the back door, rescued a cardboard box of a manageable size, and then trudged back and forth from back door to basement until the gigantic cabbages were all snug in their sawdust beds.

Next, broccoli, then cauliflower.

The corn crop alone filled the wheelbarrow ten times.

"I'm home!"

"Back here, hon."

"Wow. Still at it, huh?"

Alex wiped her face with the blue rag hanging from her back pocket. "Leo, we have six hundred forty ears of corn."

"Oh, cut it out."

"We do."

"How many corn seeds did you plant?"

"One bed, sixty-four seeds. We got ten ears of corn from each stalk, Leo."

"No way. If you get six or seven ears per stalk you're lucky, and that's from hybrids. You planted open pollinated, didn't you?"

"Sure did."

"Well, open pollinated gives a smaller yield, not a larger one, isn't that right?"

"Yeah, Leo. That's a hundred percent right. But that's not what happened. Go downstairs and check, if you don't believe me. We're going to have to knock together some more bins— I'm running out of storage space fast. I'm glad you're back. It was so quiet around here it was like being the last living cell in a dead body."

"You look all in, honey. How about a break?"

"I could use one, I think. Want some lunch?"

"Yes, but you're not making it. Howze about the diner in Southfield?"

"Oh, I like that place. I think this time I'll have a big breakfast—matzoh brie, potato latkes with sour cream, grits with butter, and a side of bacon and sausage."

"And what happens after you eat all that? Your heart dials 911?" Leo asked with a chuckle. One thing about Alex that continued to baffle him is how she managed to stay so thin. She packed food away like a trucker. "Why not just order cardiac arrest dipped in a stroke with a side of arteriosclerosis?"

She ignored him. "OR, meatloaf, gravy, peas and mashed potatoes. OR a turkey dinner with all the trimmings."

"Okay, okay, let's go then."

"Just let me grab a quick shower—I'm filthy with filth."

"Just make it fast, because I'm hungry with hunger," Leo called after her.

Fifteen minutes later, Alex was dressed and ready to roll. She put the last of the corn in the wheelbarrow into the box on the porch and shoved it into a shady area. "I guess that'll last 'til we get back." She turned, took Leo's hand, and walked to the truck, swinging his arm. "Want to skip?" she asked.

Leo guffawed at that one. "I don't think I even know how to skip."

"Want me to teach you?"

"I don't think so. A skipping Leo Renfield is a Leo Renfield who is not to be trusted. A skipping Leo Renfield is a Leo Renfield to be regarded with suspicion and dread," Leo replied.

"I take it that's a 'no'?"

"You take it correctly."

"Just for that, you get to pay for lunch."

"A bargain at twice the price."

"You haven't seen how much I'm going to eat yet," Alex laughed.

The farther away they got from their house and garden, the more they relaxed.

I guess it could have been worse," Leo said. "They could have been Triffids."

"No, no—that would have been better. Then they could have walked down to the basement and stored themselves. It would have saved me a ton of time."

Leo snorted. "The human brain has amazing adaptive abilities, doesn't it?"

Alex's smile faded. "What do you mean?"

"I mean we've got a fucking science fiction movie going on in our back yard, thanks to some deranged practical joker and what do we do? We pick what's there and go out for lunch." Leo's voice had an edge of distant hysteria that Alex didn't like; it scared her.

She stared out the window, sighing. "Well, what do you suggest, Leo? Alert the media? Move?"

Leo was silent. Alex looked over at him. He reminded her of a horse that just spotted a rattlesnake.

"Move? You want to move, is that what you're saying?" Alex asked.

Leo sat back in his seat. "Yes. I mean, no. It's a nice thought, but we signed a lease, plus we're contractually obligated to the Hamiltons, no matter which episode of the *X-Files* we currently find ourselves starring in."

"Tell you what, Leo. After we finish that job and collect our loot, if you still want to move, then I say, 'let's go.' We can get out of the lease somehow. Deal?"

"Deal," he said, genuinely smiling for the first time that day.

"But what are you so worried about? Somebody's playing games, that's all—you said so yourself, and you must be right. What happened is impossible otherwise."

"What's still bothering me is the way you planted it in that grid pattern, and how the correct number of plants are in each square. They got the plant variety in each square right because you labeled them, but somebody playing a joke would have just put one plant in each square, wouldn't they, and not the number that you planted?" Leo asked.

Alex mulled that over for a moment, then said, "Not necessarily. That grid pattern is very specific to one style of gardening, and I'm sure that there's more than one copy of *Square Foot Gardening* floating around—it's a bestseller. If I saw a grid pattern like this in any other garden, I would know exactly how the garden was planted, too. There's a chart at the back of the book that tells you how many seeds or transplants of each vegetable you can plant in each square foot. Our joker must have a copy of it, that's all."

Leo pulled into a parking space, stopped the truck, and turned to Alex. "But you know what the really big question is, don't you?"

"Uh, no."

"The really big question is, why are all the diners in the tri-state area owned and operated by Greeks?"

"It will have to be a question for the ages, I'm afraid. I'm too hungry to care," Alex said, opening her door and hopping out.

"Some people I could name have no intellectual curiosity," Leo called.

Once they were snug in their booth, a young man brought them water, set-ups, and menus.

Alex winked at Leo, and then turned her attention to the waiter. "Tell me something, if you can. Why do so many Greek people open diners?"

The waiter smiled at Alex, his eyes twinkling. "Because God is with us. I'll give you a few minutes," he said, and walked away.

As soon as he was out of earshot, Alex stage-whispered, "Leo, that explains everything!"

"How's that?"

"God is *with* them. He's an employee–probably the short

190

order cook. And since He can be everywhere at once, that's why all diner food tastes exactly the same, no matter where you are."

Leo grinned and shook his head. "You're going to Hell for sure for that one."

"Think Hell scares me after our back yard?"

That particular wisecrack had the same effect as a fife and drum corps marching across the stage during a Mozart symphony.

"Sorry," Alex muttered. "Sometimes my mouth diarrhea and my brain constipation conspire against me."

"Are you ready to order?" the waiter asked, reappearing.

"I guess so. Are you ready Alex? I'll have a turkey club with fries and a vanilla malt."

"I'd like the turkey dinner, please. With iced tea," Alex said with a smile.

After the waiter left to put their order in, Leo stepped outside to buy a paper from one of those bright yellow dispensers that trust the buyer to be honest enough to take just one copy. It always amused Alex to think that anyone would want extra copies of such bad news. That was probably why the system worked.

They read the paper quietly until their meals arrived, then they dawdled over their lunches, postponing the return home as long as they could.

After refilling their after lunch coffee mugs for the fifth time, the waiter asked, "Where are you folks from?"

"Not far. We live over in Woodhaven," Leo replied.

"Really? Woodhaven?"

"Yes. Why?" Alex asked.

"Isn't it kind of lonely over there?"

Alex and Leo glanced at each other. "What do you mean…" Alex peered at his name tag "…George?"

George said, "Well, you must know that a few years ago, the whole town b…"

"Well, look who's here!" Theodora effused, practically

191

bowling over the poor waiter. "It's Leo and Anita. How marvelous to see you both. And how are you feeling, my dear?" Theodora asked.

"I'm feeling much better, thanks, Theodora."

"Wonderful. Just don't overtax yourself. It doesn't pay to take chances with your health. I expect you'll be fit and able to work come May. Cooper will be picking you up at one forty-five on the afternoon of May thirteenth, which is a Tuesday. That will give you ten hours to settle in a bit before beginning your work. Did I mention that previously? No? Well, *so* glad I caught you now. Yes—so you'll be working midnight to six, so your work week will *seem* like it's Sunday through Thursday, but really it's Monday through Friday. Weekends off, of course."

"Would you like to sit down, Theodora?"

"Ah, Leo, ever the gentleman. But no, I must fly. Ta ta!" With that, Hurricane Theodora swept from the diner, stopping briefly at the takeout counter to pick up her order.

"Well, that was semi-interesting," Leo commented as the dust settled.

"How it can take only fifteen minutes to get to her house?" Alex demanded.

"What are you talking about? You know very well it takes a lot longer than that."

"If Black is picking us up at one forty-five, and Theodora said we'd have ten hours to settle in before we start work at midnight, then that leaves 15 minutes travel time."

"Oh. Right. And to answer your question, I have no idea. Nothing makes much sense anymore. We were gone from our house for over twenty-four hours the last time we were there. Maybe she meant one forty-five Monday," Leo said.

"That's not what she said, though."

"Yeah, I know it wasn't."

Alex gazed down at the table. "She scares me, Leo, and I don't know why. She's like the closet monster or the thing under the bed that's all tentacles and teeth. Or footsteps down the hall at midnight when you know you're the only one home.

Or a crazy-eyed grinning face, lit by lightning, that you see for a split second pressed up against your window pane. Christ! I keep expecting Rod Serling to drop in and tell me it's all submitted for my approval."

"Wow. I don't get that feeling from her at all."

"You don't? How do you feel about her, then?"

"With me, she's more like something watching you from underneath a rock," Leo said after mulling it over.

"Cruella DeVil," Alex said, grinning.

"Why does that name sound familiar?"

"*101 Dalmatians.* It was a line from the song Roger wrote about Cruella DeVil—the horrid woman who wanted the puppies' skins for a coat, remember?"

"That's right. I loved that movie when I was a kid."

Alex sang softly, "*Cruella DeVil, Cruella DeVil. If she doesn't scare you, no evil thing will. She's like a spider waiting for a kill. Cruella, Cruella DeVil.* I can't remember the rest of the lyrics right now, but I know that what you said is one of the lines from that song."

"When was the last time you saw that movie?" Leo asked.

"When I was nine, I think."

"Just that once?"

Alex nodded.

"My dear, you have the most phenomenal memory of anyone I have ever met."

She shrugged. "I liked the song, that's all."

"I'd be willing to bet you remember far more about the movie than just a snippet of a song," Leo said.

"I doubt it."

"What was Roger's wife's name?"

"'Anita,' I think."

"The bad guys?"

"'The Badduns?'"

"Roger's dog's name?"

"'Pongo.'"

"Anita's dog?"

"'Perdita.'"

"No, you don't remember anything else about that movie."

"I'm a fount of worthless information, what can I tell you?" Alex said, laughing. "And you remember more than you think, too, if you could even come up with those questions."

"What happened to George? He was just about to tell us something about Woodhaven when Theodora barged in. Where the heck is he?" Leo muttered, craning his neck to survey the restaurant. "Let's just ask for our check; they'll find him."

Alex held up a slip of paper. "Already got it. He dropped it on the table just after Theodora arrived. I think he got tired of refills."

Leo checked his watch. "Well, we'd better be headed back, anyway."

"Oooh, yes! I have to feed Harold before it gets dark."

"No you don't," Leo said. "Harold's gone."

"Aw, really?" Alex asked, secretly relieved. "How'd he get out of the pen?"

"Don't know," Leo said, studying the table, "but he's gone."

"I guess I'll take the pen apart when we get back, then," Alex sighed.

Leo smiled. "You really like turtles, don't you?"

"Usually, yes, very much. But to be honest, Leo, Harold was sort of on the strange side."

Tell me about it.

"Maybe I'll fill the pen with dirt and plant Cannas. The flowers are gorgeous," Alex said.

"You sure you want to plant anything more back there?" Leo asked.

"Whoever replaced all the vegetables didn't touch the

flowers."

"What about the sunflowers?"

"I don't count those, because they produce edible seeds."

"Then let's go get some Cannas," Leo said, standing.

They paid their check at the register and after inquiring about the whereabouts of their waiter, they were told that his shift had ended and he'd gone home for the day.

Once they arrived home, they unloaded the plants and topsoil onto the porch. And since they were, to put it mildly, overstocked with corn, and Alex had a soft spot for the two squirrels that lived in their maple tree, they'd also bought a squirrel feeder that would hold a single ear of corn. They nailed it up, added the corn, and adjourned to the porch to watch. Leo pulled up a couple of chairs and Alex went inside to pour them some wine.

Before long, there was rustling in the dry leaves they'd temporarily raked up against the workshop until they could build a compost bin. Two gray squirrels burst from the pile as if they'd been launched from a slingshot and scurried up the lone tree, immediately homing in on the huge ear of corn.

Alex and Leo had to laugh. The two rodents circled the ear looking astonished.

"'Acres and acres, and it's all ours,'" Leo captioned, in a whisper.

Alex grinned, waiting for them to pounce and devour the fresh corn, and her smile faded when they didn't. They just continued to look it over and smell it. "What are they waiting for?" she whispered to Leo.

Finally giving way to temptation, the larger, braver squirrel ventured a nibble.

Alex and Leo had never seen a squirrel make a face before; and not only did he make a face, but he spit out the corn in his mouth, and made pushing gestures along his muzzle, as if he wanted to make positively sure that it was all gone.

"He acts just like a restaurant critic," Leo said. "Maybe they don't like corn when it's raw."

"Oh, they sure do. My Grampa had to chase them out of

the corn field all the time. Finally he just planted extra corn so he wouldn't miss the ears that the squirrels ate," Alex said.

"Then how do you explain that?" Leo asked. The large squirrel was now chewing up and spitting out tree bark in what appeared to be an attempt to get the taste out of his mouth. The smaller squirrel, after witnessing the large squirrel's review, left the tree for parts unknown—probably to pursue a meal that was a little closer to three star.

"I can't. There was nothing wrong with that ear of corn. I checked it over before I put it up. It was perfect."

Leo stood up and put his chair back where it belonged. "Fussy squirrels, then, I guess."

Alex shrugged, walked to the tree, and removed the corn from the feeder. The squirrel had moved to a nearby branch at her approach and stuck around long enough to chitter at her and give her a nasty look before bounding down and away.

"Maybe the people who were here before us fed them stuff they liked better," Alex mused, tossing the ear in the garbage can.

"Hey, be sure you get that lid on tight," Leo called on his way into the house.

Considering the way the squirrels had reacted, Alex thought she could probably leave the lid on the ground with impunity.

Before she followed Leo into the house, Alex looked to her right at the house next door to see if anyone was around. It still looked just as lonely, just as deserted, as it had for months. Maybe someone was doing interior demolition prior to razing the infrastructure.

She turned away without noticing the tattered curtains in the attic window falling back into place.

"I wonder if the jokers who planted all that stuff out there sprayed it with something. Maybe that's why the squirrels reacted the way they did," Leo said when Alex walked in.

"Even if they did, I wash all fresh fruit and vegetables thoroughly, no matter where they come from. Now how about giving me a hand pulling in the rest of the harvest before it gets dark? You can do the peas."

"Just call me John, Deere."

They spent the balance of the day and into the evening picking eggplant, tomatoes, cucumbers, string beans, digging potatoes, pulling radishes, and detangling the pea vine snood from the maple tree.

At nine o'clock, they turned off the outdoor floodlights and Leo moved their last wheelbarrow load to the basement. He slowly trudged up the creaky staircase and pushed open the door to the kitchen. "All the potatoes are finally in your root cellar bins. Next are the carrots, beets, onions, and turnips that I piled up on the counter down there. That's tomorrow's magic."

"Tomorrow's magic?"

"Yeah, it's what I'm going to need to fit them in somewhere. I'll have to make a few more bins. And now I understand how well that technique of sectioning off the garden beds works. It's a great idea."

"Told you."

"And I must add that you're pretty darned clever. I had no idea it was possible to have a root cellar that wasn't actually dug into the ground."

"Well, the basement is underground. But I know what you mean. I've seen old photos of what dug in root cellars look like. This bin style root cellar is much easier, don't you think?"

"Depends on who gets stuck going up and down the stairs," Leo said.

"My Gramma had one just like it in her basement. I learned how to make them from her."

"I'd be willing to bet that hers was never as full as yours is."

"I wonder who we should thank. I know it must have been a joke, but it's also a truckload of free vegetables. Oh, and you don't have to worry about the sunflower seed heads. I'm just going to cut them off and lay them on the ground for the birds to pick at. Grampa used to have to tie paper bags around the seed heads so the birds wouldn't pick them all out before they had a chance to ripen. Of course, after they did mature, he'd give them to the birds, anyway; he just wanted the seeds to be the best they could be for his friends. The birds here will go nuts over them—just wait and see," Alex said.

"Let's hope they like them better than the squirrels liked the corn," Leo said.

"You know, it could be that those two squirrels got into something they shouldn't have and are just sick. That could account for their weird behavior."

Leo smiled. "Probably so."

"Good. Glad we got that resolved. Want dinner?"

"No, not really. I'm still full from lunch. I'll just pick. But right now, I'm going to take a hot shower and then stare at the tube for a while. Interested?" Leo asked.

Alex looked around the kitchen. "I'd love to have a bath, but what I really need to do is start canning and freezing while all this stuff is at its peak. If I don't deal with it right away, it won't be as good."

"We do have refrigeration in this day and age, honey."

"You have seen all these vegetables, haven't you?" Every flat surface in the kitchen was piled high.

"Silly me, even with all the evidence right in front of my eyes, I still don't see the harvest as being from anything but a small backyard garden."

"My father had a pithy saying about such dichotomies," Alex said.

"Do I want to know this?"

"He said, 'If you don't understand the situation by now, you are refusing to lear.'"

"You bet I am," Leo said.

Alex laughed and rolled up her sleeves. "I guess Dad didn't see the value of coping mechanisms."

"Do you need help?"

"With this, or psychologically?"

Leo shook his head. "With this, bozette."

"No honey. You go and relax. I'll be fine."

He came over and held her tenderly. Into the top of her head, he said, "Please try to remember that you have just gotten out of the hospital."

"Don't worry, I'll sit while I work."

"Good. Let me know if you want some help," he said, kissing her hair.

Alex went out to the garage and brought in the seven cases of Mason jars that Leo had deemed excessive at the time and had teased her about buying. Now she fervently hoped that eighty-four jars would be enough.

Next, how to deal with all this produce in the most efficient way? After some thought, Alex decided to puree and freeze the tomatoes, sauté and freeze the eggplant, can the string beans, pickle the cucumbers, and blanch and freeze the peas.

She immersed herself in her work, unconscious of the passing hours, and didn't look up until Leo came in to check on her.

"How's it going, babe?" Leo asked, poking his head around the corner.

Alex opened the pantry door, then stood aside. There were jars everywhere.

"Wow. I guess we won't starve this winter, will we, Maw?"

"Ayuh, Paw. Looks like we won't have to eat the young'uns after all."

"How much more do you have to do? It's midnight, y'know."

"Already? Well, you go on to bed. I'll be there as soon as I can."

"Alex, I think you need to come to bed. You're not a hundred percent yet."

"I know, Leo, but I can't just leave all this. Just let me finish up what's here, and then I'll bag it for the night, I promise."

"Is there anything I can do that would make it go faster?"

"No, honey. At this point, it's really just a one-person job, but thanks for asking."

"Can't you just put what's left into the refrigerator until tomorrow?"

Alex smiled. "It won't fit, sweetie. It has to go in the pantry or the freezer. I'm going to freeze the rest of the beans. The eggplant I'm going to slice up and cook down in this big pot here. And the tomatoes are getting pureed and frozen. The hard work's already done. I'll save the corn and the other stuff in the basement for tomorrow, though."

"What are you going to do with all that corn?" Leo asked.

"Make relish out of some, freeze some, and dry most of it."

"Dried corn?"

"Sure. When you reconstitute it, it tastes like you just picked it."

"Amazing. You are going to leave some for corn on the cob, aren't you? I love corn on the cob."

"Leo, with six hundred forty ears downstairs, I think you can probably eat corn until you start laying eggs. There's plenty for everything, believe me."

"Okay, babe. I'm going to bed. Please don't stay up too late."

"'Night, hon."

It was a matter of twenty minutes to get the rest of the beans prepared, blanched, and into freezer bags. Alex stacked them in the garage freezer proudly. Preserving homegrown food flooded her with warm, happy memories of her grandparents and their farm. "I don't have a cow, Gramma, so if you're right, and there is a God, this is how I feel close Him," she murmured, glancing upward, her eyes once again full. She still felt the loss of the old folks acutely and she found it comforting to think that they were watching over her from their well-deserved place in the Heaven that they had believed in all their lives.

Back in the kitchen, she peeled and sliced the eggplant—all

fifty of them—from her ten plants. How unheard of. One or two per plant was usual. Alex forced herself not to dwell on the gargantuan abnormalities of the garden, creepy joke or not, and donned mental blinders, focusing only on the repetitive peeling, cutting, and cooking.

At two forty-five, Alex tucked the last bag of tomato puree away in the garage freezer. Everything else, except the corn, was processed and put away, and the kitchen was spotless. Though she should have been exhausted, she found that she was energized instead. She supposed it was some ancient ancestral hunter/gatherer memory that made her feel that way—knowing that much of the food they'd need for the winter was safely stored. She knew exactly how the industrious Ant in Aesop's *The Grasshopper and the Ant* fable felt. Accomplishment like this, a thing that met a basic human need, was more satisfying than anything else she did or ever would do. Not, of course, that she couldn't drive to the grocery store in January and buy tomato puree or string beans or what have you. Perhaps it was the preparedness that made her feel good— everything at her fingertips. It also catered to her self-reliant spirit.

Yes, that was probably it; not to mention the fact that nothing tasted better than fresh, home-grown produce.

Too keyed up to sleep, Alex decided that a snack would really hit the spot. "A fresh salad and an ear of corn. Just what I need." She filled a pot with water, put it on to boil, and retrieved a lovely thick ear of her butter-and-sugar corn from the basement. She shucked it and left it on the counter. Then she slipped on her flip-flops and headed out the back door to clip some lettuce leaves, grabbing her basket and gardening shears from their wall pegs on the way out to the back yard.

She had forgotten her MagLite, but the light from the kitchen window, now that she'd cut down the forest of sunflowers, was adequate to find her way around. She disliked the over-bright outdoor floodlights, and used them infrequently.

Alex inhaled the fresh night air deeply. She'd always loved the night. Her favorite game as a child was hide-and-seek by moonlight with her many cousins, all of whom had scattered to the four winds since then. Gramma fretted that she'd hurt herself playing in the dark, but she never did. Grampa never worried. "She got owl eyes, Ma," was what he always said.

As Alex made her way to her salad garden bed, she was delighted to notice fireflies blinking all around her, though she had called them "lightning bugs" growing up. She remembered chasing them and winced at the memory of crushing one on her arm to see her skin phosphoresce. *As children we are small savages, ever so cavalier about the lives of beings weaker than we are.* Alex made up her mind to find out what fireflies ate and provide it so that there'd always be a light show in the backyard.

When she reached the greens bed, she looked across the way and saw that the lights were on again at the neighboring house, and that there was someone moving around inside.

Alex grinned. "Why not?" she said, and dashed back into the house, turned off the stove and descended into the basement. In a moment or two, she was back outside, with a basket containing ten ears of corn, a broccoli, a cauliflower, and a dozen potatoes.

Forgetting her salad completely, she strode across the lot, at three o'clock in the morning, to meet her new neighbors.

Chapter Thirty-Three

Alex dashed across the new pea gravel driveway of the neighboring house, and climbed the three steps to the sheltered back door. She paused before knocking, suddenly regretting her impulsiveness, unsure if she would be welcome at such a bizarre hour. "Christ, what was I thinking? I'm like the Welcome Wagon of the Undead!" she muttered. As she turned to leave, she stepped on a loose board that squealed her presence to those inside.

The porch light flared on.

The door opened a crack.

"Who's there?" a woman's voice asked.

Alex turned back to the door. "Hi. I'm Alex Renfield, your neighbor. Sorry about the hour, but I was up and I saw the lights, so I thought I'd welcome you to the neighborhood," Alex said, cringing inside. Even to her, she sounded completely insane.

"Well, bless your little heart. Come on in, honey. Fred! We have a visitor!"

"Oh, for corn sake!" a distant gravelly voice exclaimed. A metallic clang signaled the forceful arrival of a wrench on the basement floor.

"Maybe I should come back another time," Alex said, inching her way toward the door.

"No, no. It's not you, honey. He's been working on that furnace for hours now and just can't seem to fix it. He's too cheap to hire anyone to do it for him," the woman said, wiping her hands on her apron. "I'm Ethel, by the way."

"Your last name wouldn't be 'Mertz' by any chance, would it?" Alex asked, suppressing a giggle.

Ethel's eyes grew wide. "Now how in the world did you know that? Have we met before?"

"Sort of," Alex replied, her mouth suddenly dry.

"Gosh, darn it, Ethel, I can't get that blasted thing to run no matter what I... oh, hello," he said, stopping suddenly at the top of the basement stairs when he saw Alex.

"Uh, hi. I didn't mean to intrude, and I won't keep you. I'll just be go..."

"Nonsense. Alex came to welcome us to the neighborhood, Fred," Ethel said.

"Well that's mighty nice of yuh," Fred said. "I'd shake your hand, but I'm covered with soot."

"That's okay. Why are you trying to get the furnace running now? It's not like you'll need it until September," Alex asked.

Fred and Ethel looked at each other as if something unspoken was passing between them. "We're used to warmer weather where we're from. Once the sun goes down, it cools off too much for us to be comfortable," Ethel finally said.

"You a gardener?" Fred asked, indicating the basket.

"What? Oh! Yes! These are for you from my garden... picked today." *Oh, yeah. One ticket for Crazytown, please—all aboard!*

"Gee, that's awfully nice of you. We never got fresh vegetables like this back home or even in New York. Look how big everything is, Fred."

"Wow. Thank you kindly," Fred said. "Now I was raised on a farm, and I'm just wondering how you managed to have corn, broccoli, and cauliflower in May."

"Your guess is as good as mine, Fred," Alex said. "We think somebody is pulling a practical joke on us. Come on over tomorrow, and see my root cellar bins for yourself. Everything in my garden was fully grown."

"Use compost?"

"Uh huh."

"Must be *some* mixture."

Ethel put the basket of vegetables on the counter next to the sink. "I'm afraid I don't have much to offer you yet. Our appliances and furniture aren't due to arrive for another day or two. I've got some hot coffee, though, if you'd like."

"Oh, thanks so much, but if I have coffee now, I'll never get to sleep," Alex said, thinking once again how nuts it was to be having this conversation in the middle of the night. "How about if you both come next door tomorrow morning for breakfast? Or lunch? I'd love for you to meet my husband, Leo."

Immediately, there was that eye contact again between the two of them.

"Gee, honey, thanks for the offer, but, well, until we have the house set up, we're only out this way at night," Ethel said, with a tight smile. Her eyes had gone all glassy, staring.

"S'right," said Fred. "Maybe some other time. Thank you, though." Fred had the same stiff smile as Ethel, and the same glassy, disconnected eyes.

"Some other time, then. I'd better be getting back. It was nice to meet you both," Alex said, wanting nothing more than to be out of there.

They walked her out onto the covered stoop. "Bye now," they said in unison, then stood staring at her until she had crossed into the shadows of her own back yard.

"Jesus! The Stepford Neighbors! Holy crap, how spooky!" she muttered aloud. Back inside the house once more, her snack completely forgotten now, Alex locked up and then walked around and rechecked all the doors and windows before heading off, finally, to bed.

She snuggled up next to Leo, wondering what his reaction would be when she told him about her nocturnal ramblings over breakfast.

Chapter Thirty-Four

"Mornin', sleepyhead," Leo said when Alex shuffled into the kitchen.

"What time is it?" she yawned.

"About eleven. What time did you come to bed?"

"Around four, I think."

"No wonder you slept in. Looks like you got all the veggies done." Leo slipped his arms around Alex. "Great job, hon. Proud of you."

"Thanks, sweetie. Growing my own vegetables has always been important to me. Not only is it fun, but it makes me feel good about myself. In a folklore book I once read there were these beings who sold their souls in exchange for supernatural gardening skills—and I didn't blame them one bit."

"Of course you wouldn't. You're a real old fashioned girl—preserving, canning, pickling. You revive the lost kitchen arts that people just can't be bothered with anymore. It's second nature to you and will end up saving us a fortune in groceries."

Alex smiled up at him. "Not to mention how much better it will taste. But I finished dealing with the food around two-thirty."

"How come so late to bed, then?"

"Wait'll I tell you. Feel like an early lunch?"

Over leftover spaghetti and meatballs, Alex recounted the unsettling visit next door.

"Their names were really Fred and Ethel Mertz?" Leo asked.

"Honest to God. And what was really weird about that—I mean weirder—is that when I got back from the hospital, I remember saying that it would be nice to have neighbors like Fred and Ethel Mertz."

"Yeah, I remember that conversation. But why would they have said that it's warmer where they come from and then mention that they never got fresh vegetables in New York? New York isn't any warmer than here, and we both know there are farmers markets in the city."

"Yeah, that doesn't track too well, does it?" Alex said.

"Did they look like Fred and Ethel Mertz from *I Love Lucy*?"

"No, nothing like them. Ethel was a short, skinny lady with long, jet black hair and big round glasses. Fred was tall, blond, and looked like a body builder. If I had to guess, I'd say they were about our age. But they sounded like Fred and Ethel from the TV show," Alex said.

"How do you mean?"

"The same speech patterns and catch phrases, you know? I mean, Fred actually said, 'for corn sake'."

"Which Fred?"

"*Both* of them."

"Another thing I don't get is that comment about only coming over there at night until the house is ready. That doesn't make any sense at all to me," Leo said, frowning.

"Me, either. And you should have seen the way they smiled just before I left. It would have made your skin crawl.

"How long were you over there?"

"Not more than fifteen minutes."

"Then how come so late to bed?" Leo asked.

"Could you sleep after that?"

Leo grinned. "Probably not right away."

"The whole visit gave me the creeps and… oh, crap!"

"What's wrong?"

"I left my basket over there. I meant to take it with me after she put the vegetables away, but she never did. She just set the basket on the counter. I was so anxious to get out of there that I forgot to ask her for it."

"Is it that big a deal?"

"Normally, it wouldn't be, but my Gramma gave me that basket, and I do want it back. Sentimental value, you know?" Alex explained.

"Then that basket you shall have. After lunch, we'll walk over and get it. You said yourself that they aren't there during the day. If we can get in, we'll leave the veggies and take the basket. If not, you can leave a note on the door asking for it back. Ask them to drop it off on our back porch steps. If they're only over there late at night, it shouldn't be a problem for them. And we'll be in bed, so there won't be any lights on to encourage a visit."

"Oh, that's such a good idea. That would certainly be preferable to running into them again. Honestly, Leo, it was like a bad B horror movie."

"Sounds it. It would be funny if it wasn't so strange."

Chapter Thirty-Five

After lunch, Leo and Alex set off to retrieve the vegetable basket.

"Doesn't look like anybody's around," Alex said, shielding her eyes from the sun.

"They don't seem to have gotten much done. The place still looks like the aftermath of the Big Bad Wolf," Leo said, squinting.

The closer they got, the worse the house looked until, at last, they shuffled across the packed dirt driveway and stood on the lawn in front of the back door stoop.

The porch light had migrated from the outside wall to the top step, broken and rusted where it had landed. The kitchen door was off two of its three sets of hinges and was weathered so gray that it was impossible to tell what color it used to be—or if it was ever painted at all. Every window was broken, and the new pea gravel in the driveway was gone, too.

"Are you sure you didn't just dream the whole thing, Alex?"

"I was here, Leo. Look over there. You can still see my sneaker prints in the dirt."

"Okay, so you were here. Maybe sleepwalking?"

Alex turned to Leo, her face a mix of horror and incredulity. "Sleepwalkers don't remember anything they've done while asleep, and I remember everything about being here. No, I was awake when I was here, Leo, and I swear to you, it didn't look this way last night."

Leo had his own horrified expression, but it sprang from a new concern. "How did it look, then?"

"The door was freshly painted. It was bright red with a dark purple trim. I know that sounds awful, but really, it did look nice." Alex knew she was babbling, but couldn't stop

209

herself. "And there were antique seed glass panes in the top of the door, and that light was above the door, of course, and…"

"Alex, stop it. Just stop it." Leo took Alex by the shoulders and turned her to face him. "Nobody's lived here in ages. The door is hanging by a single goddamned hinge, can't you see that? There's not even a handset, for chrissake."

"The one on the door last night looked like an antique, and it was brass," Alex murmured.

"What is this, Alex? Is this another joke of yours? If it is, I don't get it and I don't appreciate it. As a matter of fact, you're really starting to scare me."

She searched Leo's closed, angry face for a trace of understanding and found none. "It isn't a joke, Leo!" she cried, tears falling freely now. "They were here. I spoke to them. And I don't mind telling you, I'm pretty scared myself."

Leo's expression softened. "C'mere, you," he said, pulling Alex close. She held on like a frightened child.

"What the hell is happening, Leo?"

"I don't know," he replied softly. "I wish I did."

Alex sobbed into his shoulder.

"On the brighter side, at least we won't have any trouble getting in. Let's go and get your basket, if it's there."

Leo pulled the door aside and they stepped into decades old layers of undisturbed grime. Alex couldn't believe what she was seeing. The blue gingham curtains that adorned the windows last night were now dun-colored rags. There were holes in the floor and graffiti all over the walls. All Alex could do was stand there with her mouth hanging open and disbelieving eyes so wide they looked like a couple of fried eggs.

"This is it, isn't it?" Leo asked, off to her right.

"It's certainly something, but I don't know what," Alex replied, unmoving.

"No, I mean, this. This is your basket, isn't it?"

With a concentrated effort, Alex turned her head. "Yes, that's it. I'm so glad it's here."

"I thought you said you brought vegetables."

"I did. I wonder where she put them."

"Oh, wait. I think they're still here," Leo said, forcing himself to ignore her reference to Ethel. "Let's take this out into the light."

Alex didn't have to be asked twice. Outside, after their eyes adjusted, they studied the basket.

Inside were all the vegetables Alex dropped off the night before, but they had shrunk and mummified to a fraction of their original size—as if they'd been waiting on that rickety wooden counter for a hundred years.

"These vegetables look like something you'd find in an Egyptian tomb," Leo observed.

"I wonder if the stuff in our root cellar is in the same condition," Alex said softly.

"You know, something just occurred to me. I think I know why you thought you'd met someone here last night."

"What do you mean 'thought', Leo? I did meet someone here last night—two someones. They were here and I met them."

"Then how do you explain this?" Leo asked, indicating the dilapidated, vandalized house with a sweep of his arm.

"I don't know," Alex replied tiredly. "How do you explain it?"

"I think you were dreaming *and* sleepwalking—you know, simultaneously. You remember the dream but not the sleepwalk. The basket proves you were here, the state of the house proves the rest. I mean, think about it. We talked about having neighbors like Fred and Ethel Mertz and, bam, there they are, and they have the right names and say the right things. What are the odds of that, do you think?"

A glimmer of hope shone from Alex's eyes. "You're right, Leo. The odds are nil. And I didn't think of a vivid dream along with sleepwalking. I used to sleepwalk when I was a kid. It started when I was around seven years old, but I thought I'd outgrown it."

"What causes sleepwalking, anyway? Did your doctor ever

tell you?"

"Stress can cause it. My mother was a sleepwalker, so I might have inherited it. When it first started up with me, the doctor gave me magnesium pills to take and that helped quite a bit. I remember that my father finally wound up hanging an old school bell over my bedroom door, just in case. I could move it aside if I woke up to go to the bathroom during the night. But if I was sleepwalking, I wouldn't remember about the bell and when the door hit it, the noise would wake me or somebody else up. Either way, it kept me out of trouble."

"That's a good idea your father had, and if sleepwalking becomes more than a one-time thing for you, I'll install buzzers on the front and back doors that will sound in the bedroom if you leave the house at night. But overall, what do you think? Reasonable explanation for what happened last night?" Leo asked.

"It's the only explanation," Alex admitted. "Could I have that, please?" she asked, indicating the basket.

Leo handed it to her and Alex walked back up the steps, disappearing into the derelict house. A moment later, she reappeared, basket still in hand.

"What was that about?" Leo asked.

"I just did what we said we'd do. Get the basket but leave the vegetables. I dumped them out onto the counter."

The hairs on the back of Leo's neck began to rise once again. "You left them?"

"Yes."

"For who, Alex? I thought we established that nobody lives in this dump."

"For the Mertzes—in case they come back," Alex said.

"In case they come back," Leo repeated slowly. It was true that he hadn't known Alex all that well before they got married, but that hadn't mattered to him. He was so sure of her then. But now he found himself wondering if Alex might have some psychological problems that she hadn't shared with him, stemming from either heredity or trauma of some kind. "How can they come back, Alex? They were never here."

"All I know is, I don't want to give them a reason to come looking for me, and if you'd met them, you'd agree. I gave them the veggies, so the veggies stay here. I just wanted my basket back. Do you think I should leave a note?"

Leo took Alex firmly by the arm and marched her across to their back yard and into the house.

"What's wrong, Leo?"

"I think we need to call somebody."

"Who?"

"Dr. Munson."

"Why? I feel fine?"

"I want a referral," Leo replied.

"For what?"

"For what? I think you need to talk to someone Alex, don't you?"

"Why? Because I walked in my sleep?" Alex laughed.

Leo shook his head sadly. "No, honey. Because you left mummified vegetables, and wanted to leave a note, for people who don't exist."

"There is nothing wrong with my sanity, Leo. I can't believe you want to do this just because of a weird dream."

"You weren't dreaming ten minutes ago."

Fear flashed through Alex like a lightning strike. "Do you think I'm crazy, Leo? Is that it?"

"No, honey, I don't; but we've both been under a lot of stress lately, and everyone reacts to stress differently, that's all."

"That's true. You lock yourself in the shop and build a project that you can't talk about and I make up scary neighbors," Alex said.

"Point taken."

"Are you going to commit me, Leo?" she whispered.

"Good God, no! I just thought that maybe you needed someone to talk things over with, that's all. It's not as if you're dressing like a bag lady and petting a dog that isn't there."

Alex's fearful expression was instantly replaced by one of

fury. "A bag lady with an invisible dog—well aren't you fucking clever, Leo," Alex said.

He was so surprised by her overreaction that he actually stepped back. "I didn't say you were like that, Alex."

"This could all be a side effect of nearly bleeding to death, did you ever consider that?" Alex asked, still angry, but also desperate for Leo to put down the phone, sure that if he made that call, the psychiatrist would put her away and never let her out again, just like her mother. She's spend the rest of her life the same way Mom did—locked away in a drug induced haze, unable to think or communicate until they performed the lobotomy. Then she wouldn't need the sedatives anymore. She wouldn't know who she was anymore, either, but she'd no longer care. Her mother died in that asylum while Alex spent her childhood looking after her drunken, sometimes violent father.

Leo sighed, replacing the receiver. "You're right, that hadn't occurred to me. I guess it's not too surprising. You haven't rested at all since you got out of the hospital, so here's the deal: you do nothing but rest for the next few days and I'll finish picking whatever's left in the garden and find places for it in the refrigerator or the cellar. I will buy microwave popcorn and rent a pile of DVDs from *Captain Video* in Southfield and we will watch all of them—maybe twice. Okay?"

"Just don't rent any *I Love Lucy*, and it's a deal," Alex said, obviously relieved. "How about a pile of corn on the cob and big sloppy cheeseburgers for supper?" Alex asked.

Leo grinned. "Perfect. But for now, I'll give you thirty seconds to go into the other room, stretch out on the couch, and read. Get floppy puppy, too."

Floppy puppy was a three foot tall smooshy, soft and furry stuffed dog with a happy expression and huge cuddle factor. Alex saw him at a consignment shop years ago and couldn't resist buying him. Whenever she was upset or ill, floppy puppy was usually her companion on the couch or in bed, and was a silent clue to Leo that something was wrong. When not in use, the stuffed dog sat on Alex's bureau top, smiling, waiting for the next time she needed to hug something fluffy.

"Do you think floppy puppy is weird?" she asked.

"Not in the least. I think if you had a real dog that you probably would turn to it for comfort instead of a stuffed one. Lots of people look to animals for solace, so why shouldn't you?"

"Thanks, Leo. Thanks for understanding."

"Sure. I'd better get going in the garden. When that's done, I'll make supper."

"But, Leo, cooking isn't physically taxing. I can do it."

"Are you saying you don't like my cooking, young lady?"

Alex laughed. "You win. I'll be on the sofa with James Thurber."

"Good choice. Which book?"

"*Let Your Mind Alone,*" Alex replied.

A micro-expression that most people would have missed flitted across his face, but Alex caught it. *He's still not sure of me.*

"Yell if you need me," Leo said, heading out the door.

Alex went to her bedside table to retrieve her book, and while doing so, glanced out the window at the house next door. An involuntary shiver coursed up her spine that her father, in one of his rare coherent moments, used to say only happened when a goose walked over your grave.

Could the answer be as simple as a realistic dream while sleepwalking? Or was it something else—something horrible?

Perhaps she actually was losing her sanity.

Was she afflicted with her mother's damaged genes? Were the problems they could cause just showing up now? The visit with the Mertzes seemed so real. Could it really have been all in her mind? Alex was beyond fear now, beyond panic. She knew all about the twilit Purgatory created for insane women, peopled with gibbering, drooling wrecks of humanity dressed in filthy rags, bouncing off the dirty, stained padding adorning the walls. Their screams, their moans, their hopeless sobbing that echoed through the corridors, filled with an unholy pain that the damned, trapped within their decaying minds, can only express with sound, so far is it beyond words. She can hear them scratching their broken, bloody fingernails on locked doors in the wee hours, trying to escape whatever night terrors were having a carnival inside their heads. She is assaulted by the stink of feces and urine and filthy skin and lice-ridden unwashed hair. She can see the mutilation, the cutting, the sores, the festering, self-inflicted wounds—but most of all, the neglect—eternally rampant. These are the discarded people, the rejects of a normal society which must have everything neat, clean and all tucked in at the corners. In such a world, there was no place for these living, breathing wraithlike inmates who were as good as dead, but just hadn't figured out that it was time to lie down.

Oh, sweet death, sweet peace, was infinitely preferable to such a terrifyingly confused existence.

Was this to be Alex's future? With Leo coming to visit every day, then once a week, then once a month, and finally not at all, as he gradually forgot her in order to survive, to retain his own sanity, and move on with his life? Would she become one of the growing numbers of human dead letters, and when her fervent prayer for delivery by death was finally answered—naturally or by her own hand—would she be buried in an unmarked grave in some out-of-the-way Potter's Field?

Would she be erased, with no one to mourn her, visited only in the spring by songbirds harvesting nesting materials from the dry, dead grass on her grave?

"Honey, are you okay?"

Alex turned, her face covered in tears she was unaware of crying.

"What's the matter, Alex? You've been standing there staring out the window for ten minutes now. And why are you crying?"

She hastily wiped the tears away, then smiled. "I was just thinking about how lucky I am to have you in my life, Leo. I guess I get kind of emotional about it."

"Aw, I love you, too, babe," Leo said, giving her a hug. "Now how about you go and sack out on the couch? Got your book? Good."

Alex followed him out to the living room.

Nice save, girl.

Chapter Thirty-Six

Leo finished up in the garden about five o'clock. Not only had he picked and stored everything left out there, but he'd also pulled up and chopped all the plant material, dumping it, along with all the raked up leaves, into a chicken wire container he'd assembled. Alex had wanted a compost bin, and now she had it. The beds were all neat and clean, ready for whatever his Super Gardener decided to plant in them next. He smiled at a job well done, took off his gloves and clapped them together to knock off some of the dirt; then, with corn on the cob on his mind, he wiped his feet on the mat and headed inside.

He clomped down the basement stairs to pick out four good ears of corn, thinking about the condition of the vegetables Alex left in the house next door. He was relieved to see that all appeared normal and chose four huge ears, wondering if the rest would last until Alex had a chance to process them. He had no intention of letting her up from that couch to do anything for at least a couple of days. Mental pictures of tying down a hurricane or herding cats came to mind at the thought of trying to get Alex to stay put. He smiled sadly. She was his world, and he was afraid something was terribly wrong with her. Sure, she had a great imagination, but this thing with the mythical neighbors was really frightening. He made up his mind to keep a close eye on her, and if anything like that happened again, no matter how much Alex protested, a doctor would be called who could help her. The fact that she was so sure that there were people living in that shack, to the point where she knew speech patterns... well, that wasn't quite true, was it? She knew the catch phrases of the Fred and Ethel Mertz characters from the TV show, and...

Leo shook his head once vigorously as if to clear it of further upsetting speculation and left the basement.

Once in the kitchen, he filled a pot with water, shucked the corn, and plopped it all in, along with a teaspoon of sugar.

While waiting for the water to boil, he made thick hamburger patties and sliced up mushrooms to go on top. His secret for fabulous mushrooms was to sauté them in A-1 sauce and beer. Anybody who tasted them loved them and nobody could figure out his recipe. Next he sliced the cheddar, then finally, mixed up some Fresca with cheap red wine and added ice. Alex called it "Poor Man's Diet Sangria," or "PMDS" for short. Leo called it godawful, but Alex liked it. He poured plain old ice water for himself, thought about scotch, but decided to wait.

The burgers began to sizzle and the water to boil, so Leo flipped the meat and turned off the burner under the corn. Since they both liked their burgers rare, Leo laid the cheese across the inch-thick patties and as soon as it melted, scooped them onto Kaiser rolls, added his fabulous mushrooms, and put two ears of corn on each plate.

"Hey, sweetie, are you ready to eat?" he called.

"Oh, yeah!" Alex was already sitting at the table grinning. "Bring on the burgers!"

Supper on the table, Leo buttered and salted an ear of corn. "Can't wait to try this!" he said, taking a huge bite… a bite that he immediately spit out into his napkin. "Jesus Christ!"

"What's wrong?"

"It tastes like… aughh, it literally tastes like…"

Alex, alarmed, took a bite herself. "Akkkk! Shit!"

"Yes! That's exactly what it tastes like."

Alex ran to the sink and spit out the corn, then rinsed her mouth repeatedly to wash out the taste. It didn't work. "I'll be right back. I'm going to get the mouthwash."

When she returned, they both stood over the sink, swishing and gargling until, three or four repetitions and a half a bottle of Listerine later, the taste of sewage had finally left them.

They made their way back to the table, staring at the remaining two ears.

"Leo, if these two were bad, the rest of it probably is, too."

"Well I sure as hell am not going to taste them to find out.

These were the best ears down there, though they all look good. Did you taste any of the other vegetables while you were preparing them?" Leo asked.

"No. I was so focused on getting everything processed as quickly as possible that it didn't occur to me."

"Well, eat your cheeseburger. I know there's nothing wrong with that."

They ate in silence and Leo was kind of sorry he'd decided to wait on the scotch.

***

After the supper dishes were done, Alex ventured a theory.

"Could the compost I used have made the corn taste like that?"

"No, honey. Compost is so well rotted by the time it's packaged that there's no manure odor at all, so that's not the answer. I don't know what the answer is, but that isn't it. Didn't your grandparents use compost?"

"I don't think so—at least, not that I ever saw. Gramma used to have rain barrels all around the house and she used the captured rainwater to water the garden. In the fall, Grampa would rake up all the leaves and spread them out over the garden for the winter, so I guess they kind of did use compost with the leaf humus."

"I wonder what Gramma would think of your two-day garden," Leo said.

"She probably would have burned it to the ground and called in her Baptist minister to do an exorcism," Alex said. "I'm not sure that we shouldn't do the same."

"I think sowing the earth with salt would probably be enough," Leo laughed.

"I guess we should have figured there'd be a catch when we had prize-winning produce two days after planting the seeds," Alex said. "Jesus, that still sounds so crazy!"

"It is crazy. That's why it's got to be somebody playing a practical joke."

"Well, you know what we have to do now, don't you?"

"What?"

"We have to check all the other veggies, including the ones I canned and froze."

"There is no way in hell I'm tasting anything else that came out of Rappaccini's Garden, thank you," Leo declared.

"Maybe we won't have to. Maybe we can just cut into them and sniff," Alex said.

"But didn't you already cut the beans before you canned and froze them? And you pureed the tomatoes. If that were the case, then the kitchen should have smelled like a waste treatment plant, and it didn't, did it?"

Alex sagged. "No, it didn't. You're right."

Leo brightened suddenly. "Wait a sec. I have an idea. Where are the two ears we didn't bite into?"

"In the garbage with the ones we did," Alex said.

Leo ran outside to the garbage can and returned with the corn, which he rinsed off and put on a plate. "Hand me a paring knife, would you?"

"Here. What are you going to do?"

Knife in hand, Leo made a slit down a row of kernels, and sniffed. "No smell, right?"

Alex sniffed. "Nope. No smell."

Then Leo worked up some saliva and dribbled it onto where he'd made the cut, leaned down and sniffed again.

The reaction was immediate.

"Whew! There's that stench. And there's the reason nothing smelled like Beelzebub's breakfast while you were cutting it and cooking it," Leo said triumphantly.

Alex looked confused. "I don't get it."

"The stuff reacts with saliva."

"You're amazing, Leo! I never would have figured that out in a million years," Alex exclaimed.

Leo blushed. "Oh, sure you would have."

"I wouldn't, but I'm so glad you did. I was dreading having to taste everything to see if it's good or not."

"I'm willing to bet that none of it's good, but now we know how to check."

"Guess I'd better get to it."

"What was that?" Leo asked.

"I said, 'I guess I'd better get to it.'"

"*Pardon* me?" Leo asked again.

"I said I guess I better get back on the couch and watch a movie."

"That's what I thought you said."

"I think I'll watch *Moonstruck*."

"Again? How many times have you seen that movie?" Leo asked.

"Oh, lots. It's like an old friend, now."

Leo laughed. "Okay. I have a couple of things to finish up in the shop, then I'll run out and pick up some popcorn and movies you haven't seen sixty-seven times, and while you're watching them, I'll check out the produce. Want some tea?"

"No, thanks. I still have PMDS from lunch."

***

Out in the shop, Leo assembled the necessary equipment for painting at the Hamiltons'. Knowing homeowners as he did, he was convinced, despite Theodora's assurances, that she would probably forget a number of items he would need.

He was already planning to sequester some of his favorite small hand tools under his clothes in his suitcase—screwdrivers, pliers, hammer, five-in-one tool, a FatMax saw and measuring tape, and a pair of bolt cutters that he didn't ever go very far without. Strangely enough, that particular tool had come in handy a multitude of times for a multitude of reasons. Leo shrugged. Theodora had lucky pens; she'd have to allow him his lucky tools.

As part of his preparation for any job, Leo tried to think of every possible problem that could arise on the worksite and then make sure he had it covered. He hated interrupting progress to continually run back and forth to Home Depot or

Lowe's. It made him look disorganized to the homeowner. However in this case (sigh of relief), the homeowner wouldn't be around, just that creepy dwarf—though his flame red hair, blue eyes, and milk white skin made him look more like a leprechaun. Cooper Black would be a whole lot easier to take, Leo decided, if he could speak and hear. His *tabula rasa* eyes and general flat affect made him both unreadable and unsettling—like an animated corpse. Christ, even the zombies from *Night of the Living Dead* acted more alive than Black did. Leo wondered what his story was. He loved reading biographies and considered everyone a walking book. He believed that no matter how pedestrian most people regarded their lives, something fascinating, at some point, touches each of us and is incorporated into the story that our daily living writes. Then, as our time dwindles, we look back and smile with amazement at the surprisingly eventful life that was ours.

Though lately, as far as their lives were concerned, Leo could do with a bit less amazement, thanks.

"Let's see—got the caulk, caulk gun, first aid kit, extra brushes, extra trays, rollers and sleeves, small artist brushes, clean rags, drop cloths, paint thinner, paint key, tarps, buckets, ladders. Guess that's it. He managed to fit all the small equipment into one twenty-four-by-twenty-by-twenty green plastic storage container and didn't even have to tape down the lid. He'd like to see Cooper Black fit that, plus the two ladders and all their luggage in the trunk of that Caddy. An evil smile played across Leo's lips.

I'll get to bring my truck yet.

Chapter Thirty-Seven

Alex stared, unseeing, as Cher told Nicholas Cage to "Snap out of it!"

She couldn't stop thinking about her mother. When Alex was seven, her mother, Natasha, began exhibiting frightening mental abnormalities. Well, frightening to her, anyhow. With Dad drunk and useless most of the time, Alex and her brother Sidney relied on Mom for everything—food, shelter, comfort, protection, care, and homework help—and when Mom started acting strange, Alex realized that it now fell to her to care for not only herself and her younger brother Siddie, but her mother and father, as well. Even as a child, she was responsible enough to step up and shoulder the burden.

Though understandably apprehensive, Alex accepted her lot and did what was required. At first, Siddie objected to her attempts at parenting, but after a while, even he noticed the waves of impairment that were slowly drowning the mother he so loved and idolized, and he reluctantly allowed Alex to care for him and help him with his studies.

He also began wetting his bed nightly, so Alex was doing laundry every morning before school, too.

She just hoped that Siddie could cope when he was away from home. She was afraid that if anyone else knew about their situation, they would come and take Mom and Dad away, and then where would they be?

Then again, where were they then?

The boom finally fell when Siddie acted up at school and his teacher called home to schedule a parent-teacher conference. By then, Alex had been the only adult in the house for nearly a year; but Dad managed to stay sober long enough each month to pay the bills from his pension and disability checks, so no one was the wiser.

When she got off the phone, after assuring Siddie's teacher

that Mom would call back after she got out of the bathtub, Alex stormed into her brother's room. She had tried so very, very hard to hold everything together and now, after all her efforts, it looked as if it was all falling apart.

"Siddie, why did you do that?" Alex demanded. "Why did you hit that other boy?"

"'Cuz I felt like it, that's all!" Siddie shouted, red in the face.

"But now look what happened! The teacher wants to talk to Mom and Dad! Now everyone will know! Everyone will laugh at us and call us names! Is that what you want?" Alex had been close to the breaking point for quite a while, and one more thing to handle with everything else she was juggling, was just one more thing too many for her already critically overloaded seven-year-old shoulders. She sighed, and hugged her little brother, whose eyes had filled with remorseful tears. "We'll talk some more later, Siddie. I have to fix supper now, okay?"

Siddie just nodded, a tear running down his nose as he stared at the floor.

Long before Alex came to get her brother for dinner, he had taken out his Cub Scout knife and slashed his own throat.

He was only six.

He couldn't even read or write yet.

Hell, he hadn't even lost all his baby teeth yet!

But to him, anywhere was better than where he was—even if 'anywhere' was a deep dark hole in the ground.

And Alex knew it was all her fault.

If only she hadn't yelled at him.

Since it was still early in the evening, Dad hadn't had too much to drink yet, so he was in acceptable shape by the time the ambulance arrived. The police showed up, too, and swarmed over Siddie's blood-spattered bedroom before releasing his too small, too young body. They said that the cause of death was pretty clearly suicide, but one this young was not only tragic, but quite unusual.

Alex was sure she was going to be arrested and thrown in

jail forever, but it didn't happen, and part of her was sorry that it didn't. Instead, a policeman asked her some questions with eyes full of apology and gave her his card "in case she remembered anything else or just wanted to talk." He was so kind to her. No other grownups in town who knew about Dad were like that. Or maybe he was just a new guy and hadn't heard yet.

The policemen talked to Dad for a while, then they wanted to see Mom. Dad called her and she shuffled out wearing a grimy old housedress. The garment was so covered with food stains that Alex could have boiled it and made soup. Her hair looked like a condemned rat's nest, her face lacked both makeup and affect, and her feet lacked shoes. She stared at the officers, silent.

Alex felt shame that went soul-deep.

The two policemen looked at each other. "Uh, ma'am?" one of them ventured.

Mom slowly swiveled her eyes to rest upon the one who spoke. She still didn't say anything for a few moments, as if she were processing the question with outdated software and seeking an appropriate answer from a system that had crashed long ago.

Finally, she smiled. "You'll have to pardon little TeaSnow, I'm afraid," she said. "He's always so curious about people he doesn't know, aren't you, baby?" She bent down and petted TeaSnow... their apricot poodle, dead and buried two years previous.

"Is she okay?" one of the officers asked Dad while watching Mom pet the air.

"She's been this way for quite a while, but she's not old enough for it to be senility and I don't think it's Alzheimer's— she knows who everybody is. She just acts funny sometimes," was all Dad had to say about it.

*Some*times! Alex nearly shouted. But she kept silent. Things were bad enough already.

The friendly policeman who had talked with Alex didn't miss her wide eyes and surprised expression. He ran out to stop the ambulance before it left. He spoke to the driver for a moment, and the driver said something into his radio. Then the two paramedics reentered the house with another gurney.

"Ma'am? Would you like to come to the hospital with Sidney?" the policeman asked.

"Sidney is my father-in-law and my father-in-law is dead," Mom replied. She looked at them as if *they* were crazy.

Alex beckoned to her policeman. He leaned down. "We call him 'Siddie.' He was named after Granddad," Alex whispered. The officer smiled down at her, nodded, and winked. He was really nice.

"Well, then, how about if you ride along with Siddie?" he asked.

"Oh, yes, that would be nice. I'd like that very much, thank you," she said, smiling brightly, just before she punched him right in the nose.

The crunching sound made it clear that she'd broken it.

Shock made everything stop… just for a second. Then the tableau unfroze and the dark paramedic who looked like an India import, seized the loaded hypodermic syringe he'd put on the gurney, just in case. The policemen fought to subdue Mom, who was flailing, but not making a sound. Once they had her arms pinned behind her back, the paramedic swabbed her shoulder and administered the shot.

"That'll stop an elephant," he muttered in his pleasing sing-song accent.

Nevertheless, a long couple of minutes went by before it took effect.

Alex was so sorry. She was sorry about all the trouble Mom had caused everyone. But she was sorriest about the nice policeman's broken, bloody nose. He was the first grown-up in a long time who'd been nice to her. She looked down at his card for his name. John Margaitis. She put his card in her pocket, promising herself that she'd call him later to apologize for what her mother had done.

Of course, it didn't take long for word to spread all over town about the goings-on at the Bluestones' house. The whole town already knew that Dad was a drunk, but a child suicide and a crazy mother being hauled away in the same day? Well now, that was something to chew on!

Alex stopped going to school after a week of ostracism and the cruelest taunts imaginable, which her teacher did nothing to curtail. Add to all of that Alex's truckload of guilt and she was weighed down to the point of nervous prostration. If she got an hour of sleep every night, it was a lot.

Daddy had stayed sober, on and off, for most of the time since Siddie kil... well, since Siddie died and Mom went away. During his sober moments, Alex begged him to sell the house so they could move somewhere else. Anywhere else. She was back at school after a three-week hiatus, and things were no better for her than before. Why couldn't the other kids pick on somebody else for a while?

He'd smiled sadly and said he'd work on it after the funeral.

Siddie's funeral was private and attended only by Alex and her father.

There wasn't even a clergyman.

They just stood by the tiny white coffin containing Siddie's cremated remains. Her father had insisted on a fancy child's casket, even though they could have just buried the ash-filled urn. Alex had picked a bouquet of dandelions, Siddie's favorites, to adorn his coffin. They were tied with a blue ribbon.

When Dad nodded, the skinny man with a three-day old growth of beard, the silver flask in his back pocket, and a total of four teeth, pressed the button and Siddie was lowered from sight forever.

The very air smelled like defeat; and though the sun shone, Alex shivered.

All she wanted to do was jump in after him, so great was her grief and guilt. But her sense of responsibility was greater, even at nearly eight years of age, and so she refrained. Instead, she hugged her father with the whiskey breath, wiped away her own tears, and with a single fond backward gaze at her little brother's final resting place, she murmured, "'Bye, Siddie. I love you and I'm sorry for yelling. I hope you forgive me."

Then she took her father's hand and led him back to their car to drive back to their much quieter, much emptier house.

The following day, the verdict came back on Mom's condition. She was severely schizophrenic. But what scared Alex most was that the man said that Mom's kind of craziness was hereditary (after she found out what "hereditary" meant). When the fat man who brought the news saw her go white after he supplied her with the definition, the man patted her arm and said, "That doesn't mean you *will* be that way, honey. It just means that you *could* be."

That didn't offer Alex a whole lot of comfort.

The man sitting at their table in his blue suit and his white shirt and piggy face, drinking lemonade that Alex had made, went on to say that Mom would have to be "committed." That sounded all right to Alex. If you're committed, then you're dedicated to something like, maybe, getting well. Sure, that had to be it! Mom would get well and come home and everything would be like it was—well, almost like it was.

The man was still talking to Dad, so Alex wandered off and found herself in Siddie's old room. Nobody'd been in there since he died. *Since he killed himself, you mean—and all because of you. Why were you so mean to him that day?*

The blood spatters had been photographed from every angle, but hadn't been cleaned up. The air had turned the last remnants of Siddie's life to rusty, spoiled-smelling splatters.

Alex sighed, walked into the kitchen, filled a plastic bucket with hot water and soap, found a scrub brush, and set to work.

"It's the least I can do. It's the last thing I can do for you, Siddie," she whispered through her falling tears.

As the year dragged on, Dad seemed to develop a sixth sense about when the social worker would be making her surprise visits and always managed to be sober when she did. She came away thinking that the horrible experience of losing his wife to insanity and his child to suicide had straightened him out. But she came in from the city. The rest of the town knew better. Most of the time, Dad was up to his old tricks of closing bars around town or being thrown out of them.

Though Dad had promised they'd move away after the funeral, he'd neglected to say exactly when, and it wasn't until Alex had completed seventh grade that they finally did move.

No one at her school bothered to wish Alex well or even to say good-bye to her.

She was glad of her new location, but it was another small town, and it wasn't very long before her father had transferred his title of "Town Drunk."

But she could live with that.

At least no one there knew about her mother or her brother, and that brought her a measure of peace.

Mom never saw their new house. She grew steadily worse, hallucinating most of the time, and violent all of the time. No therapy, drug, or combination thereof was making the slightest dent in her condition. She was kept calm by a pharmaceutical cocktail that could have put the entire nation of Zimbabwe to sleep, but all it did to Mom was allow her to function, after a fashion. However, she still had occasional unpredictable aggressive explosions that would burst through even the strongest of drugs, though, so when Alex went to see her, they visited over the phone with a thick sheet of bulletproof glass between them; but at least Mom remembered who she was most of the time. She always asked where Siddie was and even after all the years of therapy, never understood that her precious boy was dead.

As Mom's drug tolerance increased, so did her level combative behavior. The sanitarium couldn't raise her dosage of sedatives any higher for fear of massive damage to her internal organs; so the porcine man in the blue suit and the white shirt came to their house again for permission to try electroshock therapy.

When that didn't work, he came back for permission to take Mom away completely.

Dad signed the papers for the prefrontal lobotomy that would end Mom's violence once and for all.

After the surgery, Alex didn't have to be protected by heavy glass during her visits. Mom had an ugly scar on her forehead that was so large that it looked like an aerial view of the Colorado River. She had no recollection of Alex, her father, or Siddie. She also had no recollection of the fact that she should wipe the drool from her mouth and the mucous from her nose.

Years later, when Alex saw *One Flew Over the Cuckoo's Nest*, she understood completely why the Chief smothered Jack Nicholson's character to death, rather than allow him to continue to exist in a frightening, unfamiliar twilight until he died a natural death.

It didn't take many visits before Dad decided that they might as well stop going to see Mom altogether, since she didn't know who they were anyway, thus increasing Alex's already unbearable load of guilt.

Mom died the day Alex graduated from high school.

Again, there was a private funeral. Again, it was attended only by Alex and her father, without a clergyman. Alex picked lilacs this time and tied them with a raffia bow, upon which she wrote, "I will always miss you." They buried her right next to Siddie.

The weather was bad that day, and the drizzle perfumed the air with that deceitful fragrance that everything had been rainwashed clean and was fresh and new. Alex didn't buy it. Nothing would ever be fresh and new again... life would just go on.

"'Bye, Mom. We love you and we hope you are at peace now. Give Siddie a kiss for us," Alex said. Then Dad nodded at the skinny man, who pushed the button again... lowering yet another family member into the earth.

Alex took her father's hand. "It's you and me against the world now, Daddy."

Her father, looking old beyond his years, tried to smile, but his facial muscles just wouldn't respond. He heaved a sigh that could have sunk an aircraft carrier.

Alex continued to take care of her father, became more of an expert on alcohol addiction than she'd ever wanted to be, and life, such as it was, did go on. Alex won a full scholarship to UCONN, and commuted so she could be home at night to make sure Dad ate and didn't get dehydrated and to bring him home when the bartender of whatever bar he was at called her to come and get him.

He lived long enough to see her graduate UCONN with highest honors. A month later, without warning, his liver shut down, and by the weekend, he was gone.

At his private funeral, there was just one mourner, who laid flowers on two graves and a bottle of Four Roses on her father's. That was about as close as Dad had ever come to an interest in flowers.

On her own now, Alex and her English degree got a job as a proofreader at New Image Printers. It was while working there and living far away from her former Connecticut hometowns, that she discovered the wonderful sense of humor that had been lying dormant all her life. With the encouragement of her coworkers, she decided to give stand-up comedy a whirl on her off-hours.

And the rest, as they say, is history.

Alex never gave Leo any details about her parents, just that they were dead. She'd mentioned her brother, but hadn't told Leo that he was long dead, too. She just couldn't bear how much at fault she still felt. Maybe someday she'd be able to come clean, but certainly not now—not when Leo already had doubts about her sanity—doubts that she was beginning to share.

Her mother's schizophrenia had become evident when she was about thirty-five.

Alex's age now.

A shake of the shoulder roused her from her reverie.

"Hey! Honey, you in there?"

"Uh, yeah. Hi."

Leo searched her upturned face with eyes full of concern. "You're awfully pale, babe."

"Am I? I do feel kind of rotten," Alex said quickly to avoid a truthful explanation.

"Want to watch another movie? I rented a bunch."

"No. This one's fine."

"Alex… it's over." Leo said.

She looked at the television screen. "Oh. I must have dozed off," she ventured.

"Not unless you're sleeping with your eyes open these days," Leo said, his own eyes narrowing slightly. "You were staring at the TV when I came in just now."

"Deep in thought, then, I guess," Alex said, inwardly cringing at the stupid excuse.

"What were you thinking about?"

"Nothing important, honey. I am tired, though. Maybe I'll go lie down for a while.

"I'm getting the thermometer," Leo said, hustling down the hall.

Her temperature was below normal—ninety-seven point three degrees.

"What does it mean when you're more than a degree too cold?" Leo asked, staring at the digital readout.

"For me, it means I'm fine. That's my normal body temperature. Always has been."

Leo smiled. "Good. You go stretch out in bed and take a nap."

Chapter Thirty-Eight

Alex wound up sleeping right through the dinner hour and far into the night, waking in the wee hours of the morning to a quiet house with Leo sound asleep beside her. Her stomach growled an empty threat, so she got up quietly, donned robe and slippers, and padded off to the kitchen in search of nourishment.

Alex always enjoyed being up late at night—awake while the world around her slept. It was like having a secret. She smiled at the thought as she piled rye bread, turkey breast and a jar of mustard on the countertop. Rather than turn on the too bright overheard kitchen light, she made her sandwich by the microwave range light, set at its dimmest.

After she poured herself a tall glass of milk, she turned off the range light and stood at the sink, chewing and gazing out the kitchen window at the night-wrapped back yard.

Between the crescent moon's sailing over the whitecaps of tattered clouds and Alex's reasonably good night vision, she could see the entire yard in some detail. She stared out at the cleared garden beds and wondered if Leo had gotten around to checking the rest of the food that had come out of them. She went to the pantry and pulled the long string that switched on the bare bulb hanging overhead inside.

All the jars of string beans were gone. So were all the pickles. She didn't bother checking the freezer in the garage because she was pretty sure she already knew what she'd find.

Heartbroken at the huge waste, but also secretly glad that the harvest of that repulsive garden had been disposed of, Alex pulled the string once again, returning to her night kitchen.

She wandered back to her previous post to resume surveying her kingdom, but this time what she saw startled her and she instinctively stepped away from the window, even though the lights were off and she couldn't be seen from the outside.

Or could she?

There were two figures standing under the maple tree, looking at the house. Though the moonlight was hindered by the tree's thick branches, it illuminated the yard enough for Alex to see their eyes shining, but that was all. Beyond their eyes, the visitors were shrouded in deep shadow. A surge of fear coursed through Alex as she waited for her eyes to completely adjust.

The moment they did, one of the people in the dark raised a hand and waved... oddly... slowly... back and forth. The forearm and spread-fingered right hand moved robotically, like a pendulum metronome. It was a frightening, unnatural gesture.

"Yoo hoo!" the waver called.

It was Fred and Ethel Mertz.

"Oh, crap," Alex muttered upon realizing that they'd seen her. But *how* did they see her? The lights were off and she didn't exactly have her face pressed up against the glass.

Though she didn't really want to socialize with these unnerving people again, she realized that fate had presented her with the perfect opportunity to redeem herself and her sanity in Leo's eyes. She left the kitchen, walked to the porch and turned on the outside light.

"Hi, honey!" Ethel called from beneath the tree.

"Hi. How's the house coming?" Alex asked.

"Oh, fine, fine," Fred replied.

Neither of them moved from their places and remained shielded by the night, in spite of the sixty watt bulb in the porch fixture. The light spread outward but detoured around them, as if they were repelling it in some way.

"We don't mean to bother you, sweetie. We just saw your light on and we wanted to come over and thank you again for the delicious vegetables you brought us."

The microwave light is too dim to see at a distance, and the pantry light was on for ten seconds at most. How did they see it and get over here so fast? Plus, with the way the houses are angled, they wouldn't have been able to see it from their house, anyway. The only light from our house that they can see from their house is our bedroom light. These thoughts screamed through Alex's head, but proving her sanity to Leo was more important at this juncture than dashing back inside and shoving something heavy up against the door.

"Yeah," Fred agreed. "They sure were tasty."

"Really?" Alex asked, incredulous. "You liked them?"

"Course! Ethel boiled up that corn last night and it was the best I ever ate."

"Reminded us of home," Ethel said.

"New York?" Alex asked.

"Naw. We're not originally from there," Fred replied.

Alex decided that she didn't really want to know where they were originally from. She couldn't believe that they'd actually eaten the vegetables and enjoyed them, completely forgetting about the wizened specimens she'd dumped onto the counter when she took her basket back. "You didn't notice an odd taste?" she asked.

The shadowy couple turned to each other, then turned back to Alex. "No. No odd taste at all. It was sweet and delicious," they both replied in flat, uninflected voices.

Okay, let's get them inside so Leo can meet them. "Wherever are my manners?" Alex exclaimed. "Why don't you both come on in for a bit? I'll put some coffee on, and I've got plenty of sandwich makings."

"Well, that's mighty nice of yuh. I am kinda peckish," Fred said.

"Me, too," Ethel rejoined.

They stepped forward, allowing the light from the porch to touch them.

They were wearing the same clothes they had on last night.

But now, rather than the tight smiles and glassy eyes, they wore disconcertingly toothy grins. Their eyes were so bright with avidity that they looked like predators that hadn't eaten in a while.

If a shark could smile, that's what it would look like, Alex thought, leading the way into the house. She felt very uncomfortable with these spooky people behind her rather than in front of her where she could keep an eye on them.

She seated the Mertzes at the kitchen table, got the coffee going and made two more sandwiches.

"Sure is a nice place you have here," Ethel remarked, still grinning.

"Yep, sure is," said Fred.

Alex suddenly realized another reason, beyond the funhouse grins, that they presented such a sinister façade.

They never blinked.

The more Alex looked at them, the more she was reminded of *Jaws*.

"You have some beautiful things," Ethel said, her head pivoting mechanically.

"We bought most of it from thrift shops and refinished it. We're remodelers—did you know?" Alex asked.

"Of course I know," Leo said.

He was standing in their little library, tying his bathrobe. "What are you doing up?"

Alex smiled. "I'm glad you're awake, because I was just going to come and get you. Say hello to Fred and Ethel Mertz," she said with a note of triumph.

She chalked up Leo's stricken expression to the Mertzes creepy grins, and turned quickly back her guests to apologize, lest they regard Leo's silence as rude.

There was no one there.

Alex was afraid to look at Leo. Her heart just couldn't bear to see the same expression on his face that the attendants at the sanitarium wore when regarding her mother—that look that said, "What a pity that she's so hopelessly, irretrievably mad."

"They were here, Leo, I swear to you," Alex said in a small, frightened voice, still averting her eyes. "I... I made them sandwiches and they were telling me how much they liked the vegetables I brought them, and..."

"It's all right, honey," Leo said, hating the patronizing tone that had crept into his voice. He was now convinced that his wife needed help and needed it fast. "Why don't you come on back to bed now."

"A last night together before you have me locked up?" Alex asked, still staring at the two untouched sandwiches.

"No," Leo said. "I just want you to talk with someone, that's all, I promise. I'm worried about you. Let's find out what's wrong, okay? For me?"

"Sure, Leo," Alex replied, her voice leaden. He was being so nice, so reasonable. Just like everyone was to Mom before she went away.

Leo put the food away and shut off the lights. Alex followed him back to bed, convinced that she'd be sleeping somewhere not nearly as pleasant by tomorrow night.

Once in bed, Alex astonished Leo by immediately falling into a deep sleep.

***

Leo, on the other hand, didn't shut his eyes for the rest of the night, and at one point, even looked out their bedroom window at the house next door. His digital clock radio read four-twelve A.M. and there was no sign of lights or life in the house across the way.

He was filled with anxiety. He had no experience dealing with insanity (oh, what a dreadful word!), hallucinations, what have you, and without the appropriate coping mechanisms, he was terrified that he'd do or say something wrong and make everything worse.

He decided to call Dr. Munson first thing; before Alex woke up. Or, better still, he'd drive out to his Southfield office and catch him on his way in the door.

Yes. That sounded like a plan.

Chapter Thirty-Nine

Earle Munson, M.D., breathed deeply of the late spring air as his taupe Lexus convertible purred through the shady, sidewalk-lined streets. He loved this time of year in Connecticut. He loved the maple trees, the lilacs, and all the renewed wonders of nature that each change of seasons provided. It was impossible to be bored, and that was the way he liked it. He'd just finished planting his yearly geraniums, petunias, and impatiens around his house, and though he planted the same types of flowers every year, each season the specialty horticultural catalogs he received offered a large selection of colorful new hybrids; so his gardens had an updated look every spring, but with the plants that he knew from experience would thrive where he always planted them. And at sixty-seven years old, but still with a full head of thick, though gray-streaked, brown hair, carrying a few pounds too many and sporting a bad back from years of lifting incorrectly (when he most certainly did know better), flower gardening was the perfect outlet for him. There was nothing he enjoyed more than strolling through his wonderland of living color each evening at dusk prior to the daily drenching the garden received when he activated the complex irrigation system he'd installed years earlier. Once that was on, he'd pull up a chair on his screened-in porch, and sip on a glass of his favorite single malt scotch and soda until it got dark, watching the fine sprays of water create knee-high rainbows in the setting sun. He took great comfort and joy from such simplicity. His life was ideal.

He'd been a bit more daring than usual this year, though. He'd bought some marigolds as well as two deep purple butterfly bushes to add their mustard yellow and deep grape blooms to the yard after the wisteria and his beloved lilacs faded. At the moment, there was a riot of color everywhere at home. His gardens outside were looking lovely, his indoor cactus garden under lights was in full bloom, and most of the orchids that flourished in his little greenhouse were also flaunting their alien, otherworldly flowers.

He'd just decided to bring all his orchids indoors to display them for the cocktail party he was having on Saturday when he pulled into the office parking lot, right next to Leo's Silverado.

Leo was enjoying the balmy morning, too; leaning against his truck, sipping a cup of coffee from a travel mug. "Great day for a convertible," Leo said, smiling.

"It certainly is. But the time I most enjoy it is at night, strangely enough."

"I don't believe I've ever ridden in a convertible at night," Leo said.

"Try it if you ever get the chance. It's marvelous," Dr. Munson said, stepping out of the car. He pulled his seat forward to extract the briefcase he'd wedged behind it, then picked his Starbuck's out of his cup holder, and said, "It's 'Leo,' isn't it?"

"That's right. Good memory, Doc."

Munson smiled. "Not really. I don't get new patients very often. Been treating the same folks for a long time. Are you my first appointment? If so, you're awfully early. We don't open until nine and it's only..." he glanced at his watch, "...seven-thirty."

"I don't have an appointment at all, actually. I wondered if I could bend your ear," Leo said.

"Certainly. I come in this early because I like to ease into the day rather than jump to work the moment the door opens. My 'zero to sixty in three seconds' years are far behind me, I'm afraid, and I'm just as glad. Come on in. We'll have our coffees together and you can tell me what's on your mind. How is your wife, by the way? 'Alex' is it?"

"Right again. She's why I'm here."

After watching the doctor jiggle his key in the lock, removing and reinserting it multiple times, amid sighs of exasperation about old and finicky hardware, Leo went to his truck, returned with a can of WD-40, and sprayed some into the lock. When Dr. Munson reinserted his key, it turned smoothly and the lock opened without complaint.

"Well, I'll be," the doctor said, staring at the handset. "I'm going to try that again." And he shut and relocked the deadbolt and unlocked it, relocked it and unlocked it. He grinned up at Leo. "Young man, you have just bought yourself a night ride in Bessie over there. I've been wrestling with this lock for years and I just chalked it up to hundred-year-old crankiness. What is that stuff?" he asked, pointing at the spray can.

"WD-40. It's a spray lubricant that you can get at any hardware store or Home Depot. You can keep this one. I have more in the truck. Whenever it acts up, just give it a quick spray."

"Again, thank you."

"WD-40 is part of the do-it-yourself credo, you know," Leo said.

"Which is?"

"'If it doesn't move and should: WD-40. If it moves and shouldn't: duct tape.'"

The both laughed companionably, then entered the building.

Inside, the office was appointed more like a house than a medical establishment. The floor of the entryway was covered with a long Persian runner that looked antique. Turning left, they walked through the reception area that boasted a Queen Anne walnut kneehole desk with an inset top of tooled red leather—so much nicer than the white melamine counters prevalent in the majority of doctors' offices.

The waiting area was a large room outfitted with one comfortable-looking sofa and four sprung cushion wingback chairs. There was also a fireplace which undoubtedly burned merrily during the winter months. Leo made a mental note not to get sick once it got cold.

No one working in this office wore hospital whites, lab coats, or hospital scrubs, and the only way you'd know there was a doctor in the house at all was if you noticed the stethoscope protruding slightly from the inside pocket of Dr. Munson's sports jacket.

They arrived in his office, which looked more like a den belonging to a man's man. Leo couldn't help but comment. "I like coming here. It feels friendly."

"Do you really think so?" Dr. Munson asked, obviously pleased. "That's exactly the effect we're striving for. People shouldn't be afraid of the doctor's office. Or the doctor, for that matter," he said, with a wink. He bent to clear a pile of magazines from the consult chair. "Have a seat," he said. He then sat behind his huge, beautifully carved desk made of some exotic wood that Leo couldn't even begin to identify. The doctor looked at Leo expectantly over the rim of his coffee cup.

"I'm afraid my wife is having some sort of mental breakdown," Leo blurted out before he lost the courage to say it.

Dr. Munson looked mildly surprised, not anticipating this sort of complaint. "And what makes you think that, Leo?"

Leo proceeded to fill the doctor in on every detail of what he regarded as Alex's steep mental decline, culminating with the events of early that morning.

Dr. Munson silently took it all in. His nose was propped on the rim of the Starbuck's cup he was holding. He inhaled deeply of the sweet aroma of fresh ground Columbian, three sugars, and heavy cream and appeared to be lost in thought.

"Right!" he exclaimed at last, startling Leo. "Before we go off the deep end here, let me talk with her former physicians."

"How will you do that? I have no idea who she used to see."

Dr. Munson smiled. "Remember the form each of you filled out when you became patients here? There was a section for names, addresses, and phone numbers of past physicians. It's all in her file."

"Of course. How silly of me."

"Not silly at all, Leo. You're worried and that takes center stage in your mind. Just be careful working with anything that could injure you badly until we get this problem resolved. Your powers of concentration probably won't be as sharp as they normally are until then. Now, tell me where she lived as a child, if you know it. It's time to do some research."

"I know she lived in Litchfield first, then they moved to, I think, Norwalk when she was in Junior High School. Does that help?"

Dr. Munson took a yellow legal pad from his top drawer and jotted down some notes.

"Yes, it does. What was her mother's name?

"Natasha Bluestone."

"Father?"

"Nathan Bluestone."

"Bluestone. Sounds like that might have been Anglicized from 'Blaustein.' They were Jewish?" the doctor asked.

"It was and her father was. He spent some time in the camps as a child. I only found out about all this recently myself," Leo said.

"Does it bother you?"

"What? That her father was in a concentration camp? That he was Jewish? Or that I just recently found out about it all?"

"Any of it. Does any of it bother you?"

"No. I love my wife. I wouldn't care if she were a purple Buddist who'd been raised by chickens."

"Good to hear," Dr. Munson laughed. "Does she have any siblings?"

"One brother. Sidney."

"Are any of her family members deceased?"

"Yes. Mother and father."

"And where is the brother these days?"

Leo looked uncomfortable. "I don't know. Alex never talks about him, and I've never met him," he said.

"Bad blood between them, do you think? It's odd that you haven't met the man, being married to his sister."

"Bad blood is a possible explanation. The only thing I know for sure about him is that he's alive."

"And why are you so sure about that if you've never met

him?"

Leo briefly recounted their first conversation with Theodora at the Chinese restaurant.

"All right, Leo," Dr. Munson said, after dotting the last 'i' and crossing the last 't.' I'll get to work on this and get back to you soon."

"Could I get back to you, Doc? Alex doesn't know I'm here. She's afraid I think she's crazy and that I'm going to have her locked up somewhere."

The doctor shook his head ruefully. "I'm sorry she thinks that and I wonder why she does. These days, the only mentally defective people who are 'locked up', as you put it, are the criminally insane or extremely violent. There have been enormous advances made in medications for all sorts of mental disorders, if that's even what she has. May I ask, is she a devotee of black and white movies?"

Leo was confused by the *non sequitur*. "Yes, a big-time fan. Why?"

"I was just trying to get my mind around why she would jump to the conclusion that mental illness would lead to incarceration. Now I understand. She's probably seen *The Snake Pit* and *Bedlam*, two 1940s films about the horrors of insane asylums; and on a more recent note, *Frances*, and *In the Mouth of Madness*."

Leo sat back in his chair, amazed. "Wow. I never thought of that, but those are movies that I know she's seen more than once. She even has a copy of *In the Mouth of Madness*. You're incredible, Doc."

Munson chuckled. "Hardly. I'm a Sherlock Holmes afficionado, that's all. I've read everything Sir Arthur Conan Doyle ever wrote, and he, along with my medical training, has taught me to observe and to 'think outside the box' is the way young people put it, I believe."

"Say, your middle name wouldn't be Moriarty, would it?"

"Sorry. 'William.' But back to the matter at hand. Let me do some checking—can you give me a day or two? Today is Friday, May second, so you can either drop by again or give

244

me a call on Monday, May fifth, all right?"

"I can't tell you how grateful I am, Doc," Leo said, reaching for his wallet. "What do I owe you?"

"Not a thing. You've been very pleasant company." Dr. Munson rose and Leo stood and shook his hand.

"Any time you need any work done on your house or this office, Doc, you let me know. I like pleasant company, too."

"Noted," he said. "Have a good day, and try not to worry too much. We'll get it figured out and dealt with."

Leo left feeling relieved. He stopped on the way home to pick up some of Alex's favorite custard filled doughnuts and a couple of maple glazed for himself.

Chapter Forty

Dr. Munson closed the door behind Leo and ambled back to his office. He still had an hour before his first appointment and he decided to spend it with Alex's patient file.

He was fairly sure he knew what her trouble was from Leo's description, but wanted he check on Alex's background for himself.

It was what Holmes would have done, after all.

The doctor slid out the appropriate file drawer, stroking the rich polished walnut of the custom-made cabinet. Earle Munson loved natural wood and, wherever possible, he surrounded himself with it in all its beauty, in both utilitarian and decorative items.

His desk, for example, was solid Cocobalo from Costa Rica. He'd fallen in love with the look of it—its variegated orange, yellow, and dark red with irregular black stripes —and ordered enough to make this desk as well as an escritoire for his home. It was such a rich, warm color, unlike any other wood, and it pleased him to tell curious patients all about it. He hadn't had a patient or visitor yet who was able to identify it and he vowed that the first one to do so would be treated free that day.

Of course, that was a pretty safe vow, since the entire patient roster had been coming to him for years and had already heard the story of his marvelous desk. Well, almost all. His two new patients still had a shot.

Leo hadn't asked about the desk. Odd that, being a woodworker himself. Could it be that he didn't ask because he already knew?

Or was it because he was so distracted by his concern over his wife? Yes, that was probably it.

Dr. Munson skimmed through Alex's file, consulted the notes he'd taken while Leo spoke, then reached for the phone.

Chapter Forty-One

Alex sat at the table, a cup of cold, untouched coffee in front of her.

She had heard Leo leave at six-thirty, so she got up, showered and put herself together, poured herself some of the coffee that Leo had made, and began her wait.

She waited for him to return with... who? Would it be an Indian paramedic with a syringe behind his back? Would it be an ambulance? Or would he be the one to pack her up and drive her off to Fairfield Hills? Oh, wait. It wouldn't be Fairfield Hills, would it? It closed down in 1995, years after her mother died there. No, they'd probably ship Alex off to Connecticut Valley Hospital in Middletown. Or would it be the psycho ward of Waterbury Hospital first?

Alex's eyes were so swollen from crying that they only opened with difficulty. Her slitted view of the beautiful day outside touched her not at all.

After a while, she got up and wandered aimlessly through the house, fingering small knick-knacks, remembering where they'd bought them. She soaked up her surroundings, memorizing them, in order to recall the beauty of the life she had once had during the sleepless nights she'd be having in her locked padded cell at the asylum.

She wasn't angry with Leo. As a matter of fact, she hardly felt anything at all. She was waiting for the inevitable, and when something is inevitable, it's impossible to be either surprised by it or resentful of it.

It just is.

Chapter Forty-Two

Leo pulled into the driveway just as a truly horrible thought leaned over and tapped him on the shoulder.

Should I have left Alex by herself?

He mentally smacked himself on the forehead, grabbed the bag of doughnuts, and ran into the house.

"Alex? Honey? Where are you?" he called.

No answer.

Leo thought his heart would pound out of his chest. He put the doughnuts down and strode through the house to the bedroom.

No Alex.

Oh, God, please please please no! Leo headed for the bathroom. He knocked softly.

"Honey?"

The door was locked.

He jiggled the knob.

"Alex?"

"I'm here, Leo."

"Why did you lock the door?"

"I was afraid the Mertzes might show up again while you were gone," came her chilling answer.

"Are you in the tub?" Leo asked, trying to keep his tone light.

"If you're worried that I've slit my wrists or something, don't be," Alex said, opening the door. She exposed the underside of her arms for Leo's inspection.

"Have you been in there all this time?"

"Yes."

"Why?"

"I told you, I was afraid. Shall I pack now or are you going to do it for me?"

"Pack? Where are you going?" Leo asked.

"Wherever you're sending me, I guess," Alex said, tears falling from her swollen eyes once again.

Leo held her tight.

It was like hugging a fence post.

"You're not going anywhere, my girl. We have a house to paint, remember?"

"You're not sending me away? Really?"

"No, I'm not sending you away. I can't live without you, don't you know that?" Leo said into her hair.

"I'll be good, Leo, I promise. No more Mertzes. I'll be just fine from now on—you'll see," Alex said, too fast and too brightly, with a pleading, hysterical edge to her voice.

Leo was glad Alex couldn't see his eyes fill, then overflow. As if she were doing all of this on purpose, and now was promising to be a good girl... promising not to be insane... as if she could do it with sheer willpower. She was that desperate.

His heart broke and bled.

Chapter Forty-Three

The next few days passed uneventfully. Alex was very much herself again, and Leo was delighted. That morning, they carted all the old garden plant material off to the dump. Alex was afraid to use it for compost.

It felt good to be rid of all traces of those quiet monsters in the back yard.

"Are you going to plant anything else in the beds?" Leo asked on their way home.

"Are you kidding?"

"Why not? We know the vegetable garden was some kind of twisted joke, don't we?" Leo asked. "I mean, you could put in some flowers, couldn't you? Even if somebody swapped them out for giant ones, it would just be pretty, wouldn't it?

"Honey, I have a feeling that I could plant Morning Glory seeds in those beds and what I'd get would be Venus Fly Traps and Pitcher Plants big enough to eat stray cats. So no, I don't think so," Alex said. "I don't trust them anymore."

Leo let the comment pass. What was to trust? Someone played a practical joke. There wasn't anything wrong with the soil. "It just seems a shame not to use them after all the work that went into building them. You planted Cannas in Harold's old place."

"But I never planted any vegetables in there. Nothing horrible has come out of that raised bed," Alex said.

Except Harold Leo thought. Illogical though her arguments were, Leo decided not to debate the matter any further. "Waste of wood and soil, then. I'll take them apart tomorrow. Too bad."

"No, not yet. Let me think about it. Maybe I can come up with something else to use them for," Alex said.

They stopped at the market in Southfield center on the

way home and bought beets and asparagus, as well as a good size Porterhouse and some baking potatoes. Leo was desperate for some fresh corn, but it was too early for it, so he settled for broccoli.

Alex was putting the groceries away when the telephone rang.

"Hon, can you get that?" she called, her head in the refrigerator.

"Sure thing," Leo said, answering the phone. "Hello?"

"Leo? This is Dr. Munson. I didn't hear from you on Monday and I became concerned."

"Oh, hi. Things are fine, thanks. How are you?" Leo said, deliberately keeping his end of the conversation vague. Alex was doing so well, he didn't want to upset her now.

Meanwhile, she had turned his way, and mouthed, "Who is it?"

Leo waved a hand at her and pretended to be concentrating on what the caller was saying. In reality, he was wracking his brain to come up with a believable story about who was calling.

"She's standing nearby, isn't she? Alex, I mean," the doctor deduced.

"Uh huh."

"Fine, then just listen. I found a few very interesting, if perplexing, facts in my research and I'd very much like to see you about them as soon as possible."

"I don't see how," Leo said, sympathetically.

"Ah, I see. You'll need to have a reason to see me as well as something to tell her about who is calling, yes?"

Finally, the excuse section of Leo's brain kicked into gear. "I think I have that covered," Leo said.

"Good. Then meet me at my office tonight at, say, ten o'clock? I'd meet you earlier, but this is the one night of the week that I have extended office hours until nine. I'll give you that ride in my convertible I promised and we can talk."

"That sounds fine, Theodora. I'll pick it up at ten, then.

Thank you for calling."

"Good luck," said Dr. Munson.

"Theodora? What does she want now?" Alex asked as Leo hung up the phone.

"It seems that earring you lost has finally turned up," Leo said, hating himself for the lie.

"The blue one?"

Leo nodded, looking away. He was a terrible liar and he only hoped that Alex didn't yet know him well enough to be aware of it.

"That's great! But where? I thought lost it at Dr. Orbon's office."

"You did. She had dinner with Orbon last night and he mentioned it to her, so she told him she'd call and let us know. Want me to go pick it up for you tonight?" he asked, crossing his fingers that she wouldn't want to come along.

Alex smiled. "Sure, if you can find him. Thanks, honey. I really don't feel up to any more nighttime edge-of-the-graveyard adventures. As a matter of fact, I thought I might train it out to see Stan and Clara."

"That sounds like a fine idea. Do you good to get away. You'll stay over?" Leo asked.

"Oh, yeah. Woodhaven to Gloucester and back again is a pretty long trip to make in one day. I'd never have time to visit. I'd ask you to go, honey, but I know how you feel about Stan, so I won't," Alex chuckled.

"Thank you."

She had to agree that Stan Blenowski was a blowhard jerk, but his wife, Clara, was one of the sweetest people Alex had ever met. They had relocated from the City at the same time the Renfields did, but they landed in Gloucester, Massachusetts instead of Connecticut. Alex could never figure out how they got a pronunciation like "Glahster" out of such a spelling, but that was New England for you. Stan had secured a job in the accounting department of *The Boston Globe* and Clara spent her days throwing and firing pottery for an impressive number of upscale stores and private collectors in New York, Boston, Los

Angeles, London and Paris, if you please. Her work was exhibited in several important museums, the Guggenheim among them, but Stan treated Clara's remarkable achievements as if they were part of nothing more than a time-killing hobby that kept her occupied while he was at work. It infuriated Alex that Stan undervalued and underappreciated Clara's incredible talent. Her use of color with the special glazes she formulated was nothing short of astounding. And the graceful, fantastic shapes her creations assumed, the sheer organic look of some of them, bowled Alex over every time she saw them.

One would think that the fact that even her smallest pieces sold, and sold vigorously, for thousands of dollars each might have made some sort of impression on that blockhead of a husband of hers. She was the primary breadwinner in their household, but Stan chose to ignore that little slice of reality, and instead, would regale anyone with a working ear with story after dull, pointless story about Stan Blenowski, Super Accountant. Alex had not the slightest clue as to why Clara stayed with him. Talk about hitching your wagon to a tree stump!

She picked up the phone to call her friend and once she reached her, was delighted to discover that Stan was away at a convention in Miami, so it would just be the two of them.

Hurrah!

Selfishly, Alex didn't tell Leo that Stan would be absent. Some girl talk would be just what she needed.

She dialed the phone again, this time calling the train station to book her tickets.

Chapter Forty-Four

Leo dropped Alex off at the Waterbury train station at three o'clock and didn't envy her all the train changes she'd have to make to get to Gloucester. Since Alex wouldn't be home for supper, he didn't see much point in cooking for one, and so planned to grab a pizza at *Goombah!*, a Soprano's-themed Italian hole-in-the-wall pizzeria in Southfield.

As he drove, it occurred to him that neither he nor Alex patronized any of the Woodhaven businesses.

It wasn't for lack of trying, however.

He found the one-man-show Home Depot in town so disconcerting that he couldn't even walk through the door anymore; and the small shops and markets along Main Street, well, they just weren't *right* somehow with no one around. Anyplace that was usually bustling with activity, like playgrounds or shopping center parking lots, always struck Leo as creepy when no one was there. Such lonesome places reminded him of horror movie sets.

Woodhaven was beginning to give him the same feeling. Though all the store signs read, "OPEN," during business hours, they had a dead, abandoned feel that was so strong that it kept both Alex and Leo from venturing any closer than the sidewalk.

The whole town was kind of like that. Though there was the *suggestion* of people everywhere, they never actually saw anybody else around. Nobody out washing their cars on a sunny weekend afternoon. No kids outside riding bikes or bickering over toys. Nobody gardening or doing outdoor fix-ups on their houses.

Nobody.

Though he'd initially shrugged it off as people keeping themselves to themselves; now that they'd lived there a while, it was becoming unnerving.

At the far end of town there was a small bridge, no more than twenty feet above the water it spanned, under which the Pomperaug River lazily flowed. There was obviously a swimming hole just down and to the left of the bridge, as evidenced by a two-inch thick piece of knotted rope tied to a sturdy tree branch that overhung the water. Leo remembered just such ropes and swinging out high over the water to let go at the height of the outward swing. He could still remember the coarseness of the knot on his bare feet and the scary/thrilling split second feeling of weightlessness as he let go. Sneaking off to go swimming with his buddies was the best part of his childhood summers and he remembered it fondly.

The bridge itself was even low enough for the braver kids to leap from safely; but he never saw anyone there. This was odd, considering how warm it had been for the past week. When he was a kid, the whole neighborhood hit the nearest body of water on the first day over seventy degrees—at least to wade in if not to swim.

Oh, yes, he definitely preferred Southfield; and after their lease was up, he wanted to find a place in Southfield and get out of Woodhaven as fast as possible. But in the meantime, he decided to work on a project he had in mind for Alex's garden beds; so after running several minor errands, he made a stop at a specialty building supply warehouse in Watertown just before they closed, loaded up his purchases, and drove home.

Upon arrival, he looked at his watch. Five-thirty. He had about an hour and a half before sunset, and so decided to spend the remains of the day unloading the truck. He'd start his project the next morning.

Leo stepped inside the house to grab a cold drink, and was just pouring his Arizona Iced Tea over a tall glass of cubes when the phone rang. He grinned, lifting the receiver.

"Duffy's Tavern, where the elite meet to eat. Duffy speakin'," he said.

"Hi, honey." It was Alex and she sounded very subdued.

"Uh oh. When you don't laugh at that, something's up," Leo said.

"I can't talk too long. Clara's an absolute wreck. I'm going to have to stay for a while. I don't want to leave her alone like this," Alex said.

"Like what? What happened?" Leo asked, concerned.

"It's Stan…"

"Is he dead?"

"No, but we both wish he were."

"Say no more. Stay as long as you need to and fill me in when you get back. It doesn't sound like you can talk freely right now."

"Thanks, sweetie, I knew you'd understand."

"Are you okay? How are you feeling? How was the trip?"

"Yes, fine, and long," Alex replied.

Leo laughed. "All right. Call when you can and don't overstress yourself. I love you."

"Love you, too, honey. Be safe, be careful while I'm away."

"You bet. Give Clara a hug from me. 'Bye." Leo hung up the phone and lifted his now ice-cold, sweating glass of tea and drained it in three gulps. While rinsing out his glass he contemplated the long shadows in the back yard and decided that since he now had more time to complete the garden bed alteration before Alex came home, he'd forego even unloading the truck today and just be a couch potato until he went to have his pizza.

At eight-fifteen, Leo was awakened by an annoying diatribe delivered by one Dr. Gregory House. He sat up and glanced at the window. Not only was it dark, but the distant earlier grumblings of thunder were now much closer. As he watched, the skies opened up and a torrent of water poured earthward escorted by lightning bolts. He hadn't seen a storm like this since he left Phoenix, and the monsoon season there had nothing on this New England storm.

"Well, there goes my convertible ride." Leo pushed himself up off the sofa, called *Goombah!*, then showered, dressed, and grabbed his keys. There was a pizza waiting for him and he was starved.

Chapter Forty-Five

By the time Leo finished his dinner, the rain had stopped and the night sky was clear and strewn with stars.

He strolled to his truck through the fresh scent of rainwashed air and spice ferns from the wooded area behind the parking lot that infused the evening with their earthy tang of wild cinnamon.

A scant ten minutes later, he was pulling into Dr. Munson's nearly empty parking lot. The top was up on the Lexus.

Before Leo could ring, Dr. Munson opened the office door. "Good evening, Leo," he said. He craned his neck around the roofline to get a look at the sky, and smiled. "Come on. You shall have your ride after all." He reached just inside the office door, extracted a Harris Tweed jacket, and as he walked to the car, removed the car keys from the inside pocket and then folded it into the back seat. He wore a lined trench coat, and regarded with skepticism the windbreaker Leo wore over his sweater. "I do hope you'll be warm enough."

"This is cashmere, Doc," Leo said, touching the camel colored turtleneck. "Alex gave this to me last Christmas and it's plenty warm. Between this and the windbreaker, I'll be fine."

The doctor pushed a button on the key ring, and the roof of the Lexus soundlessly retracted into a chrome frame above the trunk. "Hop in," he said.

Leo complied. "It's a good thing the top is down," he said. "Otherwise, I'd never fit."

"You'd be surprised at how much head room there is. How tall are you, again?" the doctor asked.

"Six-five."

"Well, perhaps not *that* much headroom." He looked Leo up and down. "Especially since your height is equally distributed between your torso and your legs." He slipped behind the wheel. "I'm glad the evening's so clear."

Leo grinned. "Well, so far, that's the only thing that is. What'd you find out, Doc?"

Without answering, Dr. Munson pulled out of the lot onto Old Waterbury Road and set off at a good clip. Leo loved it—the wind, the night, the openness, the feeling of freedom. "This is great."

"Ah, another convert," Munson said. "I'll take you to a place in Middlebury where all we old crocs meet up. It's about twenty minutes from here if I take a less direct route, which I assume you'd prefer. A quiet place and a good scotch will be in order, I think."

"Only if you let me buy, Doc," Leo said.

"Done. Now sit back and enjoy the ride," the doctor said.

Leo slouched down in the seat, leaned back against the headrest and watched the starry sky through the budded, bare branches on the trees that lined both sides of the two lane road. Traveling this way, after dark, was brand new and exciting in a world that, after passing a certain age, seemed to be all out of fresh takes on things.

He glanced across at Dr. Munson to see him smiling to himself. *What a nice guy he is to do this. Convertibles at night—go figure.*

Long before Leo was ready to stop, they arrived at *Mood*, which, from the outside, looked like a quietly elegant pub. A contemporary structure, it stood by itself, all angles and points with triangular windows, of all things. Even though ultra modern architecture usually left Leo cold, there was an indefinable something about this place that appealed to him.

When they walked in, Leo realized his mistake in thinking that this place was any kind of a bar.

It was an exclusive men's club.

Dr. Munson greeted the woman behind the front desk, presented his membership card, and signed in as "Earle Munson and Guest."

The anteroom was sparsely furnished, but with pieces that

Leo knew were antique and probably worth a fortune.

Next, they stopped at the check room. The young woman took charge of their coats, but never gave the doctor a claim check, and the room was filled with outerwear.

"You don't get a chip or a check or anything?" Leo asked in a low voice as the woman went to add their coats to the multitudes. "How will she know which ones belong to us?"

Dr. Munson smiled. "Our Harriet has an astounding memory. No matter how busy it gets, she hasn't yet mismatched coat to patron. Isn't that right, my dear?"

Harriet had returned from the back of the closet. "Yes, that's right," she said.

"One time, just to test her, a group came in, all about the same size, wearing identical coats. Remember that, Harriet?"

Harriet snorted, but in a ladylike way. "Remember it? I'll never forget it."

"Were you able to match all the coats and owners later?" Leo asked.

"Yes. Of course. That's what I get paid to do, after all," she replied, a twinkle in her eye.

"And that evening, she was paid quite well, indeed, when each of the fifteen members lost their wagers that our Harriet would fail," Dr. Munson laughed. "What was your 'tip' that evening?"

"He just loves to tell this story," Harriet said with a smile. "My 'tip' was three thousand dollars."

"Wow," Leo said. "But I don't understand why you got the winnings if you weren't even aware of the bet. Isn't a bet usually between two agreeing parties?"

Dr. Munson coughed softly and turned away.

"This is the part of the story he doesn't like me to tell, but I'm going to anyway," Harriet said. "Dr. Munson is the reason I went home with a wallet I couldn't close that night."

Leo turned a questioning look on the doctor, whose face was red with embarrassment. "Oh, I told them that if they were going to perpetrate such nonsense that I would hold the money and if they lost, which I was confident that they would, then Harriet was to receive the proceeds. So you see, there were two agreeing parties, it's just that Harriet wasn't one of them."

"So you really didn't know anything about it? Weren't you kind of suspicious?"

"Not really. I've been working here for a long time and I just thought it was one of their jokes. I nearly fainted when Dr. Munson handed me an envelope full of hundreds and explained." She looked at the doctor. "Now stop blushing this minute! I don't think there's anything wrong with other people knowing what a fine person you are."

This only made Dr. Munson blush all the more.

Harriet grinned at Leo. "I give up." Then she turned to the doctor, and said, "Why don't you two go on in? Your place is ready. I saw you pull in and I alerted the staff."

"How very thoughtful. Thank you, Harriet." He reached into his pocket for a tip, but she stayed his hand with a vigorous shake of her head.

"I don't ever want to see your hand reach for your wallet again on my behalf, please, Dr. Munson," she said.

"Harriet, it was your skill at your job that won you that money, not I."

"Perhaps, but it wouldn't have come my way if not for you, and don't think I'll ever forget that, sir." She turned to Leo and added, "I was finally able to put a new roof on my house thanks to this man. Now I can enjoy listening to the rain on my roof, instead of on my floors."

Dr. Munson shook his head ruefully. "May I at least have the privilege of sending a drink your way, then?"

She smiled. "Yes. A Campari and soda, if you would be so kind."

He patted her hand. "My pleasure entirely."

Leo expected to see a room full of tables covered in fine linen when they entered the main hall. The threshold itself was the height of two men and the width of five, so Leo knew that the space beyond it would be large, probably with a cathedral ceiling.

His estimation of size and height were both correct, but he guessed wrong elsewhere, and was surprised to see that the huge open space contained not tables but large brown leather Chesterfield sofas and George III library chairs with matching upholstery. Subdued lighting was provided by antique brass-based Tiffany lamps centered on blocky Gothic walnut end tables placed next to each chair. It was a hodgepodge of periods, but the effect was cohesive and elegant, exuding an atmosphere of quiet comfort. Most of the available seating was already occupied by older gentlemen reading newspapers or books, going over paperwork, writing, or conversing quietly over their cocktails. Almost all of them were smoking cigars.

"I do hope you don't mind cigar smoke. I meant to ask you earlier and it slipped my mind," Dr. Munson said. "If it bothers you, we can go somewhere else."

"Not necessary. I've never smelled cigar smoke that was anywhere near as pleasant as this. It's wonderful—like brandy and old wood," Leo said.

"What an apt description. But it's not surprising... the aroma, I mean. This club stocks only the best smoking materials. There is a walk-in humidor in the back filled with Cuban cigars. Nothing finer, in my humble opinion."

"I thought they were illegal in this country," Leo said.

"They are. I have no idea how they manage to get them, but I don't question it, either," the doctor replied, with a wink. "It's probably one of the reasons that membership here is so damnably expensive."

On their way in, several of the gentlemen looked up to acknowledge Dr. Munson with a smile and a nod, which he returned in kind. The hostess led them to two leather library chairs, with ottomans, directly in front of a glowing fireplace.

Leo was instantly tense.

"No, it's not a real fire, in anticipation of your question," Dr. Munson chuckled. "It's a bit too late in the year for an actual fire. This artificial one is comprised of light only, but it's pretty convincing, isn't it? We have real fires in the colder months—it's very cozy."

With an inward sigh of relief, Leo made settled into his

chair and was glad he'd put on his dress slacks. Almost immediately, a waiter appeared, not to take their order, but to drop off a bottle of single malt scotch, two glasses, a pair of silver tongs, and a matching small silver bucket filled with ice cubes.

"You looked like a scotch drinker to me, so I took the liberty. We old timers have reached the point where, after a lifetime of experimentation, we have arrived at the one drink we consume exclusively. Mine is the bottle you see here. However, if you'd like something else, it's no trouble."

Like something else? This is only the best scotch there is. "Oh, I think this will be just fine, Doc... really."

"I remember that you mentioned on your new patient form that you had an ulcer at one time—I trust you can drink now without aggravating it?"

"It hasn't given me trouble in years, so pour away," Leo said.

Munson grinned, using the tongs to quietly place three ice cubes in each glass. He poured generously, handed Leo a glass, then settled back into his chair with his own. "There is a cigar for each of us in the little drawer there; however, tonight I find I'm not in a cigar mood. But please do help yourself," he said, indicating the small drawer in the end table between them.

Leo opened it and inside there were two cigars, a silver cigar cutter and a silver cigar lighter.

Talk about class.

Leo had quit smoking at age seventeen (he'd begun at twelve), but this cigar was worthy of backsliding, and he didn't feel the least bit guilty about unwrapping it and cutting it.

Lighting it was another matter entirely.

Dr. Munson noticed Leo's distress. "Something I can help with?"

Leo's face fell. "I want to smoke this cigar, Doc, I really do. I probably won't get another chance in my life to taste a Cuban cigar. The problem is, I have trouble with open flames— even if it is just a lighter."

"Is that all? If you'll allow me?" he said, with his hand out.

"I assure you that I am disease free."

Leo laughed, handing him the prepared cigar and lighter.

"I shall be back momentarily. There's something I have to fetch, anyway." With that, he rose and stepped down a narrow hallway and out of sight.

Leo felt the tension drain away and his high opinion of the doctor was reinforced once again. He didn't ask him why he couldn't light his cigar. He didn't ask any questions at all. He simply did what was necessary to put his guest at ease.

After a few minutes, Dr. Munson emerged from the hallway puffing Leo's cigar. "I just lit it, so you haven't lost much of it, and you're welcome to another if you like, but it can't leave the premises, so you'll have to smoke it here."

"Thanks, Doc, for... you know."

Munson's smile was kindness personified. "Actually, I don't know, but I imagine you'll tell me when or if you care to."

"It's a story for another time... but I will tell you someday."

"Then I'll wait," he said, fumbling through his pocket. "Ah, here we go." He withdrew a Meerschaum-lined calabash pipe and a small pouch of tobacco.

Leo observed him with fond amusement. "Is that black shag?"

"It is," he replied, preparing his pipe without looking up.

"Then shouldn't it be coming from the toe of a Persian slipper with a nail hole in it instead of a leather pouch?"

The doctor laughed. "Caught in my own affectation."

"The pipe was a dead giveaway, Doc."

"Ah, yes, I suppose that, second only to the deerstalker cap, the calabash is the item most associated with Holmes," he said. The pipe now properly prepared, he stood. "Be right back."

Leo knew he was going back to the hallway to light his pipe out of sight.

When he returned, they both settled into their chairs for a

few moments of quiet contemplation amid sips and puffs.

Finally, Leo looked over at Dr. Munson. "You know, Doc, you even look like him."

"I thank you for that, Leo, but I am painfully aware that I look far more like Watson than I do Holmes."

"Well, look at it this way, Holmes wouldn't have kept Watson around if Watson wasn't just as brilliant in his own field. And the Watson in the books was much more intelligent than the clownish character that Nigel Bruce portrayed. Hollywood made Watson into such a buffoon that he became Basil Rathbone's comic relief."

"You're absolutely right, Leo. I always disliked those films because of just that character defamation. We appear to have a great deal in common, you and I." The doctor sighed. "But I'm continuing to postpone the reason for this meeting, which is to tell you what I discovered about Alex's background. Would you like to hear it now, or would you prefer to wait a bit?"

"I think I'd like to hear it now."

"All right." Dr. Munson set his drink on the table coaster and, as gently as possible, filled Leo in on Alex's father's death by liver failure, her mother's insanity and eventual death in confinement, and, lastly, her younger brother's suicide.

Leo took it all in without a word. When Dr. Munson finished the horror story that had been Alex's life, he reached into his pocket and discreetly passed Leo a handkerchief.

Leo wiped his free-flowing eyes and, just as discreetly, handed it back.

Neither man said anything for many minutes.

When Leo finally did speak, he asked softly, "Is this why you brought me here, Doc? To a public place? Were you afraid I'd flip out in your office?"

Dr. Munson smiled sadly. "No, dear boy. I hoped a treat would ease the swallowing of a rather bitter pill, that's all. I suppose that was foolish of me. There's no way to sugar-coat what I've just told you. You've no idea how sorry I am."

Leo was instantly ashamed. "No, Doc, not foolish at all, and I'm the one who's sorry. Of course that wasn't why you brought me here, and yes, the treat did help a lot, believe me. It was a wonderful, thoughtful thing you did for me tonight, and the motives I just attributed to you were way out of line. Please forgive me. I'm really very grateful for everything you've done for me and for Alex, and I would be proud, not only to call you my doctor, but my friend, as well," Leo said.

Dr. Munson's smile lost some of its sorrow. "Why, thank you, Leo. I'm pleased that our outing tonight helped buffer the news, however small the measure. And I would deem it an honor to be a friend of yours."

"I'm glad." Then his face clouded once again. "Doc, why do you think she let me believe that her brother was still alive?" Leo asked.

"Usually, when someone refuses to accept or divulge a reality, it's because there are unresolved feelings of guilt. I imagine she hid his death from you for fear that you, or anyone she tells about it, would judge her harshly, thereby adding more guilt to a load that is undoubtedly too heavy already," the doctor explained.

"But you told me it was a suicide. It's not as if she killed him."

"Perhaps she feels responsible for it in some way. Please understand that I'm not saying that she drove her sibling to suicide, but it could be her perception that she did. And as you know, Leo, our perceptions are our reality, accurate or not. Also remember that she was only seven years old at the time, and, in light of what I've told you about her mother and father, they probably didn't do much in the way of helping her cope with Sidney's death. If blame is to be laid at anyone's door for the suicide of an innocent child, I would say it belongs with those unfit parents of hers. But to the mind of a youngster, who was likely forced into an adult role far too early in life, this sort of sophisticated reasoning comes hard or not at all. In light of all that, I'm not the least bit surprised that she hasn't shared her brother's death with you. Do you understand what I'm saying?"

"Yes, I do, Doc," Leo replied.

"And if 'friends' is what we are, Leo, perhaps you should

call me 'Earle.'"

Leo smiled. "Thank you, Earle."

"Now, as to her mother's insanity," Earle said, getting back on track, "it seems that she was severely schizophrenic. Had it been caught earlier, before she required institutionalization, medication and psychotherapy might have mitigated it and made it manageable."

"Were there pills for that back in 1980?"

"Indeed there were. But Alex couldn't have been expected to know about them—or have any idea what was wrong with Natasha. The home situation being what it was, I have my doubts that her family did much entertaining; so that left Alex without any other adult in whom to confide who might have interceded and procured help for her poor mother. No, Alex probably just kept her head down and did her best to hold her disintegrating world together," Earle said.

"It's amazing how things change, isn't it?" Leo asked. "If this sort of thing were going on now, an army of social workers would have descended on that house to take those two children away. Might have saved a life."

"They were living in a small New England town, my boy, and though everyone in such small towns knows everyone else's business, they are content with knowing it rather than minding it, if you know what I mean. In these little burgs, interference in the lives of others, even now, must usually be summoned."

"What are the symptoms I should be looking for?"

"From what you've told me, she already has some of them. She is seeing things that aren't there, hearing voices, and is fearful. As time goes on, you might see paranoia, and a belief that others are reading or controlling her mind. She might sit for hours without saying or doing much, be emotionally flat, seem to take no pleasure in everyday life, withdraw from interacting with others, have delusions or disorganized thoughts, and have difficulty starting and completing even the simplest of tasks."

"Gee, is that all?" Leo asked dryly.

"I know it's a lot to take in all at once. If you have a computer at home, you can do some additional research on your own."

"Is schizophrenia hereditary?"

"There have been studies that suggest so, yes; however the odds aren't as high as you might think. The child of a schizophrenic mother has a likelihood of about nine percent of developing schizophrenia in his or her lifetime, as opposed to the one percent likelihood a child of a normal mother has. At least that's what the scientists tell us. As a matter of fact, over in Norway, researchers think they've isolated the chromosome responsible."

"Which chromosome is that?" Leo asked

"Chromosome number five."

"Of course."

"Why 'of course', Leo?"

"Oh, it's just that Alex is into numerology and five is a bad number."

"Signifying?"

"Change and upheaval."

Earle smiled. "Change isn't necessarily bad. Some changes prove to be very good. But change involving upheaval, I agree, is not so hot," he said. "But how wonderfully appropriate that the anomalies should appear in the fifth chromosome. Schizophrenics are nothing if not changeable—sometimes within seconds. I shall have to read up on numerology. How fascinating!" He glanced at Leo and saw the chagrined expression on his face. "Oh my, do forgive me. I sometimes get so caught up with a new and interesting idea that I completely forget myself."

"No problem. That facet of your personality is probably one of the things that makes you a great doctor," Leo said.

"You are most kind."

"Nine percent odds—that doesn't sound too bad. And even if she does have it, we're catching it early, right? So medication could cure it?" Leo asked with eyes that begged.

"Unfortunately, there is no known cure for schizophrenia. It's a disease of the brain that we do not yet understand how to eradicate. The good news is that with the rapid advancement in medicine, it can now be controlled so as not to disrupt the daily life of the sufferer. Today, schizophrenia is regarded and treated as a chronic illness, much like HIV is these days."

"Well that makes me feel a whole lot better," Leo said, expelling the breath that he was unaware of holding.

"Exactly. Things are far from bleak, Leo. Just bring her by the office, and we'll formulate a plan of action."

"You can't just give me a prescription for her that I could crush up into her orange juice?" Leo asked.

"I'm afraid I can't. She really needs to be evaluated by a competent psychiatrist before a prescription can be discussed."

"The thing is, I went behind her back coming to you. If she is schizophrenic and possibly paranoid, wouldn't she think we were plotting against her and refuse the help? Wouldn't stress like that make her even worse?"

"That's a good point, Leo," the doctor said. He swallowed the dregs of his scotch, then sat back, regarding Leo with that mildly surprised look Leo had come to know. "You're very impressive, do you know that? You not only listen carefully, but you analyze well, too. Bravo. I'm going to pour us another round and mull it over while we sit here, all right?"

"Suits me," Leo said, holding out his empty glass.

After further rumination, Earle finally turned to Leo. "How about this: A friend and colleague of mine, Jack Henderson, is a top drawer psychiatrist. Suppose I set up a meeting in my office... now, wait... and present him as someone who is interested in moving to Woodhaven. Since you and Alex are my only two patients from Woodhaven, you could say that I asked you, as a personal favor, to give him a tour of the town, and perhaps some lunch at your house afterward. I'm hoping that will be long enough for Jack to evaluate Alex's condition and advise us how to proceed. What do you think?"

"But why can't you just see her?"

"I'm just an internist who reads psychology books, Leo. This is a matter for a psychiatrist, and a good one. I don't know enough about schizophrenia to make an accurate diagnosis, and a misdiagnosis on my part could do much more harm than good. No, I believe this is the best course of action for now."

"All right. You have my total trust, or you wouldn't be my doctor. What does this guy charge, by the way?"

"Hmmm. Well, you'll have to pick up his round trip train ticket from Boston—he won't fly and he doesn't enjoy driving great distances—so that will probably cost you a hundred or so. I happen to know that he charges one-fifty an hour for consultations, so if you give him a tour for an hour and lunch for another, you're probably looking at a four hundred dollar day or thereabouts. I know you don't have health insurance. Can you manage it?" Earle asked.

"Three months ago, I couldn't have, but a client from years back recently made good on a very old bill, so yes, now I can."

"Wonderful. I'll call him tomorrow. You'll like him, Leo."

"No doubt," Leo said, feeling better than he'd felt in weeks. He took another long velvety drag on his delicious, dwindling cigar, knowing that he'd remember this evening, and the deep gratitude he owed his new friend, for the rest of his life.

Chapter Forty-Six

The ride back to the office was over far too quickly. Earle hadn't allowed Leo to pick up anything more than a ten dollar tip for their server and twenty dollars for Harriet, since she refused to take money from the good doctor. Leo felt the evening would have been cheap at twice the price for the hours spent with this caring and concerned gentleman, and he said so, embarrassing Earle once more.

"Again, Earle, thank you very much for everything," Leo said, shaking Earle's hand and exiting the vehicle.

"Glad to do it, son. Is there a day that's better for you for our ruse?"

"The sooner the better. The thing is, Alex is up in Gloucester visiting Clara, a friend of ours who is going to pieces about something or other, so Alex may be staying there a while. How about if I call you as soon as I find out when she's coming back?"

"That's fine, then. Have a safe ride home. Oh, and do you have a cellular telephone? It might be easier for you, if I need to get in touch, than if I call on your land line."

"Yes, I have a cell phone, but I'll still have to come up with an excuse about who's calling. We're usually together," Leo said, fishing a business card out of his wallet and handing it to the doctor.

"Let me think about getting around that, too," Earle said. Leo stepped away from the convertible, and with a final wave, the doctor drove off into the night.

It was all Leo could do to keep his eyes open on the drive home. He hadn't felt tired earlier, but between unwinding with good scotch and the profound relief that something could be done to help Alex, he was bone tired. Once he got in the door, he checked voice mail (no messages), shucked his clothes, fell into bed and was snoring in no time.

Leo slept solidly through the rest of the night right up until nine-thirty, when the phone woke him up. "Hullo?" he said, his voice rough with sleep.

"Leo? Are you still asleep?"

"Not anymore. How are things going up there, sweetie? How's Clara?"

"I'm more concerned with how you are. You never sleep this late. Are you feeling okay?" Alex asked.

"Oh, I'm fine. Stayed up too late, that's all. You weren't here to put me to bed."

"I know. You need supervision," Alex laughed. Then her tone changed. "Oh, hi Clara. I'll be right with you."

"So how's Clara? What's going on? Can you talk?"

"Oh, all right. I'll call back later, then," Alex said.

"I take it that's a 'no.'"

"That's right."

"Can you tell me when you'll be coming home?" Leo asked.

"The five-and-ten store? Yes, I know where that is— though I guess they call them 'dollar stores' now, don't they?" Alex replied.

Leo pulled the phone away from his ear and stared at it, bewildered. "Five-and-ten store?" Then he smiled, and put the phone back to his ear. "Do you mean May tenth?"

"Yes."

"Have you already got your ticket home?"

"Uh huh."

"Morning , afternoon, or evening train? Just say one for morning, two for afternoon, and three for evening," Leo said.

"Two."

"Okay, honey. I'll be at the station to meet the afternoon train out of Boston on Saturday. Can't wait to see you. I miss you," Leo said.

"You, too. And please tell him that I called," Alex said, hanging up the phone.

Leo wondered why she still couldn't explain what was going on up there, but he knew that if Alex couldn't talk, there was a good reason, and so put the question aside.

Now that he knew when Alex was coming back, Leo called Earle to let him know. He couldn't reach him so he left a voice message then dressed in his work clothes, shifting his focus to breakfast. He cooked up a monstrous portion of scrambled eggs along with a pan fried rainbow trout. He wanted caffeine, but didn't want to wait for the coffeemaker to slosh, burp, and fart out a pot of his favorite French roast; so, with a slight nod to the waistline, he had a Diet Coke instead.

It wasn't the same, somehow.

Afterward, he rinsed and stacked his dishes in the sink, thinking for the fourth or fifth time about how much better breakfast tasted when Alex made it; then went outside to unload his truck. He wheeled the hand truck out of the workshop and carefully stacked his purchases on it, then pulled the heavy load around to the back yard. It took several trips to empty the truck bed completely.

Next, he set to work with a shovel and a large roll of Contractor's Extra Heavy Duty trash bags. He had a lot of work to do before the nearly two cubic yards of concrete he'd ordered arrived.

Leo shoveled out all the soil in each garden bed into the contractor's trash bags. He tied the tops off tightly and stored the soil-filled bags in the empty shed at the far corner of the back yard, knowing full well that Alex would someday have a use for them. He'd never seen anyone get so excited about dirt.

He finished up reinforcing the garden beds, which were now, in concrete pouring parlance, 'wooden forms,' with rebar just as the concrete truck arrived. The day had turned unseasonably hot and after directing the truck as it backed around the side of the house, Leo offered the grateful driver, Manny, a cold beer and a thick ham and cheese. By the time they were finished eating, they were fast friends; and after Manny poured the concrete, he stuck around and helped Leo with the screeding—leveling the top of each bed.

"You're gonna need to let this 'crete cure for four days,"

Manny said around the unlit cigarette hanging from his lips. "You can take out the forms on day five."

"Oh, but I'm not taking out the forms – they're staying just like this. And I can't give it four days. I need to tile the tops by Saturday, and that's just three days away."

Manny scratched his chin and considered the situation. "Prob'ly won't be a problem to set your tiles if you wait'll Satiddy mornin' to do it. I'm not doin' nothin' that day—could prob'ly come by and help ya, if ya want."

Leo grinned. "You know how to tile?"

"Mista Renfield, my papa was a tiler, and his papa before him. I don't got blood, I got grout. What time ya want me? You make the coffee and I'll bring the doughnuts."

"Okay, then, Manny. Here's what I want to do." Leo showed Manny the detailed drawings. "This is a surprise for my wife who's coming in on the three o'clock train on Saturday, so I figure I have to get the tiling done by two, so I can clean up and go pick her up. What time do you think we should start?"

"With two of us workin'? We can get this done real nice in four hours or so, but just to be sure, how about nine o'clock?"

"Works for me. I'll see you then." Leo shook Manny's hand. "And please, Manny, call me 'Leo.'"

"You got it, Leo." He climbed back up into the mixer's cab and finally lit his cigarette. "Later," he called, then drove carefully out of the yard and back onto the street.

Leo grinned after him. Even if he forgets all about it, it was nice of him to offer. He checked his forms one more time, then went inside to clean up.

Chapter Forty-Seven

Leo checked and rechecked the cement over the next couple of days, and by Saturday morning, just as Manny said, it was hard enough to tile.

He was up early and had a quick breakfast of a bagel with cream cheese and coffee before adjourning to the back yard. From eight o'clock forward, he moved each set of tiles next to its designated box, then laid them out on the ground in the pattern in which he'd be mortaring them onto the concrete.

He'd just finished the last pattern and looked up to see a half-ton pickup truck, so old and filthy that its color was anybody's guess, pulling to a stop at the shoulder of the side road. Out jumped Manny, waving with one arm and carrying a Dunkin' Donuts box in the other.

"'Betcha thought I'd forget!" he exclaimed, grinning.

Leo grinned back. "Of course not!"

"Howya like that truck, huh? Nearly thirty years old and still runnin'."

"What color is it?"

"It's a two-tone—rust and dirt."

"How long since you washed it, Manny?" Leo chuckled.

"Long time. Now I can't. The dirt's all that's holdin' that heap together. You say somethin' 'bout coffee?"

"No, but it's all made. Come on in. Oh, and I picked up some ground beef and grinder rolls, so we'll have meatball grinders for lunch. How does that sound?"

"Depends on the gravy, I guess," Manny said.

"Gravy? What gravy?"

"Oh, sorry—'talians call tomata sauce 'gravy.'"

"Ah. The 'gravy' in that case, is homemade by my wife who, though not Italian, is a fabulous cook," Leo said.

"What is she, your wife?"

"What do you mean?"

"What is she? Y'know, where do her people come from?"

"She's Russian, German, and I think there's a smattering of Spanish in there somewhere."

"The Spanish part may just save the gravy, we'll hafta see. Be intristin', anyhow," Manny said with a shrug.

Leo smiled, knowing that Manny would love Alex's 'gravy,' since it was a recipe she'd wheedled out of Sofia Viviani, an old Italian woman who ran a hole-in-the-wall restaurant in the North End of Boston. She'd taken an immediate liking to Alex on the afternoon that they stopped in there a year ago for a bite after the Boston walking tour. The old lady had made her sign a paper that kept her from passing the recipe on to anyone, however. Old, she was. Stupid, she wasn't.

He and Manny stepped into the kitchen. Manny scanned the premises and gave a low whistle. "I ain't seen such a jungle since 'Nam!"

"Yeah, my wife has a green thumb, all right,"

"Green thumb? She's got green from her fingers to halfway past her elbows, and I don't even want to think about her feet!"

Leo laughed. He'd never met anyone who could speak as bluntly as Manny did, but at the same time, not offend. It was quite a talent.

Manny sat down at the kitchen table while Leo got the coffee pot, a trivet, and a couple of mugs. "How do you take your coffee, Manny?"

"Black with two blacks and a dash of black," Manny replied, opening up the doughnut box. "I got a 'sortment—that okay?"

"Bound to be. Any glazed?"

"Yeah, there's a couple in here. You like those? I always feel like I'm eatin' a soggy egg carton with sugar on it." He made a face. "They're all yours. I like the Bavarian cream ones," he said, withdrawing two from the lineup in the box. Leo handed him a plate and put one down for himself, poured

275

the coffee and they spent the next twenty minutes discussing the state of the world and consuming enough sugar and carbohydrates to meet their RDA for the next month.

The doughnuts served them well, however, and they had completely tiled seven of the ten concrete slabs by noon.

"Hey, Manny, you ready for lunch?" Leo called.

"Born ready. But you still have to make the meatballs, right?"

"Yeah, I do. Don't you want to take a break, though?"

"Tell ya what—if you wanna bring me a cold beer, I'll keep goin' out here 'til lunch is ready."

"You got it," Leo said. He had given Manny a Coors the other day, but today he brought him a bottle of Killian's Irish Red. He took a big gulp and looked surprised. "Damn, 'at's good beer!" He turned the bottle over in his hand to read the label. "Irish beer—figures. The Irish know what they're doin' even better'n the Germans do when it comesta this stuff. *Grazie*, Leo."

"*Prego*, my friend," Leo said, returning to the kitchen.

He rolled up his sleeves, conscious of a self-imposed pressure to impress. He turned the ground beef into a large stainless steel bowl, then added the usual suspects of oregano, freshly pressed garlic, basil, an egg, salt and crushed red pepper, and set the bowl aside. In a frying pan, he heated olive oil, and used it to sauté sweet onions and sliced mushrooms. When they were done, Leo folded them into the meat. He washed his hands well, then moved to his favorite part of the proceedings—mixing and rolling the meat by hand.

Once the meatballs were rolled and had started to sizzle, Leo poured the container of Alex's 'gravy' into a pot and set the heat low. Fifteen minutes later, lunch was ready.

"Hey, Manny, come and get it!" Leo called.

While Manny washed up, Leo slit the foot long grinder rolls and stuffed them with six meatballs each, spooned on Alex's simmering sauce, then he draped thin slices of Mozzarella cheese on top of all that, and melted it under the broiler. He dribbled more sauce over the mozzarella, set two more bottles of Killian's on the table, along with a roll of paper towels and sat when Manny, who looked considerably less sweaty, joined him.

"Okay, now let's see how a Russian German lady with a little bit of Spanish makes gravy," he said, taking a huge bite. His eyes widened as he chewed. Then they filled with tears. He swallowed, staring.

"What's the matter, Manny? No good?" Leo asked.

"No, it's good. Better than good. It tastes just like my mama's," Manny replied, his voice breaking with emotion.

"If it's that good, why does it make you so sad?"

"I always asked my mama for that recipe, and she said she'd give it to me if I came and helped her in the family business. Recipe or not, I was gonna move back up and surprise her just before Christmas," Manny said.

"So what happened?"

"She died two days after Thanksgiving."

"Oh, no. I'm so sorry, Manny."

"*Grazie*, Leo. I miss her so much, and tastin' this, well, it's like she's in the room with us. It's nice… real nice."

"So you decided to stick around Southfield, then?"

"Sure. What do I know about runnin' a restaurant?"

"What's your last name, Manny?"

"Viviani. Why?"

Leo smiled sadly. "Just curious. But say, how would you like a copy of my wife's gravy recipe? I know she'd love for you to have it."

"It would mean more to me than you c'n possibly imagine," Manny said, his eyes still shining with unshed tears.

"Okay. Let's finish lunch, then I'll clean up in here and write it out for you," Leo said.

"Leo, *siete l'amico del mio cuore e l'amico della mia anima. Milione ringrazianment*," Manny said.

"That sounds beautiful, whatever it means," Leo said.

"It means, 'You are the friend of my heart and my soul. A

million thanks.'"

"And how do I say, 'I'm glad to know you and you are always welcome in my home'?"

Manny grinned. "You just did."

After lunch, Manny went back to work and Leo put the dishes in the sink and flipped through Alex's recipe card file until he found what he was looking for.

There was no signed paper in the world that would keep him from giving a copy of that recipe to Manny.

The two men finished up at two o'clock on the dot, then walked from slab to slab admiring their work. Manny had done an exemplary job and certainly had a future in tiling if he wanted one.

"I can't begin to thank you enough, Manny. I never could have gotten this done in time without you," Leo said. "You do beautiful work. If you're interested, I'd love to hire you if I get any tiling jobs. Do you realize that you could go into business for yourself and make a bundle?"

Manny was obviously pleased. "Ya really think so? I mean, I dint go to school or nothin'."

"My friend, you've already forgotten more than any tiling teacher ever knew. Take my advice and think about it, and if you decide to do it, let me know. I'd like to help you in any way I can. Great tile guys are hard to find. Oh, and here's your recipe," Leo said, handing Manny the transcribed index card. He accepted it as if Leo were handing him the Mona Lisa. "And I want you to have this, too."

Leo stuffed a folded hundred into Manny's shirt pocket.

Manny pulled it out and looked at it. "What's this? I don't expect you to pay me. You gimme lunch and you gimmie my mama back for a little while. I don't want your money, Leo." He held it out for Leo to take it back.

"Do you have a freezer in your house, Manny?" Leo asked.

Manny was thrown by the abrupt shift in subject. "Huh? Yeah, I gotta freezer—a big one. I do a lotta fishin'. But what does that have to do with…"

"Here's what I want you to do with that money. Go out and buy as much of each of the ingredients for the gravy as that hundred allows, then go home and made up a big batch and freeze it in individual portions. That way, when you get to missing your mama, you can just boil up some pasta, heat up some gravy, close your eyes, and there she'll be."

"You're one of the nicest people I ever met, Leo. All right, I'll do that, then," Manny said, slowly pocketing the cash. "And maybe you and the missus will come to my place for dinner sometime."

"We'd love to."

The two friends shook hands warmly and exchanged telephone numbers and 'thank-you's, amid promises to get together soon, then Leo watched Manny drive off down the road until he was lost to sight.

Chapter Forty-Eight

When Alex saw Leo waiting for her, she rushed into his arms as if they'd been apart for months, not days. She was so much like her old self that Leo wondered if he'd been overreacting to previous events.

"That's the kind of greeting I like," Leo said after a long kiss. "Do I know you, by the way?"

Alex laughed. "Well, you do now."

"Come on, I'll take you home with me. My wife's away," Leo whispered.

"What a moron she must be to leave a hunk like you at large," Alex giggled. "I really missed you, honey."

"Missed you, too, babe."

"I tried to call you last night around ten."

"I didn't feel like cooking just for myself, so I went to out to the diner for some grub."

"That late?"

"Open all night," he said.

On the drive back, Alex filled Leo in about the goings on in BlenowskiWorld. There was some pretty big news.

"Clara dumped Stan, and she's filing for divorce," Alex revealed.

"And sanity makes a comeback in Gloucester! Good for her. She give you a reason? Not that you couldn't give *her* twenty or thirty."

"She caught Stan doing things behind her back."

This mist of happiness surrounding Leo suddenly evaporated.

"What was he doing?"

"Oh, going out at all hours and not telling her where he was when he came back; or where he was going when he left, for that matter. Apparently, he was on the phone at all hours of the night, too. You don't exactly have to be a windsock to know which way the breeze is blowing in that scenario," Alex said.

"Stan and another woman? *Stan*?"

"Seems that way."

"Stan *Blenowski*?" Leo was incredulous.

Alex laughed. "I couldn't believe it, either. It's so Lifetime TV, isn't it? He was damned lucky to have talented *and* gorgeous Clara; BUT, he just turned forty, so my guess is that he found some twenty-year-old chippie who thinks that dating an older man is romantic. I'm sure she doesn't know that he's married, and she probably thinks he has money, too."

"*Stan Blenowski*?"

"I know, I know!"

"So how come you couldn't talk to me about it over the phone?" Leo asked.

"It took Clara a day or two to remember that all men aren't pond scum, and until she did, I didn't feel right about discussing her situation with you. Everything's fine now, though, and she sends you a hug and a kiss. As a matter of fact, I talked her into signing up for Yahoo Personals. Maybe she'll meet somebody decent."

"So what's she going to do now?" Leo asked.

"Same thing she always has. The great thing is that Clara bought herself a store on Main Street that has a huge loft above it, and that's where she's living now. The store space is gigantic, so she had a partition put up to section off her new studio area from the front sales area. The retail part of the store is now about twenty-by-twenty, with shelves all over the walls and a scattering of pedestals for her larger, heavier pieces. It's a perfect set-up for her. You should see the location, Leo—it's practically on the water."

"So you didn't see Stan at all?"

"Nope. He's supposedly at a week-long convention in Miami. Clara did all that in just a few days—he doesn't even know they're kaput yet. She's already put the house on the market, since it was in her name only. She said she doesn't need a big place like that."

"Oh, boy. Put you two together and you move mountains. Is she all right financially? We can send her some cash if she needs it."

"Not necessary, Leo. She makes a *lot* of money. When things started to go south with Stan, she was smart enough not to confront him, but to cash and hold back some of the big checks that came in for her. Since she did the bills anyway, Stan didn't notice."

"That's strange. Stan's the accountant, but Clara does the bills?"

"She said he never wanted to do any accounting that he wasn't being paid for."

"Yep, that's Stan," Leo said.

"And yesterday, she took half the money out of each of their accounts," Alex said.

"That was restrained of her. Don't most 'women scorned' just clean the accounts right out?" Leo asked.

"You know Clara. She's more than fair—always has been. The fact that most of the money was put there courtesy of her talent didn't matter to her. 'Marriage is a fifty-fifty proposition,' she said, so she just took that fifty percent along with the money she held back and opened new business and personal accounts. She only intends to take fifty percent of the proceeds from the house sale, too. Stan doesn't have a damned thing to complain about as far as I can see," Alex said.

"Just that his meal ticket is gone."

"Well, screw him. And I hope Clara finds a guy who's worthy of her this time."

"From your lips to God's ear," Leo said.

"Oh, speaking of ears—did you get my earring?"

"Sorry, honey. False alarm. It was blue, but it wasn't yours."

Upon arrival at home, Leo grabbed Alex's overnight bag, and Alex carried in the large bag she'd placed carefully on the back seat.

"What's in there?" Leo asked.

"A present from Clara. A late wedding gift, actually."

"One of her pieces?" Leo's eyes lit up. He loved Clara's work, but despaired of ever owning any due to their justifiably high price tags. Though he knew Clara would have sold him whatever he wanted at a severe discount, Leo had always vowed never to take advantage of friendships that way, and so admired her pottery from a distance.

Alex nodded excitedly.

Once inside, she removed the gift from its shopping bag and carefully unwound the many layers of bubble wrap safeguarding the handmade artwork at its center.

Leo picked up the shopping bag and guffawed. "'Crackpots'? This is the name of her store?"

"Uh huh. Cute, isn't it?"

Leo nodded. "How'd she get them printed up so fast?"

"She has a friend who's in the silk-screening business. He did fifty of them for her to hold her over until the printer gets her order done. 'Crackpots' is strictly for the tourists, though. She doesn't market herself that way to her serious buyers," Alex said, unwinding the last of the bubble wrap. The piece she held was a bud vase shaped like Fountain Place, the angular, ultra modern Dallas, Texas building that I. M. Pei designed. But the really remarkable thing was that, due to the glazes that Clara created, the vase appeared to be a different color depending upon not only exposure to light, but how much light and what type of light it was. In some light it would glitter, in some the color would appear to have a matte finish, and in others it would appear to be slick. Nobody understood the relationship of color and light like Clara. Nobody.

"Every day it's a different piece," Alex marveled. "It looks one way in full sun, one way in partial sun, one way at dusk, one way at dawn, one way on a cloudy day, one way in fog, moonlight, you name it! And then, of course, there's incandescent, halogen, and fluorescent light, too."

"Yes, but doesn't that happen with everything, though?

Different light always makes colors look slightly different," Leo said.

"There's no 'slightly' about this, Leo. Look." Alex drew the drapes closed. Before she did, the vase had been a deep, rich, royal purple with a matte finish. "Now watch," she said as she placed it beneath the lamp and turned it on.

"Incredible!"

The vase was now bright green and so shiny that it looked wet.

"That's absolutely mind-boggling!" Leo exclaimed. "I'd have said it was impossible if I hadn't seen it myself."

"That's why she gets sixty-five hundred for a piece like this," Alex said.

"Sixty-five hundred! Really? Gee, should we even be accepting a gift that's worth that much? I hate to think of Clara just giving away sixty-five hundred dollars," Leo said, still unable to take his eyes off the vase.

Alex laughed. "That's my Leo."

"What do you mean?"

"Always looking out for other people. And I want you to know that I voiced the same concern when she gave it to us, so you must be rubbing off on me."

"What did she say?"

"Nothing. She just handed me her ledger. She made a hundred twenty-five thousand dollars last month, Leo, and about the same for each month previous. She can afford this," Alex said, pointing at the vase.

"Jesus—she makes over a million a year! I had no idea."

"Feel better now?"

"Oh, yes. Now I can enjoy it without feeling guilty. Can you put a live flower in it? With water? Or is it just for artificial?"

"It's glazed inside, so yes, you could, but why would you want to?"

"You're right. A perfect rose would actually detract from it. Ever think you'd hear anybody say that about a vase?"

"But *what* a vase," Alex sighed.

"Do you realize that, outside of the truck, this is the most valuable thing we own?"

"Hey, the way Clara's work appreciates, keep it for twenty years, and it will be worth four times the value of the truck… new."

After Alex found a home for the vase of many colors in the safety of the hutch, and Leo got off the phone singing its praises to a delighted Clara, she poured them both a Wild Turkey on the rocks.

"What are we celebrating?" Leo asked when he saw the special rocks glasses.

"I think we have a lot to celebrate, don't you? We have a kind and generous friend who's given us *and* herself a wonderful gift. And I'm celebrating the fact that I don't have to worry about you sneaking around like Stan. I just wish Clara could find a man as decent as you are, Leo," Alex explained, her eyes shining with love.

Leo's smile turned slightly green around the edges. "I'm not that terrific, hon."

"Oh, yes you are. You let me work things out for myself instead of calling for the white coats. I'm really grateful for that, Leo," Alex said, clicking her glass against his.

"So you've worked things out, then?" he asked.

"Yes, I think I have."

"Then here's lookin' at you, kid," Leo said, putting the issue aside for the moment. Nobody conquered the kinds of demons Alex was grappling with on their own in just a few days. The bourbon, which he normally relished, was like acid on his tongue.

"Hey!" Leo exclaimed. "In all the excitement, I completely forgot about *your* surprise! Come on!"

"What surprise?"

"It's in the back yard."

Alex felt the color drain from her face. "Oh, Leo, please don't tell me you planted anything back there."

"Didn't you say that you didn't want to plant anything in those raised beds?"

Alex nodded.

"Then why would you think I'd do it anyway?" Leo asked.

Alex sighed. "I'm sorry, honey. I know you'd never do that. The back yard still has me spooked, I guess."

"Well, come on. I've 'de-spooked' it for you." He took her hand and drew her outside. "Close your eyes, first." She did and he led her to the nearest garden bed. "Okay. Open 'em."

"Oh, Leo, it's just beautiful!" She scanned the rest of the yard. "All of them?"

Leo nodded, a huge grin spreading across his handsome face.

"It's gorgeous." The slab they were standing in front of was tiled with Italian marble in swirling pastels. She ran to the other slabs.

Each was different.

One slab was done in black tiles with a scattering of silver flecks that made the surface look like a night sky. Another had tiles the colors of the Mediterranean Sea. Another sported tiles in bright fire tones, and another the warm browns and greens of the earth. There was also a neutral-toned bed in subtle shades of taupe, beige, and ecru, a bed of antique rose and burgundy, another of purples and grays, and finally, one with black and orange tiles as a tribute to Alex's favorite dual purpose day – Halloween and her birthday.

"I'm absolutely agog, Leo. It looks great."

"Do you really like them?"

"Of course I do. You know, you remind me of Clara sometimes. She's always surprised when people like what she does, too. What shall we use these for, do you think?" Alex asked.

"I thought they'd be a good place to put all your house plants for the summer."

"That's a wonderful idea. We can have plants back here, without actually growing them out of the ground. We'll have to put up some shade cloth, though, because the sun will burn them."

"Already thought of that. There's shade cloth and frames to attach it to in the garage."

They spent the balance of their day putting up the frames and moving the potted plant jungle that filled the house outdoors.

When Alex started keeping potted plants years ago, she decided that they would each have pots that were nicer looking than the basic run-of-the-mill terra cotta flowerpots, and so bought many different shapes, colors and glazes of the more expensive ceramic pots as she needed them. This worked in Alex's favor now, as she was able to coordinate the pot colors with those of the tiles on each bed, and create a surprisingly cohesive look to the back yard. By nightfall, Alex had them beautifully arranged on each tiled surface.

"It would appear, my dear, that you know a thing or three about color yourself," Leo said, marveling at the result.

Alex kissed him. "Thanks for doing this, hon. It will be nice to be able to enjoy the back yard again. I hate being afraid to look out the window."

Chapter Forty-Nine

After a slap-up dinner of hot dogs, three-bean salad, and leftover spaghetti, they settled back to watch the tube.

Alex's eyes closed during *Bobby Flay's Throwdown*. The excitement, the traveling, the plant hauling and arranging, and the previous unsettling days had finally caught up with her. When *The Cake Boss* came on, Leo picked her up and carried her into the bedroom. She didn't stir, so he removed her shoes, socks, and pants and tucked her in into bed in her panties and tee shirt, then went back out to watch Buddy create the most amazing cakes known to man, and have a lot of fun doing it. They'd have to take a trip to Carlo's, the Cake Boss' bakery in Jersey one day, just for the Italian cookies.

He watched a while, then switched over to BRAVO to catch *Project Runway*. He was a closet fan—only Alex knew. It was sort of an unwritten no-no for a straight guy to admit out loud that he likes the show, but Leo found it absorbing. The talent and creativity of the contestants and the beautiful things they could make in such a short time astounded him. He loved to pick the weekly winner and loser and was correct more often than not. He got a pad and pencil so he could jot down the winner and loser for Alex. She'd be sorry she missed it.

Seated again, he glanced at his watch. Remembering that Earle hadn't yet returned his phone call, he picked up his phone and called him again to let him know that Alex was back and their plan to get her evaluated could now move forward. After five or six rings, the doctor's voice mail answered, so Leo left a brief message asking the doctor to return his call, whatever the hour, and hung up. Turning back to the television, Leo set his cell phone to vibrate only, and dropped it into his shirt pocket.

***

The next thing Leo knew, the late movie was on and his shirt was vibrating, startling him out of a sound sleep. He fumbled the phone out of his pocket, stood and walked quickly out to the shop, answering it along the way.

"Hello?"

"Hello, Leo, this is Earle. I do hope it isn't too late, but I thought that Alex would certainly be asleep by now."

Leo glanced at his watch. "It's one A.M. I had no idea you were such a night owl, Earle."

"I'm not, my boy. I set my alarm clock and have been awake for exactly thirty seconds."

"You don't sound sleepy at all."

"A doctor trick. One learns to fall asleep immediately when going through internship, whether it's in a bed or a hospital gurney in the emergency room hallway. It's an ability that remains long after twenty-hour shifts are a faded memory."

Leo laughed. "I won't keep you long. Did you get my earlier message?"

"Yes, I did, I apologize for not returning your call before now. Jack Henderson, my psychiatrist friend, will be at my office tomorrow morning at eight o'clock. I'll call you on your house phone at seven—will you be up?"

"Yes."

"Good. You can tell Alex the story we agreed upon, then come to the office to pick Jack up around nine, all right?"

"Great. I can't tell you how much this means to me, Earle," Leo said.

"We do what we can, dear boy, we do what we can. See you later," Earle said, softly hanging up the phone.

Leo folded up his phone and went to bed.

For the first time in a long time, he didn't bother to look across the way at the abandoned house.

If he had, he would have seen that the lights were on.

Chapter Fifty

Alex and Leo were enjoying a breakfast of sausage links, potato pancakes with sour cream, and a breakfast radish salad when the phone rang.

"I'll get it," Leo said, standing.

"No, you finish your breakfast. I'll go," Alex said. "Pretty early for a phone call."

When she answered the phone, her face instantly brightened. "Hi there!" She mouthed 'Dr. Munson' to Leo, who did his best to look surprised. He was glad that she'd answered the phone; now he wouldn't have to lie to her again—she'd get the story from Earle.

"What's that? No, not really. Pretty much hanging around the house. Why?"

Another lie on the way, Leo thought miserably.

"Well, I don't see why not. Let me check with Leo, though. Hang on." Alex put her hand over the mouthpiece. "Dr. Munson has a friend in town who's thinking about moving to Woodhaven. Feel like doing a tour and having a stranger to lunch?"

Leo smiled. "It's okay with me."

Alex returned her attention to the phone. "That would be fine, Dr. Munson. We'd be glad to show him around. And if he'd be interested in cold salmon and hot German potato salad, he's got a deal for lunch, too."

A pause.

"He does? Oh, good. What's his name?" Alex asked. "All right. See you soon." She replaced the receiver.

"Did you know that we're his only patients who live in Woodhaven? Alex asked.

"Seems kinda odd, doesn't it?"

Alex shrugged. "Everything about this town seems kinda odd. Oh, well. We have to pick this guy up at nine at Dr. Munson's office, so we've still got plenty of time to finish breakfast. More coffee?"

"Please. What's his name, this fellow?" Leo asked, in an effort to pretend he didn't already have all this information.

"Jack Henderson."

"Does he have a family?"

"I don't know anything more about him than his name at this point. I guess we'll find out later, huh?" she said, spearing a piece of sausage. "It'll be fun. I like meeting new people and it would be nice to know someone else in town," she said. *Someone besides the Mertzes, that is.* The thought made her shiver.

"You cold?"

"Goose walked over my grave," she replied, with a wink.

***

For some reason, all the way to Earle's office, Leo kept picturing Dr. Henderson as looking like Howie Morris when he played a Viennese art appraiser on the old *Dick van Dyke Show*—sort of a Sigmund Freud caricature with a hokey Austrian accent. He knew that Alex would tumble to their plan right away if he gave off "doctor" vibes even slightly.

And if she figures it out… Leo pushed the thought away. The consequences of that were too black to examine.

"So where shall we take him—on the tour, I mean?" Alex asked, jolting Leo back to the present.

"Let's see. What are the points of interest in town?"

"The Pomperaug and the Weekeepeemee," Alex said, naming the two rivers in the area. "Did you know that 'Weekeepeemee' means 'twisting and turning' in Pagasett or Pootatuck, I forget which."

"Pagasett or Pootatuck?"

"The Indian tribes who lived here in the 1600s," Alex explained.

"Since when did you become such a historian?"

"Since you bought us the computer. I can pretty much find out about anything I want."

"So what does 'Pomperaug' mean?"

"'Town of huge vegetables that taste like shit.'"

Leo chuckled. "As appropriate as that is, I have a feeling you're funnin' me, girlie. What does it really mean?"

"It's the name of the Pagassett chief that sold the town to the settlers."

"Then where do the Pootatucks come in?"

"As nearly as I can figure out, the town had to be resold to the settlers later by the Pootatucks on some technicality or other."

"This is good. We have two rivers and some town history. What else?" Leo asked.

"I guess if he's going to live here, we should show him where to shop for groceries, clothes, hardware, and stuff like that."

"But we don't even shop here, Alex. We go to Southfield."

"Let's just show him where things are and let him make up his own mind."

"Fine. Rivers and shopping. Check. What else?"

"There's a bowling alley on the other side of town, Willy's Ice Cream, and Canfield's Corner pharmacy. If he's Catholic and religious, he'll have to go to Southfield. There are no Catholic churches in this town—only Protestant. They probably still call them 'Papists' here."

Leo laughed. "Typical old New England community."

"Oh, and let's not forget all the antique shops."

"Right. I have a feeling that whenever somebody dies in this town, a new antique shop opens up."

"There's also Dr. Orbon, as long as you get sick at night, and Harry Wang's. We could take him up Grassy Hill Road, if you want—it's pretty up there. I don't know if he has kids or not, but if he does, he'll probably want to know where the schools are." Alex paused. "He'll need to know where the Post Office is, too."

"I think it would be safe to just point it out as we drive by as fast as possible. He wants to explore that piece of magic, he can do it on his own," Leo said.

They lapsed into silence, remembering their box rental experience.

***

The Woodhaven Post Office was the first place they went after they signed their lease. It was a squat brick building that was located about five hundred yards from their new home, so they walked over to rent a box, since they lived too close to the Post Office for their mail to be delivered.

It had appeared to be closed—the interior lights turned down to minimal illumination. But they tried the door anyway, and it opened, so they entered. To their left was the typical wall bank of windowed combination mail boxes; to their right, another glass door with a deserted counter on the other side. Concluding that the counter personnel were off sorting mail or taking a bathroom break, they opened the glass door and walked in, prepared to wait. The interior of the shadowy post office was ghost-town silent, and exuded an off-putting musty odor similar to a dirty, wet dog.

"Hello?" Alex called, hoping no one would answer.

No one did.

They looked at each other. Leo shrugged. It only took a fraction of a second, but when they faced forward again, their eyes widened and they backed away a step.

There was now a man standing behind the counter.

He hadn't made a sound on his approach. He stood, motionless, and stared fixedly at them, without a word. There was not much remarkable about him—he was of average height, of spare build, with a head shaped like a light bulb topped with receding fine, dark brown hair, clipped short. His only arresting feature was his eyes. They were deep brown, small, and set so far back into his head that his brow resembled an awning. The bloodshot orbs were surrounded by raccoon-like circles so dark that it looked as if he hadn't slept in a year. His skin was the unhealthy color of parchment, and he exuded a resinous odor.

Recovering somewhat, Leo had the presence of mind to glance at the man's name tag. "Uh, good afternoon, Mister... Darling."

"Hi," Alex said, "Are you the Postmaster?"

Darling swiveled his eyes in Alex's direction, but they stopped before they quite made it, as if they were too tired to reach their destination.

"Yes," he said hollowly, staring at the institutional green wall that was visible between Alex and Leo.

"Um, we just moved into town and we'd like to rent a box," Leo said.

The Dale Carnegie graduate behind the desk reached down and withdrew a form without taking his eyes off the spot on the wall or moving any other part of his body. The parts he did move operated in slow motion which, under normal circumstances, would have irritated Leo; but today, any comment withered on his tongue.

"Small, Medium, Large?" Darling inquired of the green paint. His voice sounded rusty from disuse.

Leo made a Robert Goren of *Law & Order CI* signature move by bending ninety degrees sideways in an effort to redirect the Postmaster's gaze.

"A small one will be fine," Leo replied, filling the man's field of vision and forcing him to finally look at him. After more interminable slowness, the box was finally assigned, paid for, and the combination handed over.

"The mail is up by two o'clock. If you get a parcel, I will put a note in the box."

"Thank you," Leo said, turning to leave.

The peculiar official continued to stare at the place where Leo had been, as if unaware that he was no longer there.

They hustled into the lobby.

"What's our box number?" Alex asked.

"Dunno." Leo shuffled through the paperwork and looked up, confused. "One."

"One? How can that be? Having box number one is a point of pride and bragging rights in these New England towns. It shows who's been here the longest."

"Maybe the patron who had it died. Do you want to go back in there and ask Mr. Personality for an explanation?"

"Let's go look at our box," Alex said.

It wasn't hard to find, being nestled in the top left corner of the wall of boxes. Leo shuffled through the papers until he found the combination. "12 left, 15 right, 13 left."

"Bad number, Leo. It adds up to 41, which is a numerological five," Alex said, shaking her head.

"Now wait a minute. 12 plus 15 plus 13 is 40, not 41. You're one short."

Alex pointed to the front of their new mail box.

"Want to go ask for a different box?"

Alex looked at the now deserted counter and seriously considered it for a moment, but at last shook her head.

"Somebody once told me that change isn't necessarily a bad thing," Leo said. To be sure the combination worked, he spun the dial and opened the box, which contained a pile of first class dust.

"If the previous renter died, it looks like their ashes were scattered in their damned mail box," Alex observed.

Leo smiled at her and pulled a clean handkerchief from his pocket, intending to wipe it out. When he turned back to the box he was, once again, startled by the Postmaster. His eye filled the other end of their open box as he pressed his face against the back opening and peered through at Leo.

"Is everything... all right?" he asked. His voice was flat and uninflected, so the question came out sounding like a statement.

"Yes, fine," Leo replied, once his heart decided to remain in his chest. "Uh, just out of curiosity, who had this box before us?"

"No one." The eye, an uninhabited island in a sea of pale skin, continued to stare.

"Oh… well, thanks," Leo said, gently closing the box.

Even after the box was closed, Postmaster Darling continued to stare through the back of it. The Renfields beat a hasty retreat.

Outside once again, Alex was indignant. "How can that box never have been assigned?"

"Maybe they assign them in reverse order here, so that box number one would be the last box to go," Leo hazarded, not believing a word of it.

"I guess that's possible, but I don't think it's true, do you?" Alex said.

"Not really."

"Leo, did you look through the little windows on any of the other boxes?"

"No. Why would I do that?"

"I guess I'm just nosier than you are, because I did, and I didn't see any mail in any of them."

"Yeah, that is pretty weird. Maybe we should go back and talk to this guy," Leo said, reaching for the door handle.

"Oh, please, no! It gives me the creeps just to think of that zombie handling our mail. I really don't want to talk to him anymore. Oh, and Leo? If you're going to order anything, be sure it's delivered by UPS or FedEx. I know I could lead a happy and fulfilling life without ever stopping at that front counter again. Where do they find people like that? I guess to pass a civil service exam around here all you have to be able to do is breathe."

Leo truly hoped Postmaster Darling at least met that qualification. "Did you hear him walk up to the desk? I didn't."

"No. And the floor back there is all tile, did you notice? We should have heard footsteps," Alex said.

"Maybe he was wearing gum-soled shoes or sneakers."

"Gum soles squeak on tile, Leo. Sneakers do, too, if you don't pick up your feet—and if he picked up his feet, we certainly would have heard him."

"Then I have no answer."

Alex made a mental note to collect the mail daily so that the box would never be so full as to necessitate a trip to the counter. *Also because I can't stand the idea of calling him Postmaster* Darling*!*

***

"Yeah, let's skip the Post Office," Alex said, emerging from her reverie with a shudder. "I think we've covered everything. If he wants to go to the movies or clubbing, he'll have to do it out of town. Dr. Munson said he's down from Boston. I hope he's not expecting too much."

"If he likes a quiet life, though, this is the place for him," Leo said, pulling into Earle's parking lot. *I have to remember not to call him Earle today.*

Right on time, they rang the bell and opened the door.

"Back here—in the office!" the doctor called.

They threaded their way back and upon arrival, discovered Starbuck's coffee and a selection of doughnuts from the Southfield bakery, *Yeast of Eden*, waiting for them. Dr. Munson already had his coffee and a cruller in hand and greeted them with a warm smile.

"Oh, isn't this nice," Alex said, accepting the proffered coffee. She looked over the doughnut selection and chose a Boston Cream. Leo snagged a jelly doughnut and they took the two vacant chairs by the doctor's massive desk.

"Where is your… oh, there you are. Hello. I'm Alex Renfield and this is my husband, Leo. You must be Jack."

Jack Henderson, Leo was relieved to see, in no way resembled a Viennese Howie Morris. He looked more like a favorite uncle, with a round face and a rounder body. He had an open, kindly expression that appealed to Leo and no doubt stood him in good stead with his patients. He was clean shaven, and what was left of the hair on his head was a monk-like tonsure, a dignified gray at the temples, and black elsewhere. He looked about as much like a psychiatrist as Santa Claus did.

Henderson stood, smiling, and extended his hand to Alex.

297

"That's me. I really appreciate your going out of your way like this—and for someone you don't even know. How unusual in this day and age." He shook Alex's hand, then Leo's. "Hello, Leo. Again, thank you for this."

"Glad to help," Leo said sincerely.

Settled into their chairs, Alex searched his face and asked, "Do I know you? You look very familiar to me."

"Oh, I don't think so. I seem to have that kind of face though—everybody thinks they know me from somewhere," Jack said.

"Except that I remember faces, and I know I've seen you somewhere before," Alex said. "So what do you do, Jack?"

Henderson smiled. "I'm a printer."

Alex shook her head, an amused smile on her lips. "I don't think so."

Leo and Earle were sure the game was up, but Jack's gentle smile never faltered. "And why don't you think so?"

"Your hands are all wrong, for one thing. The way you shook our hands, just clasping the fingers above the knuckles, tells me you have arthritis, and shaking hands in the usual way would be painful for you. Additionally, your hands are soft, moist and don't appear to be very strong. When I was working as a proofreader in a print shop, I saw what printers' hands looked like—muscular, dry, and cracked from moving paper around all day. The paper took every bit of natural oil out of their skin, no matter how much Corn Husker's they used. Finally, your hands are clean. Printers hands always have traces of ink on them."

Leo and Earle expected Jack to come as clean as his non-printers hands were and blow their whole scheme to bits. Instead, he sat back in his chair, looking pleasantly surprised.

"Very good, Alex. You're quite observant, and though you are correct about my arthritis, the hands you have described are those of a *pressman*. I said I was a printer."

"What's the difference?" Alex asked.

Jack winked at her. "I own the place."

Alex laughed and Leo and Earle relaxed. "You got me

there," she said. "What kind of presses do you have?"

Leo prayed that this guy knew enough about printing to fool her.

"We're a smallish house. A couple of Heidelberg six colors and a Miller two color."

"So you do books, then?" Alex asked, though it was more of a statement.

"That's right. And how did you divine that?" Jack asked.

"You referred to your business as a 'house.' That means book publishing. A commercial printer would have called it a 'shop'."

This is actually a good thing that's going on here Leo thought. *He's finding out right away that Alex is no fool and listens very carefully. He won't be able to put one by her easily.*

"Do you have a bindery in-house?" Alex asked.

"Oh, yes. Small staff, though."

"What sorts of books?"

"We're a vanity press. You pay, we print. It's surprisingly lucrative," Jack said.

"You've come to the right place, then. I don't believe you have any competition here. At least, I've never noticed a printer in town," Alex said.

"Young lady, if you haven't noticed it, then I'm quite confident that there isn't one," Jack chuckled.

"Want to scout a potential location this morning?" Alex asked, sipping her coffee.

"That sounds fine."

"Do you have a family, Jack?" Leo asked.

"Am I married with children, you mean? Alas, no. I'm on my own."

Leo wondered if that was true or if it was part of the persona the psychiatrist had adopted for the day.

Earle had been quiet throughout the conversation, content to watch and listen. After a bit more small talk, everyone had finished both coffee and pastry and it was time to go.

As they stood, Alex smiled at Dr. Munson. "Oh, Doctor, I meant to tell you the last time we were here that I think your desk is one of the most beautiful pieces I've ever seen."

The doctor, ever proud of his desk, said, "Why, thank you, Alex. I'm very proud of it."

"As you should be," Alex agreed. "I've never seen a desk made from Cocobalo before. Well, see you later."

She and Leo headed out. Dr. Munson hung his head and laughed quietly through his nose. When the Renfields were out of earshot, he said, "A quick word, Jack?"

"I'll be right with you," Jack called to Alex and Leo. Then he turned back to his colleague. "What is it?"

"Make sure I get your bill for today."

"For everything?"

"Everything," Dr. Munson replied, absently stroking his desk.

Chapter Fifty-One

Following a drive through their odd hamlet that covered all the hot spots *except* the Post Office, the tour concluded at the Renfields' house on Judson Avenue.

While Alex prepared lunch, Leo and Jack sat at the kitchen table. "So what do you think of our town?" she asked Jack.

Jack thought for a moment. "Actually, I'd be more interested in hearing what you think of it, Alex," he said.

Alex chuckled. "Turning a question back to the one who asked it. You'd make a good psychiatrist, Jack."

The moment the words were uttered, Alex's smile faded and she bowed her head. When she looked up again, her eyes were brittle with fury.

Jack's face fell.

She smiled tightly at him. "Gotta admit, you had me going, Doctor. Is 'Jack Henderson' even your real name?"

Jack returned her hostile smile with a sad one of his own. "Yes, it is." Then he turned to Leo. "It would appear that our convivial time together has come to an end. Would you mind driving me back to Dr. Munson's office? I do apologize to you both, for different reasons. I've never been very good at subterfuge. You have no idea what a great pleasure it was to meet you, Alex. I'll be outside whenever you're ready, Leo."

After Jack left the kitchen, Alex searched Leo's face with tear-filled eyes. The pain of her perceived betrayal made her look smaller, somehow—smaller and vulnerable—like her best friend had just bitten her on the leg.

"Alex, honey, if you'll just…"

"Get him out of here… right now," she whispered, looking away.

"Come with us? Please?"

"I'm not planning to commit suicide while you're gone, if that's what you're worried about," she said.

"But..."

"Just go."

When Leo pulled out of the driveway, Alex rushed to the bathroom and vomited until she was too weak to do anything but curl up on the tile floor and go to sleep.

***

Neither man said a word most of the way to Munson's office. Finally, it was Leo who spoke.

"Don't blame yourself, Jack. I, for one, think it's great that you're not good at this kind of nonsense—you'd be the psychiatrist I'd go to because of it. I just wish Alex would have given you a chance."

Jack heaved a sigh pregnant with regret. "At this point, all I'm hoping is that I didn't just ruin your marriage."

Leo looked grim. He hoped not, too. "It was probably a bad idea from the get-go."

"She has a wonderfully quick mind."

"That she does. She was a popular stand-up comic."

"Yes, I know," Jack said. "It isn't every day one gets to meet Alex Bluestone."

"Oh, she told you?"

"No. I've seen her perform in Boston. I'm a very big fan of hers. I've caught her act and all its iterations twenty or thirty times at least. Each time she appeared at the Comedy Connection at Faneuil Hall, I got tickets for every show, front and center. And you married her, you lucky dog. I had my eye on her myself, you know," Jack said, eyes twinkling.

"No kidding!" Leo hoped that after today she wouldn't suddenly be available again for somebody else's eyes. "She has a terrific memory for faces. I'm surprised she didn't place you."

"Oh, I imagine she probably will if she chooses to think about it. I looked familiar, at least. She'll figure it out sooner or later," Jack said.

"Tell you what, Jack. You give me your address, and when all this blows over, I'll send you an autographed picture of her. I know she's still got a stack of publicity shots around somewhere. After she calms down and I tell her what a fan you are, she'll be happy sign a photo for you, believe me," Leo said.

"I'll look forward to that. And I'd also enjoy it if, the next time you find yourselves in Boston, you'd allow me to take you both out to dinner and a show afterward… perhaps at the Comedy Connection? Alex could see who's not nearly as funny as she is these days. Is she still killing the people?"

Leo laughed at the show biz terminology. "Not anymore."

"Good heavens, why not? I just assumed she'd switched circuits. I had no idea she'd stopped performing."

"I don't know. She doesn't talk about it."

"Tsk. A great loss to comedy," Jack said.

"But dinner and a show is a definite date."

"Good." Jack jotted his home address and phone number on the back of his business card and Leo tucked it into his shirt pocket. "And please tell her again how sorry I am."

"She'll be fine, don't worry," Leo said. He was worried, though—enough for the both of them. He didn't want an autographed head shot to be all he had of Alex, too.

They pulled into Dr. Munson's lot. Leo stopped the truck and turned to Jack. "Before you go, Jack, what did you think?"

"You mean about Alex's condition?"

"Yes."

"It can be difficult to diagnose in just a couple of hours. If she's in early stage schizophrenia, she won't exhibit symptoms constantly, so a pinpoint diagnosis could take weeks or even months sometimes. In early stage, she'll have more good days than bad. To just go by today, there doesn't appear to be anything wrong with her. But I'll tell you what I'll do—I'll give Earle the name and dosage of a good, non-sedating medication that would be appropriate if she's inherited her mother's problem. If she begins seeing things again, if those night visitors… what did she call them?"

"The Mertzes."

"Ah, yes, a flavor of the sixties. At any rate, if Fred and Ethel show up again, call Dr. Munson for the prescription. Have her take it for a while and if it helps, we'll go from there, all right?"

"Sounds good." Leo leaned forward and took his checkbook out of his back pocket. "What do I owe you, Jack?"

"Nothing. Before we left the office this morning, Earle told me to send my bill to him."

"Well, that's not right. Come on. I'll walk in with you."

The office was bustling with activity. Phones were ringing, people were standing at the desk waiting to sign in, patients in the waiting room were chatting sociably, and Sally, Dr. Munson's nurse-slash-receptionist, was doing her level best to keep everything humming right along.

"Are you a new patient?" she asked Jack when he and Leo reached the head of the line.

"Oh, no," he said. "I'm a colleague of Dr. Munson's, down from Boston. I have to leave and I'd very much like a quick word with him before I go," Jack said.

"Would you be Jack, then?"

"Yes, that's right."

"He told me to expect you. And you're in luck, because he's due to take his fifteen minute lunch break right about now. If you'd like to follow me, please?" Sally led them to Earle's closed office door and tapped softly, then stuck her head in to announce his guests.

"Just go right in," Sally said, holding the door open for them.

Earle looked up from his newly-unwrapped tuna on rye with a dill pickle spear and big pile of chips. "Am I safe in assuming that this rapid turnaround does not bode well?"

"In spades," Leo said, flopping down dejectedly in the nearest chair. Jack sat too, and recapped the morning.

Earle sighed heavily. "Would you like me to speak with her, Leo? The whole scheme was my idea, after all."

"Probably not right now, Earle. She's none too happy with

any of us," Jack answered for Leo.

"Is this going to make her worse?" Leo asked the two men. "Doesn't stress cause it to act up?" Leo just couldn't bring himself to say 'schizophrenia.'

"It certainly can," Jack said, "but it's fairly unlikely in very early stages. When was the last time she saw the Mertzes?"

"About ten days ago."

"Nothing since?"

"Nothing she's mentioned."

"Any deep depressions, dramatic mood swings?"

"No."

"Hmmm. I'm going to revise what we talked about earlier, Leo. If our good country doctor here will write you out a prescription for olanzapine…"

"What is that the generic of, Jack?"

"Zyprexa."

"I can do better than that," Dr. Munson said. "I have a closet full of samples of Zyprexa, and the rep leaves more every time he comes. So I'll start you with a thirty-day supply and you can just stop by here and pick up more whenever you need them."

"I'll need enough for the whole summer, Earle. We're starting a big job on May thirteenth, and we're going to be living on the premises with no wheels. Won't be back until September first."

"With the bag of samples I have, I'm sure I can cover four months for you," Earle replied.

"Oh, this is good news, Earle," Jack exclaimed. To Leo, he said, "It's very effective, but it's also very expensive, even in the generic form. I find it amazing that we have the finest medical care and pharmaceuticals in the world, but then we turn around and price them so that they're unaffordable for the citizenry."

"Wow. That's the first time I've ever heard a doctor say that," Leo said.

"Oh, I've felt that way for quite some time," Jack said.

"What Jack isn't telling you, Leo, is that, though he's very well known and very busy, he charges on a sliding scale, so the rich folks from Back Bay, who just want somebody to complain to about breaking a nail or a sweat, pay more so that the hard working people with no health insurance can be treated for minimal or no payment. He leads a pretty modest lifestyle compared to most psychiatrists," Earle laughed.

Jack laughed, too. "I don't need very much, and selfishly, it makes me feel great about myself to do what I do."

Leo smiled. These were definitely two of the good guys.

"But back to the Zyprexa. Earle, if you'll jot down dosage?" Jack directed.

Earle grabbed a pen and blank pad. "Shoot."

"One by mouth daily. Let's start with five milligrams for the first five days, then up it to ten milligrams once a day. It's going to take a week or two before the Zyprexa builds up in her system enough to notice a change. Alex won't feel anything, but her thoughts will clear up, and she'll stop hallucinating and hearing voices. If she's unreasonably fearful, that should go away, too, and she'll have more energy. Keep in mind, though, that once she starts on these, she can't just stop them, even if she feels better. Understand, Leo, that if she's schizophrenic, she'll have to be on medication for the rest of her life. Schizophrenia, unfortunately, is not curable, only manageable. If these pills work, problem solved. If not, there are other things we can try; but let's jump off that bridge when we come to it," Jack said.

"And how do you suggest I get her to take them?" Leo asked.

"If you'll permit me just one more idea?" Earle asked.

They both looked at him.

"How about if I remove the tablets from their sample packs and put them in an empty prescription vial? Then you can tell her that they're antidepressants, which, truthfully, is one of the areas they address, and you could leave schizophrenia out of it. Would that be helpful?"

"I'll take the samples, Earle, but I'm not going to lie to her or even stretch the truth anymore. I intend to go home and tell her everything I know. We're going to have a long talk, after which I will either be sleeping at the Southfield Bed & Breakfast or she'll be willing to try the meds. And I understand, Earle, that all you're trying to do is to find a way to get her well without turning her world upside down in the process, and I'm very grateful, believe me."

"Well said, my boy."

"You have a truly devious mind, Earle," Jack said wryly.

"I blame Arthur Conan Doyle."

"All right, Watson," Jack said.

Earle sighed. "See? I told you," he said to Leo. "I'll get those samples for you, now."

When Earle returned from his supply cupboard and handed over the paper lunchbag stuffed with enough Zyprexa to see them through the summer, Leo shook his hand warmly and said, "Thank you so much. And before I go, what's all this about Jack giving you his bill?"

"Yes. I was mystified by that myself," Jack said.

Earle explained. They all laughed.

"Sally couldn't believe it when I told her somebody finally identified it."

"That's my Alex," Leo said, with pride.

"I have news for the both of you," Jack said. "When I found out that it was Alex Bluestone I was going to be observing, I never had any intention of charging either of you for the privilege, anyway."

"Oh, come on. Jack," Leo cried. "I can afford to pay you... really."

"Nonsense. I would consider it more than enough payment if you, Alex and I could have dinner together at some future date—perhaps in the fall, after your summer job is done."

"And where do you know Alex from, if I may ask?" Earle asked.

Jack looked aghast. "Alex Bluestone is only the funniest

comedienne to grace any stage, anywhere."

"I had no idea," Earle marveled.

"Jack was sweet on her, too," Leo teased.

"My, my, the things I don't know about my oldest friend."

Leo said good-bye and left them divvying up Earle's lunch.

Chapter Fifty-Two

Leo was not looking forward to going home.

He thought about buying a big bouquet of roses for Alex, but then decided she'd probably just use them to beat him to death. He considered playing to her sense of humor, but then figured that she'd just grab something else to beat him to death with. In the end, he opted for the roses. They were softer.

He pulled into their driveway, shut the truck off, and listened to the ticking of the engine for a moment as it cooled. His stomach growled a reminder that he hadn't had lunch, so he picked up the two dozen lavender roses, said a silent prayer, and walked into the house.

"Alex? Honey? I'm home," he called.

No answer.

Alarmed now, he double timed it to the back of the house. Not in the bedroom. Experiencing déjà vu, he knocked softly at the bathroom door. "Alex?"

"What?" She sounded groggy.

Leo turned the knob, expecting it to be locked, and was glad to find that it wasn't. He opened the door to find Alex getting up from the floor, where she'd been asleep for the past hour and a half. He dropped the flowers in the hall and went to help her up. "Honey, what happened?"

"I'm fine, Leo. I got really sick after you left, and I was too weak to move, so I slept here. I feel a little better now."

He held her and she didn't resist—a good sign. "Honey, I can't tell you how sorry everyone is about what happened today. Nobody blames you for being mad, but please realize that we only did what we did to try to help you without upsetting you in the process," Leo said.

"Guess that backfired, huh?" Alex said.

"Do you feel like you could eat something?"

"Maybe just soup for now. There's some Tomato in the pantry."

"All right. I'll make us some lunch and we'll talk to each other like people who still love each other, okay?"

"People who love each other don't do what you did, Leo."

"Sure they do—all the time. Best of intentions, piss poor execution."

Alex smiled at that. "Couldn't have said it better myself."

Leo smiled, too. "I have a bribe for you," he chuckled, picking up the flowers and presenting them to her with a flourish.

Alex accepted them—lavender roses were her favorites—and, smelling them, she said, "Wow, some bribe. You must really be sorry."

"I am, honey. And so are Jack and Dr. Munson. These are from the three of us."

"You make lunch, I'll put the apology in water, and we'll talk—like people who still love each other," Alex said.

Leo's heart sang.

***

Over soup and onion and cheddar sandwiches, Alex seemed less inclined to talk, so Leo jumped in, explaining that he, Jack, and Dr. Munson now knew all about her horrific childhood and all the waking nightmares she'd lived through.

When he finally finished, Alex stared down into her now cold bowl of soup because she was too ashamed to look at him. "Now that you know what kind of craziness I come from, do you want a divorce, Leo?"

"Honey, if I wanted to divorce you, I'd be just as crazy as they were. I love you. And this is not as big a deal as you think it is. If you have what your mother had, it's in its real early stages and we can control it with pills. You'll have to take them for the rest of your life, but so what?"

"Really? There's a pill for this?"

"Sure. Got 'em right there," he said, indicating the paper

bag on the counter. You want to try taking them?"

Realizing that her salvation was as simple as a pill and the relief that came with that realization allowed Alex to finally drop the guard she'd had up for so long and release the dread she's been holding down for decades. She burst into tears. Leo came around the table and held her until the sobbing subsided. If she was willing to take the pills, and it looked as though she was, he was convinced that things would be back to normal soon.

"And as far as your brother goes, Alex," Leo said, "you didn't have anything to do with his death. You were seven years old! It was your mother's and father's craziness that did it. He was six. He needed his mother. His father was supposed to protect him. It was a world that he didn't understand. He was probably afraid and hurting all the time, and just wanted it to stop. It wasn't you who pushed him, Alex."

"I yelled at him when I shouldn't have," she hiccupped, wiping her eyes on a napkin.

"Honey, when anybody, especially a child, decides to commit suicide, it's a decision that's made as a result of a long, unbearable ordeal, not just because somebody yelled at them once. Don't you see that? It was a devastatingly tragic thing, but it was not your fault. If you hadn't been there, he probably would have done it a lot sooner. Or he would have just died of neglect. Or your mother might have killed him. He had you to protect him for however long he lived, and you have to try very hard to find solace in that, sweetie. You need to let go of all this guilt you've been carrying around."

"I have to pay more attention to you, Leo. You get really smart when I'm not looking," Alex said, smiling through her tears. "And you're right in everything you say. You have no idea how debilitating it's been carrying around a hideous secret like that for so many years."

Leo made a decision. "Yeah, Alex, I do. I've got one, too, and I think it's about time you heard it. No more secrets between us."

She blew her nose, then leaned back in her chair. "Okay, if you want to tell me."

Leo hoped he was doing the right thing, and plunged ahead. "You know that my family is gone, but what you don't know is that they died in a house fire that I was responsible for." Leo held up a hand. "Please let me finish before you say anything. Anyway, I was in the middle of fixing our stove—the gas line was leaking—when my mother came into the kitchen to tell me that our dog had just taken a crap in the living room and to ask me why I hadn't walked him. Well, let me amend that. Mom never just 'asked.' Mom 'demanded' at a decibel level that would curdle milk. Here I was trying to save the old man the cost of a plumber, and I just about had it done when the old lady 'asked' about the dog, using a broom handle on me. Now keep in mind that I had just gotten off my after school job packaging and loading concrete mix, it was nine o'clock at night, I hadn't had anything to eat since noon, and my mother was standing over me beating me with a boom handle. So I crawled out from behind the stove and said, 'You want the dog walked, I'll walk the dog, and *you* can fix the stove for all I care' and I grabbed Lefty's leash, whistled for him, and off we went. The problem was, I didn't have the gas line secured as well as I thought, and I guess it got dislodged when I was trying to get out of the way of that broom handle. Lefty and I were two streets away in the park and had been gone about a half hour when my father walked into that miniscule kitchen and lit a cigarette. The whole house went up. Everybody was home at the time... except Lefty and me. And now you know why I can't deal with open flames or dogs."

"Oh, Leo, none of that was your fault, either, honey! But I know exactly how you feel. We've both been carrying around a truckload of guilt over nothing more than being human. I see that now. I was at the end of my rope, and I did something human. I yelled at Siddie. Your mother was beating you over walking a dog when you were hungry, exhausted, and trying to save the family some money. It's no wonder you didn't double-check that line or even see it when it dislodged. You were trying to keep your head from getting knocked off your shoulders. We were both put into untenable positions as kids and expected to behave like Jesus Christ. You do see that, don't you, Leo?"

"Yes, I do now. It's amazing the perspective you get from discussing things. The guilt will take time and effort to get rid of, but I do feel better for having talked about it. How about you?"

"Much better. Maybe we should both make appointments with Jack," Alex said.

"Probably so. In the meantime, we have each other to talk to, right?"

"Always, Leo."

"By the way, have you remembered where you know Jack from yet?" Leo asked.

Alex shook her head. "I've been wracking my brain, but I just can't come up with it."

"Want a hint?"

"You know where I know him from? Then, yeah, gimmie a hint."

"He's from Boston, right? Think 'Comedy Connection.'"

Alex's eyes opened about as wide as her mouth as her memory finally cooperated. "Oh my God. He's 'Front and Center.' Of course!"

"Did he ever get up the nerve to talk to you? And what do you mean, 'front and center?'" Leo asked.

"No, he never said a word to me. He was there at every show, though. I was always hoping that he would introduce himself so I could have an engraved brass nameplate attached to the back of his chair. He was in the same seat every time. I can only imagine what that kind of preferential treatment must have cost him. He sent me flowers backstage a few times, and always signed the card, 'Front and Center.' When I went out onstage, I'd acknowledge them by either waving or nodding and mouthing 'thank you' over the applause, and I guess that was enough for him. He never tried to meet me."

"Too shy, I guess. He didn't mention the flowers. What'd he send?"

"Always Stargazer lilies—a huge bunch of them each time. They smelled wonderful."

"Stargazers for the star he was gazing at, huh? I could get jealous, here… he had a crush on you, you know."

"Well that was pretty obvious. If he had ever introduced himself… who knows? But he didn't." Alex shrugged.

"Would you have been interested if he had?" Leo asked.

"I don't know. Maybe, maybe not. Since he didn't, it's really a moot point, isn't it? Besides, shy men really don't do much for me from the romance standpoint. I tend to intimidate them. I don't mean to, I just do."

"I'm not surprised. You're an extrovert, and that doesn't usually mix too well with 'shy.' I think he's still carrying a torch for you; although now that you're married, it's probably more like a lighter."

"Sounds like you are jealous."

"Not a bit. I think it's really nice, actually—the affection your fans still have for you. Maybe you should think about doing a show now and then," Leo suggested.

Alex smiled. "You can't just 'do a show now and then,' Leo. It's a tremendous amount of work, and if you're not doing it all the time, your popularity drops and nobody wants to hire you. To do it well is to do it full time. There's a reason there are no successful stand-up hobbyists."

"Oh. Well, anyway, Jack wants to take us out to dinner and a show at the Comedy Connection whenever we want. He's sorry to the bone about what happened today, and wants to make it up to you." Leo said.

"He doesn't have to do that. All is forgiven. It isn't necessary for him to take us out."

"He genuinely wants to."

"Okay, then, why not? Hey, maybe we could fix him up with Clara."

"They'd probably get along great," Leo agreed. "But let's wait until her divorce is final first, okay?"

"Who was that jerk she was married to, again?" Alex asked.

"Stan somebody or other," Leo replied. "Oh, hey, I'd

better call Earle and let him know that your plans to mine his flowerbeds are off."

"Since when do you call him 'Earle'?"

"Since we had a boys' night out while you were up in Gloucester… when we concocted today's idiocy."

"Kids!" Alex said, shaking her head. "By the way, what was the bill for today's entertainment?"

"Nothing."

"Can't be."

"Really. You identified the wood Earle's desk is made of."

"So what?"

"So you're the first one to do it."

"And for that there's no charge?"

"No, for that Earle was going to pay Jack's bill. But there wouldn't have been a charge anyway. Jack was so thrilled to finally meet you that he waived his fee."

"So because I can tell one piece of wood from another and can make people laugh, there's no charge?"

"Essentially, yes."

"Too bad I don't sing and juggle, too," Alex said.

"Why?"

"Because then *they* might have paid *us*."

Chapter Fifty-Three

"Will you be okay to work the day after tomorrow?" Leo asked Alex, after a brief phone conversation with a mightily relieved Dr. Munson.

"Sure. I haven't felt this good in a long, long time—maybe never. There's a lot to be said for a sympathetic, non-judgmental ear, but I do want to try the pills."

"I think it's a good idea. You just take one a day. Jack said it'll take a week or two before you notice any difference."

"You know, in a way, I'm glad we're staying at the Hamiltons'," Alex said.

"How come?" Leo was breaking the Zyprexa out of its blister packs and into a small empty green glass jar that formerly held capers. Alex saved everything.

"Would you really want to be riding back and forth in Lucifer's Limo every day?"

"No. I'd really rather be riding back and forth in my truck every day," Leo said.

"Well, that won't be happening," Alex said.

We'll just see about that…

***

The Renfields spent the thirty-six hours getting the house ready for their three-and-a-half-month extended absence. Since they didn't know anyone the in area, Leo called Manny and asked him if he'd mind stopping by once a week to give Alex's plants a good drenching. He offered him payment, but Manny declined and said it would be his privilege to water Alex's plants for her. He also told Leo that he was so inspired by the story of how he met Alex that he'd gone home and signed up for Yahoo Personals himself. He explained that he'd done a lot of thinking and, now that his mama was gone, he missed having a lady in his life, and it was about time he got married and started that tiling business he and Leo talked about.

"Maybe when the summer's over, we can go out on a double date with you and your new girlfriend," Leo said.

"Sounds like a plan. I'll probably find somebody in three months, doncha think?"

"Manny, a nice guy like you, I don't think it will even take that long." He rang off with a promise to call when they returned home.

Alex was on food detail, and spent time cleaning out the refrigerator and making sure all the food in the pantry was buttoned up tightly enough to discourage any rodents or bugs that might decide to stroll through the uninhabited house looking for a snack.

When she had the kitchen taken care of, she moved on to the bedroom to get their packing done. She'd never had to pack for a three-month stay before. Even when she was on the road doing stand-up, she was never gone for more than a couple of weeks at a time. However, assuming that there was a washer and dryer somewhere on the premises, she let go of the temptation to pack the whole closet, and limited items to one week's worth of work clothes, three changes of nice casual clothes, a week of socks and underwear, two sweatshirts and a couple of cotton sweaters. She paused, mid-fold, when an image of that house oozed into her mind. The resulting shiver urged Alex to include one heavy wool sweater, as well; even though summer was rapidly approaching.

Somehow, the idea of warm summer weather didn't fit with that house at all.

Shaking off her gloomy reverie, Alex placed her open, packed suitcase across the room on the floor. Then she wrote a checklist of the last minute things, like her toothbrush, hair dryer, and items of that ilk, and laid it across her folded clothes. It was a foolproof way to keep from running off without something vital, as long as the list was complete.

Make-up was not on Alex's list. When they reviewed their contract at home, they discovered that make-up and perfume was prohibited, that appropriate substitutes for her usual products would be provided, and that neither of them was to arrive at the house wearing deodorant, hair care products, or skin cream.

"No deodorant!" Alex had exclaimed at the time. "What the hell am I supposed to do, put a bay leaf under each arm and hope I smell like stew?"

"It's only until we get there. Then we can take another shower and use what they give us," Leo had said.

Next, Alex packed for Leo, and left his case open next to hers. Leo always made his own "last minute items" list.

They spent the balance of the dwindling time before reporting to the Hamiltons' Carpenter Gothic cleaning their Cape Cod until it shone.

Chapter Fifty-Four

May thirteenth finally arrived and Alex dragged their two packed suitcases out to the porch, then returned to the bedroom and filled her canvas briefcase with her journal, a dozen yellow lined legal pads, and another dozen of the black pens she favored. She was looking forward to spending her off hours either reading or writing in the library in front of a roaring fire.

Then she thought of Leo.

Perhaps not a roaring fire, then, but maybe now he'd be willing to try a small one. Oh, and that kitchen! She could tell that Leo was just itching to do some cooking in there.

All in all, it was shaping up to be a fine summer—easy work, big money, a larder full of food; and at the end of all of it, enough money to begin house shopping. *But not in Woodhaven*.

Alex was roused from her musings by Leo shouting from the kitchen.

"Hon? Limo's here!"

Alex picked up her bag and on the way through, she stopped briefly at one of the bookcases, where she grabbed two essential writing books: Robert McKee's *STORY* and *Words into Type*. She was sure that there'd be a dictionary in their library, so she left hers behind.

"All ready for camp?" she asked Leo brightly when she joined him. "I did a full-blown Niagara on the plants outside."

"I saw that. It looks like you flooded the whole yard."

"Manny probably won't have to come by too often, since it rains so much around here. And it looks like it's just about to start," Alex said, peering up at the now overcast sky.

The sky became darker still as they left their house and faced the funereal Cadillac. The driver's door creaked open and Cooper Black disembarked with as much dignity as his awkward little frame allowed, then walked to the rear and popped the trunk. He stepped to the side, silently waiting and staring straight ahead.

Leo lugged the suitcases out to the black limousine and set them down next to the trunk. Then he retraced his steps, locked up the house, and opened the workshop door that faced the driveway. *He'll never fit our suitcases and all this stuff into that trunk; I don't care how big it is. I'll be able to bring my truck after all.*

Cooper Black effortlessly lifted the two suitcases and Alex's briefcase into the trunk, much to Alex's amazement. She and Leo had struggled with them and this little person hoisted them up as if they were paper bags filled with feathers.

Leo put the first load of his equipment on a hand truck and wheeled it out to the driveway. Black stopped him with a raised hand and a slow shake of his enormous head.

Leo looked at Alex. "How the hell do we communicate with this guy?"

"Wait a sec." She reached into the trunk and pulled out a pen and a pad. "Let's hope he can read English," Alex said, and wrote:

We need that to do our job!

Black focused on the words as though he were examining a decomposing frog, then looked up at Alex and shook his head again.

"Okay, let's try this." She wrote:

Is everything we need already at the house?

Again, the dead frog look, but then he closed his eyes and slowly nodded.

"The good news is that he reads English, Leo. The bad news is that you can't take anything—it's all there already. I guess your ploy to bring the truck is shot. Sorry."

"I know that's what Theodora said, but I can't believe that she thought of everything," Leo retorted.

"He's not going to let you bring it, hon."

Black reached up and grabbed a strap, no doubt specially installed for his convenience, and pulled the trunk closed. He moved past Alex to open the door while Leo trudged back to the shop with the loaded hand truck, happy, at least, that he managed to get his favorite hand tools past Black by packing them in with his clothing.

Black stood by the rear door until Leo locked the workshop and joined his wife in the back seat. Once aboard, the door slammed they were plunged in darkness. Alex reached over and took Leo's hand. "Sorry about your truck, hon. It was a good try."

"I really hate being without wheels."

"But why would you need them? Everything's there. And think of the amazing meals we can make. And all those miles of books in the library. It's going to be the best summer ever—it'll break all previous records," Alex said.

"Who are you trying to convince, me or you?" Leo grumbled.

Alex sighed. "Me, I guess. It's a creepy goddamn place, Leo."

"I know. Let's just get this job done as soon as possible. We work all six hours that we're allowed to work per day with no breaks except for bathroom, okay?"

"I'm all for that," Alex replied with a yawn.

Within seconds, they were both sound asleep.

***

About the last thing Leo wanted to open his eyes to was psycho munchkin shaking him roughly by the shoulder.

"Okay, okay, I'm awake!" he said, shrugging off the unwelcome hands. "Alex, we're here," Leo said, patting her leg.

"Oh." Through force of habit, she looked at her watch, only to discover that it had stopped, just like the last time. Surprise, surprise.

They piled sleepily out of the black nightmare and retrieved their suitcases from the trunk. Their diminutive driver closed it up, then pointed at the front door of the house.

"I think he wants us to go inside," Leo said.

"What kind of a hotel is this, anyhow? We have to carry our own bags? Ohhhh, Travelocity shall hear of this, my friend. This dump will lose at least two stars," Alex said.

Leo looked over his shoulder at Cooper Black, who was standing there glaring at them. "It's a good thing he can't hear you. I don't think he likes guests as it is."

Once they started walking toward the house, Black got back in the Caddy, turned it around, and drove down a pathway that they hadn't noticed previously, and into the woods that extended off to the far left of the expansive yard. He soon disappeared from view.

"S'pose the garage is down that way?"

"A garage... or a big cage," Alex said, shifting her briefcase strap from her hand to her shoulder. "A really big cage."

"Where's the sign, though? I don't see the sign."

"What sign?" Alex asked.

"The one that says, 'I'd turn back, if I were you'."

"I don't know. I'm busy checking the sky for 'Surrender Dorothy.'"

The engine noise of the Caddy died away to be replaced by an uncanny stillness, the like of which they had never experienced, causing them both to stop and unconsciously strain to hear something... anything. Not a leaf rustled. Not a bird sang or flew past. Alex felt as though she were standing in the middle of a photograph. The woods surrounding the black house were unlovely, dark and deep, and kept secrets rather than promises. The sky was a bilious gray, and couldn't have found a better setting for a thunderstorm. Alex idly wondered if she'd run into Rochester's insane wife in the attic—until she had another, more appropriate thought.

"You know, of course, Leo, that 'no one lives any closer than town. No one will come any nearer than that,'" Alex said. "'In the night. In the dark.'"

"Stop with the *Hill House*, Alex. You're freaking me out!"

"'And whatever walks here, walks alone.'"

Leo shivered. "*The Haunting of Hill House* is the scariest

book I ever read—trust you to use it like *Bartlett's Familiar Quotations.*"

"I think that that book has the best opening paragraph of any book ever written."

"Yeah," Leo agreed, looking up at the house again. "Shirley Jackson probably wrote it right here."

"What do you want to bet there's a copy of it in the library? Probably leather bound."

"I don't make it a habit of betting against a sure thing. Let's get moving. I want to get unpacked and then have a drink before dinner. How about you?" Leo asked, grunting as he hefted the two bags.

"Sounds good," Alex said, then added, "You're no Cooper Black."

"What the hell is that supposed to mean?"

"He lifted those suitcases like they were empty. I guess all his strength is in his upper body."

Leo cursed the heavy suitcases up the front steps. "What did you pack, Alex? A second car?"

She chuckled. "Guess we'll have to wait here for Black. Door's probably locked."

"Why? Who would even think about robbing this place? Take a look around. Who'd want to get close enough?"

"'In the night. In the dark,'" Alex said, with an impish smile.

"At least try the door so we don't look like idiots if it is open."

Alex did and it was. She had to put every bit of her back into overcoming the inertia of the twelve foot solid Macassar ebony front door. When she had it open, Leo chugged through with the bags, which he unceremoniously deposited on the floor in the middle of the front hall.

They stood in the silent foyer. Neither noticed the door closing behind them until it shut with a sonic boom that echoed through the shadow-silent house.

"Doors that close by themselves are not hung properly,"

Leo said, not even flinching.

After Alex peeled herself off the ceiling, she said, "They're going to have to stay that way, then. Can you imagine taking them down and rehanging them? You'd need a crew, a crane, and prayers from the Pope. I guess we should wait here for Cooper to… jeez, I don't like calling him 'Cooper!' It makes him sound like the friendly local barrel-maker and he's anything but!"

"What do you want to call him, then?"

"Just 'Black,' I think. 'Mr. Black' to his face, though, in case he reads lips. Anyway, what I was starting to say was, should we wait for him, or just go ahead and unpack and make ourselves at home? I mean, we do know where our room is. Maybe we should take our luggage and get settled in."

"'Lug' being the operative part of that word," Leo said.

Alex laughed. "How about you just leave the bags in our room and meet me in the library? I'll go to the kitchen and whip us up some preprandial drinks and…"

"Preprandial!"

"It's a perfectly good word that I acquired with considerable effort and personal expense, and have wanted to use on many occasions in many places," Alex said.

"What stopped you?"

"The occasions and places were not perfect enough for the use of such an expensive word. I'd have been frittering it away, and you know how I hate waste."

"So now the time is right, huh? What's so perfect?" Leo asked.

"This huge gothic house shrouded in mystery and slopping over with intrigue? Yes, I'd say it's the perfect place. I may even end up dusting off a few more words from my Bronte vocabulary before we're through here."

"While you're dusting, Charlotte, I think I'm just going to leave the cases right here."

"I don't know, Leo. He might trip over them right there."

"Never happen. They're nearly as tall as he is. Come on."

When they strolled into the library, they were pleased to find a full decanter and a bit less pleased to find a typed note from Theodora, which read:

Dear Leo,

Welcome.

I've taken the liberty of providing you with some Wild Turkey Bourbon, as I understand that this is your celebratory drink of choice. There is a wide variety of libations in the Billiard Room bar, and board games in the Games Closet. Please feel free to help yourselves to whatever you find there. Should you require wine, there is an extensive selection in the basement. The freezer is fully stocked and Cooper will shop for fresh fruit, vegetables, and any other incidentals once weekly, on Saturday morning. Leave a list of anything you require on the kitchen table for him each Friday evening.

In the manila envelope on the tray, you will find $10,000 in cash. I will be releasing additional cash to Cooper when payments are due, and he will see that you get it.

A REMINDER! Do not stray beyond the first floor! And please note that, though you may open the drapes and windows in your own room as you please, kindly refrain from doing so in the Library—the sunlight is damaging to the books, many of which are quite valuable. The rarest editions are locked in an airtight Lucite box on the top shelf of the central bookcase, and though it will keep smoke from the fireplace out, alas, it will not repel sunlight.

Cooper will let you know what time to begin and end your work day. Though there are no working timepieces in the house, Cooper studies the movement of heavenly bodies and as a result, his timekeeping is accurate within a second or two. He was once a ship's navigator, and that is where he acquired this rather astonishing ability.

You may build a fire in any fireplace if you wish—all are clean and safe. I make the offer, though I am aware of your fire phobia, Leo, so build one or not, it is your choice. I just wanted to let you know that you may, because even at the height of summer, it gets very chilly indoors when night falls, for some reason, and the house has no central heating system; so when we are here, we usually get necessary heat from burning the fireplaces. The woodpile is at the left side of the house as you face it from the driveway and is stacked against the outer wall of your bathroom, should you opt for fireplace heat. If not, then I can only hope that you brought enough warm clothing with you.

There is no cellular phone reception either inside or outside of the house. There is a single land line telephone located in the kitchen, should you need it.

The washer and dryer are in the basement, as are all the laundry supplies you will require. Please use only these supplies.

You'll find all your work supplies in the foyer closet.

Have a pleasant summer. And remember that if you do go for a walk, it is imperative that you do not wander off any of the established paths.

Sincerely,

Theodora Hamilton

Alex snorted derisively. "'Dear Leo' of course! What am I? Mugwamp? And how, may I ask, did she know about your problem with fire, when I only just found out about it?"

"Must have been Orbon. He had to draw my blood wearing night vision goggles, I was so panicked by all the candles."

"Oh, right. I forgot how thick she is with him. How unethical, violating patient confidentiality like that. I'm surprised."

"We'll sue him later," Leo chuckled. "Come on, let's get our bags put away. I don't feel right about just leaving them in the middle of the hall anymore." He turned to retrieve the suitcases, but before he could exit the Library, Alex burst out laughing.

"Oh, mother! Get a load of this!"

Leo turned back. "What?"

Alex pointed at a bust on a pink alabaster pedestal. "Know who it is?"

Leo came closer and studied the sculpture. "Damn! He looks so familiar!"

"Remember *Cannonball Run*?"

"No!"

"Oh, yeah."

It was a bust of Dom DeLuise as Captain Chaos.

Leo stared at it. "Actually, that's even creepier than if it was Poe or Dracula or someone like that. It just doesn't fit."

"I know what you mean," said Alex. "Every time I think I have things figured out around here, something else gets tossed into the mix that throws me off balance again. You'd think they'd have a bust of Shakespeare or Beethoven, wouldn't you? As pretentious as they are?"

"Too normal," Leo said. *It doesn't make sense. Theodora is so particular about décor and a less formal room would be a much better place for this—a media room would be perfect; even the kitchen, since he's such a well-known cook. But here? Why?* To Alex, he added, "But yeah, Beethoven or Shakespeare would work better with this room. Or maybe some small but pricey Italian sculptures."

Alex was about to comment about Her Nibs' money fixation when she spied another bust, smaller than Dom's. She walked over to examine it. "This one looks like the guy who played Superman, but in his Clark Kent phase, glasses and all," she said.

"Hey, there's another one over here." Leo got closer. 'Oh, you're gonna love this one."

"Tell me."

"Mel Blanc."

"Got Muggsy Bogues over here, too," Alex said

"Who?" Leo asked.

"Muggsy Bogues—that pro basketball player who's only five feet three inches tall." Alex shook her head as if to clear away the confusion. "What do these people have in common?"

"Why would you assume commonality?" Leo asked.

"There has to be. It's too weird otherwise."

"They're all in entertainment," Leo ventured.

"I don't think that's it, Leo," Alex said, suddenly serious. "I think the *tchotchkes* in this room are a tribute to people and things that aren't what they appear to be. See the painting of the coral snake above the fireplace? Looks harmless, but in reality one of the more deadly snakes. And the botanical print of Oleander next to it? A pretty flower on a fast-growing shrub. Lots of people in warm climates grow them as hedges, but every single part of that plant is poisonous. And finally, the polar bear trophy to the right of the Oleander print. Looks cuddly and cute, but cuddle one of those and you'll be looking for your arms and legs; they're really nasty. And there's a deflated blowfish in Lucite on the bookcase right there. Not a scorpion or a black widow, but a blowfish. When they're deflated like that, it's hard to notice the spines. Strange, isn't it?"

"Not really," Leo replied. "All houses reflect their owners' tastes and interests. And considering what a freak show these homeowners have been so far, you can't tell me you're surprised."

"Not 'surprised,' exactly. Maybe 'disturbed,' would be a better word," Alex replied, a thoughtful expression on her face.

"Why?"

"The subtlety bothers me. It's like a cat with pockets."

Chapter Fifty-Five

"Don't you just love a bedroom you can launch the space shuttle in?" Alex remarked, after getting a good look at their quarters in the light.

Theodora's version of 'small but adequate' accommodations turned out to be a mammoth bedroom containing a carved king size sleigh bed, oriental rugs on the floor, antique gold leaf on the ceiling medallions, and a magnificent fireplace made from large pieces of natural rose quartz set so close together in the pink-tinted mortar that it looked as if the fireplace was made entirely of the semi-precious gemstone. Alex couldn't take her eyes off it.

"Can you just imagine how this would look by firelight?" Alex marveled.

"I've never seen anything like it. It's magnificent," Leo said.

Also in the room, but less to catch the eye as to provide service was a small, minimally stocked bar, a sizeable antique desk made from the same wood as the bed and bar, and an ornate bookcase crammed with contemporary paperbacks.

"You know, I love these pieces individually, but putting them all in one room seems…"

"A bit much?" Leo asked.

"A little gaudy, yeah. I think it's better to have one great piece in a room instead of six or seven all fighting for your attention, don't you?" Alex asked.

"Less has always been more to me. And you're right—one piece should be the star," Leo said. He pointed at the desk. "What kind of wood, oh expert?"

"It's an antique, so it probably isn't exotic. Let's find out." She opened the top drawer and inhaled deeply. "Walnut, I think," she said, closing the drawer. She laid her briefcase gently on the thick piece of beautifully etched glass that protected the desk top, and looked around again. To the right of the bed was a door.

"Hey, look at this," Alex said. "What is that, about eighteen inches wide?"

"Looks that way. If there's a closet in this room, that's probably it. This is an old house, remember. The closet's probably as small as the door."

"Oh, great. Where are we going to put all our clothes?" Alex said as crossed the room to the undersized door. "Not that we have much with us, but I don't think even that is going to fit."

Alex turned the knob and her look of exasperation turned to pleasant surprise. "It's a walk-in, Leo, and it's huge," she exclaimed.

Leo stuck his head inside. "Huh! They must have expanded it. No way was it originally built like this. But why not enlarge the door, too, while you're at it?" He withdrew and said, "I'm gonna hit the head, then make us a couple of drinks. How's that? I'll mix, you unpack," he proposed, stepping into their immense bathroom.

"Deal," More cheery about unpacking now, Alex flipped their bags open on the bed and started sorting.

She heard the toilet flush, followed by running water, followed by, "Oh, honey, you've got to see this."

Abandoning her chore, she stepped into the blindingly white bathroom and noticed something that she hadn't picked up on during Theodora's house tour. "Where's the toilet?"

Leo dried his hands. "Right here," he replied, opening the door near the tub.

"The toilet has a room of its own?"

"Nothin' but class, sweetheart! Stick with me, and I'll have ya fartin' though silk," Leo said, in his best Robert Mitchum.

Alex laughed. "You can take the boy out of Bridgeport, but you can't etcetra. Hey, great. A magazine rack." There were multiple issues of *This Old House*, *Popular Photography*, *Mother Earth News*, *Countryside*, *Writer's Digest*, *Bon Appetit!*,

MAD Magazine, *Hobby Farms* and *Crosswords and Cryptograms*. Alex's face clouded as she flipped through them. "Leo, these are all our favorite magazines, and I was planning to subscribe to *Writer's Digest* this fall."

"Yeah, I know."

"So how did *they* know?" Alex asked.

"Maybe they like those magazines, too." It sounded stupid to Leo even as he said it.

"But there's not one misstep. These are exactly the subjects we read about and enjoy. There's no *Popular Mechanics*, no travel magazines, or the *Robb Report* or *Newsweek*, or anything like that. It's exactly what we read, and that's all. I mean, do these people really strike you as *MAD Magazine* readers? Alex picked up one of the half dozen issues in the rack. "And these *MAD*s are decades old, Leo, way before Bill Gaines died, when the magazine was at its best. They've even provided my favorite era! And while we're at it, how did they know about the Wild Turkey?"

"One of us must have mentioned it," Leo said.

"I know I didn't."

"I must have, then."

"When? When we were here last and Theodora buttonholed you for the whole time?"

"Must have been."

"Magazines, too?"

"Maybe she figured out what we'd like from the subjects we chatted about, I don't know." Leo said.

"Yeah, maybe. I guess it's nice that they've gone to so much trouble to make us comfortable," Alex said with a relieved smile. "You going to fix those drinks, or not?" she asked, stepping back into the bedroom to resume unpacking.

The next sound she heard was Leo clinking ice cubes into Waterford rocks glasses in the Library.

Leo didn't feel anywhere near as relieved as Alex did. He'd gone through the entire magazine rack and knew damned well that he hadn't divulged this or any other kind of personal information to Theodora, pry as she might, and he'd had no intention of pointing out the spot-on reading material to Alex, in the hopes that she wouldn't notice how well selected the periodicals were. He'd just wanted to show her where the toilet was. But notice she did and rapidly got that 'deer-in-the-headlights' look that Leo was coming to recognize, and knowing that stress was the absolute worst thing for Alex right now, he dismissed the issue the way he did. But truthfully, the magazine rack and its contents bothered him more than a little.

Drinks in hand, they settled back into the couch in front of the Brobdingnagian stone fireplace.

"Think maybe you might like to try a fire in the fireplace sometime?" Alex asked.

Leo smiled. "Maybe a little one... later in the summer. I'm not up for it quite yet."

"What time do you suppose it is?"

"No idea, but I bet we can fit in another one of these before dinner," Leo said, hoisting his drink. "What is for dinner, by the way?"

"You don't want to make it? I thought you couldn't wait to get into that kitchen."

"I'll get there eventually. We have all summer. To be honest, I just don't feel like cooking tonight," Leo said.

"Well, since I haven't given it any thought before now, it's probably too late to defrost any meat; but if we have some shrimp in there, I can make some scampi over linguini with a tossed salad and garlic bread. How's that?"

"Sounds great, assuming we have the ingredients," Leo said.

Alex put her drink down on a nearby coaster on the end table. "I'll go check. Want to come?"

"Normally, I would; but I'm just too comfortable to move."

"Relax and enjoy. I'll be right back."

Leo sipped his drink and sighed. *I could get used to this*. He studiously avoided thinking about the reason he had that particular booze in his hand. Instead he glanced around the room, studying the furniture.

He was sitting on what he was sure was a Meeks masterpiece of a rosewood sofa, probably dating back to the mid-1800s. It was upholstered in fuchsia linen and was surprisingly comfortable for a Gothic Revival antique.

The coffee table in front of him was hand carved and also made of rosewood. The top was fine white marble with the cookey corners that were original to the piece. It, too, looked like it came from Meeks & Sons of New York.

Behind him and to the left was a sizeable card and games table; but though it wasn't a Gothic Revival piece, it combined Classical, Gothic and Rococo elements skillfully enough to blend well into the overall room décor. Its fluted legs and stretchers supported two top boards which, Leo knew, would open to form the table top. The pie crust moldings that edged the table, again, reminded Leo of Meeks & Sons work, but, taken as a whole, was more like something Alexander Roux would have come up with.

The pedestals scattered throughout the room were either carved stone or gothic-style carved wood—very heavy and ponderous looking. The wooden ones appeared to be made from oak.

But it was the four armless chairs in the room that were, in Leo's opinion, the most breathtaking. In true Gothic style, they looked as if they had been plucked straight out of a medieval castle, with their sophisticated foliated crockets, center finials and turreted side finials, not to mention the highly detailed, cathedral-like tracery that served as the chairs' backs. The seats were upholstered in deep indigo velvet, and they stood at attention within each of the four corners of the room like sentries on guard duty.

Two comfortable-looking nineteenth century English library armchairs, upholstered in ecru faux crocodile accented with nickel studs were angled into another sitting area at the back of the huge room, the centerpiece of which was an additional sofa that looked like late nineteenth century and, of all the pieces in the room, it was the one that Leo would have taken home with him if offered his choice. The lines were so elegant and graceful that it almost hurt to look at it, and he relinquished his comfortable seat to study it up close.

The wood frame appeared to be bleached cherry, but he wouldn't know for sure unless he had Alex sniff it, and it was well sealed and lacquered, so that wouldn't be happening. The upholstery was, again, linen, but was slate blue and deeply buttoned. It looked inviting and comfortable, but when Leo sat in it, he discovered that it was anything but. To start with, the seat was only fifteen inches off the floor; and between that and the high back, he felt like he was sitting in a hole. It was also difficult to get out of, which Leo did after a bit of struggle.

He returned to his former seat and decided that his new choice would be the four Gothic chairs.

Then his thoughts moved to the fireplace in front of him. He knew that Alex would love to have a fire in the evening, and he supposed, now that Alex knew his secret, that he really ought to make the effort to put the past truly behind him. Besides, Theodora assured them that the fireplaces were clean and safe, so why not?

He hoped he could. Alex deserved the full treatment in this *Wuthering Heights* throwback, including a fire in the fireplace. He'd like to get her a dog someday, too. He knew she wanted one, but she was willing to let go of that because of Leo's stated dislike of them. But did he really dislike them? He didn't think so, when he examined the question fully. He'd loved Lefty, and cried like a baby the day the little fellow died of old age in his doggie bed.

I guess I just lumped him in with all the rest of the pain and guilt I was feeling at the time. Maybe I blamed him some, too. Or maybe I didn't want another dog because any *dog would be a constant reminder of the fire.*

A breakthrough!

Chapter Fifty-Six

While Leo was enjoying his drink, Alex was exploring the kitchen. Her initial stop was the walk-in freezer, first making sure that it could be opened from the inside, should the door close.

There was an astounding array of food that could probably meet the household requirement for a year or more. Inside she found every cut of aged beef imaginable, including milk-fed veal (which she wouldn't touch for ethical reasons). There was an impressive selection of poultry including chicken, turkey, duck, quail, partridge, grouse, and pheasant. In the pork arena, there were hams, two-inch thick chops, slab bacon, salt pork, and sausage, as well as crown roasts and tenderloins galore! Nearby there were legs of lamb and lamb chops. And next to that was exotic meat—venison, buffalo, ostrich, boar, alligator, rabbit, and, would you believe it, rattlesnake! Seafood was at the back and included Dungeness crab, halibut, swordfish, cod, trout, perch, salmon, rockfish, lobster tails, sea bass, haddock, yellow fin tuna steaks, sole, flounder, catfish, shark, squid, octopus, and finally, bags and bags of shrimp.

Alex was overwhelmed. "We are gonna eat great this summer!" she exclaimed, selecting a two pound bag of prawns and moving it out to the refrigerator... which was another adventure.

Inside, she found fresh mussels, steamers, and quahogs, as well as scallops. There was also a large package, wrapped in brown kraft paper and labeled "Abalone." Alex lifted it. It was heavy—at least ten pounds. *Abalone? I* know *that's a protected species. How disgusting* she thought. *We won't be touching that, either. Maybe Black eats it.*

In light of a refrigerator full of perishable shellfish, Alex decided that a change in supper menu was definitely in order, and replaced the bag of frozen shrimp in the walk-in.

The rest of the fridge held a mixture of both expected and unexpected items. There were dozens of brown eggs, condiments, milk, and cold cuts and white button mushrooms on the expected side; with persimmons, breadfruit, dragon fruit, and star fruit, as well as chanterelle, morel, portabella, and oyster mushrooms among the unexpected. The double set of extra-large crispers contained heirloom tomatoes of every shape, size and color; fresh dill and parsley, celery *and* celeriac, breakfast radishes, haricots verts, white asparagus, Belgian endive, broccoli rabe (Alex's favorite), several ears of yellow and white corn, Boston lettuce, peppers, eggplant and cucumbers.

Moving on to the pantry: there was a root bin at the bottom, which held potatoes, onions, turnips, carrots, beets, Jerusalem artichokes, and several heads of cabbage. The upper shelves housed every known canned, jarred, or bottled delicacy, as well as the perennial pasta, tomato paste, all baking needs, cereals, snacks, dried beans, nuts, and grains.

Whew!

"Change in plans," Alex said, flopping down on the sofa next to Leo.

"What'sa matter? No shrimp?"

"There is enough shrimp back there to sink Forrest Gump's boat! No, the problem is that the fridge is full of fresh, very expensive shellfish, and I don't want it to go bad, so I thought I'd make a big pot of chowder that we can eat for supper tonight and for lunch over the next few days."

"Ooooooo, that sounds great. Got some crusty French bread you can warm up to go with it?"

"I haven't checked the bread situation yet (she'd noticed a huge bread box on the counter), but if we don't, I'll be shocked… and after I get over my shock, I'll just make some myself. Either way, French bread is on the menu." She then filled Leo in on the gastronomic wonders she'd discovered.

In the middle of Alex's description of the pantry, they heard a soft whirring.

"What's that?" Alex said, interrupting herself mid-syllable.

"Sounds like a motor." Leo got up. "It's coming from down the hall."

They both went to investigate.

The sound turned out to be a black velvet upholstered stair chair that had obviously been custom made for Cooper Black. The stair risers were probably too far apart for Black's short, bowed little legs to handle easily, and even if they weren't, the chair gave him an air of dignity that would be absent if he were forced to use the stairway in the usual manner in concert with his cane.

When he arrived at the bottom, Alex noticed that he was actually seat-belted in. *Boy, he's not taking any chances. I bet he's one of those people who wears a belt* and *suspenders.* After Black extricated himself from his conveyance, Alex smiled at him, and, exaggerating the words so it would be easier for him to read her lips, since she was without her pad, she asked, "Do you know what time it is?"

Black's stony expression never changed as he held up first six fingers, then three, then four.

"I think he means that it's six thirty-four," Leo said, *sotto voce.*

"Thank you, Mr. Black. I'm making chowder tonight. Would you like to have dinner with us?"

Again, the same granite affect. After a moment, he shook his head.

"If you change your mind, there will be plenty."

He just stared, and continued to stare until Alex became uncomfortable enough to get out of his way and leave him alone.

They went back to the library, finished their drinks and poured another round.

Alex sipped the smooth bourbon. "We've got about five and a half hours before we start, so that will be plenty of time to get the chowder made and have a nice, leisurely dinner. Do you want to nap a while? We're going to be up all night and we haven't gotten any extra sleep to prepare for it."

"No, no nap. Tonight will be tough, but we'll adjust before

you know it. We'll sleep late tomorrow—probably until mid-afternoon. Those heavy curtains in the bedroom will keep it dark, so it'll be easy to sleep during the day." Leo said. "Just don't make the mistake of drinking a lot of coffee to try to perk back up when you run out of gas tonight."

"I was planning on a sugar fix for quick energy. It metabolizes faster than caffeine."

"And what are you planning to do, girlie, spoon it from the bowl?"

"Nope. There are about two dozen boxes of Lindt chocolate in the pantry. But you can spoon it from the bowl, if you want to," Alex laughed. Leo would wrestle tigers for Lindt chocolate.

"Very funny, McGee. Since we're having a second round here, I guess I should skip the wine with dinner, huh? We'll be too relaxed to get anything done."

"Probably so, but I will need some dry white for the chowder," Alex said.

"Then I guess we'll have to make a trip down to the wine cellar and rustle up a bottle," Leo said.

"Yeah, I haven't been down there yet. Let's go check it out."

It wasn't nearly as nice as the rest of the house. Leo and Alex expected to descend into a well-appointed finished basement, but what they got was something out of a Vincent Price movie, though it smelled densely clean—like newly turned earth. The foundation was hewn from solid rock and provided such efficient natural refrigeration that Alex made a mental note to wear a sweatshirt the next time she came down here.

"Where's the light switch?" she asked.

"Isn't one. I'm looking for a... ah, here we go." Suddenly, there was light.

"A bare bulb with a pull string? I feel so pampered," Alex said. "This is a different world from upstairs. You'd never think it was part of the same house. It looks like a photo shoot for *Martha Stewart Dying* down here."

"Kind of creepy, isn't it?"

"If we had more light, maybe it wouldn't be so bad." Alex gazed at the tiny puddle of light the fixture shed. "I had no idea they made two watt light bulbs."

"Bright enough to see all the cobwebs, though. Take a look."

"Abandoned for quite a while, it seems. There doesn't appear to be much down here in the way of bugs. No wonder the spiders left." She looked down. "For packed dirt floors, they're pretty well maintained. Not a lot of dust when you walk on them. Where do you suppose the wine is?"

Leo spied a darkened archway festooned with the labors of what had to be at least three generations of spiders... and big ones from the look of it. The webs were so thick that they hung down like dusty Spanish moss. "I bet it's in there," Leo said.

"Naturally."

They stepped through the stone archway and into another gloomy Hammer Films set. There were hundreds of bottles of wine, but instead of being neatly racked, each bottle had its own cradle cut into the stone. The two long walls were peppered with line after line of wine bottle holes.

"Some wine cellar," Alex whispered.

"Wine cellar? It looks more like a wine mausoleum," Leo whispered back. "Let's get what we need and get out of here," he said, feeling for a light source.

Nothing.

"I can't find a light... oh, wait a minute. Here it is, I guess."

He flicked on a flashlight with batteries that had seen brighter days. "Great. Let's shake a leg before this thing dies completely."

There was no order whatsoever to the way the cellar was arranged. The varietals were all mixed together, as were the bottling years. It was as if the cellar were fully stocked just for show, not for consumption.

"Here's a Chardonnay. That'll be dry enough. Let's go," Alex said. They made their way back to the stairs as quickly as possible, and Alex took them two and a time. When she opened the door at the top, Leo noticed something that didn't quite belong.

"Now what could be the purpose of that, do you think?" Leo asked, pointing.

There was an iron rod affixed to the back of the door panel, running from the upper right corner to the bottom left corner.

Alex snorted. "Maybe Theodora sharpens her teeth on it. I'll get going on dinner if you want to hang out in the library," Alex said when Leo closed the door behind him. "Did you turn out the Little Light Bulb that Could down there?"

"Damn, I didn't. I'll go back."

"Don't get lost."

Leo clomped back down the open slatted stairway. *Maybe while I'm down here, I'll scout out the washer and dryer for Alex.* He walked out of the five-foot area the bulb illuminated and into the gloom, cursing himself for not bringing a light. He walked back to the foot of the stairs.

"Hey, up there!"

The door opened.

"Oh, take it away, I'll buy bonds!"

"Tee hee. Do you have any idea how old that joke is?" Leo asked.

"Kindly remember that it is this old jokester who is preparing your food."

"Do you have any idea how funny that joke is?" Leo asked.

"Much better. You bellowed, sire?"

"Yeah. Toss me down your MagLite, will you?"

"Sure." She disappeared.

Leo continued to look though the open doorway, waiting for Alex.

Suddenly, his brow furrowed.

Someone's shadow passed slowly through the kitchen.

Someone who wasn't Alex.

"Alex!" Leo called, mounting the stairs.

"Patience is a virtue, Leo," Alex called, returning to the kitchen. "I have to cross the equivalent of a football field to get to our room, remember?"

Leo, panicked, was scanning the kitchen for the uninvited guest and trying to do it in such a way as not to alarm his wife.

There was nobody there.

He hadn't heard any door open and shut, so a hidden intruder was unlikely.

As a matter of fact, he hadn't even heard any footsteps—there was just that shadow. He glanced out the window at the shrubs surrounding the house. Could it have been a shadow cast by the plants outside in the westering sun?

Had to be. Didn't it? Sure.

Leo relaxed. *I'm letting this place get to me.* He started back down the stairs again.

"Uh, forgetting something?"

He turned at the foot of the stairs. "Toss it."

Alex threw the MagLite into Leo's waiting hands.

"Anything else?"

"Go cook, wench."

She closed the door, giggling.

Now that he wasn't on a wine mission, Leo stopped and took in more details of his subterranean surroundings.

The basement was gigantic.

The room at the foot of the stairs was bare, representing thirty-by-thirty of the total underground area, and apart from its size, he'd never seen a basement so clean in his life. Nothing stored, no rusty, moldering junk, no boxes filled with forgotten papers.

No nothing. Clean and empty.

The right side of the room, as he faced the stairs ended in a blank stone wall. The passage to the wine dungeon began at the far left wall; but he'd noticed that it continued well past the wine doorway and straight off into the darkness.

He had the light now. Why not?

Approximately one hundred feet down the passage, he came across a door that had a big gouge in the wood, next to the hand set, and Leo made a mental note to come down and fill it in with some wood putty later. When he tried the knob, he found that the door was unlocked, and opened it to find a powder room all done up in pink frou-frou. Without taking his eyes from the startling sight, he ran his hand up and down the wall inside the strange room, feeling for a switch.

"Shit!" He pulled his hand back. He'd just cut it on something in there. Stepping inside to the double sink, he spun the tap.

Nothing. Then he noticed that there was also a faucet installed in the smaller adjoining sink, so he tried that one.

Fortunately, the water ran and it looked clean, too; not brown and rusty from disuse as he was expecting. But who was using it? Cooper Black? And if so, why?

Leo set the MagLite on the sink and rinsed his hand beneath the running water, stinging the deep open wound. The bathroom was stocked with pink hand towels, and mentally apologizing to Theodora, he grabbed one and wrapped his freely bleeding palm with it.

He shone the light around before leaving and saw that even the toilet paper was pink. There was also a pink magazine rack containing, of all things, hunting and fishing magazines. On the sink, there were hard-milled sweet-smelling pink guest soaps in a pink shell-shaped dish. The floor was carpeted in pink shag.

And there was not a speck of dust anywhere.

He walked to the pink toilet and lifted the lid. Sparkling clean, as was the pink sink before he bled into it.

Leo shone his MagLite on the ceiling, looking for a light fixture.

There wasn't one.

So how did whoever used this bathroom read the magazines?

Finally, he directed the strong beam of the small flashlight to the wall where he'd felt for a switch to find out what it was that had cut him so badly.

It was a knife… well, a knife blade, anyway, big and broad and protruding about four inches, sharp side up, from the stone wall. Leo looked at the outside wall for the hilt, but it was nowhere to be seen.

This wall had been built with this knife purposely embedded into it.

What the hell*! A booby trapped powder room?*

Exploration terminated, Leo unwound the blood-soaked towel, rinsed it out, and rewrapped his hand before heading back to the kitchen.

Chapter Fifty-Seven

Alex chuckled. Sometimes she thought Leo had a better sense of humor than she did. She made a note on the pad in the kitchen for Black to pick up spare MagLite batteries, as well as an additional MagLite. Leo was always losing his, so a spare would be a good thing. Oh, and D batteries, too, for the dim specimen in the wine crypt.

Alex selected the potatoes and onions for the chowder and stepped across the kitchen to the alcove where the wet and dry waste containers lived. Since she didn't know where to put the full liners for pick-up or disposal, she assumed that this was one of the chores that Black took care of.

She flipped up the top of the garbage can and was halfway through peeling her potatoes when she remembered that there was a garbage disposal in the sink.

"Who are you? Eliza Doolittle?" she asked herself. "Not used to all these modern conveniences?" Sighing, she bent over and picked all the peelings out of the garbage to dispose of them properly in the sink. When she stood, she noticed a vertical stack of frames behind the dry trash bin. Curious, she moved the container.

They were paintings.

Original paintings.

The Hirschfeld, *two* Rothkos, the Agam, the Modigliani, the Chagall, and the Max—seven pieces by six artistic greats, all loosely bundled together with twine, with a large note attached that read, "TO BE THROWN OUT!" and signed, "Theodora."

What?

Alex reflected back on conversations on their first visit here. *Gifts or no gifts, I guess they decided against hanging onto artwork by Jews.*

Well, if they *don't want them…*

Alex took the treasures, with their accompanying note, and tucked them away in their bedroom.

She was just walking back into the kitchen when Leo burst through the cellar door.

"Hey! You'll never guess wh…" She saw Leo's bloody bandage. "Jesus, Leo, what happened?"

"You wouldn't believe me if I told you. Are there any bandages in our bathroom?" he asked, holding his wrapped and dripping hand over the sink.

Alex flew to the medicine cabinet and was relieved to find all manner of first aid waiting there. She snatched up gauze, adhesive tape, a bottle of some kind of no name alcohol-free disinfectant and butterfly clamps, and dashed back out.

Leo was rinsing off what had rapidly gone from being an Egyptian cotton hand towel to a bloodstained rag. His palm was still bleeding freely.

"Lemme see, Leo."

The gash was deep and about two inches long, looking small in Leo's huge paw of a hand. But it wasn't anything Alex couldn't handle. "If we were home, I'd say go have Dr. Munson stitch it up; but since we don't have wheels and you would probably bleed to death while we tried to locate hell's little angel…" She opened and shut kitchen cabinets until she found the spices and crossed her fingers that the one she needed would be there.

It was.

She extracted a squat glass jar from the riot of flavors within.

"Got it," she said, unscrewing the cap. "Rinse your hand slowly once more, Leo."

"What are you going to do?"

"First I'm going to pour on some of this stuff from the medicine cabinet that is supposed to be a disinfectant, then I'm going to stop the bleeding."

Leo shrugged and did as he was directed.

Alex blotted the gash with a paper towel, then poured some disinfectant over the wound. "Does it sting?" she asked him.

"No. The soap probably did a better cleaning job than that stuff."

"I can pour some bourbon over it, if you want."

"The only way bourbon is entering my body is through my mouth."

"Just a thought." Alex blotted his hand again, then dumped a spoonful of a rust-colored spice on the affected area, and used her index finger to gently push it into the gash. She continued to add a little at a time until the bleeding slowed.

"That stings a little. What is it?"

"Cayenne pepper."

"*What?*"

"Relax. See, the bleeding's nearly stopped already. Wait a few minutes more, then soak your hand in ice water. That will clean the cayenne out without starting the bleeding up again. Then I'll butterfly it and wrap it up for you."

"I'll be damned," Leo said. "How did you know about that?"

"What, the cayenne? I read it somewhere. Cayenne pepper does something to normalize blood pressure, even locally—like that," Alex said, indicating Leo's hand. "This is the first time I ever tried it. I guess it really does work."

"Good thing for me you have a good memory."

Alex ran the hot water over the hand towel, then wrung it out.

"Hey, won't that set the stain?" Leo asked.

"Honey, the only thing that will get this stain out now is peroxide, which we do not have—I checked. When I do the wash, I'll try bleaching it, that is, if there's any Clorox down there, which I also doubt, with their obsession about their pipes. I just want to get as much blood out of it as possible, otherwise it's going to smell bad."

"Bleaching won't solve the problem, anyway. It was pink

to start with."

"Then it's going to become a bleached white hand towel for our bathroom. And how did you happen to come by a pink hand towel down there, anyway?"

Leo filled her in. "And I still haven't found the laundry room," he concluded.

Alex was incensed. "Is that some sick asshole's idea of a joke—building in a knife blade sticking out of the wall? Who does that?"

"I have no idea."

"And a frilly powder room. What do we have down there? Gay vampires?

"Who like to hunt and fish, apparently," Leo said.

Alex was baffled. "What's the deal with a pink powder room down there, anyway? Why is it there at all—especially decked out like that?"

"All I know is, I was so surprised by it that I didn't even notice the knife until I got cut."

"Are you going to be able to work tonight?"

"Oh, sure. I'm right handed, so no problem."

"Yes, but I'm afraid you'll open up that cut again by holding a bucket or a paint tray. You'll have to set stuff like that across the top of the two-foot ladder instead of carrying it around."

"I can do that. As a matter of fact, while you're getting dinner, I think I'll go case out where we'll start priming tonight. Too bad they want the walls charcoal gray. It's going to make this place even more unwelcoming than it already is," Leo said.

"Just try to keep your left hand somewhat elevated," Alex cautioned his retreating back. In all the hubbub, she'd completely forgotten about the treasures nestled in the corner of their bedroom.

Leo wandered the first floor, feeling more than slightly ridiculous with his hand up in the air. He looked like he was trying to hail a cab in the hallway.

After surveying the gallery, he thought that the best

starting point would be the front foyer, moving forward from there. Tonight he expected to get that area and part of the living room/art gallery primed, hoping that a generous layer of charcoal gray would minimize the white paint bleedthrough. He reflected that most people didn't realize how long a good interior paint job took. First you have to take everything down off the walls, then you have to wash all the walls, then tarp floors and furniture, then blue-tape the baseboards, then remove all the outlet covers and switch plates—and that's all before you even get started painting. Next is cutting in with the primer, then rolling the walls, then priming the trim with a paint brush. Then you have to do the same steps with the paint. Theodora said that one coat would be enough, but Leo was skeptical. They'd see. Black may end up going out for more paint before they were through. When he and Theodora were chatting prior to the contract signing, she had reminded him, rather firmly, not to scrape the walls under any circumstances; that she just wanted him to paint over what was there; but Leo couldn't imagine that they wouldn't need to clear away old, peeling paint *anywhere*.

However, in the final analysis, it was, in fact, her dime.

Leo could hear Alex humming in the kitchen as she worked. He smiled. It was such a homey, warm and comfortable sound.

Leo decided to take down paintings until Alex called him for dinner. Though many of them were small, all could be managed with one hand and a bit of patience.

By the time dinner was ready, the walls were bare and the artwork was stacked carefully out of harm's way in the Library.

Chapter Fifty-Eight

"This chowder is great, hon!" Leo exclaimed. All the different kinds of clams really give it a rich flavor."

"Thanks. I'm glad you like it, because I made a huge pot of it. We'll be eating it for lunch all week. Breadstick?"

"Oh, fantastic—you made breadsticks." Leo withdrew two of Alex's soft garlic breadsticks, tore one in half and dunked it into the soup. "What happened? No French bread?" he asked, through a full mouth.

Alex grinned. If there was anybody in the world she loved to feed, it was Leo Renfield. Nobody enjoyed her food more. "Yeah, there was; but I thought you'd rather have these."

"Always. Thanks for going to the trouble. You should make these more often. That salad's good, too. What's the dressing?"

"Salt, pepper, a squeeze of lemon juice, and olive oil."

"That's it?"

"Uh huh. You get to taste the vegetables instead of a heavy salad dressing."

"What's the white stuff?"

"Hearts of palm."

"And these?"

"Chopped pignoli nuts."

"I thought they tasted familiar. Haven't had `em in a long time."

"When they cost twenty dollars a pound, I should say you haven't," Alex said. "They are good though, aren't they?"

"Man, this is livin'!"

They ate in silence for a while, then Alex said, "I wonder where the laundry room is."

"That's what I was trying to find when I went down there.

Theodora's note said it was in the basement; and I have to tell you, it goes on forever. How about we just plan on staying really, really clean?"

"We're bound to run out of underwear sooner or later. We can't put it off for long."

"Sure we can. Just put 'underwear' on Black's shopping list."

Alex laughed, but Leo was only half joking. He hated that basement. There was something not right about it. Mainly, the girly pink powder room. That room, in that location... it was like putting lipstick on a tarantula.

When the gooseberry pie and espresso with lemon peel arrived for dessert, Leo temporarily drowned his concerns with exotic berries and some top quality caffeine.

They both decided to have a second espresso, even though they spoke earlier about limiting their caffeine intake. It was just too, too delicious, and they lingered over it, unwilling to break the satisfied, relaxed mood that invariably follows a well prepared meal. But the longer they sat in contented silence, the easier it was for unsettling thoughts to slink back in.

"What do you suppose is with that pink room down there?" Alex asked.

Leo sighed and shook his great head. "I don't know. I wish I did. Want to see it?"

"Sure," Alex replied.

"I'll get the flashlights."

MagLites in hand, Alex and Leo clomped down the rickety staircase. It occurred to Leo that there would be no way anyone could enter the basement undetected by someone who was already down here with all the noise the stairs made.

Hmmmm. An early warning system?

He resolved to see if it would be possible to quietly sneak down these stairs later.

Alex reached for the pull string. "It's almost a waste of energy to turn this teeny bulb on for all the light it sheds."

"I disagree. It's useful to help get your bearings when

you're coming back from there," Leo said, indicating the dark passage.

"Good thought. We should probably check around upstairs for a higher wattage bulb to replace this piddly one, though."

Leo shone his light upward and examined the fixture. "Sorry, sweetie, but that's not an option. This fixture is three days older than dirt. Put a more powerful bulb in it and we'll either blow a fuse or start a fire. Let's just leave it alone."

They set off through the thick darkness. "I haven't been very far down, but I saw some side passages that connect to this main artery. No idea where they go yet," Leo said.

Their flashlight beams bounced off every surface like mad fireflies. Neither of them spoke further until they arrived at the powder room door.

"This is it. Just don't touch the inside walls," Leo said, pulling the door open for Alex and standing aside.

Alex stared, confusion suffusing her pretty face.

"Weird, isn't it?" Leo asked.

"Leo, this is a cleaning closet."

"*What?*" He pushed himself off the wall he was leaning against to see for himself.

Alex was right. It was a large cleaning closet; as neat as the rest of the basement and filled with cleaning rags, a tub sink, mops, brooms, buckets, carpet sweepers, and a shelf of cleansers and polishes.

Leo was stunned.

"Are you certain that this is the right door? There are a couple more, farther down."

"This is the door, Alex."

"How can you be so sure?"

Leo closed the door. "See that big gouge next to the handset? That's how I know. This is the door," he said, opening it again, half hoping that the pink powder room would be there this time.

It wasn't.

Who was living down here? Penn & Teller?

"Let's see what's behind door number two and door number three," Alex suggested.

"I somehow doubt it's going to be a new car or a trip to Europe," Leo muttered.

Door number two was locked as was door number three.

"Had enough, or do you want to look around some more?" Alex asked.

"Oh, I've had more than enough," Leo said. "It was there, Alex. It was."

"Are you sure that maybe you didn't walk farther than you thought and got turned around somehow? Maybe the pink powder room is in some other part of the basement. Or you just got the wrong door of these three and the powder room door locked when you shut it." Alex said.

"What about the gouge?"

Alex trained her MagLite on door number three. "This one has a gouge, too. Let's check the other one." She ran back to the other locked door. "Same here, Leo. Maybe somebody was moving something heavy and awkward, and bounced it off the doors and the wall on the way to wherever they were going with it down here. The gouges all look the same and they're in the same spot on each door."

Relief washed over Leo. "You could be right. I wasn't paying a lot of attention to where I was walking."

"That's got to be it, honey."

Leo nodded, though still not completely sold. He resolved to bring something with him to mark his way the next time he visited the basement.

Chapter Fifty-Nine

Back in the kitchen once more, Alex banished Leo to the Library to rest and read while she cleared up the supper dishes. She was still concerned about his hand.

She opened the refrigerator to make some space to put the soup away and was surprised to discover that an appropriately sized vacancy was already waiting for her.

The ten-pound package of abalone was gone.

Alex slid the tall stock pot into the open space. *Black must have taken it.* But she couldn't imagine tiny Cooper Black eating ten pounds of anything; and it disturbed her vaguely that he was insinuating himself into what she regarded as "their" area of the house. Didn't he have his own refrigerator and kitchen up there?

Knock it off, jerko. He lives here. He can go wherever he wants, Alex berated herself. Searching her feelings, she came to the unattractive conclusion that she just didn't like the man; someone who had done absolutely nothing to her to merit that dislike. How heartless! He had a hard enough road without others recoiling from his appearance and his handicaps.

Guilt rapidly set in. Alex, feeling ashamed of herself, resolved to go out of her way to be nice to Cooper Black, no matter how he behaved toward her, from that moment forward.

Leo sat before the cold fireplace, staring down at the open book in his hands, reading none of it. His mind was still on the basement.

What the hell was going on? Could inattentiveness really have caused him to wander farther into the warren of passages down there without realizing it?

It's a pretty sad state of affairs when a grown man has to bring a bag of breadcrumbs with him when he goes for a walk.

Then a truly devastating thought struck like a scorpion.

Could it be early onset Alzheimer's?

Most people have a particular disease that they fear above all others, and this one was Leo's.

Oh, God, please, no.

Remembering that crossword puzzles were supposed to be good for keeping the mind toned up, Leo set his John Adams biography aside and went to the bedroom in search of Alex's puzzle book.

He found it tossed on the bed, so he picked it up and thumbed through it, noticing that Alex had already done all the cryptograms. He didn't see how anybody could solve those things, but Alex said it wasn't hard if you "re-tooled your thinking."

Most of the crosswords hadn't been attempted yet, so Leo turned to pick up a pencil from Alex's night table and saw the stack of paintings leaning against the wall.

Crosswords forgotten, he picked up the bundle and headed for the kitchen.

Alex smiled as he walked in. "Almost done, sweetie. Can I get you something?"

Leo held up the bundle. "What are these doing in our bedroom? Have you taken up grand larceny?"

He was serious, but Alex just laughed. "Didn't you see the note?" She pointed to the front of the stack.

He read it, no less confused. "I don't get it. They're throwing them out?"

"It seems so. Do you have any idea how valuable these are?"

"None whatsoever," Leo said.

"Well, I bet, conservatively, that these are probably worth $100,000—maybe more."

"A hundred grand for seven paintings? Wow."

"A hundred grand *each*, Leo."

"Well, we certainly can't keep them!" Leo cried.

"Why not? Theodora wanted them thrown away." Alex

filled Leo in on where she found them.

"I noticed the blank spaces on the wall when I took the paintings down earlier, but I figured that they just relocated the ones that were missing."

"They did. To the trash."

"But why the trash? If they decided to dispose of this artwork, why not sell it?" Leo asked, mystified.

"Maybe they don't want anyone to know that they own paintings by Jewish artists. Take it from me, Leo, Theodora is living proof that Eva Braun made it out," Alex said. "And when did you take all the paintings down, by the way?"

"While you were making dinner. I figured I might as well—to get ready for tonight."

"Did you diagram their positions on the wall before you took them down?" Alex asked.

"Nope. They can re-hang 'em when we're done. The more you handle valuable stuff like that, the more of an insurance risk it becomes. I'd rather not chance damaging them. Plus, I don't trust the way they were hung up and I wouldn't want to re-hang them the same way."

"Why? How were they hung?"

"With duct tape. They were taped to the wall," Leo said.

"Cut it out."

"Really. Not one single, solitary nail or hook in the whole wall. Even the big, heavy pictures were taped. I had a devil of a time trying to peel that tape off and not take any paint with it."

"I gotta see this," Alex said.

They both turned to leave the kitchen and were brought up short.

Cooper Black was standing in the doorway, watching them.

Alex put her hand on her chest and forced a smile. "You startled us," she said slowly. She reached for the pad and pen she'd left on the counter earlier and when she looked back, it was to see Black staring pointedly at the bundle of paintings. Rather than speak and hope he understood, Alex wrote:

I found these by the trash bin with a note from Theodora that they were to be thrown away.

Is that right?

The small man stared at her note, then at Alex. He slowly nodded his head.

Alex wrote:

If no one wants them, could we have them?

An unblinking stare at the note, then at Alex. Again, a slow nod.

Are you sure?

Black sighed, nodded again, pointed at the bundle, and made a shooing gesture with both hands.

Thank you!

"Leo, they're ours! The paintings are ours!" Alex cried with wide-eyed delight.

"Ho. Lee. Shit," Leo muttered, grinning.

Black shrugged his shoulders, looking bored. Then he turned to Leo, who was deep in thought about their newest acquisitions, and snapped his fingers rapidly three times to redirect Leo's attention, and when Leo looked at him, Black held up the index finger of his left hand, then quickly opened and closed both his fists three times.

At sea, Leo looked to Alex for clarification.

She smiled. "Don't worry. I think I've got it." She scribbled furiously on her pad, then tapped Black on the shoulder. When he turned, she handed it to him.

An hour and a half before we are to start working?

A look. A nod. Then he handed the pad back to Alex.

Alex grinned at Leo. "It's ten thirty, babe. He just told us we have an hour and a half before we get started.

She turned back to thank him again.

He was gone.

"Did you see him leave?" Alex asked.

Leo shook his head. "But I wasn't looking at him, either. I was off in the ozone thinking about what these paintings are going to do for our future.

She was about to say something, then closed her mouth with a snap. "Hey! I just figured something out." She walked over to the range. "I know how to keep track of time in this place."

"How?"

"Watch." She set the oven timer for seven and a half hours and pressed START. "In seven and a half hours, it will be six A.M. It's ten thirty now, so all we have to do when we want to know the time is to come in here, subtract the elapsed time from seven and a half hours, add that to ten thirty, and Bob's your uncle!"

"Though I do applaud your inventiveness, it sounds like an awful lot of trouble to go through just to know what time it is," Leo said.

"Not for me, it isn't. It drives me crazy not to know the time."

"But isn't there a built in clock on any of the other appliances here?"

"Sure there are, but none of them works. This is the best we're going to do. So what do you feel like doing for the next ninety minutes? I mean, besides putting these paintings back in our room. Do you believe this? Isn't it fantastic?"

"We don't have to worry about our retirement anymore," Leo said. "Money in the bank."

"You said it." Alex picked up the bundle. "So what do you want to do until midnight?"

"How about cards?" he ventured. "Gin Rummy?"

"You're on; but first I want to see the backs of those paintings you took down."

"I put them in the library. There's so much room, I figured that they'd be safe and out of the way in there," Leo said.

"Good. That's where we're going, anyhow. Let's put these away first, though."

They decided on a high shelf in their closet as the safest place for their canvas treasures and once they were safely out of harm's way, Alex and Leo returned to the Library.

But when Leo brought Alex to where he'd stacked the gallery artwork, it was gone.

"You didn't appropriate those, too, did you?" he asked.

"Of course not," Alex laughed. "Quit playing around, Leo."

"Damn it, I put them all right here, Alex, and I should know; all the trips it took to do it. Jesus, what happened to them?" Leo looked like the jury had just returned a death sentence for jay walking as he dashed out of the Library and down the hall to the gallery with Alex at his heels... where he stopped so suddenly that she plowed right into his back.

The paintings were all back in their places on the wall.

The Renfields could only stand there and gape.

Behind them, two fingers snapped three times. When they turned, an irritated Cooper Black pointed at his wrist, then shook his finger at them in an admonishing fashion.

"What the *hell*..."

"Let me have the pad and pen in your pocket, Leo."

He handed them over. Alex wrote:

Why are all the paintings we took down back on the wall?

Black repeated his previous gesture.

Alex's brow furrowed, then she snapped her own fingers, and wrote:

Is this because the paintings were taken down before midnight?

He nodded, lips pursed in disgust. Then, mission evidently accomplished, he waddled to the foot of the stairs, buckled himself into his plush chair, pushed a hidden button, and slowly dissolved into the shadows of the upper floor.

"I'll say it again. What the *hell?*"

"He was telling us that we started working too early. Remember? No work before midnight or after six?" Alex explained.

"But how did he get all those paintings back up? Do you see a ladder? A couple of those pieces were almost too big for *me* to manage alone."

"He's pretty strong, Leo, so I don't doubt that he could handle whatever they weigh. What I don't understand is why we didn't hear a ladder being moved around. He obviously had to have used one. Those larger pieces are ten feet off the floor."

"So this means that we can't even do prep work before we start priming?"

"Guess so."

"Hoo boy. Well, nothing says we can't experiment, right?" Leo asked.

"What do y…"

"Wait here." Leo ran to the supply closet and pulled out a ladder. "Okay. Go back into the kitchen and tell me if you hear anything."

Alex did. "Ready. Go ahead."

Leo moved the ladder down the hallway and set it up as quietly as he could.

"Hear you!" Alex called.

"I thought so!" Leo said, folding up the ladder and returning it to the closet. *Could he have put all the pictures back up while we were in the basement?*

He didn't see how. They weren't down there long enough.

Mystified, they both adjourned to the bedroom to change into work clothes. Alex donned her paint spattered black AC/DC tee shirt that a fan had given her because she had parodied the song *Dirty Deeds Done Dirt Cheap* in a monologue chunk one night. It rode atop equally spattered black Levis. She tied her long blonde hair back and stuffed it up under a green canvas ball cap.

Leo pulled on his favorite Blue Oyster Cult concert tour tee and an old pair of jeans that had seen better days but not participated in them.

They both wore steel-toed brown leather work boots. Alex had painted pink bows on hers "to give them the feminine touch they need." They never failed to make Leo smile.

The Renfields adjourned to the Library to play cutthroat Gin Rummy for the hour or so they had left before beginning their first night of work.

Searching a drawer or two, they located a deck of cards, pulled up a couple of chairs to the now unfolded Gothic card table, and got down to it.

At one point, Alex was just about to pick up the ace she needed to complete a run when fingers snapped three times behind them.

Leo looked over his shoulder and nodded at Black, who was making hurrying gestures at them. "Time for work, babe," he said, gladly putting down his lousy hand.

"I'll beat you later, then," Alex said.

"You are the Gin Rummy Queen, I admit it," Leo said, standing.

They walked down to the hall closet and liberated buckets, tarps, brushes and all the other implements they needed, piling them off to one side. They occupied the next two hours painstakingly peeling duct tape off the walls in the gallery in order to take down all the artwork... again.

"Did you see any TSP wall wash in the closet?" Leo asked.

"No, but there's a gallon of a substitute version in there, and it's concentrated. I'll take a couple of buckets and mix some up for us in the kitchen." Alex disappeared down the hall.

Leo moved the stacked artwork back to its storage spot in the Library. He despaired of getting much done in their first six-hour stint. Just getting the walls washed and ready for primer was going to run about three hours. That duct tape was a bastard to lift off without damaging the paint underneath. You needed the patience of a safecracker. He couldn't figure out what the Hamiltons found so unacceptable about picture hanging hardware.

"All set," Alex said, setting the buckets with their sudsy contents carefully on the tarp-covered parquet floor. She picked up two car-washing sponges from the equipment pile and dropped one into each bucket.

"Thanks, hon. You know, I never thought I'd ever say this, but I'm really beginning to hate duct tape," Leo said. "If these jokers knew how to use nails, we could be priming by now."

"Why do you suppose they did that?"

"No clue. It would certainly have been easier to use nails. Faster, too. Maybe they're paranoid about hitting electrical wires in the walls—some people are," Leo replied. "Not that it's a realistic worry. Picture hanging hardware wouldn't even come close to touching the electrical."

"Maybe they rearrange their artwork frequently. This way, they don't have to keep patching holes," Alex said.

"I don't think that's it, Alex," Leo said. "Look at the walls."

She did, and could see the outline of every picture. "Man, don't these people ever clean their walls?"

Leo laughed. "Most people don't think about washing their walls unless noticing something like this motivates them to do it. When was the last time you washed a wall?"

"Just prior to painting it. You're right."

"Hey, could you grab some Goof-Off out of the supply closet? We're going to need it to get rid of the adhesive residue from all this duct tape."

Alex returned a few seconds later. "Sorry, hon, no Goof-Off—just this stuff—another one of Theodora's 'green' substitute products."

"You mean those 'green' substitute products that don't work nearly as well as the ones they're supposedly just as good as?"

"Those would be the ones, yes," Alex replied, producing two soft rags and pouring a liberal amount on each. Handing one to Leo, they both began dabbing at the walls.

After a while, Alex said, "I just thought of something. We're not supposed to put even the tiniest holes in these walls—it's in the contract, remember? Maybe the reason we can't do it is the same reason they don't do it. We just don't understand why, since that clause was never explained to us."

"Another mystery," Leo grumbled. "Never in my life have I done a job that had so many crazy commandments attached to it."

As they continued to dab, both missing the Goof-Off that would have removed the adhesive in a flash, Alex asked, "How much do you think we'll get done tonight?"

Leo sighed. "Not a lot. I sure hope we'll be able to leave everything set up when we quit. If we can't, it's going to add a half-hour setup and a half-hour breakdown to our day, so we'll really only end up working five hours. I don't see how we can get all this work done if we have to cut an hour a day off our already short work time. Hell, finishing up by September first is going to be a near thing as it is."

"Don't worry about something that you don't have enough information on yet, honey. When our alarm clock shows up, I'll ask him," Alex said, patting her back pocket.

"I thought Jim Carrey was the only one who could make his ass talk."

"Hilarious, Leo." She pulled the spiral bound pad and pen out of her back pocket and waved it at him. "But that reminds me of a joke."

"Oh, God."

"Did you know that you can get AIDS in your ears?"

"No, Mr. Bones. How can you get AIDS in your ears?" Leo asked.

"From listening to too many assholes."

Leo snorted and shook his head. "I bet I could give you a word and you'd have a joke for it."

"Let's try it. Nouns only," Alex said.

They worked away happily for the next few hours. Leo threw word after word at her and couldn't stump her. He was ready to try, "spatula," when their human alarm clock sounded.

Snap, snap, snap. Then he made the gesture that baseball

umpires use to indicate "safe."

"Uh, I think we're done for the night, Alex," Leo said.

Before she even acknowledged Black's presence, Alex reached for the pad and pen, and wrote:

Is it OK to leave our equipment set up?

She walked over to Black, who was standing in the doorway. He was wearing what looked like a very dressy outfit from his part of the world, sporting an ivory white Nehru jacket and matching trousers. The color of the outfit offset his dark skin, making him look more like a well-dressed shadow than a man. His huge, hyperthyroid eyes gleamed like headlights; with about as much life in them. She showed him her question.

He looked up her, his DOA eyes staring a beat too long. Alex was instantly uncomfortable and made aware, with a certainty that she couldn't explain, that her communications were unwelcome. To her relief, he finally did look down and read the note, after which, he closed his eyes, as if fighting a nasty headache, and sighed deeply. Alex recognized the gesture for what it was: something school teachers did to communicate student stupidity without actually saying the words. Her previous "make nice" resolution evaporated instantly. She was infuriated, and was withdrawing the pad to let him know exactly how she felt about his attitude; but before she could, Black reached out suddenly and grabbed her wrist.

It was everything Alex could do not to rudely shake off his iron grip. His hand was Alaskan tundra cold—so cold that it felt like he was burning her skin. Instead, she gave him her undivided attention, hoping that once he had it, he'd let go of her.

Once they had made eye contact again, he did let go. Her wrist throbbed painfully, but she didn't look at it yet—only at him.

He pointed to the note and nodded slowly, then looked back up at her, waiting.

"Good news and bad news, hon. Good news is that we don't have to break our stuff down."

"What's the bad news?" Leo asked. He was glad that Alex

was dealing with Black. The little guy gave Leo the creeps with a capital C.

"He seems to be waiting for something from me. I don't know what he wants."

"Ask him. You have the pad there."

"He doesn't like written messages," Alex said.

"How do you know that?"

"I just do." She looked back down at Black, and said, "Would you prefer to read my lips rather than a piece of paper?"

Black nodded. Then he took the pad out of Alex's hand, and walked down the hall. The next thing they heard was the purring of his electric stair chair as it outran the overcast early morning light tiptoeing onto the first floor.

"Of all the damned nerve!" Alex cried. "He took the pad!"

"I saw. Guess you were right about his not liking your notes. How did you know, though?" Leo asked.

"Just a feeling. It just came to me, all of a sudden."

"I guess his lip-reading preference makes sense. It must be the way Theodora and the other storm troopers around here communicate with him. I mean, can you honestly see Theodora having patience enough to write notes to him all the time?"

"I didn't think about that. He probably resents note writing because it's a reminder of his handicap. If he reads lips well, he fits in better. Understandable," Alex said.

"I don't know how he'd fit in anywhere but a costume party, with the way he was dressed," Leo said.

"Yeah, that get-up was unusual, all right; but I liked it. It looked sort of good on him."

"You think so? He's not historically accurate, you know."

"What do you mean?"

"Napoleon was never that short. He was 5'8", as a matter of fact."

"What does Napoleon have to do with this?"

364

"Alex, he was all dressed up like Napoleon—hat and all!" Leo cried.

"No, he wasn't! He had on a white Nehru suit that looked great against his dark skin!"

"What do you mean? That he was made up and dressed like he was from India?"

"It's not make-up, Leo. He's Indian."

Leo started at his wife, horrified.

"Honey, his skin is whiter than white, and he has blue eyes and red hair."

"Oh, my God," Alex said, a knot of panic tightening in her stomach. "Am I losing it, Leo?"

"You really see an Indian in a white suit?"

"You really see an Irish Napoleon?" Alex asked.

"I do. He has the same coloring as my mother did. Matter of fact, he even looks a little like her."

A thick wave of nausea rolled over her and Alex's hands began to shake. "To me, he looks like a miniature version of the Indian paramedic who took my mother away." She dashed down the hall, through the Library and their bedroom, arriving at the toilet just in time.

Chapter Sixty

As Alex rinsed her mouth, she stared at her pale reflection in the mirror. *One of us is losing it, and it's probably me.* She patted some cold water on her face and neck, then remembered that she forgot to take the magic pill that her number one fan had prescribed, and heaved a huge sigh of relief. *It is me. But what happened to the meds? I'm sure I left them right here by the sink.* She popped open the medicine cabinet and there they were. She withdrew the green glass jar and stared at it, knowing that she hadn't put it there. When she was taking prescriptions, she never put them out of sight, because she'd forget to take them if she did. Alex shrugged and tipped a pill into her palm, then drew a glass of water and washed it down, thinking that pills that were purported to do something as dramatic as these did should be followed by a fanfare of some kind.

"Ta da!" Alex supplied, grinning. "Well, at least it doesn't have a vile aftertaste, like antibiotics." It was nice to take sweet-tasting pills for a change, and Alex wondered why the pharmaceutical industry didn't flavor them all this way. She let the water run for a minute, then refilled the glass with ice cold water and greedily drank it down, feeling its path from her throat to where it spread in her now empty stomach.

Alex hoped the pills would take effect sooner than the projected one- to two-week waiting period. She made a final check in the mirror, turned with the intention of rejoining Leo, then stopped. Something made her turn back to stare at the frieze that ringed the bathroom walls—all those white plaster faces. It was disturbing. And what bothered her about these faces was the same thing that bothered her about all sculptured countenances in general—the eyes. By the nature of their art, sculptors usually limited eye detail to the eyelids and eyeballs, with no irises or pupils depicted. Alex felt that it sapped the life from them and made the carvings appear zombie-like. That was why she liked the Venus di Milo—no face. She despaired of ever being able to relax in a hot bath or use the spa, with all those faces looking down at her like perverts at a peep show. The fact that all the faces were men only served to add to the vague sense of obscenity—men, from Alex's best guess, who ranged in age from late teens to early sixties. No matter where she stood in the large room, there were always a couple of them staring directly at her.

They gave the impression that she was being judged and was found wanting.

Alex decided that she'd use the shower in the half-bath off the Billiard Room for bathing. It was just too disquieting in here—like being alone in an art museum in the middle of the night. Suddenly, Alex desperately needed to be somewhere else that wasn't quite this quiet. She turned and ran back to her husband, who was just walking through the Library door.

"Are you okay? I was just coming to look for you," Leo said.

"Yeah. I just threw up, that's all."

"Why?"

"Scared, I guess. Afterward, I remembered my pill and took it. I'm sure it was my perception that was off and not yours, honey. I just wish these pills Jack prescribed would get to work."

Leo smiled, inwardly quite relieved himself. "This is your first dose—give 'em time. Then you'll be just fine." He gave Alex a single arm hug and kissed the top of her head.

"You do that a lot."

"What? Kiss your head?"

"Yeah."

"I like the way your hair smells," Leo said.

"Oh. I was about to draw you a map to my lips."

"Oh, *those*. I can find those," he said, and proved it.

Alex smiled up at him. "I think we'd better finish cleaning up, don't you?"

"Yes, dammit."

They had just put their rags, sponges, and buckets in the

large kitchen sink when—

Snap snap snap

Alex turned to find Cooper Black standing in the doorway shaking his head. He was still in his white Nehru get-up, and was still very much an Indian. She wondered if Leo still saw the Emperor.

"I don't think he wants us to use this sink to clean up," she said to Leo out of the corner of her mouth. Leo shut off the taps.

"Where do you want us to clean up, then?" she asked him.

Black pointed at the floor.

Oh, shit

"The basement? You want us to use the sink in the basement?" she asked.

Black closed his huge eyes, and nodded once.

Alex turned to Leo. "Why don't you go relax in the spa for awhile, hon? I'll go."

"Are you sure?" Leo asked, eyebrows raised.

"Yes. Now that I know I'm just seeing things, I'll be fine. What's not really there can't hurt me, right?"

"Right, but it can scare you. I'd be glad to go down there with you."

"Not necessary, Leo. Don't treat me like a girly girl, okay?"

He laughed. "All right. But you're *my* girly girl and I don't want you to be afraid."

"I'll be fine. Go," she said, giving him a playful shove.

After Leo left, Alex gathered all their soiled equipment and stacked it so that she could manage everything in a single trip. She took the flashlight from the counter, stuck it under her arm and opened the basement door with her free hand.

Stygian darkness yawned below her. She cocked her head, listening, and heard what sounded like running feet with long, scratchy claws.

She really didn't want to go down there.

She thought for a minute.

Then why should she?

Black had already returned to his upper domain, so screw it.

Alex closed the basement door, put the flashlight back, and headed for their bathroom. *I'll clean this stuff out in the bathtub, then join Leo in the spa*, she thought, forgetting about the faces on the wall.

She laughed out loud when she walked in. Leo had brought in tarps and covered the entire frieze.

He was stretched out in the bubbling, steamy spa. "I don't like people looking down on me, literally or figuratively."

"I'm glad you did that," Alex said. "I hate that thing. Bathroom functions are not spectator sports."

"You decided against the basement, I see."

"Yeah, okay, I didn't feel like going down there. I'm cleaning this stuff right here," she said. "All we used tonight was that 'green' crap Theodora's so in love with. The drains will take it and so will her sainted pipes."

Leo chuckled. "Gonna join me when you're done, girly girl?" he teased.

Alex rolled her eyes and shook her head, sighing. "I deserved that, I guess. And, yes, I'll be right there as soon as I get this stuff cleaned up," she said, dropping her load loudly into the bathtub.

She ran the water and bent to her task, concentrating on doing a thorough job. The entire undertaking took about twenty minutes, and when she shut the bathtub faucet off she realized that the spa wasn't running any longer.

Alex looked over her shoulder. Not only was the spa off, but it was vacant, as well.

"Hey! I thought you were going to wait for me!" she called.

No answer.

She stacked the clean supplies next to the tub. Her knees popped as she stood.

"Leo?"

Silence.

She crept to the spa and looked in.

Leo was lying across the bottom, two feet below the surface with the peaceful, composed countenance of the drowned.

Alex screamed his name...

Chapter Sixty-One

…and Leo's eyes opened.

He sputtered to the surface. "Whatsa matter, hon?"

"Jesus Christ, Leo, I thought you drowned!"

"I'm sorry, babe. I was just seeing how long I could hold my breath. I used to be able to stay down for nearly three minutes."

"Just warn me next time!" Alex demanded, color beginning to return to her face.

"I promise. You done cleaning? Come on in," Leo said, turning on the jets.

"Not for too long, though. I'm exhausted and I want to get to bed soon."

"Me, too, but this will help relax you. You'll sleep better."

"The water smells nice. Did you put something in it?" Alex asked, taking off her work clothes.

"Yeah. There's stuff in that cabinet over there—essential oils, I think. There's 'Tranquility, Serenity, Calm, Peace, Relaxation…'"

"Nothing to wake you up, huh?" Alex joked.

"Actually, there is. 'Invigorate, Awake, Pep, GetUpandGo,' and a couple of others."

"That's funny. I've never associated soaking in a spa with feeling energetic."

"'Energy.' That was another one," Leo said.

"Which one did you put in?" Alex asked, stepping into the churning water.

"'Soothe.'"

"It smells just like freshly laundered flannel pajamas—the kind with the feet in them," she said, settling back into the hot water.

"You're right. I went through many a pair of those when I was little. They were my favorite pajamas. That's why it smelled so familiar."

Fifteen minutes later, two extremely 'Soothe'-d people got out of the spa, toweled off and tottered into the bedroom which, as Theodora had warned, was surprisingly chilly. They bolted under the covers, spooned together for warmth, and fell asleep almost immediately.

Alex's sleep was anything but soothing. Her rest was plagued with sound bytes from hell that ran behind a stuttering Kinescope of horrific images parading continuously across the movie screen of her mind.

Leo was standing at the open front door. Alex begged him not to go outside. There were things moving beneath the lawn, but Leo didn't see them and stepped off the porch. Clawed hands erupted from the ground and pulled him under.

Then she was standing in the kitchen when Cooper Black appeared in the doorway, snapping his fingers three times. When Alex looked at him, he pointed to the basement door, which was opening by itself. Suddenly, Black was across the room, standing next to the now open basement door. He grinned at her showing teeth that were far too sharp, and pointing down into the dark, said, "*Vestri posterus specto*" in a high speed Alvin and the Chipmunks kind of voice. He jumped up and down gleefully, like an Oompah Loompah on PCP, chanting, *vestri posterus specto* over and over again until Alex couldn't bear it anymore. She clapped her hands over her ears and squeezed her eyes shut.

She awoke with a start, the caretaker's words still ringing in her ears. He sounded like he was talking backward. She reached for the pad and pencil that she put on the night table, all the while repeating the nightmare words so they wouldn't evaporate from her sleep-hazed mind before she wrote them down.

"*Pestry posterus specto, pestry posterus specto, pestry posterus specto*," she muttered, flipping on the lamp.

She dropped the pencil, which rolled under the bed.

"*Pestry posterus specto, pestry posterus specto*, dammit!" She retrieved the pencil, but discovered that the lead had broken off when it hit the floor. She pulled on her robe and padded into the Library in search of a replacement.

The Library, of course, was shrouded in tomblike darkness, due to the heavy blackout curtains.

"*Pestry posterus specto, Pestry posterus specto*," Alex muttered as she felt for the light switch and turned it on.

The Library lights went on, but very dimly. Alex hadn't noticed a dimmer switch anywhere, but at least there was enough light to find the exquisite Lalique thistle vase—a vase that cost more than her last car—filled with sharpened pencils on the end table. She crossed the room and carefully withdrew one, writing her nightmare message on the spiral pad.

Fully awake now, the idea of a snack appealed to her and she made her way to the kitchen, but was unprepared for the wash of bright sunlight suffusing the area beyond the Library door. Squinting, she traversed the main hallway, thinking that the concept of a "midnight snack" was ruined by daylight, when she saw something that opened her eyes, sunlight, or no.

The basement door was standing wide open.

Snack forgotten, Alex tiptoed to the head of the stairs.

"Hello? Anybody down there?" Even as she said the words, she felt ridiculous. If Black was down there, he wouldn't hear her—and who else could it be but Black? Maybe he was doing his laundry or something.

"So you dreamed about an open door, and here's an open door. What are the odds of that?" she asked herself. "Stop making grand opera out of nothing and get back to bed."

She was about to take her own advice when Cooper Black entered the kitchen from the hallway. He seemed irritated to find Alex there, and with various gestures, urged her to return to her bedroom.

"Why is that door open?" she asked him.

Black sighed, walked across the room and shut it. Then he turned to Alex, spread his arms wide and arched his eyebrows, to convey, "It's closed now—happy?"

"I want to know why it was open in the first place," Alex

said.

Black just shrugged, walked to the pantry, removed a jar of caviar and a box of Carr's crackers, then left the room. His chair grumbled up the stairway, leaving silence to reign once more...

...until the basement door slowly yawned opened by itself.

That did it for Alex. She never moved so fast in her life. Sprinting across the hall and through the shadowy Library, she buried herself under the blankets and cuddled up next to Leo. She still clutched her little pad but rather than stick any part of her body outside the mock safety of the blankets, she sequestered it under her pillow; but not before remembering that she'd left the Library lights on and hadn't shut the bedroom door after her, so she forced herself back out of bed and took care of it, not only closing but locking their bedroom door.

With everything all battened down, her anxiety faded and she returned to bed for the third time. She turned onto her left side and fell asleep within minutes, dreaming, this time, that she was outside the house at dusk gathering firewood. When she looked down at the stack, she saw that she carried not cordwood but dead and blackened human arms. Sensing her shocked realization, the dry and brittle fingers reached out for her.

**

Hours later, Leo awoke slowly, feeling groggy and disoriented. The room was far too warm and his whole body was slick with perspiration. When the flickering light fully registered, he bolted upright, his heart jackhammering in his chest.

There was a fire burning in the fireplace.

"Alex! Alex, wake up!" he shouted.

"I'm up, I'm up! What's wrong? Why is it so hot in here?"

"Alex, the fireplace!" Leo shouted. He was crippled with fear. Further movement was impossible.

Alex leapt out of bed and ran for the buckets she'd left in

the bathroom. She threw one into the bathtub and spun the faucet on full. It only took a moment to draw a bucketful, but to Alex, it took years. She heard a distant high keening sound that she knew was coming from her terrified husband.

She pounded back into the bedroom and threw the water onto the fire, dousing it at once; then pulled aside the curtains and forced open a window to release the smoke to the outside.

"What's going on, Leo?"

Trembling with an even mixture of fear and anger, Leo shouted, "That's what I'd like to know! Why did you do this?"

"Do what?"

"Start a fire in the fireplace!"

"I *didn't!*"

Leo marched over to their door and twisted the knob. "Well, guess what? The door is locked from the inside, so if you didn't do it, who the hell did?"

"Honey, calm down!"

"What did you do, wait until I was asleep, then go outside and bring in a pile of wood?" he cried, indicating the small stack of logs beside the hearth that weren't there when they went to bed.

"Leo, there's got to be another explanation," Alex said, throwing the blankets back prior to climbing back under them again.

"Another explanation, huh?" Leo snarled.

Alex's side of the bed was full of dirt, leaves, and bark chips, and so were her feet.

"I can't believe this! Not only are you selfish and insensitive enough to light a fire when you know how it affects me, but then you lie to me on top of it! Do you think I'm some kind of moron? Jesus Christ!" Leo yelled. He grabbed his robe and slammed out of the room.

Alex was in shock.

She didn't really do that, did she?

She reviewed her night, then remembered the nightmare about gathering the logs that turned out to be arms. Could she have gone sleepwalking again, and that was how her mind had processed it?

It had to be.

The door was locked from this side.

She remembered locking it.

And poor, poor Leo. She couldn't imagine how frightened anyone would have to be for that kind of paralysis to set in.

She pulled on her own bathrobe. Without looking, she knew Leo left the Library door open because she could hear him clearly out in the kitchen. She idly wondered what time it was, because she'd forgotten to reset the range timer at six that morning.

Leo wasn't so much making breakfast as throwing things around. The din he generated sounded like *The Washington Post March* as performed by The Little Rascals. Alex watched him in silence, waiting for him to wind down.

It took a while, but he finally did.

"What do you want for breakfast," he asked, refusing to look at her.

"I want us to talk—you know, like people who love each other?" Alex said, quietly.

"It doesn't seem like you love me very much, Alex. You took personal information and used it against me. Was it supposed to be one of your jokes? Did you get a good laugh?" Most of the anger was gone now, and what was left was just sad and deflated.

It about tore Alex's heart out. "Don't you know that I'd never do anything like that on purpose?"

"The evidence would seem to suggest otherwise." He stared past her out the window, hearing her voice, but ignoring her presence.

"Honey, there may be another explanation here. I think I might have been sleepwalking again. I don't remember getting out of bed, going outside, or starting that fire. And I had this nightmare about getting firewood. That has to be it and I can't tell you how sorry I am. You must have been scared practically to death. I'd rather cut off my arm than hurt you, don't you know that?" Alex pleaded.

He looked down at her and Alex saw the tracks of undried tears on his cheeks. "I didn't think of the sleepwalking. I didn't know what to think," he said.

"Of course you didn't, sweetie, and I don't blame you a bit. Maybe it's being in a strange new place that's setting me off, I don't know. But what I do know is that I want you to go through the first floor of this house and find all the matches and lighters there are and either hide them or throw them away. Then if I sleepwalk again, at least I won't be lighting any fires, okay?" she said.

Leo smiled and nodded. "Okay. What do you want for breakfast?"

Alec returned the smile. "Surprise me." Judging from the afternoon shadows outside the kitchen window, Alex guessed that it was about two o'clock—ten hours until work began again.

***

They took their time over breakfast.

"It's amazing what people can do in their sleep, isn't it?" Leo asked.

"It's pretty scary, too, if you happen to be the sleepwalker. People have cooked meals, driven places, and carried on conversations and they don't remember a thing when they wake up. One guy supposedly even killed somebody while asleep."

"So what's the answer to keeping you in bed, then?" Leo asked. He didn't like the sound of that "even killed" part. "We never did get those magnesium pills for you before we left to come here."

"Let's put 'em on Black's shopping list, then," Alex said. "And in the meantime…"

"Get rid of the matches and lighters. Right. First thing after breakfast," Leo said, refilling his coffee mug.

They sipped their beverages, reveling in the luxury of a whole day stretching before them in which they could do whatever they wanted.

"What do you say we have a picnic supper outside and watch the sun go down?" Alex ventured.

"That's a good idea. It's such a beautiful day."

"I'll clean up and you go outside to scout out a spot."

"You got it," he said, and leaned over and kissed her.

"I'm really, really sorry, Leo," she said again.

"All is forgiven, honey. You didn't mean it and you couldn't help it. I'll hide the matches when I come back in."

Alex smiled as he headed out. She was relieved that they'd resolved things, and she'd gladly give up a million candlelit dinners and wine by a romantic fire if it would put Leo at ease.

After the dishwasher was loaded and the coffee pot and pans were clean and dry, Alex made her way to their bedroom, intent on changing the soiled bed linens.

She hunted through the bathroom, noting happily that Leo's tarps were still in place, looking for a linen closet.

Not in the bathroom.

She searched the bedroom.

Not there, either.

There didn't seem to be any spare linens or towels anywhere. The linen closet was probably upstairs, where the family slept. The Library bedroom was obviously a seldom-used guest accommodation. Since they couldn't sleep on the soiled sheets, and she didn't have any spares...

...she'd have to wash them in the basement.

Alex toyed with the idea of hand washing them in the bath tub, but abandoned the thought, uncertain that she'd be able to remove all the stains by hand.

The brightness suddenly gone out of the day, she grimly stripped their bed and in so doing, came across her little note pad under her pillow. She'd forgotten her dream until she flipped it open and read the mysterious phrase inside. Making a mental note to show it to Leo later, she replaced the pad on her night table.

Alex crammed the linens into one of the pillowcases and

set off for the basement, stopping in the kitchen to check under the sink for laundry detergent. Finding none, she remembered Theodora's note about the washing supplies being in the basement. She stood and turned.

The basement door was wide open.

Her heart jumped. Now she *really* didn't want to go down there. *The door's not hung right, that's all. That's the reason it keeps opening. It's just a goddamn dark basement, nothing more, so knock this off! If you back out again, you'll never hear the end of it from Leo. You'll be called a girly girl for the rest of your life.*

But it was more than just that. If there was something she couldn't or wouldn't do, then that meant that Leo couldn't count on her completely and he'd have to pick up her slack. She wouldn't have that. Equal partners meant equal partners, so Alex took a calming deep breath, which failed miserably to calm her, swallowed hard and made herself cross the kitchen, pick up the D-cell flashlight that Leo had packed along with his "lucky" tools, and slowly descend the slatted stairway, certain that she'd feel a hand wrap itself around her ankle through the middle of an open riser before she reached the bottom.

Thus began her search for the elusive laundry room.

The basement smelled different this time—like old, wet dirt, not the clean, freshly turned garden smell that she experienced the last time. This was corrupt-smelling dirt, conjuring images of dying and rotting flesh riddled with carrion beetles. It was as old as the pyramids and as rank as night soil.

It smelled just like the cell her mother had called home for the last horror-ridden years of her life.

You're all grown up now, Alex, so start acting like it. A bad smell can't hurt you and the memories it calls up are nothing more sinister than history. Get moving, she told herself.

Her stomach wasn't paying a great deal of attention, however, and began a forward roll before she reached the bottom of the stairs.

Deep breaths, deep breaths. Goddammit, I will not allow a memory to incapacitate me!

She reached up and tugged the pull string to light the tiny

bulb at the center of the room.

Nothing happened.

Perfect.

Alex resolved to pay close attention to where she walked, since she wouldn't have this beacon, however dim, to guide her back to the stairway. She slung the pillowcase over her shoulder and trundled after her flashlight beam, looking for all the world like a second-storey man with a pitiful sense of direction.

She passed the wine crypt on the right and farther down, the three doors on the left wall. Try as she might to think happy thoughts, her mantle of unease only grew heavier the farther away from the kitchen stairway she wandered. The basement was immense and seemed to stretch away to a surreal distance. Alex shone the light straight ahead and ran out of illumination long before she ran out of basement.

I know the foundation of the house can't be this big.

There was a passageway off to the right and another off the left a bit farther down. Or, she could continue straight ahead down the main hallway.

Choices... great. And me without a map. Why all the passages, anyway? What were these people, bootleggers? Alex hoped she'd be brave enough to explore the side passages at some point, but right then it was all she could do just to put one foot in front of the other.

Her mouth was too dry to whistle, so she tried distracting herself with thoughts that were unrelated to things with claws and big pointy teeth hiding in the dark. *I should have worn my sweatshirt. It's cold down here.*

The whispers and susurrations that were building around her were so soft and low that Alex didn't notice them at first; but when she took a couple of steps inside a tunnel to her right, and they suddenly made their presence known.

The sounds were varied. Alex could distinguish whispers, but no words, fingers drumming on wood—*onetwothreefourfive pause onetwothreefourfive pause*—and scratching on stone. Something near her shoulder, close enough to whisper in her ear, moaned a wordless threnody so frightening that Alex's bladder nearly let go. The sound of hysterical sobbing echoed off the walls ahead of her. It was like listening to a child who had just discovered her mother's dead, mutilated body in the pile of autumn leaves in which she was playing. Beneath these, and other sounds that were unidentifiable, but equally terrifying, was a swishy rustling that called to mind a woman in a taffeta and crinoline gown walking across a thick carpet.

Alex felt her breathing go shallow and rapid and her pulse pound. Her fingertips tingled with pins and needles. When her brain finally got the message down to her legs to move, she stepped back out of the side passage and into the hall again.

The noises stopped.

She stepped back in again and the sounds resumed with one addition… metal scraping along the stone wall and heading her way.

She stepped back out to the hallway, and the noises stopped once again. Alex decided that she'd stay out of that passage this time and not up the ante by stepping in again.

Put your left foot in, pull your left foot out, put your left foot in… Jesus, it's like a demented version of the Hokey Pokey. She made a Herculean effort to suppress the rising hysterical giggle that the thought provoked.

All quiet now, Alex continued to move forward until she came to the passage on the left side.

Put your right foot in, pull your right foot out, put your right foot in, and shake it all about…

She did step in, and this time her presence was greeted with hideous maniacal laughter that didn't sound as if it were too far away.

She stepped out quickly.

Silence.

That's it. I've had it with this carnival spook house. We can just sleep on a bare mattress as far as I'm concerned. She pivoted, ready to run.

The sounds were directly in front of her now; animals shrieking in pain, the insane gibbering of a mind gone to mush, and uninterrupted, hoarse screaming that bespoke of psychological devastation so complete that it was far past human understanding.

And what was worse, her batteries were dying.

Oh, how fucking cliché is this? She gave the flashlight a couple of good whacks and the beam brightened considerably, revealing that absolutely nothing stood in her way in any direction. However, the beam of light seemed to amplify the already horrid sounds.

She didn't know what compelled her to do it, but she turned around, as if to continue her quest for the laundry room.

The sounds stopped again.

Oh my God. I don't have to be a sheep to know when I'm being herded.

Afraid to move at all now, Alex stood, trembling. Who knew what would happen if she disregarded the sounds and walked back through them? As long as she remained facing in her present direction, there were no terrifying noises—but she couldn't stand there forever, either.

She remained stationary for quite a while, and at last her breathing slowed down and her pulse quit its drum roll. *If somebody wants me to keep going, I guess I'd better. It's a good thing I'm looking for the laundry room, because I'll probably have to clean out my underwear by the time I get there.*

Alex continued down the hall and proceeded around a gentle curve to the right. There were more side passages, but Alex kept to the main hall and didn't venture into them, figuring that if her tour guides wanted her to change direction, they'd let her know. After another hundred yards or so, the hallway bent into another curve to the left.

I've been walking a long time. These passages must extend way out under the lawn.

Fifty feet farther and the hall opened into a large cavernous room. Alex had finally reached her destination. Though the air in the room was disagreeably stale and reeked of stagnant water, it did contain a large washer and dryer, a sorting table, an ironing board, an iron and a shelf full of detergents and fabric softeners. Back in the far left corner, there was even a comfy chair and a floor lamp… right next to the sump pump.

How charming.

"Thanks for helping me find this place, whoever you are," Alex called to the noisemakers. She found the wall switch, flipped it, and wasn't the least bit surprised when nothing happened. She tried the floor lamp, which did work; but it was fitted with the same five watt bulb as the overhead fixture at the bottom of the stairs.

Coincidentally, as she turned the floor lamp on, her flashlight batteries died for good and all. "Shit!" Alex pounded the flashlight repeatedly and got nothing but a sore hand for her trouble. "How in hell am I supposed to get back to the kitchen now?"

There was barely enough light to see by and she foolishly hadn't thought to bring her MagLite as backup. The stone laundry room was steeped in shadow. Alex sighed, opened the washer, and with unsteady hands, added the soap and soiled linens, shivering. *It's like a meat locker down here,* she thought, again missing her sweatshirt.

As she reached out to shut the top loader, she saw a shadow out of the corner of her eye.

A shadow that moved.

A shadow that was person-sized.

She whipped her head around.

Nothing.

Oh, man. The walls are gonna start breathing next. Get a grip, girl. She tried another deep calming breath, which didn't work any better than before, and looked back at the washer.

And at the edge of her vision, another shadow moved across the threshold.

Alex slammed the lid of the machine, punched START, and looked around. The shadows were gone.

She looked away and her peripheral vision revealed several more man-sized shadows moving into the room. Alex had always scoffed at screaming women, feeling that a clear head always served one better than high-pitched vocalizations, but now she was ready to revise her opinion. She had never screamed in her life, but watching the room's only exit filling up with what could only be described as Shadow People, it was difficult for the clear head to prevail; but prevail it did, though it was a near thing. Alex exerted a huge effort and forced the useless scream down, but her terror remained for three reasons: Number one, the Shadow People might really be there; Number two, they might only be the creations of her impaired mind; and Number three, she couldn't tell the difference. However, whatever these Shadow People were and wherever they came from, they had scared her badly, but they hadn't hurt her and they had helped her to find the laundry room—that is, if they were the same ones responsible for all the noise earlier. *No, let's not think like that.* She cleared her throat.

"Who are you?" she asked in a quavery voice she didn't recognize.

WE ARE YOU YOU ARE WE

The response was a multitude of breathy whispers that crept through the dank air and slithered down the stone walls.

She looked directly at them.

They vanished.

She looked away and there they were, hovering at the edge of her vision... and there were many more of them now.

"What do you want?"

TO LIVE

"Do you need help?"

YES

"How can I help you?"

WE DO NOT KNOW

"Why are you here?"

WE DO NOT REMEMBER

"Do you intend to harm me or my husband?"

WHO ARE YOU

"Alex Renfield."

WHAT DO YOU WANT

"To work and be paid."

PAID WITH WHAT CURRENCY

"I don't know what you mean."

WHY ARE YOU HERE

"To work."

DO YOU NEED HELP

"I think so," Alex replied, realizing it was true.

HOW CAN WE HELP YOU

"I don't know."

DO YOU WANT TO HARM US

"No! How could I possibly harm you?"

THERE IS A WAY

"Why would I want to?"

WE DO NOT KNOW

"What do you want?" Alex asked again.

TO LIVE

Suddenly, the already frigid air in the room plummeted to below freezing, and something at a very primal level in Alex urged her to get out… now.

"May I pass? I must go back upstairs." Her teeth were chattering and her breath was thickly visible. Her nasal passages and eyes were on fire from the cold.

STAY STAY WITH US YOU ARE WARM WE ARE COLD YOU WARM US YOU WILL STAY AND LIVE WITH US WARM IN THE DARK

"I can't. I must leave now."

YOU ARE WARM WE ARE COLD WARM US

"Some other time."

WHAT IS 'TIME'

"I must go," Alex cried, facing the Shadow People. Though she could no longer see them, their whispered pleas filled the frigid air around her.

STAY

WARM US

WE ARE COLD

STAY

STAY

STAY

Alex bolted through the doorway and as she passed through the shadowy aggregation, she was brought to her knees by a wall of impossible coldness. She felt her heart freezing, her eyes turning to ice.

WARM

TO LIVE

STAY

IN THE DARK

LIVE WITH US

WARM

She crawled out to the middle of the main passageway just before she lost consciousness.

Chapter Sixty-Two

Leo stood on the sun-splashed front porch for a moment, just admiring the day. The breeze ruffled the treetops and the afternoon air was suffused with a delicious mixed floral scent, the sources of which were nowhere in sight.

Deciding that this might be a better time to hunt for the garage rather than a picnic spot, Leo stepped down from the porch and set off toward the dirt road that wound into the woods at the left side of the property.

The gravel of the driveway crunched beneath his boots as he crossed it. Leo smiled, suddenly realized why so pedestrian a sound should be so comforting.

It was a sound of life.

He stopped walking half way to the narrow dirt road and stood very still.

Quiet.

Unnatural quiet.

Christ, aren't there any birds around here? Or bugs? Or squirrels?

He couldn't even hear any distant noises, like traffic or sirens. Even the breeze had moved on, and the landscape held its breath, watching and waiting.

Leo shuffled his feet in place, just for the sake of the noise, then continued on his journey, but uneasy now. Once he walked off the driveway and down the rutted dirt road, even the sun went out of the day.

Normally, a dense tree canopy bestows an atmosphere of shelter and protection for those walking beneath it, but these heavily intertwined bare branches above Leo made only made him feel captured, not comforted. The black, spiky limbs joined at the midpoint above the path like folded skeletal hands, impeding the light and reducing what little did get through to a dull mottling here and there. Leo identified the elements of the huge interweave as ancient oak, chestnut, and black walnut, with some old growth maples thrown in. There probably used to be elms here, too. New England was rife with them at one time; before the Dutch Elm Disease brought most of them down in the 1950s. The damage was so extensive that, for a while there, it looked like New Haven would have to change its sobriquet from "The Elm City" to "The Swamp Maple City." Leo smiled at the thought of the Chamber of Commerce trying to sell *that* one to New Havenites.

The brush on either side of the road was overruled by the poison ivy majority. *There's a shocker,* Leo thought, glaring at the innocuous-looking vines to which he was so highly allergic. He hurried on his way, his formerly lazy stroll now more a mission than a pleasure. Rounding the bend up ahead, he came upon a squat concrete block building that was large enough to house the Caddy, but didn't look like any garage Leo had ever seen. It was about fifteen feet square, and he was right about its not being a garage. The usual double-wide doors were absent. Instead, this concrete bunker sported an incongruous exterior raised panel door typically found on a house.

Curiosity piqued, Leo slipped quietly up the narrow tributary path leading to the building. It didn't have conventional windows, but sported arrow loops—much like the type seen high on castle parapets and used by archers to repel an approaching enemy; but on this crouching toad of a structure, they were completely out of place.

He cupped his hands around his eyes, more out of habit than need, and peered in the nearest slash of a window.

The room, and it was a single room, looked sort of like a movie set to Leo, and was crammed with devices he did not recognize. The good news, however, was that no one was around, so he went to the front entrance and tried the knob.

Locked, of course. He rattled the knob in frustration, and was thinking about trying his credit card on the lock when he heard the first rustling in the shrubbery that surrounded the weird building. It was off to his right, then moved across to the left, then back to the right. There seemed to be only one of whatever it was initially, but it was shortly joined by more... many more, all below brush height, all moving back and forth through the overgrown shrubbery as if they were pacing.

Leo chuckled at his initial threatened reaction. *Glad that something actually does live out here. Gotta be grouse or partridge— these woods are probably full of them. Could be squirrels, too. Maybe they live back here because the lawn at the house is too exposed for them to feel safe. Well, let's see what we've got...* Leo stamped his foot hard on the cement stoop, then yelled, "Geddouddahere!" in his best Tony Soprano.

It worked. Whether bird or squirrel, the hidden animals fled; but his sudden shout hadn't flushed them into view, so he still didn't know what it was that he'd frightened away. Profound silence reigned once again.

Leo wasn't sure which was worse.

The question now was: find the garage or go back to the house?

He opted for the garage and after a final gape through the windows, trying to commit every detail of the odd room to memory, he set off again down the dusty road.

***

Leo arrived at the garage after another ten minutes of stepping quietly but briskly.

He was surprised to see that it was in a terrible state of repair and appeared ready to fall down in spots. The roof sagged alarmingly and Leo thought that it might be worth his while to reinforce the roof beams, since the Caddy they sheltered was the Renfields' only connection to the outside world. No, more than that. It was their lifeline to the rest of humanity. This epiphany rattled Leo to the core of his being. *How scary is that? We're depending on a hunk of metal for survival.* But was that really what scared him? *No, that's not it. It's the fact that our survival depends on Cooper Black driving this hunk of metal... and he doesn't seem too interested in us.*

Unlike the building he'd just left, the garage was made from wood rather than cinder blocks; and Leo idly wondered if he'd find another building made out of straw if he kept walking. The whole place had the same melancholy air of slow disintegration as the forgotten ghost towns dotting the oldest areas of the southwest—that sad, down-at-the-heels look that made the observer understand why the previous residents had left no forwarding addresses.

There was a small wooden outbuilding behind the main garage, so Leo followed the path to it, proceeding as stealthily as his large frame would permit. Fortunately, the brush here had been cut back, so this path was easier to navigate quietly.

Closer now, he heard voices coming from the structure. He couldn't make out any words clearly, but he definitely heard the mumbling of quite a few different people—but the building was too small to fit more than two or three. It sounded like a meeting was going on in there. But with whom? For what? And why all the way out here?

Leo decided that the better part of valor was, indeed, getting the hell out of there. Garage exploration could wait. As a matter of fact, the idea of exploring it with Alex suddenly seemed like the best idea since rock 'n' roll."

He left the way he came, unconsciously holding his breath, fearing that his every broken twig would alert the occupants and call who knew what down upon him; and he was quite far into the woods, after all.

Space isn't the only place where no one can hear you scream.

Chapter Sixty-Three

Alex came to sometime later, completely disoriented in the utter blackness. She didn't move at first, just listened to herself breathe, her mind a blank. But when the sounds began again, she remembered where she was, and clambered to her feet. She ran as fast as she could to escape the basement, but she was facing the wrong direction and charged into the stone wall at the far end of the hall.

Dazed and bleeding, she turned around and extended her arms until she found the right direction, then ran like alligators were lunging at her ankles.

The sounds of the Shadow People followed her down the hallway, bringing their unbearable cold with them. Alex was losing her wind in the subzero temperature and it seemed like she'd been running forever. She needed help, and used some of her rapidly dwindling energy to scream for Leo, hoping he was back in the house by now and would hear her.

Chapter Sixty-Four

Leo emerged from the forest at a trot, glad, for once, to be under the aegis of the manicured lawn and the brooding gothic house. He dashed across the grass and took the front steps in a single leap, feeling giddy with relief.

He'd had other things on his mind before reaching the porch, but now he glanced at the sky. The northern New England sun had been captured by an army of rebel gray clouds, leaving Leo fairly certain that their picnic was going to be a washout.

Anxious to discuss his adventures with Alex, he put his back into opening the ridiculous front door and stepped into the chilly stillness of the house.

It didn't last long.

"Leeeeeeeeooooooo!"

The voice was close to his ear. So close he imagined that he felt the speaker's breath. He pivotted, scanning the hallway.

Nothing.

"Leeeeeeooooooooo!"

There it was again.

"Alex?" he called. The expected answer didn't arrive. He remembered the laundry and headed for the basement.

"Leo?"

It came from behind him.

I'm imagining this. It's not there. Leo directed himself with all the pragmatism he could muster. Still, he turned, searching.

"Leeeeooooo!"

It was coming from the art gallery.

He backtracked, then ran to the gallery. The door was closed but something stayed Leo's hand when he reached for the knob. He stood quietly, listening instead.

"Leo?"

He jerked backward. The voice was so clear that it was obvious its owner was standing directly behind the closed gallery door.

"Who's in there?" he demanded, sounding much more intimidating than he felt.

"Come in and find out," the voice suggested, with a silky edge that immediately called spiders to mind. Big spiders.

"Never mind the games! Who are you and what are you doing here? The owners are away."

"And that's when the mice will play," the voice replied in a high childish sing-song. "Mice… or something larrrrrrgerrrrr."

Leo had his hand on the knob when a shriek from the basement drew his attention, and his footsteps, back down the hall.

He threw open the basement door with such force that it bounced off the wall and caught him hard on the shoulder as he moved forward. He didn't even feel it.

"Alex! Alex! Where are you?" he called down the stairs. He searched for the big flashlight before he remembered that Alex would have had it with her; but then he spied her MagLite on the counter, so he snatched it up and turned it on.

'Leeeeeoooooo! Help!" she screamed.

It sounded as if she was right at the foot of the stairs. Why wasn't the light on?

Leo clattered down the stairs and just about knocked Alex flat when he reached the bottom. She fought him, not realizing who he was.

"Alex! Alex, honey! It's me! It's Leo!" he shouted, pinning her arms.

"Oh, God! Leo. Thank heav…" Alex rasped, slumping into his arms.

It took him a moment to realize she'd fainted. He laid her down gently on the basement floor and retrieved the still lit MagLite from where it had landed when he ran into his flailing wife. He located the pull string and added a bit more illumination to the murk.

Though he knew before he turned the light on that something had frightened Alex badly, he was completely unprepared for what he saw. "Jesus, Alex, what happened to you?" he murmured.

The tips of her fingers, nose and ears were purple and her lovely blond hair was now a startling snowy white.

Leo carried his unconscious wife up the noisy stairway and into their bedroom, where he laid her down on the bare mattress. Then he sat on the edge of the bed, took her pulse, and found it to be strong and steady. He brushed her long white hair aside and was surprised to see that Alex's face was a study in Buddha-like serenity. He patted her cheeks. "Alex? Honey?" Wake up, sweetie."

She came around as if waking from a deep, relaxing sleep. "Leo? Why am I in bed?"

"You passed out in the basement, but not before you screamed your head off. Don't you remember?"

"Some. I found the laundry room. It's at the far end of a really long tunnel." She sat up. "Oh, gosh, the laundry's still down there. I have to put the sheets in the dryer."

"What happened down there, Alex? Look at your fingers. They're purple. Is that paint or stain or something?"

"It was cold down there, Leo. I remember that. So cold I thought I was dying. This must be frostbite. I can't feel anything when I touch it."

"Alex, it doesn't get cold enough in a basement to give anyone frostbite—not even in the dead of winter."

"It was like the North Pole down there, Leo, I promise you."

"Okay, assuming that's so, then it's on the tops of your ears and the tip of your nose, too. I'd better get you into a hot bath so you can put face cloth compresses on those areas," Leo said, pushing himself up off the bed with a grunt and disappearing into the bathroom. The next sound she heard was water splashing into the tub.

Alex, wanting to assess the damage herself, slowly got out

of bed and followed Leo into the bathroom, stopping at the vanity. "Oh no!" she cried, eyes saucer-large.

Leo turned. "What are you doing in here? You should rest until I get the tub filled."

"My hair! Oh, Leo, look at my hair!" Alex wailed.

Leo stepped behind her and held her because she wouldn't turn to face him. She couldn't pry her horrified eyes from her reflection.

"How did this happen?" she asked in a small voice.

"I have no idea. Something must have scared you pretty badly," Leo said.

"Is that really true? That a bad scare can turn hair white?"

"Seems so."

Not only had her hair color changed, but the texture had changed, too. No longer was it silky and baby fine. Now it was thick and coarse, horrible to touch.

"I look like a hag."

"No you don't, but if it bothers you, put some hair dye on 'The Black List.'"

"That's a great idea, Leo, but I've never dyed my hair before. I wouldn't know what to tell him to buy." Then she sighed. "But anyway, we can't. Not on the product approval list, remember? We must preserve the pipes! I'll have to wait until we get home. Can you live with it until then?"

"Honey, I wouldn't care if you were bald. While we're waiting for the tub to fill, let's put some compresses on your nose," Leo said, handing her a steaming face cloth.

Alex looked in the mirror again, this time at the frostbite on her face. Sighing, she applied the hot cloth to her nose, and quickly pulled it away. "It burns, Leo. It really hurts."

"Yeah, it's going to hurt; but you need to get your circulation back in those areas as quickly as possible before the tissue dies."

Alex gritted her teeth and though intense pain shot through her face, she held the cloth in place.

"Sorry about your hair," Leo said. "I should have warned

you."

"It won't be this way long, don't worry," she replied nasally.

"What scared you, babe?"

"I honestly don't remember, Leo. I wish I did."

"Why didn't you turn the light on down there?"

"It doesn't work. I tried."

"Sure it works. I put it on when I came down to get you. Which reminds me, it's still on and I'd better go turn it off and save it. I don't think they even make bulbs like that anymore, so if it burns out, we're out of luck."

"The light's on? Right now?"

"Yeah."

"Keep an eye on the tub, will you? I'll be right back," Alex said, tossing him the face cloth.

She ran to the kitchen. The basement door was still open and she could see the tarnished glimmer of the little bulb in the darkness. Intending to go down to shut it off, Alex picked up the MagLite that Leo had tossed on the counter and started down.

She experienced a curious sensation that grew deeper as she descended—a medley of desire and repulsion. She stepped across the hard pan floor and shone her MagLite down the vast passage where she had so recently won the 100-Yard Mortal Terror Dash.

But in mortal terror of what?"

She had no idea.

Alex was tempted to take a walk and put the linens in the dryer, but she remembered that her frostbite required immediate attention. When she pulled the sting and plunged herself into near darkness, she found that something new had been added, and she switched off her MagLite.

She could now see, quite clearly, in total darkness.

Somehow, she knew with certainty that she had been given a gift; but from whom, and why, she had no idea. She also knew, without being told, that it was hers only as long as she kept it to herself. And far from being terrorized, she felt happy in the dark without knowing why.

She smiled. "Thank you," she whispered into the darkness, then turned and left the basement.

Now why did I do that? Who was I thanking? And for what? I probably hit my head—that accounts for the night vision. It'll probably go away soon.

But deep down, she knew it wouldn't.

"Turned out the light for you," Alex said, walking back into the bathroom. "Water ready?"

"Yes. All you have to do is get your delicious body out of those clothes and hop in," Leo said, leering.

"Aren't you supposed to offer me a piece of candy first?" Alex asked, shucking her jeans and tee shirt.

"That's right! Oh, please don't tell anyone. I'll be drummed out of the Dirty Old Men's League."

"Really? But aren't you the president?"

Leo threw a face cloth at her. "Get in there!"

Alex put her foot in. "This is going to hurt a lot, isn't it?" she asked.

In answer, Leo held out four aspirin and a glass of water.

"Could I wait for them to start working before I get in?"

"It's vital to get the circulation restarted ASAP, babe. I'm really sorry."

Alex took the aspirin and sat down in a tub that would normally have been a perfect temperature if she wasn't treating frostbite.

"It's going to take about a half hour for the affected areas to thaw out, so you're going to be in pain for a while. What I'd do if I were you would be to lie back and let the water cover your ears. I'll put compresses on your nose so you can keep your hands submerged. That way, you'll at least get all the pain out of the way at once," Leo said.

"How come you know so much about frostbite?" Alex asked.

"I was an Eagle Scout, my love. I know many things about

many things, and I have the merit badges to prove it... or, I did."

"Lost them in the fire?" Alex asked gently.

"Yes, along with everything and everyone else," he replied.

"Do you want to talk about it some more?"

His smile was both tired and sad. "Not right now, but thanks. Want me to stay with you while you soak?"

"Yes, that would be great," Alex said.

"Okay. I'll get something to read. Are you finished with that Westlake book?"

"Uh huh. It's on my night table. It was his best Dortmunder novel yet." John Dortmunder was a burglar who couldn't have had worse luck if he stepped on a crack while walking under a ladder to break a mirror over a black cat. Neither Alex nor Leo could get enough of Dormunder's hilarious capers, and eagerly awaited each new release.

When Leo returned, he carried, not only the Westlake book, but Alex's spiral bound pad, as well. "What's this for?" he asked, holding it up.

"In case I get any story ideas during the night."

He smiled. "Anything brilliant yet?"

"Check it and see," she replied.

Leo flipped it open, and looked puzzled at what he read.

"What?" Alex asked.

"This phrase. '*Pestry posterus specto*.'"

"Oh, yeah! I meant to show that to you and forgot all about it. It was from a dream I had. I don't remember any of the details now, and if I hadn't written that down, it would be gone, too. Wonder if it means anything. Reading it out loud, it sounds like you're talking gibberish," Alex said. Though her ear for comedic timing was fine tuned, it was pure tin when it came to languages other than English.

"I think this is Latin," Leo said.

"How can it be? I've never studied Latin, so why would I

dream in it?"

"I don't know. This is Latin, though," Leo said.

"I had no idea you were multilingual," Alex said, surprised.

"Twelve years of parochial education would teach Latin to a doorstop, kiddo. You didn't learn it, you got a ruler across the knuckles—and not gently, either."

"They really did that?"

"You bet."

"And at the end of each term, did you have tests or inquisitions?"

"Cute. Did someone write this out in your dream or did they say it?"

"Why?"

"Because I think there's a spelling error or two."

"I dimly recall someone saying it over and over."

"Well, *pestry* is the problem here. For one thing, it would end in an 'i' not a 'y', making it '*pestri.*' Are you sure it wasn't '*vestri*'? Could it have been a 'v' that you heard rather than a 'p'?"

"It could have been, I guess."

"The reason I ask is that it makes more sense if you misheard '*vestri.*'"

"Why? What does it mean with the 'p'?"

"Something like, 'your pestilence looks back at you.' It doesn't make any sense.

"What about the other way?"

"It means, 'Your future awaits.' And what awaits your future, my dear, is to bite the bullet and soak your frostbite. Now come on, you've stalled just about enough."

Leo set the timer he'd liberated from the kitchen to ring in 30 minutes. As the ticking began, Alex closed her eyes, steeled herself, and reclined until her ears were beneath the water. She dropped her hands below the surface, then Leo placed a hot compress on her nose.

The pain was excruciating, but Alex bore up like a Navy Seal.

It was the longest half hour of her life.

***

When the timer finally dinged, Alex sat up. "How does it look?" she asked Leo.

"Lots better. I think we got it in time. You'll have to put some Vaseline on it for a few days, and a thick coat of it if you're going anywhere even slightly chilly."

"Like the basement?"

"Very much like the basement, it would appear."

"But, Leo, the sheets are still down there."

"Then I'll go get them," Leo said, absently pocketing Alex's spiral pad.

"They need to be dried first."

"I'll do that, then."

"Okay." Though Alex expected to feel relieved, she didn't. Rather, she felt as if her territory was about to be violated. *Why do I feel so proprietary about that spooky old basement? Why can't I remember? And why can I see in the dark now?*

"You look funny. What are you thinking about?" Leo asked.

She snapped back to the present. "Funny, is it?" She pulled an outrageous face from her mental filing cabinet and put it on. "How about now?"

"Why, Alex, wher*ever* have you been?" Leo cried.

She bounced a loofah off his forehead.

"Be right back. Way at the end of the straight hallway, you said?"

"Yes, but really, Leo, I can take care of it." The logical part of her brain threw up its hands and rolled its eyes.

'You're joking, right? This is a joke," Leo didn't ask so much as state, his deep voice carrying a warning edge.

"Uh... yeah. See you later, then." If she couldn't remember anything else, at least she hadn't forgotten when to quit.

Chapter Sixty-Five

Before going downstairs, Leo gathered up all the fire starting implements he could find, and stuffed them into a small garbage bag. *I'll stick them in the basement—scared as she was, she'll be staying out of there for a long while.* Smiling at his cleverness, he switched on the small MagLite and reminded himself to keep an eye out for the missing D-cell flashlight while he was down there.

He clomped down the stairs and pulled the string dangling at the center of the room. He felt kind of sorry for that poor little bulb—it tried, but only threw off about as much light as a candle would... maybe less. *Hang in there, buddy. Vegrandis tamen validus.*

Before long, he was outside Door Number One. Without thinking about it, he tried the knob and found it unlocked. He opened it cautiously and shone the light inside.

The pink powder room was back—the same as it was, including, Leo was careful to note, the knife blade sticking out of the wall. This time, however, something new had been added.

There was writing on the mirror.

𝔠hapter 𝔖ixty-𝔖ix

As is often the case with adults in bath tubs who find themselves without a book to read or a companion to talk to, minds tend to meander off onto more juvenile tracks. Weary of trying to call up a memory that refused to come, Alex turned down this childish spur line herself and, inspired by Leo, wondered how long she could hold her breath under water. She took a deep inhale of the steaming air, then hastily submerged, mentally counting the one-Mississippi, two-Mississippi seconds.

At fifteen-Mississippi, Alex started to feel uncomfortable.

At thirty-one-Mississippi, she could hear her heart pounding in her ears and her lungs were hurting.

At forty-seven-Mississippi, her lungs were on fire and she gave it up, sputtering to the surface.

She took a huge lungful of air.

She wiped her eyes.

She gasped.

While she was underwater, the tarps had fallen and every face in the frieze was looking directly down at her.

Chapter Sixty-Seven

What the hell? Leo's brow furrowed as he stared at the writing on the surface of the mirror. As a matter of fact, upon closer inspection, it looked as if the words had been painted on with a fine artist's brush. The script itself was old style and antique looking, and what was written was a poem.

Leo remembered Alex's pad in his pocket, so he took it out, grabbed the pen clipped next to it and copied out the curious missive—after hiding the bag of fire-making supplies under the sink.

"Weird," Leo muttered, putting the pad and pen away. Then he realized that Alex must have done this while sleepwalking. Her calligraphy was impeccable and Leo remembered that she'd given a Poe-obsessed friend of theirs a calligraphic rendering of *The Raven* and the lettering was very similar to what he was looking at.

At least she wasn't starting fires anymore. This, he could live with.

Still staring at the bizarre message, he let his right hand drop to rest on the edge of the sink.

Yelping in pain, he pulled it back.

A whole series of cuts crisscrossed his palm and were bleeding profusely. He held his hand over the side sink and with his previously injured left hand, shone the light down to find the culprit this time.

It didn't take long. The top of the sink was coated with small shards of clear broken glass, all carefully glued in place to point upward, like miniscule stalagmites. He'd have noticed them earlier if the writing on the mirror hadn't captured his full and immediate attention.

Leo washed the punctures and cuts with care in the small sink, lest he retain pieces of glass in the wounds. He ran the water as hot as he could stand it, hoping to get the blood to clot and stop the bleeding; but it continued to flow freely, which struck him as odd. He'd never ever been one who was quick to bleed. His clotting factor had to be halfway decent, too, because whenever he did cut himself, he never bled long.

But lately…

He sighed, selected another fine Egyptian cotton had towel to ruin, and wrapped it around his right hand this time.

Shaking his head, he stepped out of the garish room and shut the door, using his pocket knife to cut his initials into the door at eye level. He then continued on his way to the laundry room, resolving not to upset his wife by confronting her with the message she'd written on the mirror.

After all, it was harmless.

Chapter Sixty-Eight

Alex bounded out of the tub, snatched up her bath sheet and charged into the bedroom, slamming the door behind her. She wrapped herself in the huge towel and perched on the edge of the bed, willing her heart to desist its tap dancing.

What's going on here?

Damp and uncomfortable, she began a slow burn. *I am so tired of being frightened to death every time I turn around. This is stupid. I can't just never go into the bathroom again.* She wondered, too, if perhaps the faces in the frieze were actually moveable in some way. As put off as she was by the carvings, she'd never examined them closely. Maybe they were. *Maybe there's a gizmo somewhere in the house that moves them—on a timer.*

But for what purpose?

"Well, they didn't move by their own damned selves, idiot. And were you hurt? No. So get back in there and find the mechanism," she ordered herself.

The only thing missing when she threw open the door was the melodramatic "Aha!" that should have accompanied it. Instead, her gran…

"Alex! Wake up, sweetie."

"Oh, Leo, what a horrid dream." She looked quickly at the frieze and was happy to discover that it remained covered, and all was right with the world.

"Your water's getting cold; you must have been asleep for a while."

"I guess. I'll be out in a minute. Hey, how about a game of Scrabble?" she asked.

"Sure. I'll go set up the board," Leo said, and left the bathroom.

Alex got out of the tub and dried off; but the fright from the dream, though receding, was still hovering at the back of her mind, like a vaguely foul odor. So, to put her mind at ease, she crept up to the first covered face at the far end of the bathroom, and lifted the end of the tarp.

The face was fixed and unchanged… until it turned toward her and screamed.

All she could do was…

"Alex! Wake up! You're having a nightmare!" Leo said, shaking her shoulder.

"Wha?"

"Well, a tubmare is more like it," he laughed.

"Am I really awake this time?" Alex asked.

"What do you mean?"

"I mean I had a nightmare within a nightmare—a double whammy. I just want to be sure I'm not going to try for three. I dreamed that you already woke me up once."

"You're really awake this time. I promise. What did you dream?" Leo asked.

"It was about those faces on the wall. Glad to see they're still covered." Alex filled him in.

When she'd finished, Leo asked, "Want me to check them for you?"

"I don't think so. As long as they're covered, I'm okay with them."

"Oh, and I meant to tell you—I think a picnic supper is going to be out of the question for tonight. Storm's coming," Leo said.

"Too bad. Another night, then. You were out for a long time, though. Where did you go?"

"Garage hunting."

"Did you find it?"

"Yes. I'll tell you about it when you get out. Want to play Scrabble?" he asked.

"Sure." *Wish I'd thought of that,* she laughed to herself.

***

Squeaky clean, frostbite Vaselined, dressed and ready for Scrabble, Alex walked into the Library to the pleasant surprise of poured cocktails and a plate of warm brie with green grapes and sliced pears.

"Wow, that looks great," Alex said with a grin.

"I probably should have served you a Chardonnay with this, but I didn't feel like going down into that damned basement again."

"You, too, huh?"

Leo held up his newly bandaged hand.

"*Again*? What happened? Oh, Leo, are you all right?"

"Yeah, I'm fine—good as new. Just needed some soap and hot water and a bandage."

"Do you want some cayenne?"

"No, the bleeding seems to have stopped," he replied. *Sure it did, after eight ounces or so went down the drain.*

"How did it happen?"

Leo gave Alex a version that was so abridged that, if it were a skirt, it would have caused traffic accidents and arrests. "I scraped it on something."

"On what?"

"I don't really know—it's so dark down there. The MagLite doesn't help too much."

Alex stared at the dressing. "Did you find the pink powder room again?"

"Yep. It's down there, all right. And this time, I marked the door so I can find it again."

"Why do you want to find it again?"

"So I can show it to you."

"Good. Oh, did you put the sheets in the dryer?" she asked.

"No. I didn't want to bleed all over them."

"That's all right; I'll take care of it later. Does it still hurt?" she asked, nodding at his hand.

"Nope. I'm tough."

Alex smiled.

The truth was it hurt like a sonofabitch. Leo wondered what that glass was coated with, besides his blood.

"And what have we here?" Alex asked, picking up a glass.

"We have bone dry Bombay Sapphire martinis with five Spanish olives in each."

She laughed. "I think the only reason you ever drink martinis is because you like the gin-soaked olives." She took a sip. "Lovely. How did you get them so cold without diluting the gin with ice?"

"Easy. Right after we got here, I took three bottles each of gin and vodka from the Billiard Room and put them in the walk-in freezer."

"Brilliant. Don't you feel sort of silly referring to it as 'The Billiard Room' though?"

"Yes, I do. I always imagine that I should say it like Thurston Howell the Third, underslung jaw and all."

They took their drinks and snack, and settled back into the rosewood sofa that faced the cold and empty fireplace.

"So tell me about the garage," Alex said.

"It's falling down," Leo said.

"Was the Caddy in it?"

"Uh huh."

"That's odd," Alex said. "They're so fussy about the way everything else looks, you'd think the garage would be in tip top shape, too, wouldn't you?"

"You'd think."

Alex studied Leo's face. "So what bothers you?"

"Think about it. That car is our lifeline. If the roof falls down on it, nobody's going anywhere for a long time."

"Let's fix the roof, then," Alex said.

"It would be in our interest to do so," Leo said. "I'll put the lumber I think we'll need on the list. Black can figure out how to get it here. We can take a walk out there tomorrow and get a few measurements—or, at least, a better materials estimate. We'll have to do it on our own time, though. That okay with you?"

"I think it better be," Alex replied.

"I found a couple of other things out there that I can't explain, too. Weird shit," Leo said. He filled Alex in about the small concrete structure and the mumbling building.

A small smile spread over Alex's face.

"What's funny?" Leo asked.

"I think I know what's going on in your mumbling building."

"You do? What?"

"I'd rather wait until tomorrow and see. I might be wrong."

"All right, Miss Inscrutable. Ready for that Scrabble game?"

"Sure. You'll probably win, but I don't care."

"Why do you say that?" Leo asked.

"Because I have no head for strategy. You, on the other hand, can put down a couple of tiles and get sixty-five points—I've seen you do it."

"You could do it, too," he said.

"No. I'm perfectly happy with the way I play. I may not win, but I usually have the most interesting words."

They left their empty glasses and cheese plate and moved to the game table across the room. Leo had already set up the game.

Alex studied all the face-down tiles. "There are way too many tiles here. There are only supposed to be a hundred in all, but this looks closer to two hundred."

Leo grinned. "Two hundred exactly, Rain Man. I bet they just combined two games so they could play longer."

"But the board is still the same size. It has two hundred twenty-five squares on it, and there'd never be enough open space to use all these tiles, or to even come close." Alex explained.

"Well then, maybe they were using the extra letters to teach the kids how to play when they were little. You'd need more vowels than the game provides for children to play it."

"Must be it."

They each chose a tile to determine who would go first. Leo got and E, Alex a W. They each chose six more and began.

Leo put down:

Alex built from the L:

"That's not too interesting so far, my dear," Leo said.

"I know. I don't know what's the matter with me. Did you slip me a Mickey or something?"

Leo laughed and built from Alex's L:

"Into bugs tonight, are we?" Alex asked.

"Seems so," Leo said. "Your turn."

Alex added tiles to Leo's U:

"'You?' C'mon. You can do better than that!"

Alex focused on her tiles and said nothing. Leo used the first W in WEEVIL:

"'Welcome.' Good one," Alex said quietly without lifting her eyes from the board.

Leo was growing concerned. Scrabble games were always so much more fun than this—more lighthearted with lots of banter. This game was bordering on funereal.

Alex built off the last E in LOUSE:

"Oh, Alex, you aren't even trying," Leo gently chided. "We can do this another time if you don't feel like playing."

"No, Leo. I have to… I mean, I *want* to play."

"All righty, then. Watch this one:"

"Double word. Nice," Alex said. She put a U above the S in SATED:

"Alex, are you letting me win?"

"Of course not."

"Then what's with the elementary school words? 'will,' 'you,' 'help,' 'us'… oh my God…"

"Somebody's talking to us, Leo," Alex said, her face as pale as her hair. "It feels like a pulling inside me, and I think whatever's doing it is controlling what I put down on the board."

"Do you want to stop? I'll put it away right now if you want," Leo said, his blue eyes filled with alarm.

"No, let's keep on. It's sort of like a new take on a Ouija Board, isn't it?" Alex said. Her eyes were way too bright.

"Okay." Leo added to the M in WELCOME:

Alex drew tiles and spelled, from the D in MODERN:

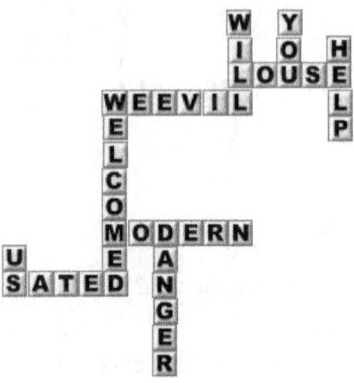

"I wonder if I can ask questions," Alex muttered.

"Try it," Leo encouraged, as he used the L in WELCOME for his word:

"'Danger' from whom?" Alex asked the board. Then she placed tiles at the R in DANGER:

"'Restrain,'" Leo read. "Who is restraining you?" He chose tiles and used the N in RESTRAIN:

"Well, that makes no sense. I guess they don't want to talk to me," Leo said. "Your turn."

"Who restrains you?" Alex asked. She chose fifteen tiles and placed them on the board.

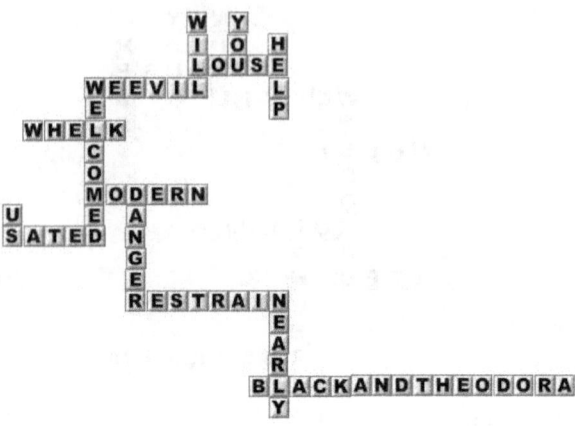

"'Black and Theodora,'" Leo read.

"How do they restrain you?" Alex asked. She waited and found she had no desire whatsoever to even touch the tiles. "I'm getting zip, so go ahead."

Leo used the P in HELP:

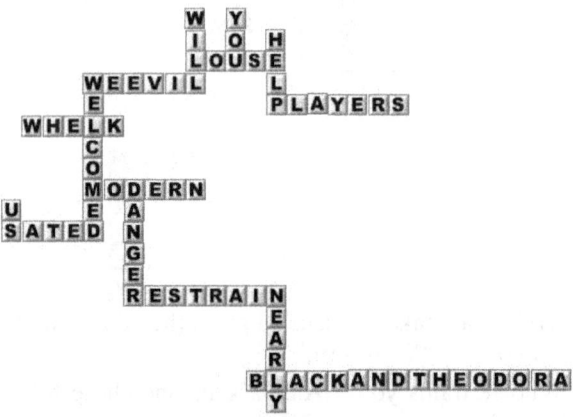

Alex asked again. "How do they restrain you?" Now her fingers nimbly chose and placed tiles once again, using the W of Leo's WHELK:

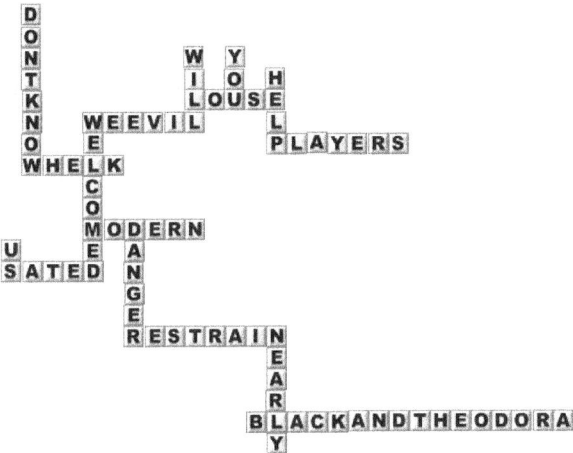

"'Don't know.' I think we have to continue playing," Leo said. "It doesn't look like they want to talk to you *or* me when it isn't your turn." Leo used the S in PLAYERS:

"Do you need help?" Alex asked.

"I think they already said that, didn't they?" Leo asked, pointing out the WILL, YOU, HELP, and US. Alex didn't respond, she just picked up tiles and placed them on the board, using the E in PLAYERS:

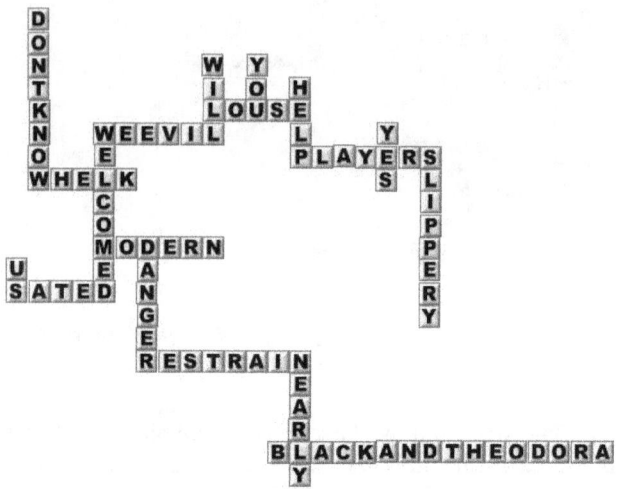

"'Yes.'" Leo quietly added OUS to DANGER:

"How can we help you?" Alex asked. She picked tiles and laid them on the board at Leo's word, SLIPPERY to spell:

"'ONLYOU.' I could challenge that, you know," Leo whispered.

Alex looked up, her face expressionless. "Who would you challenge, Leo?"

"Sorry. A joke. A coping mechanism. Not the time or place," he said, using the S in DANGEROUS:

When Alex ignored it and failed to make the usual quip that he'd left himself open for, Leo realized fully that they weren't playing the game at all anymore, and just going through the motions so that Alex could continue to communicate with whatever was out there in the ether. Fear spread through him like Kerrygold butter on hot brown bread.

"Just me? Not Leo? You just want me to help you?" Alex asked, her attention riveted on the board. She chose tiles and laid them out, using the E in MODERN:

"'YES' and 'AS.' Good one," Leo whispered to a wife who was way past hearing him. The back of his mind registered the humming of Cooper Black's stair chair on its way to the first floor. He used the K in BLACK:

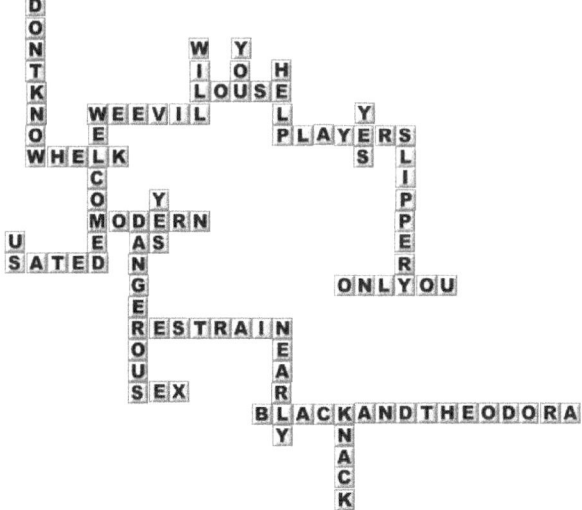

"What do you want me to do?" Alex asked. Using the A in KNACK, she spelled:

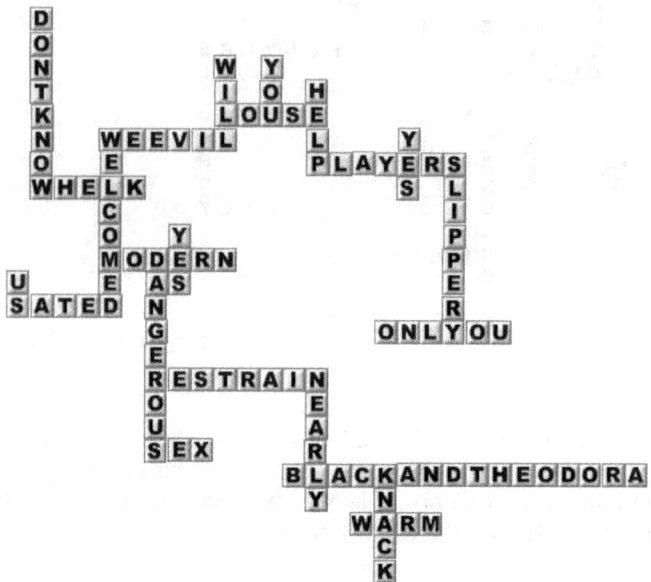

Alex swept the board from the table as the memory of her basement experience came flooding back.

Chapter Sixty-Nine

"Oh God, Leo, I remember now! I remember what happened in the basement!" She was about to tell him all about it, but suddenly, the story died on her lips.

If she never before thought that a dwarf could have not only an imposing presence but an intimidating one, seeing Cooper Black standing in the library doorway made a new believer out of her. He was obviously very angry about something, his already dark visage made even darker with what seemed like barely suppressed rage.

Leo followed Alex's gaze, but wasn't put off in the least by the man's incendiary expression. He was, however, annoyed that Black had interrupted a private conversation, even though he couldn't hear a word of it. "Something we can do for you?" he asked, slowly forming the words to facilitate lip-reading.

Black indicated, with a pointed finger that he wanted the spilled game picked up, pronto. As Leo nodded and got up out of his chair to retrieve the scattered tiles, Black continued to stare at Alex, his face contorted with wrath. He held the look for another second or two, then put his index finger vertically across his lips, still glowering at her. After a moment, he dropped his arm and walked away. The next sound she heard was his chair as it thrummed back up into the darkness of the second floor.

"What in the hell was that all about?" Alex asked, turning from the door herself, to help Leo. "We couldn't have disturbed him. He's deaf."

"I dunno. Don't ask me to explain anything that goes on around this place."

But she continued to be bothered by Black's gesture.

Maybe he was telling her to keep her mouth shut.

Finally, the game was restored to its box and replaced in the Billiard Room Games Closet. Leo poured them both lemonades, and they sat together outside on the top step of the front porch, each leaning against a thick railing baluster, facing each other.

"So now that you know, tell me. What happened down there in the dark?"

Alex recounted her disturbing adventure but omitted any mention of the gift she'd been given.

Leo sat, transfixed, as she talked on, and when she finished her story, he still sat in silence.

"Well?" she asked.

Leo sighed. "Did you take your pill?"

"Yes."

"Good. Well, Jack did say it would take a while for them to build up in your system."

"Leo, this was real! They're down there, I swear to you."

"I believe that you believe it, honey. You believed it so much that your hair went white. But I've been down there a couple of times, too, and I haven't heard a thing."

"They don't want to talk to you, remember?"

Leo looked tired. "Yes, I remember."

"Well, explain the Scrabble game, then," Alex demanded. She couldn't decide if she was angry or anxious.

"It's easy enough to answer your own questions, sweetie," Leo said, trying to be gentle.

"Leo, there was something making me put those tiles down like that. It wasn't me!"

"And isn't that kind of thing another symptom of schizophrenia?" Leo asked, continuing to meet her rising panic with calm reasoning. "Don't worry, babe. When the pills go to work for you, everything is going to be fine. How's your lemonade?"

"Great," Alex murmured, forcing back her tears. *It's better than I am.*

They sat together a few minutes more, watching the skies get progressively darker and more threatening, each lost in different thoughts. Finally, Leo drained his glass and stood, stretching. "If it's all right with you, I think I'll make supper tonight. I've been dying to get my hands on that kitchen for a big meal." His joviality couldn't have been more forced, and Alex knew it.

She got up from the step. "Sure, Leo, whatever."

"Don't be that way, Alex. You know what an imagination you have. Put that together with the condition you're being treated for, and a basement full of talking shadows isn't so unlikely, is it? You've just got to be patient, babe. Everything will be fine once the pills start to work."

"I sure hope so, Leo." It was everything she could do not to tell Leo that she didn't think schizophrenia accounted for her sudden ability to see in the dark, but she managed to quell the urge. He'd only say it was an aberration from hitting her head, and he might be right.

Hell, maybe she *was* crazy. She just didn't want to think about it anymore, and so she resolved to keep any further hallucinations, if that's what they were, to herself. Real or not, though, Leo had made it clear that he didn't believe her; and that was worse—much worse.

She was on her own if the Shadow People did exist, and crazy if they didn't.

Swell.

While Leo prepared their supper, Alex browsed the library in search of a new book to escape into. She despaired of finding any Westlake, and chided herself for not thinking to pack more of her preferred reading material.

Scanning the shelves, she discovered that the majority of the Hamiltons' collection was comprised of histories—never a big interest of hers, though Leo would be pleased. There was a leather bound set of the great literary classics, all of which she'd read several times. There was also the complete works of William Shakespeare that people always put on their bookshelves to look highbrow, but never read. The Shakespeare snobbery always amused Alex, because Shakespeare wrote for the uneducated masses, not for the elite intelligentsia of his time. So people getting all nose-in-the-air over plays geared toward entertaining the likes of butchers, farmers, and fishmongers never failed to bring a smile to Alex's face. In the final analysis, it was like getting all uppity and imperious over the *Lifetime* movie channel.

There was also an extensive collection of obsolete gardening books published in the 1800s, numerous volumes of poetry by poets Alex had never heard of, and volume after volume of equally dry and, for Alex, uninteresting nonfiction and other obscure literature.

"Okay, nothing out here," she murmured. "Our bookcase is it, I guess." She legged it to the bedroom and browsed through the more contemporary offerings, hidden away as they were, like a shameful secret. There was a wealth of entertainment biographies, as well as books by Shirley Jackson (with *Hill House* conspicuously absent), Robert Benchley, T.M. Wright, J.K. Rowling, S.J. Perelman, James Thurber, Dean Koontz, P. G. Wodehouse, and a dozen books by an author Alex hadn't heard of before—Maeve Binchy. Curious, she withdrew a thick paperback entitled, *Scarlet Feather*, read the first couple of pages, and was hooked.

By the time Leo called her to supper, she was a hundred pages into it, previous cares and worries mercifully forgotten for the moment.

***

The storm broke just as they sat down before Leo's beautifully prepared meal of Chicken Française, Brussels Sprouts Hollandaise, and thin-sliced potatoes fried with garlic, green onions, and clarified butter. There was also a warm side salad of radicchio, arugula, and broccoli rabe that had been lightly sautéed in crushed garlic and olive oil, then laid across a bed of baby Romaine and garnished with capers.

"Gee, Leo, is this it?" Alex asked, looking disappointed. Leo's devastated expression was so priceless, she had to laugh or her teeth would have exploded. "Leo, I'm only kidding! I can't believe you got all this done so fast. It smells wonderful and looks even better." They both took their seats.

"You got me. I owe you one," Leo said with a good

natured grin. "Getting windy out there," he said, indicating the scene out the kitchen window.

Alex turned to look. The treetops were thrashing in every direction, but her overriding interest was on her supper and she quickly refocused her attention. She had taken her first bite and was about to give Leo a rave review when a huge bolt of lightning touched down alarmingly close to the house. It was immediately followed by a thunderclap that shook the entire building.

"Let's go watch!" Alex cried, getting up and heading for the front door. She just loved a good storm. Leo lagged behind, coming along to keep her company, but really not interested— especially when lightning was involved. The gourmet meal was forgotten for the moment.

It took a bit of doing to get the door open, between its leaden heaviness and the opposing forces of the high winds that seemed to be fighting their efforts to move it; but when they finally did, their view was obscured by a torrential downpour. It was a wall of water so dense that nothing could be discerned beyond the covered porch.

"It used to rain like this in Phoenix during the monsoon season!" Leo shouted over the downpour. "It never lasted much more than fifteen minutes or so. Let's go eat before everything gets stone cold."

They tried to ease the door shut, but the wind ripped it from their grasp and slammed it so loudly that it rattled their teeth. They went back to their meal.

Supper was both delicious and noisy. The tumultuous rain continued, as well as the too close lightning, which bothered Leo so much that he got up and closed the window blinds and pulled the curtains. The thunder continued to boom, almost simultaneously with the lightning strikes now. The storm was directly overhead, and the cascading rain continued to pour down long after Leo's initially estimated cutoff time.

He was amazed. "I've never seen it rain this hard, this long, anywhere!" he shouted over the *sturm und drang* outside. "We'll probably be able to start a trout hatchery in the basement by the time this is over! Did you happen to notice if there was a sump pump down there anywhere?"

"Yes! In the laundry room!"

"Nothing like putting it as far away from the stairs as possible! I'll have to wade down there after supper and see what's what!"

"I'll go, Leo!" Alex yelled.

"After your last trip down there, I don't think that's such a good idea, do you?" Leo shouted back.

Alex, for a reason that eluded her, was desperate to return to the far reaches of the basement, so she said, "I need to go, Leo! I need to prove to myself that the last time was just my imagination and nothing more!"

"Do you want me to come along?"

"No!" she answered, too emphatically and far too quickly. Recovering, she added, "It's something I have to do myself, that's all!"

"Fine, but what do you know about sump pumps?"

"Plenty! Oh, hey, the storm must be letting up—we don't have to scream at each other anymore. Anyway, the basement of the house I grew up in always filled up after a storm. I know how to fix them, unblock them, get them started and stopped, and I could probably rebuild one if I had to," Alex replied.

"Who taught you all that?"

"No one. You learn to figure things out when there's nobody else sober enough or sane enough to do them."

"How did you ever live through all that? You're the strongest person I've ever met, Alex," Leo said.

"You think so? Well, keep reminding me every now and then, will you? I'm feeling kind of shaky lately," she said.

Leo's smile warmed the room. "You're going to be just fine, Alex, so stop worrying. And if you're set on going down there, toss the sheets in the dryer while you're there. That mattress will be pretty rough to sleep on without them."

"Sure thing. What's for dessert?"

The storm returned to a semblance of its former fury just before Leo set down two portions of Crème Brulee, along with strong coffee and an after dinner Napoleon brandy. They found they could have a normal conversation that didn't involve shouting themselves into a ruptured aneurysm if they timed what they said between the rolls of thunder.

"How lov…" was as far as Alex got before the lights went out.

"Oh, crap," Leo said.

"Look at it this way," Alex said, "we may have a night off. Can't very well paint in the dark. And I don't know how you're going to be able to work with two bandaged hands, anyway. How are they doing, by the way?"

"I'll survive. If I pad them out enough with gauze, I'll be fine to work."

Alex shook her head. Leo would continue changing a tire if he had a sucking chest wound from a drive-by shooting. He would not consider quadruple bypass surgery reason enough to skip mowing the lawn or washing the truck. He was the Energizer Bunny of the human race. Leo Renfield—the *real* reason they nail coffins shut.

"Where are the MagLites?" Leo asked as he bumped into something and swore softly.

"On the counter, just to the left of the range," Alex replied.

"How'd they end up all the way over there?"

"Don't know."

"Good thing you have a great memory," Leo said, caroming and cursing his way across the kitchen.

Memory had nothing to do with it. She could see the two flashlights quite clearly, and she wished she could have saved Leo all the punishment his shins were taking, but she had this gift for a reason and didn't want to jeopardize it.

Leo stopped moving. "Did you hear that?" he asked.

"Hear what?"

"Shhhh. Listen."

"All I hear is thunder, Leo," Alex said.

"Shhh."

Knock, bump... knock, bump... knock, bump... knock, bump...

"Oh, now I hear it."

"It's getting louder," Leo whispered.

"Whatever it is, it's out in the hall," Alex whispered back. "Should we go look?"

"I expect so, yeah," Leo replied. "Ah, here we are." He activated both the MagLites. When Alex walked over and took one, he hazarded, "You don't suppose the house has been hit by lightning, do you?"

The tremor in his voice told Alex that that was exactly what he thought. "I doubt it, hon. We'd have heard the strike inside and by now we'd be smelling it, too; both the ozone and the smoke. An old house like this would burn like tinder, but I imagine the roof is loaded with lightning rods, so don't worry." Alex said.

Leo suppressed a shiver.

Knock, bump... knock, bump... knock, bump... knock, bump...

"Let's go see what's going on," Leo said.

The curious sounds were coming from the hall staircase. "I know what it is. It's Black coming down the stairs the hard way. His chair is out of juice." Leo whispered.

"Of course. Well, let's get out of sight. The way he's navigating these risers sounds like it might be pretty undignified. As much as he irritates me, I don't want to be cruel and humiliate him. C'mon."

They backed off to just inside the kitchen doorway, switching off their lights until the odd descent ceased and they heard Black's feet on the floor.

Alex turned her light back on, and swung it down the hall to reveal Cooper Black all buttoned up in bright yellow foul weather gear, looking like a parody of Gloucester's *Man at the Wheel* statue; the only deviations being that he had a headlamp strapped to his hat, and he carried a five gallon, obviously empty gas can in each hand, which he proceeded to place to one side. After that, he shot a dirty look back down the flashlight beam, then turned and stalked to the front door as fast as his malformed legs would carry him.

The storm raged, but Black reached up with one hand and flung the front door wide, with no difficulty whatsoever, retrieved his cans, and lurched out into the storm.

Alex didn't even have to look at Leo to know that his mouth was open wide enough to swallow a Buick. "I told you he was strong!" she shouted, not waiting for the thunder to subside. "Where the hell is he going in this weather?"

"My guess is that there's a big-ass generator out there," Leo replied. "There must be a gas tank sunk somewhere on the property, too; probably near the generator. It'd have to be around 10,000 watts to power this house, and if so, he's going to have to fill those two cans five times."

"So once he gets the generator going, all the power will be back on, right?" Alex asked.

"No. Hollywood leads us to believe that a generator can run everything, but at a fraction of the power, which isn't accurate. For a place this size, there's probably a transfer station out there, too. What that does is monitor the line to the main power grid. When that line loses power, the transfer station here automatically switches over to generator power, and the generator should go on in fifteen or twenty seconds."

"It's been longer than that already, Leo."

"Then somebody forgot to fill the gas tank," Leo said.

"So what will be running once the generator gets started?"

"The transfer station has a panel on it that runs lines to specific places in the house. What you'd want to keep running here would be things like the refrigerator, the walk-in freezer—which is a power guzzler, by the way—and the sump pump. That would probably leave just enough power for a few house lights, and that's it. Black will know which outlets and lights have power. Meanwhile, let's just wait for him."

Twenty minutes later, the lights still weren't on and Alex was getting impatient. "Should we shut the door?" Alex asked.

"I don't know. He left it open, so maybe we should let it alone. The wind isn't blowing this way, so no rain is coming in."

"Then let's go back and have our dessert," Alex said.

At that moment, Black stepped out of the rain and back under the cover of the front porch, looking very much like a wet cat. Water poured off his cheerful yellow rain hat, and his oversized slicker hung to his ankles, running with rain. He looked thoroughly disgusted. When he glanced through the open door and realized he was being observed, he favored the Renfields with a look you'd normally reserve for something that just crawled out of a pipe.

They took the hint and MagLite-d their way back to the kitchen.

"Did you ever see so much hate in such a small package?" Alex asked.

"Hate? What do you mean?" Leo asked.

"The filthy looks he gives us!"

"*What* filthy looks, Alex?"

"Come on now, Leo. You can't have missed those."

"I didn't see any filthy looks. When he got to the foot of the stairs, he may not have smiled, but he did nod. It wasn't nasty at all," Leo said.

"I didn't see any nod, Leo."

"Honey, this is probably part of what the pills will correct. I know you're aware that mild to severe paranoia is also a symptom of schizophrenia. I also know you don't like Black, and so your mind tells you that he doesn't like you either. In reality, I don't think he cares about us one way or the other."

"But what about the way he looked when he came to the Library door after the Scrabble game? He looked like he wanted to kill us!"

"No, honey, he didn't. He made picking up gestures, I nodded that we would pick the game back up, and he went on his way. He has no reason to hate us," Leo explained. "I think that you're probably nervous about spending the summer in a house that I have to agree, is somewhat on the creepy side, and this is the result of it. It's aggravating your condition. But don't worry…"

"…the pills will start working soon, and then you'll be just fine," Alex finished for him. 'I know, Leo, I know." She dropped the subject.

The next sound they heard was the front door slamming shut. This was followed by the grumbling of Black's stair chair creeping upward to be swallowed by the mysterious second floor.

"Sounds like his chair has full power. I wonder what else has power around here," Leo said, embracing the change of subject.

"The only things that are really critical are the fridge and the freezer, but how can you tell if they are fully powered up?" Alex asked.

Leo stepped to the fridge and opened the door. The light went on brightly. "That's how. Then he checked the walk-in freezer. "Motor's running here, too, so I'd say that everything critical is running up to speed."

"But how are you going to work without light?" Alex asked.

"What do you mean 'you?' Do I sense a mutiny?"

"Of course not. I meant 'we.'"

"I guess we'll have to wait for Black to give us a yea or nay on tonight's work, which ought to be happening soon. It feels like it's about ten. What do you want to do until midnight?"

"I found a really good book in the bedroom bookcase. I think I'll read if there's a working light."

"What about the sump pump?"

"Forgot. I'll go down right now and check it. I sincerely hope it also has full power, since I don't have any galoshes with me," Alex said. She ran back to their bathroom and applied more Vaseline to the affected areas of her face, then stopped in the bedroom to don her heavy gray hooded sweatshirt and to stuff a pair of pliers, a couple of wrenches, and two screwdrivers into her back pockets. Trust ever-prepared Leo to pack some critical hand tools with his clothes—it was his hardware security blanket. On the way back to the kitchen, she grabbed her book in the library. She smiled up at Leo as she picked up her MagLite. "I'll just stay down there and read until the sheets are dry."

"Before you step off the bottom stair, check for water on the floor. If it's deep, don't step into it," Leo said.

"Why? I'm not going to be able to fix the pump if I can't get to it."

"You're not going to be fixing anything if you put your foot into deep basement water. If there's four inches or more on the floor throughout the basement, you stand a good chance of being electrocuted."

"Electrocuted! Why?"

"Because the washing machine pump and all the its internal electronics are located at the bottom of the machine, about four inches above floor level. If the sump pump quits and water rises to that level and the machine is still plugged in... zappo! You're a crispy critter."

"I'll keep that clearly in mind."

"Sure you don't want me to go with you?"

She smiled. "I think I can handle it. You relax."

"Okey dokey. Don't forget the sheets," Leo reminded her.

Chapter Seventy

Alex stepped down two stairs and turned back to shut the door behind her. She peered at the floor, found it dry, then headed downward, accompanied by equal proportions of anticipation and dread. She turned her MagLite off and stowed it in a pocket in her hoodie. No sense in wasting the battery.

It came to Alex that being able to see clearly in the dark is one of the powers humans often possess in their dreams, along with invisibility, flight, super speed, walking through solid objects, shape shifting, superior strength, living beyond death, and breathing underwater. Alex thought it odd that all these abilities have been traditional attributes, mainly, of monsters. The Invisible Man was human, but an insane criminal. Dracula flew and shape shifted. Ditto that last for the Wolfman and Dr. Jekyll. The Creature lived underwater. King Kong had superior strength. Ditto that for Dracula and the Frankenstein Monster. Living beyond death included Dracula, the Frankenstein Monster, and the Mummy. Though Superman and other superheroes could be put in many of these categories, they were all monsters and misfits in their own right, too; whether or not they worked for the power of good or evil really didn't enter into it. How very interesting that we, as humans, have these wish fulfilling dreams.

We envy the monsters.

And now Alex had joined them.

Oddly enough, this epiphany didn't faze her at all.

"Hello," she called softly into the gloom as she began the long walk to the laundry room.

HELLO

A Shadow Person was right beside her.

Alex turned in the direction of the greeting, and was pleased to discover that she could see it standing next to her and it didn't vanish anymore when she looked directly at it. Its features were distorted, however, resembling a smudgy pencil portrait or a watercolor that had been carelessly left out in the rain.

"Was it you who was talking to me through the Scrabble game?" she asked.

WHAT IS 'SCRABBLE GAME'

"It's a word game played with lettered tiles."

WORDS WITH QUESTIONS YES

"Not normally, but in that case, yes. Was it you?"

NO IT WAS ALL WE EACH HAVE LITTLE MEMORY SO MUST COMBINE TO PLAY WORD WITH QUESTIONS GAME

"I see," Alex said, as she continued to walk. The shadow kept pace. The whispering and other noises were growing loud enough to notice, but Alex wasn't afraid of them anymore. Now they were more like a message from an old friend or the happy thump of a big dog's tail.

Alex was surprised to realize that the basement was the only place in the entire house where she felt comfortable now. Any residual fear she had was completely gone.

The walk to the laundry room went quickly this time. *Time flies when you're not scared shitless,* she thought. The first thing she did was to transfer the sheets from the washing machine to the dryer. She crossed her fingers and punched the START button, and praise the Lord and pass the potatoes, the dryer began to spin. She then walked across the room to place her book on the small end table next to the chair and the floor lamp; but before she did, she opened it to a random page, and found that her newly acquired night vision was sharp enough to allow her to read in the dark, too. Smiling, she set the book on the table, and went back to check the sump pump.

There was no standing water on the floor now, but there had been. The packed dirt was damp and water stained, but the dampness was fresher smelling than when she was here last. Alex reasoned that the sump pump must be working, since the water that was on the floor was now gone, but she knelt and raised the float valve to double check. Sure enough, the pump growled to life. When she stood and turned around, she discovered that the entire room was filled with Shadow People. She felt like a housewife whose husband had invited everyone in his office over for a barbecue, but had neglected to mention it to her.

There were so *many* of them. They stood there, in a big crowd, waiting.

"It's good to see you all again," Alex said, and was surprised to find that she meant it.

She received no worded response, but elation suddenly suffused her. It must have been some sort of vibration or energy from the Shadow People. Alex thought, from the happy energy they sent to her that they must glad to see her, too. "Is it difficult for you to speak? Is communication this way easier for you?"

Another elation bath.

"All right. I don't see why we can't do it your way."

She suddenly tasted cotton candy on her tongue. *How interesting.* She tried an experiment. She thought a question, waited, and got nothing from them. No mental images, no emotions. *Now I know they're not telepathic.*

"Why did you want only me to help you? My husband would have been willing to help you, too," Alex asked.

In answer, she was abruptly rendered completely blind. Rather than panic, Alex thought a moment, then asked, "Are you trying to tell me that he's blind—that he doubts his own eyes?"

Cotton candy flavor again and restored eyesight. She was getting concerned about the flavor they'd use to convey 'No.'

"How are Black and Theodora keeping you here? You said in the game that you were restrained by them. How?" Alex asked.

Instantly, she felt a gag being tied over her mouth and wetness on her thumb and first two fingers of her right hand. She reached up with her left, touching her face. There was no gag there, but she could feel it, all the same. After a moment, the feeling disappeared.

"Something keeps you from telling me—is that right?"

Cotton candy.

"Well, if you can't tell me, how can I help?"

A picture of Sherlock Holmes suddenly occurred to her.

"Detective?"

Very slight cotton candy, and a mental picture of Holmes gazing through a magnifying glass.

"Clues?"

Strong cotton candy and elation.

"Okay. I'll do my best," Alex said.

A burning fireplace popped into her mind.

"Did you light fireplace in our bedroom?"

Taste of spoiled milk.

"Akkkk!"

Image of a group of people sitting around a fire.

"Are you cold?"

Cotton candy.

"Do you want me to warm you?"

This time, the fragrance of summer roses.

"How?"

She felt a cold presence pass through her then, and some of her body heat went with it.

"You get warm by moving through me?"

Jasmine, this time.

"But the last time you did that, I nearly died."

Nauseating stench of sulfur.

"The only way I will agree to this is if you move through one at a time, and will promise to stop when ask you to."

Spring lilacs.

"All right, go ahead, but pause for a moment after each."

Hyacinth.

One at a time, it wasn't too bad, but she could feel her body heat diminishing quickly, and after the first four had been warmed, she said, "Please stop now."

She felt four set of lips place a brief gentle kisses on her forehead and cheeks.

"You're entirely welcome. I'll warm you again when my own warmth returns."

Mental image of Alex feeding a starving dog. The dog looks up and licks her hand.

"How does the warmth help you? Is it just that it makes you more comfortable?"

Mental picture of a finger with a string tied around it.

"I see. It allows you to remember?"

Taste of chocolate, this time. Alex assumed that that meant 'yes,' too; because how could chocolate possibly mean 'no?'

"Remember what?" she asked.

String-tied finger again.

"I don't understand."

The air surrounding Alex immediately turned artic cold and her thoughts clouded so much that she couldn't speak. Then it pulled back and she was warmer again.

"That was so cold I could hardly think!"

Chocolate.

"Oh! Being cold keeps you from remembering. Warmth clears your minds. Is that it?"

Chocolate cotton candy!

"What are you trying to remember? I don't understand."

YOU ARE COLD COLD BRINGS CONFUSION

A room full of echoey, whisper-soft voices replied, abandoning, for the time being, the sensory responses.

"But once I'm warm, I still won't understand."

PERHAPS NOT

"I thought it was taxing for you to speak."

WE ARE WARMER NOW IT IS EASIER

"Suppose I set up a portable heater down here for you?" Alex asked.

FOR WHAT PURPOSE

"To warm you."

YOU ARE WARMTH FOR US WARMTH IS YOU

"I wish I knew why you are all here."

WE REMAIN HERE WE CANNOT LEAVE

"But why?"

WE CANNOT SAY

"There must be a way."

THERE IS

"Then tell me."

WE DON'T REMEMBER

"Maybe you will. I'm feeling warmer now. Send the next four through," Alex said.

Chapter Seventy-One

"Hello, you," Leo said with a smile as she closed the basement door behind her. He was sitting at the kitchen table enjoying another cup of coffee and using his MagLite to read a copy of *This Old House* he liberated from the rack in the bathroom. "I thought you fell asleep down there, you were gone so long. How was the sump pump?"

"No problems—seems to be working fine." Alex adjusted the sheets folded under her arm. She had the missing large flashlight in one hand and her book in the other.

"And a good thing, too. I don't know how they'd deal with a flooded basement that they couldn't walk through. How would you pump out the water?" Leo commented.

Alex set her sheets, book, and tools on the table and sat. "They must have figured that out. Probably some arcane method that you and I would never think of."

"What's that on your hand?" Leo asked, noticing the dark spots on her fingers and thumb.

"I don't know."

"Bring your hand into the light. Let's see."

Alex did, and the light revealed three purple bruises, one on each digit.

"What is that? More frostbite?" Leo asked.

"I don't think so. It wasn't that cold down there."

"How did that happen, then? Do they hurt?"

Alex touched her discolored fingers. "No, not at all. If they did, I'd have noticed it before now, with the things I've been carrying."

"Then what is it?"

Alex looked closely at them. "Looks like ink. But I haven't been writing anything, and especially not in purple ink—that's

441

so high school."

"Did you get any cleaning products on your hand? With the weird crap they use here, it could be some kind of chemical reaction."

"The only thing out of the ordinary that I touched was the float valve on the sump pump," Alex said.

"Well, that can't be it."

"Why not? Maybe they put something in the water."

"Nobody does that. A sump pump goes on several times a day, whether it's raining or not. It's all about keeping groundwater from flooding the house, so it's regularly pumping out, and changing, the water in its well. Anything put into the sump well wouldn't be there long."

"Then what about the ground water itself?" Alex asked.

"That could be. There could be something in the ground water that caused that reaction. Try some bleach to… damn."

"What?"

"I forgot. No bleach here. We're a *'green'* house. What a load of crap. All the gray water goes to a waste treatment plant anyhow. It all gets cleaned in the end, so it doesn't matter what kinds of cleaning products you use. It's just an excuse for vendors to charge you twice as much for products that don't work half as well."

"I'm sure it will wear off, Leo," Alex said, studying her fingers. "I'm not worried about it. I don't have any hand modeling photo shoots this week. I think I'll put AA and D batteries on the Black List before I forget. If these storms come up often, we'll be going through them like toilet paper."

After making the list entry, Alex poured herself a cup of coffee and joined Leo back at the table. "Probably be starting work soon. I see you already got changed. Guess I better, too." She picked up her book, the sheets, and the hand tools. I'll make the bed, while I'm at it."

"What about your coffee?"

"It's too hot to drink anyway. It'll be perfect by the time I get back." She used her MagLite to leave the kitchen, then switched it off when she was out of Leo's sight. She loved her gift, and now she understood why cats act so superior—they know that they *are*.

In the bedroom, she placed the tools carefully on a paint rag so as not to scar the etched glass on the desk. She left her book on her night table, then she extracted the fitted sheet and held two ends to snap it open. She tucked it in, ever alert for the sound of Leo's footfall. *It's not everyone who can make a bed perfectly in total darkness.*

She snapped open the flat sheet next, and gasped aloud.

There was something written on it.

Alex smoothed the sheet out over the bed, then stood on the seaman's trunk at its foot for an aerial view and read:

Remember me
When next you see
My face in the Book of the Dead
Everyone there
Was placed without care
And now we are merely well-read

You'll know my face
You'll know the place
Where there are others like me
So do what you must
My death was unjust
The Reaper did not strike me

Witness and till
Screen and refill
First taking a piece from each core
Then ne'er to return
Set them to burn
Memento Mori no more

Alex's flashlight beam and her shout for Leo filled the bedroom simultaneously, and too late, she realized her mistake in calling him. She shifted her steel trap memory into high gear and read the poem again with all the concentration she could summon as she heard Leo coming closer.

The writing faded away the moment Leo crossed the bedroom threshold.

"What's up?" he asked.

"Just wanted some help putting the comforter back on—it's kind of heavy."

"At your service, m'dear."

While Leo was smoothing out the heavy blanket, Alex reached down for her spiral bound pad and found it was gone. Undaunted, she pocketed a pen from the Royal Doulton Toby Jug next to her lamp, and resolved to snag another pad from her briefcase the second Leo was out of the room. She wanted to transcribe the poem on the sheet at her earliest opportunity.

"Anything else?" Leo asked, giving the already smooth comforter a final tug.

"Don't think so. I just have to get changed—it must be nearly twelve," Alex said.

"Need any help with that?"

"After work, yeah."

"Can I watch, at least?" he asked, leering.

"Sure. But if Black comes looking for us to tell us to get to work, then he'll be watching, too."

"Not good. I'll meet you in the Library," Leo said, as he shut the door.

The second she was alone, Alex seized a small pad from her briefcase, pulled out her pen and scribbled furiously, managing to transcribe the message on the sheet before forgetting any of it. After a quick change of clothes, she tore the odd verse from the pad and folded it into her back pocket for later consideration.

"Alex! Time to get started," Leo called.

She opened the bedroom door. "Just coming!" she called

back.

She found Leo and Cooper Black setting up work lights in the gallery.

"Is there power in here?" Alex asked.

"Nope. These run on batteries," Leo said, switching one on. "Guess this kind of thing happens a lot around here."

The three battery-powered lights were affixed to telescoping tripods, and were bright enough in their own right, but in a room as large as the gallery, they threw more shadows than illumination.

Once all the lights were on and in place, Leo surveyed the room and shook his head.

"What's wrong?"

He pointed at the ceiling. "Tonight we have to finish cutting in with the primer up there. All that crown molding has to be primed, and with this kind of lighting, we're going to go blind doing it and probably make a mess of that beadboard ceiling besides."

"Tell you what, Leo. Let me do all the crown and the cutting in below it. I've always had good night vision, so shadowed areas won't be as much of a problem for me. Then you can start rolling the walls with primer down here."

"Why in hell would anyone want to have ceilings twenty feet high, anyway? What a huge amount of wasted space, not to mention what it must cost to heat."

"I doubt they heat it at all. Do you see a thermostat anywhere?" Alex asked.

"No central heating... right. So no thermostat."

"The height of the ceilings is ugly for a room like this, isn't it? It throws all the proportions off," Alex said.

"How do you mean?"

"Well, in this art gallery, paintings are hung up to ten feet, which is really too high. Artwork is supposed to be fifty-seven inches on center from the floor, which is normal gallery level and average eye level. But even hanging them as high as they do here, that still leaves a ten-foot band of empty wall space around the whole room. It makes me feel like I'm at the bottom of an avalanche."

"Wait until we paint the charcoal gray over it. Then you'll feel like you're at the bottom of a coal bin. The only thing that color has going for it is that it will make the room seem smaller."

"It will probably be a better background color for the artwork, too. But why does she want the rest of the first floor painted dark gray? The place will be as cold and unwelcoming inside as it is outside. It will be like walking into a cave," Alex said.

"Did you say 'cave' or 'grave?'" Leo asked.

"Take your pick."

"Somehow I doubt they have a lot of people dropping by. As a matter of fact, I'm pretty sure even the Jehovah's Witnesses stay away from this place," Leo said.

Snap snap snap

They had forgotten about Black, who had been standing in the doorway the entire time. He made irritated gestures that indicated that they'd better stop yapping and get to work. Leo nodded, and Black turned on his heel and disappeared into the gloom. They breathed a sigh of relief at the thrum of his chair.

"Let's set up the extension ladder for you, then. I really wish we had a Baker—it would make the job go faster and would be a whole lot safer for you," Leo said.

"What's a 'Baker?'"

"Somebody who makes bread."

"*Sonofabitch!* Got me good!"

Leo laughed. "Actually we do need a Baker, but not that kind. A Baker looks sort of like building scaffolding on a smaller scale, and it has a wide wooden platform. You can roll it around and it's a lot more stable than a ladder… and if you're prone to vertigo, a whole lot safer."

"Lucky for me I'm not,"

"It is lucky, because I am," Leo said.

"Really? You never told me that."

"I've always tended to stay away from jobs where I had to get on a ladder much higher than six or eight feet, and so far, I've managed. I don't mind telling you that when we came here and I saw how high the ceilings on this floor were, I considered backing out."

"Why didn't you?" Alex asked.

"I want to buy you a house, that's why."

"Oh, Leo, I don't ever want you to take chances like that for anything—least of all, me. If you have vertigo, you have vertigo. It's nothing to fool around with."

"Don't worry, hon, I wasn't going to do anything stupid. I got a prescription from Earle, just in case I needed it."

"Good. Now you won't have to use it, though."

"You sure you don't mind?"

"Nah. I like being up high."

"Okay, then. Let's get going before *Il Duce* comes back."

"Who?"

"*Il Duce*. Mussolini," Leo replied.

"Why Mussolini?"

"Because that's how he's dressed tonight."

"Is he still white with blue eyes and red hair?"

"Uh huh."

"I'm still seeing him in the white Nehru suit and he's still an Indian."

"Forget it. When the pills go to work you'll see him the way I do."

At that moment, there was a loud knock on the front door.

Leo and Alex looked at each other, unsure if they really heard it, but after several seconds, it came again.

"Should we open it?" Leo asked.

"Oh, I don't know, Leo. It's after midnight and somebody's knocking at the door of a spooky old house on a stormy night out in East Nowhere. If this were a movie, we'd both be yelling, 'Don't open the door!' at the screen."

Leo laughed.

The knocking resumed and it sounding like whoever was out there was using a Louisville slugger to get their attention.

He shrugged. "Well, Black isn't going to hear it. I guess I better see who it is." Leo walked to the door and opened it about twelve inches, then stepped back so quickly that Alex was convinced that the visitor had shot him with a silenced weapon. She ran forward as Leo staggered back.

"Honey, are you all right?"

"Yeah, I'm fine. Go back to work. I'll take care of this," he snapped. It was clear that Leo didn't want her to see who their uninvited guest was, and planned to get rid of him or her as soon as possible. Trusting that Leo would explain later, Alex turned on her heel and went back to the gallery.

"Good evening. I have a delivery for Mr. Cooper Black," the man on the stoop said.

"What the hell are you doing here?" Leo hissed.

"I'm making a delivery." The man was dressed in a basic brown uniform common to area delivery services, and was holding a parcel.

"Yeah? Where's your truck?" Leo demanded in a low voice.

"It's parked at the bottom of the driveway. I just love walking in the rain, don't you?"

"The bottom of the driveway is about a mile away. Where's your umbrella?"

"Umbrella?"

"Yes, umbrella. That thing that keeps the rain off," Leo said.

"I have no umbrella, as you can see."

"Then why are you dry?"

The deliveryman's response was a slow, malevolent smile. "If you'll sign for this, I'll be on my way," he said, holding out a receipt pad and a Mont Blanc pen.

Leo accepted both, and examined the pen. "These pens seem to be pretty popular around here," he said, scribbling his signature.

"Indeed," he said, accepting the pen and signed pad. "Here's his package. Put it in the refrigerator for Mr. Black, if you would… and no peeking."

"Are we done now?" Leo asked.

"Yes, we most certainly are… now." The deliveryman tipped his hat and strolled off into the night.

Leo shut the large door on the retreating figure of the Client.

Alex heard the door close and emerged from the gallery. "So what was that about?" she asked.

"I was just a delivery," Leo said, holding up the butcher-paper wrapped package.

But Alex would not be fobbed off. "No, Leo. Not 'just.' Nobody delivers anything normal at this hour. What shows up at the door at after midnight is the Four Horsemen of the Apocalypse, not UPS."

"He wasn't UPS," Leo said, lamely.

"No kidding! Really?"

"It's something for Black. He told me to put it in the fridge."

"It looks like some kind of meat, the way it's wrapped. Let me see," Alex said. She turned the heavy package, searching for a label, and finally found one. "It's more abalone, according to this. Christ, he must live on the stuff. No wonder they're nearing extinction. Cooper Black is eating them all. Want me to put it away?"

"Yeah, hon. Thanks."

"Who was that guy, Leo?"

"A really weird deliveryman, Alex, that's all." And Leo's tone made it clear that the subject should be dropped.

She had to do some rearranging to fit the ten pound package of abalone into the refrigerator. She had been using the space opened up by the previous package to store her chowder, which she now took out and set on the range, intending to heat it up for a quick snack after work. She put the bundle in its place and, shuddering, closed the door, wondering if the next knock would reveal a door-to-door banshee selling cut-rate burial plots.

"Okay, all put away. I took out the chowder for later."

"Great. Grab the end of this ladder, will you? Sucker's heavy, and I can't get a good grip with all these bandages. Christ, I feel like the Mummy."

"You look more like the Daddy. How tall is this ladder extended?"

"It's fifteen feet and extends to thirty. They must use it outside, too, for washing windows," Leo said. "Grab an end."

"Ugh! This must weigh a hundred pounds! I thought aluminum ladders were supposed to be light," Alex exclaimed.

Leo laughed. "This amount of aluminum is going to be heavy, and this model weighs, if memory serves, just over eighty pounds, Miss Hyperbole."

Alex would have had a smart aleck comeback, but in trying to maneuver the awkward extension ladder across the sheet covered, highly polished parquet floor, she slid and fell, face first, into the wall. Impact was accompanied by a forceful and copious blood splatter.

"Oh Jeez! Alex!" Leo cried, carefully placing his end of the heavy ladder on the wooden floor, then rushing to his bleeding wife.

Alex found her footing and pulled away from the wall, which was running with her blood. She ripped the clean painting rag out of her pocket to catch the stream pouring from her injured nose. "I'm okay," she said.

"If that's 'okay,' I never want to see 'badly hurt,'" Leo said. "Is it broken, do you think?"

"I don't think so. It's just a nosebleed. I get pretty bad ones sometimes, especially if I whack my nose."

"Let's get you cleaned up and put some ice on the back of your neck. Come on," Leo said, taking her by the arm. He tried not to think about the gouge that the ladder had put into the wall when Alex slipped. He just hoped there was some spackling paste or Durabond in the supply closet.

After Alex cleaned her face off and it was clear that the nose, though bleeding, was intact, Leo wrapped a large bag of frozen peas around the back of her neck, supplied her with a clean paint rag, rinsed the old one out repeatedly in the sink, then walked back to the gallery to assess the damage. He was relieved that they were painting dark over light. At least if there was a stain, the paint would cover it.

It was worse than he thought. It looked as though someone had filled a balloon with blood and thrown it against the wall. And the gash the ladder had made! Not good... not good at all, especially when he considered the fact that these people didn't even use nails or tacks.

Leo used the damp rag to wipe away the rapidly drying blood, being careful to fully clean out the foot-long gash so that the spackle would take. There was a large amount of blood there. He didn't think Alex had bled quite that much, but apparently, she had. Leo had to rinse the rag a couple of times before rendering the gouge clean enough to repair. When he inspected the damage more closely, he pulled away, confused by what he saw. Thinking it might be a trick of the poor lighting, he went back to the kitchen to get his MagLite and check on Alex. She was doing better, so he returned to the gallery wall, and examined the sides of the gash under a bright light.

He wasn't mistaken.

There were what looked like fifteen layers of built up paint... layers that alternated white and charcoal gray. *I don't get it. Why in hell do they keep switching between the two colors like that? And anyway, didn't Theodora say that the lower floor had never been painted before?*

Lost in thought, he stepped down the hall to look for some kind of repair compound in the supply closet.

There was nothing, and he began to panic.

He for sure didn't want Cooper Black to see that they'd damaged the wall, and he could easily repair it before quitting time at six.

But there was no spackle.

What to do, what to do?

Then he remembered an old trick he'd learned from a bunch of frat boys who had trashed a house they'd leased. Leo had been called in to restore it to rentable condition and discovered that they'd patched some of the larger holes they'd made in the walls with toothpaste. If they'd been a bit more skillful with their application, Leo could have painted right over it without a problem—that was how hard it dried.

He rushed down the hall and grabbed a couple of tubes from their well-stocked bathroom vanity, and rushed back, stopping off in the kitchen to say hello to Alex and to pick up a butter knife.

The gash was about half an inch deep at its deepest point, so Leo uncapped the toothpaste and began filling from there outward. In a couple of minutes, he had the gouge repaired so beautifully that it was invisible. He expected that it would probably crack when it dried, and he'd have to do a second fill job, but it shouldn't be a big deal.

He brushed his fingertips lightly over the faint stain left on the undamaged wall. Then, startled, he placed his palm flat against it.

The wall was warm.

And he realized something else.

Hey, wait a minute. The whole room is warm, and nights are chilly in this house. It was cold in here last night. There isn't a central heating system, Theodora said so. Any heat is from fireplaces. Had Theodora lied to them to keep them from looking for a thermostat—a thermostat that was, perhaps on the upper floor? Could Black have turned on the heat? Leo listened, but he didn't hear a furnace running.

He made a third trip back to the kitchen. Alex was up and around, and though swollen, her nose had mercifully stopped bleeding.

"Oooooo, that's gonna leave a mark," Leo said, looking at her.

"Anyone who knows me will have no trouble believing that you punched me," Alex said, with a giggle.

"Seriously, sweetie, if it's really painful, why don't you go lie down and I'll work solo for tonight. I don't mind—really."

"No, I think I'm all right. It still hurts, but working will help keep my mind off it."

"It's up to you. If you don't feel right, don't tough it out. You don't want to take chances on a ladder."

"I didn't get the opportunity to. I got all bloody just picking the damned thing up and walking with it."

"Maybe I should take my pills and you should stay on the floor level for tonight," Leo said.

"Leo, I wouldn't take a chance on climbing a ladder if I wasn't sure I was up to it, all kidding aside. Please stop worrying."

"Okay. There's just something I have to check first." He switched his light on and opened the basement door.

Alex was immediately anxious. "Why are you going down there?"

"Damndest thing. The walls in the gallery are warm—all of them. It's actually comfortable in there for a change."

"So why do you need to go downstairs, then?"

"I want to look for a furnace. I think Theodora lied to us about no central heating. The room is warm, but I didn't hear a furnace kick on; and in an old place like this, you'd hear it, believe me."

"Oh. Well, just be careful," she said, her anxiety for him growing by the second for no good reason. The beings down there, whether they were all in her mind or actually existed, didn't seem to be interested in Leo, so that wasn't a worry. She had no idea *what* she was worried about, but worried she was.

***

Leo rattled down the slatted stairway and down the corridor. He found what appeared to be a furnace in an alcove about forty feet past the far side of the wine crypt.

It was the craziest setup he'd ever seen. It was a freestanding metallic Medusa with overhead ductwork snaking off in every direction. He studied it from all sides and traced a few of the myriad of pipes overhead, then, muttering to himself, went back to the kitchen.

"So?" Alex said when he shut the door behind him. "Find a furnace?"

"I did, but it will take a better mind than mine to explain that mess," Leo said.

"Why?"

"Let me check something else first," he said, dashing off down the hall.

Leo checked the walls in every single room on the first floor, then came back to the kitchen, even more mystified than before.

"*What*, Leo? You're killin' me here," Alex said.

"Sorry. How much do you know about furnaces and heating systems?"

"Not a lot," Alex admitted.

"I'm no big authority, either, but I know when something's not right."

"And?"

"Something's not right."

"*Le*o!"

"Sorry. Every heating system has three major components: the heat production component where your fuel is converted to heat—and that means any fuel—whatever you're burning. Then there's the distribution system. This gets the heat to where you want it in the house. The last thing is the control that regulates the demand for heat."

"I'm with you so far."

"The problem, Alex, is that the system for this house only has one of those three critical components, yet the walls are all warm. Haven't you noticed how comfortable it is in here?"

In answer, Alex pointed to her sweatshirt draped over the back of a kitchen chair.

Leo continued. "There are no heating grates or grilles on this floor anywhere—not in the walls, the floors, or the ceilings, so there's no way for the heat to be delivered. And there are no thermostats on this floor, either, so the controls that regulate demand for heat are missing, too."

"But the walls are warm?" Alex asked.

"Touch them and see for yourself."

She crossed the room and placed her palm flat against the tasteful wallpaper. "You're right! Well, could it be some kind of radiant heating system in the walls, with coils?"

"That's normally used to supplement a central heating system, and is mostly used in floors in places that have really cold winters, like Canada. Radiant heating is horribly expensive to install, but is pretty efficient once it is. That would explain the lack of a distribution system, though. But what about the thermostat?"

"Probably up on the consecrated second floor somewhere."

"Okay, so we may have solved those problems, but that's not the weirdest."

"Lay it on me," Alex said.

"The pipes running to and from the production component were made of copper."

"Isn't copper piping just used in plumbing?"

"Exactly."

"Well what if the coils in the wall were full of hot water? Do they make radiant heating coils like that?"

"Yeah, come to think of it, they do. Hydronic systems. The water gets pumped from a boiler, usually through polyethylene tubing, but you could use copper pipes if you wanted to. The only problem with that kind of a system is that you can't use it under a hardwood floor because the heat can crack it and cause warping. They'd have had to put down a laminate—and can you see our Theodora settling for laminate flooring?"

"Oh, please don't call her 'our' Theodora."

"Sorry."

"And maybe they don't have a system under the floor.

Maybe it's just the walls. Anyway, let's talk about it while we're working before Black comes back downstairs as Hitler and decides that we are not a part of his Master Race."

They adjourned to the gallery once again, and the first thing Alex did was feel the floor. "It's warm, too," she said. "This has to be radiant heat, Leo. Probably that hydro thing you were talking about."

"Hydronics. Well, maybe they like to replace the floor as often as they seem to like to paint the walls." He told her about the many layers of previous paint he'd discovered in the gash.

"Oh, I forgot all about the mess I made out of the wall," she exclaimed, searching for it. "I could have sworn it was right here."

Leo chuckled. "It was. You're standing right in front of it."

She bent down and peered at the wall. "Leo, you are a true artiste," she said with admiration.

"I live to impress you, babe."

"Seriously, this is incredible work. You can fix anything. Isn't it great that the spackle is exactly the color of the wall?"

"Didn't use spackle. There wasn't any."

"No? So what did you use?"

"Toothpaste."

"So now we have a wall that's not only repaired, but cavity free and minty fresh, too?"

"So it says on the tube."

"Where did you ever learn about that?"

"Frat boys. I was…"

"Stop. I withdraw the question. What I want to know is what you think about all the layers of paint when Her Nibs said that the first floor hadn't been painted before."

"I'm more interested in knowing why some of the copper piping on the boiler or whatever it is seems to end in sinks and tubs."

"Maybe that's how you fill the cockamamie thing."

"Could be. I don't know enough about hydronic systems to say for sure, either way. If you're sure you're up to working, let's get going. We've already blown away an hour." He helped Alex set up the ladder and sent her upward with a bucket of primer and admonitions to be careful; all the while, in spite of the logical explanation they'd arrived at, thinking that there was still something very wrong about that furnace.

Outside of Alex's nosebleed starting up again with a vengeance about three hours into the morning, and the grid repairs that restored full power to the house moments later, the balance of their second night of work was uneventful.

Chapter Seventy-Two

After Cooper Black released them from their labors, Leo and Alex sauntered down the hall to the kitchen for a bowl or two of chowder. Alex's nose had swollen alarmingly, and bruising had appeared across its bridge, as well as beneath both eyes. When she spoke, she sounded like she had a bad cold.

"To ask a stupid question for the sake of hearing my own voice, how's the nose?" Leo asked. "It really looks like you broke it, hon."

"My sinuses feel like they're stuffed with concrete and should be sleeping with the fishes," she replied, dialing up the heat beneath the black Spatterware stock pot. "And no, it's not broken. It would probably hurt less if it were."

"How about if I go rustle up some aspirin for you? There are bottles and bottles of it in the medicine cabinet in our bathroom. I guess that's all they use around here for pain relief."

"I'll just grin and bear it, thanks. Along with relieving pain, aspirin also thins the blood, and I don't think that would be a good idea right now."

"Right. I forgot about that. Are you going to be able to sleep?"

"It hurts, but it isn't like I haven't smacked my nose before. I'll be all right." Alex put the bread in the oven to warm it, and grimaced as the pain in her face informed her that bending over was not a good idea.

It didn't take them long to polish off two bowls of soup and several pieces of buttered baguette each.

"Let's get to bed. I'll take you out and show you the garage when we get up," Leo said, yawning hugely.

"Deal."

They stacked the dirty dishes in the dishwasher, then, arm

in arm, set off for their bedroom and what they hoped would be sweet dreams.

***

Once Leo's head hit the pillow, he was out cold. Alex, on the other hand, couldn't get comfortable, even as tired as she was. She usually slept on her side, but with her facial injury, all that position did was aggravate it with unbearable bolts of pain and throbbing; and she also worried about smearing the pillowcase with the Vaseline that covered the tips of her ears and nose. Lying on her stomach was out of the question, so she found herself on her back, which wasn't much better, since the residual blood and mucous that had pooled in her sinuses was now dripping down the back of her throat. To make matters worse, she never slept on her back anyway. After a frustrating hour of struggling for sleep, she threw in the towel and got up.

I wish I knew what time it is. She picked her bathrobe off the back of a nearby chair and shrugged it on, stepped into her big fuzzy pink slippers, then left the room, quietly closing the door behind her.

Since she wasn't dressed warmly enough to go downstairs to spend time with the Shadow People there—if, in fact, they were there at all and not mental figments—she opted to get out the Scrabble game and have a chat with them that way.

Alex shuffled down the hall to the Billiard Room. The closed door even had a small gold plaque that was engraved: Billiard Room. *Good thing they did that. God knows when you walk in you might mistake it for a stable or a grand ballroom,* she thought disgustedly as she opened the door and flipped on the lights. *There are three pool tables, a full bar, cues and other pool playing implements lining the walls, along with framed posters of Minnesota Fats, Jackie Gleason, and the Rat Pack* playing *pool. Sure, I can see where a sign might be necessary. These people are such snobs, I can't believe it!* She opened the closet (also tastefully labeled: 'Games Closet') and scanned the selection for Scrabble.

It wasn't there.

Qu'elle surprise, she thought, remembering the anger suffusing Black's face the previous evening. *You can't stop me so easily, Mr. Black.* Alex shut the closet door, turned off the lights and left the room.

She had an idea.

Back in the Library once more, she found a pair of scissors in the long drawer in the coffee table, as well as several sheets of white paper. A black Sharpie was the only other thing she needed and she found one in the Lalique vase. Alex sat at the game table casting her memory back to when she was nine or ten for a moment or two, nodded, and began cutting the paper.

After she had thirty-six one inch by one inch squares and three one inch by three inch rectangles, she put the scissors and remaining paper aside and popped the top off the Sharpie.

The end result was a makeshift Ouija Board, with twenty-six squares, each with a letter of the alphabet, and ten more with numerals one through zero. On the three rectangles, she wrote "YES," "NO," and "GOOD-BYE" respectively, and arranged all of these components on the game table in their correct positions, to the best of her recollection. She didn't have a planchette, though, and couldn't use a wine glass, because the pieces of paper weren't affixed to anything so the glass would destroy the "board" on the first transmitted letter.

The only thing that would work well in this situation would be a pendulum, which she also did not have... yet. Alex looked gingerly through the pencil vase and found a stub at the bottom. She sharpened it, then rounded up some string from the kitchen. Once back in the library, she unwound a paper clip, stuck it through the pencil's eraser, then knotted each end of the string to the wire protruding from each side of the eraser. She put her index finger through the closed loop at the top, and she had a balanced, if unattractive, pendulum which she then held above the board.

"Are you there, my Shadow People?" she whispered.

The pendulum turned in a small circle, then moved to *YES*. Then, additionally, spelled out, letter by letter: *BE CAREFUL WHAT YOU SAY*

"Why?"

YOU WILL BE HEARD

"By whom?"

YOU WILL BE HEARD

"How shall I communicate if I can't speak?"

WRITE YOUR QUESTIONS

Alex shrugged. It wasn't like Cooper Black could hear her if she shouted the house down, but she got some paper and a pencil, and wrote:

Why are you afraid of Cooper Black? Can he hurt you?

NO HE CAN HURT YOU BEWARE

Was the message on the sheet from you?

YES

Is that what I need to do to help you?

YES

What is the Book of the Dead?

ONE THING THAT KEEPS US HERE

What are the other things?

PAPER BONES

What are paper bones?

TWO THINGS

Alex had no idea what this meant, so she tried a different tack:

Where can I find the Book of the Dead?

NEAR

What should I do with it when I find it?

YOU WILL KNOW

Why can't you be direct with me and just tell me how to help you, without all these strange clues?

WE CANNOT

Why?

PAPER

Paper keeps you from giving me direct, detailed information?

YES

What kind of paper?

THE SAME KIND YOU SIGNED

Suddenly, the multiple layers of paint made sense to Alex. She wrote:

Did all of you work here before you died?

YES JUST BEFORE

Alex sat back, staring at her makeshift Ouija Board. She had dropped her pendulum on the floor beside her chair, unaware that she had done so.

What the hell? She didn't have to be a genius to realize that if she and Leo signed the same contract as the Shadow People in the basement, that the Renfields would be joining them sooner or later—probably sooner.

That is, if the Shadow People even existed.

She'd only been on the pills Jack had prescribed for one day; not enough time for them to be changing her point of view yet.

So she and Leo were either in terrible danger or none whatsoever.

Alex fervently wished she could reliably distinguish reality from fantasy, but she had to accept the fact that she couldn't. Leo was already convinced that she was living in the Land of the Seriously Bewildered, and she was pretty damned close to joining him in his conviction. More and more, it seemed as if her imagination had run away with her and hadn't brought any food or water along for the trip.

On the other hand, what if it was all true and she ignored the warning and did nothing?

After an inner battle that resembled the Normandy landing, Alex decided to err on the side of caution; so she picked up her pencil and pendulum once more.

Where are the contracts?

NEAR

In this room?

YES

Hidden away out of sight?

PURLOINED LETTER

Hmmmm. Interesting. "The Purloined Letter" was a brilliant story by Edgar Allen Poe at his most clever. A thief had hidden a stolen letter in a desk pigeonhole, which contained many other letters. It never occurred to the searchers that it could possibly be hidden in plain sight, and so they overlooked it in favor of every other conceivable hiding place.

Hidden in plain sight. What do we have the most of in this room? Books, of course. All the contracts must be in a book somewhere. Let's see if we can narrow down the search.

Which bookcase?

The pendulum swept to *GOOD-BYE*

You're kept from answering this question, so you respond with GOOD-BYE?

YES

Aha, getting warmer. Alex thought for a moment, then tried something more general.

Behind the books?

NO

On a high shelf?

The pendulum swung to *GOOD-BYE.*

Good-bye. I'll talk more with you later.

BURN

Right away.

She gathered up all the papers she'd written on to communicate with... with *whom*? Hallucinations? Her own subconscious? She pushed such thoughts and doubts from her mind. If she was going to assume that what she was experiencing was real, then all other doubts had to be put aside, and she had to commit to her assumption. If she kept torturing herself about every move she made, and vacillating between belief and incredulity, then everything was going to go down the toilet, including her sanity.

That is, if it hadn't already.

Alex laid the sheaf of papers on the log holder in the fireplace and, with a pang, remembered that Leo had gotten rid of all the fire starting materials. She went back to her board.

Matches?

MANTEL PIECE SIDE DOOR

There was no side door by the mantel piece.

Maybe they meant *in* the mantel piece.

She checked the right side, but found no door. She didn't find one on the left side, either, until she punched it in frustration and a drawer popped open, revealing a small box of wooden matches inside.

After she opened the flue and set the papers alight, she looked back at her board. Should she burn it, too? Probably. Alex thought hard, to be sure she didn't have any further questions, then she fed the pieces of her paper Ouija Board to the flames, as well.

Once the fire was out, she stood, smiling, her eyes cold. The contracts were somewhere on a top shelf of one of these bookcases. She moved to the center of the bookcase-lined room.

How in the world can you have twenty-foot high, floor-to-ceiling bookcases and not have a damned library ladder? Then she noticed the subtle ceiling track ringing the room. *They have a library ladder all right—somebody took it out. All the better to keep us away from things they don't want us to find. I'm definitely on the right track, with or without a ladder to put in it.*

Alex continued to scan the many feet of the top shelves. She didn't see any papers or anything unusual, just book after book, lined up like silent soldiers. And the Shadow People did say that the contracts were not hidden behind the books, so that was out. They had to be inside of a book.

At the top of the center bookcase in the wall that the Library shared with the hallway, Alex eyes fell upon the clear Lucite box that Theodora said housed rare books. It was equipped with metal hardware and a good sized padlock for security.

Bingo! Rare books my pointed ears! That's where the contracts are!

But how was she going to get up there?

And once she had the box, how was she going to open it?

Alex scooted down the hall to get a ladder. She figured she could put it on tarps and drag it into the library; but when she arrived in the partially primed gallery, the ladder was gone.

Now why would Leo collapse that huge ladder and put it away when Black already told them they could leave everything set up? She shrugged and walked down the hall to the supply closet, which was locked and dead bolted, and realized that it wasn't Leo's doing.

Stupendous. Time for Plan B, once I come up with it.

She shuffled back down the hall to the Library and sat down to give the problem a bit more thought.

She considered stacking the books up into a kind of platform, but rejected it immediately because the higher a stack like that grew, the more unstable it would become.

Then she thought of removing some of the non-exotic hardwood doors to use as platforms to lay across the book stacks every three feet to stabilize them. But how would she haul up the last couple of doors when the stack got to be eight or ten feet high? She didn't have any rope, anyway. No, that wouldn't do. Neither would building a stairway shaped stack out of the books—there was still that problem of instability at the top.

Overlapping and screwing together four doors to make a walk-up ramp? No good, either. Though she was no heavyweight, the angle at which the door ramp would have to be propped for her to walk up safely would lead to certain collapse once she was halfway to her destination. Plus, the noise would wake Leo.

Alex was despairing of ever coming up with anything workable when it suddenly hit her.

Get rid of the books and walk up the empty shelves!

Normally, this wouldn't work, either, but these huge old bookcases were built with a wide center stile—that long vertical piece of wood at the front of the bookcase that served to divide it in half and provide stability for the shelves. Fortunately, there was no solid partition attached to the back of the stile to separate the adjoining bookshelves within the bookcase, and that was why her plan would work.

Alex lost no time in emptying the shelves as high as she could reach. She only needed to remove a couple of feet of books on either side of the stile. To continue higher, she would need something to pack books into so she could climb back down with them and stack them on the floor. She couldn't just throw them down from a great height—she loved and respected books far too much for that. Not to mention the noise factor.

Quietly, she crept into their bedroom and picked up her small duffle bag and Leo's bolt cutters, then tiptoed back out, closing the door softly behind her. She grinned, thinking back on all the times she teased him when he packed the odd tool, no matter where they were going. She owed him a big apology.

Alex closed and locked the Library door, then set to work on the shelf just out of her reach. She held onto the stile, then placed her right foot on the first shelf from the bottom to the right of the stile. Next, she put her left foot on the same shelf to the left of the stile, so it looked as if she was climbing up the center of the bookcase. *They don't build 'em like this anymore* she thought, marveling at the ease with which the lone center stile supported her weight.

Carrying books down from the upper shelves was a slow business and it took her two more hours before she had a clear path to the Lucite box. She intended to use her empty duffle bag to carry the box down with her, but much to her chagrin, when she tried to move it, it wouldn't budge. It was either cemented or screwed into place.

Alex sighed. *Nothing is ever simple.*

She climbed back down, draped the bolt cutters around her neck, and climbed back up to the box. It was tricky maneuvering the cutters while trying to keep from killing herself in a twenty-foot fall. She needed two hands to use them, as the handles were long because leverage was crucial to the way they worked. Alex put her right arm through the stile and held on with the inside bend in her elbow, allowing her two hands free to manipulate the bolt cutter.

It took several tries and a great deal of *sub spiritus* cursing, but Alex finally managed to get the tool properly positioned; so with a quick prayer to whatever deity was listening happened to give a crap, plus a little force, a snick of the blades announced that the box was now open for business.

She placed the padlock on an empty area of shelf and withdrew a three-inch thick red leather bound book. The temptation was strong to look at it immediately, but Alex elected to put it away in her duffle bag and get the room back in shape before either Leo or Cooper Black discovered what she'd been up to.

She chose another red bound book that was about the same size and placed it in the box, then carefully draped the cut lock through the hardware in such a way that anyone would have to be right on top of it to see that it had been tampered with.

Alex climbed back down. She'd placed the books she took from the shelves in orderly stacks so that she could replace them in their former positions on the shelves.

By the time everything was put right, Alex was so exhausted that she couldn't even think about looking through the red book. She put her duffle bag in the bedroom closet, then fell into bed, and a deep sleep, right around noon.

Chapter Seventy-Three

Alex awoke several hours later with Leo shaking her shoulder.

"Hey, are you hibernating, or what? The sun's going down. I figured you'd be up way before this. Are you feeling okay? How's your nose?"

Alex yawned. "Leo, I mean this in the nicest possible way when I tell you that there are many decaffeinated brands that taste just as good."

"Sorry," he said sheepishly. "I missed you, that's all. Get up and get dressed and we'll take a hike out to the garage, if you feel up to it. I think there's just enough time to get there and back before dark."

"But Leo, I haven't even showered yet... or eaten anything." He had obviously been up for hours.

"I made you an egg and bacon sandwich. Shower when we get back. Let's go!"

Alex hopped out of bed and threw on her jeans, t-shirt, and work boots from the previous evening. She really hated being rousted out of bed like this—like it was a fire drill or something. She liked to ease into the day over a book with a couple of cups of coffee first—and if possible, complete silence; but she'd never tell Leo that. He'd be hurt beyond measure, so she'd kept her preferred morning routine to herself, and smiled and breathed deeply when he woke her each day like an excited puppy jumping all over the bed. She reasoned that if that was the worst complaint she had about Leo Renfield, then she was indeed a fortunate woman.

"It's a beautiful day. Meet you on the porch," Leo said.

Alex stepped into the bathroom to comb her hair and tie it back in a pony tail. The tarps over the frieze were gone, so all those creepy faces were exposed. She wasn't surprised—they needed the tarps in the gallery. It took too much time to move the few they had left around the room as they worked.

She concentrated on leaving the bathroom as quickly as possible and didn't allow her eyes to linger on the frieze that so unnerved her. If she had, she would have noticed a change.

All the faces were smiling.

***

As Alex stepped out into the bright afternoon, Leo handed her the sandwich he'd made for her, and a small thermos of coffee. "That sandwich was made with love, I'll have you know."

"I know." Alex bit into it, and noticed an unpleasant flavor.

"What did you put in this, Leo?" she asked.

"Just the usual spices, herbs. Why?"

"It tastes kind of funny, that's all."

"'Funny' how? I had scrambled eggs when I got up and I didn't notice anything," Leo said.

"You load your eggs up with so much Tabasco sauce that it probably got by you. Taste it and see for yourself," she said, holding out the sandwich.

Leo took a bite, chewing thoughtfully. "It doesn't taste *bad*, exactly. Maybe the bacon is from a wild boar instead of a domestic pig. That might account for the different flavor. There's boar meat in the freezer. Maybe this is the bacon from it," he said, handing the sandwich back. "If you don't like it, don't eat it; but I don't think it's spoiled."

"Exotic bacon. Could be. As long as it isn't spoiled, I'll eat it. New experience," she said, smiling.

"Can you eat while you're walking?" he asked.

Alex laughed and pointed to her head. "Leo, my natural blondeness, though it happens to be *in cognito* these days, is a hair color, not an IQ. Of course I can walk and eat at the same time. I can even chew gum, watch TV, and knit at the same time."

"Such a multitude of talents. I don't deserve you,

Blondie," Leo said as they set off. They entered the woods quietly, Leo giving Alex a chance to eat her breakfast in what he regarded as peace, but what Alex regarded, between holding a sandwich and trying to drink a cup of coffee while attempting to keep up with Leo on a deeply rutted pathway, as a balancing act worthy of the Ed Sullivan Show. She managed to get most of her breakfast in her mouth and minimize the clothing stains by the time they walked into the crepuscular forest. She decided that she would not be repeating her excursion into exotic sandwich meat.

Leo looked at her. "Done? Looks like you're wearing a lot of it."

"I know. It's all the rage," Alex said. "I think I'll leave the rest of the coffee right here." She tucked the thermos next to a gnarled tree root. "It's not as if anybody will bother it."

The surreal silence closed in around them, putting Alex immediately on guard. She'd explored enough wooded areas in her time to know that this kind of stillness wasn't normal. No birds calling, no leaves rustling, no bugs making noise, no tree frogs chirping. Forests are alive with all kinds of residents, but this place was like a wooden version of the Dead Sea.

"Nothing lives here, Leo," she whispered.

Leo said nothing, but quickened his stride, so she had to hurry to keep up.

"Hey, slow down a little, will you?"

Leo's face had turned grim. "I just want to show you what I found, and get the hell out of here. It feels different today than it did before."

"Different? How do you mean?"

"The other day, it was just a nice stroll in the woods. Pleasant, you know? Today there's a kind of... what's the word I want?"

"How about 'threat?'"

"No, not that so much. It's like everything's waiting for something."

"Perhaps 'anticipation?'"

"That's the word."

Before Alex could respond, they arrived at the concrete building. They crept up to it as quietly as the dry underbrush would allow and peeped through the vertical slits.

"What the hell is it?" Leo asked. "Do you have any idea?"

"I think it's a morgue."

"A *what*?"

"Sure. See that long silver thing with the sharp point on the end? That's a trocar—it's used to remove body fluids from the dead."

"And you know that how?"

"Didn't you ever watch *Six Feet Under*? From what I understand, it was pretty accurate where the funeral business was concerned. This room looks like it could have been a set for the show."

"What I want to know is, why is it here?" Leo said.

"That's a question, all right."

Leo was moving to the front door of the building. "If you want to see what lives around here, come on."

Alex joined him on the steps as he grasped the doorknob and jiggled it a couple of times.

The rustling in the surrounding bushes began almost immediately. Alex peered into the dimness to catch a glimpse of the animals, but they moved too fast for her to focus on.

"This is some kind of signal to them, Leo. By making that sound with the doorknob, you called them, whatever they are. And if they're moving that fast in response, you know what they're expecting, don't you?"

"What?"

"Food, Leo. Food."

The sounds were all around them and moving closer.

"What do we do now? How do we get rid of them?" Leo asked. "I yelled at them the other day, but there weren't nearly this many."

"Well, we can't run. If we run, they'll probably come after us, so whatever you do, relax and don't be afraid—animals can smell it. We have to stand our ground. They seem to be pretty small, but I don't know for sure, and there seems to be a lot of them. If there's a pack mentality working here, it makes them very, very dangerous. Yelling was good thinking. Out here, I wouldn't think they're used to loud noises. Let's add some unpredictable body movements, and see what happens. Do what I do."

Alex growled and shouted, stamping all over the front steps and feinting attacks with sudden sharp forward upper body thrusts. She was doing her best to bully and intimidate, and if that didn't work, they were SOL. Leo joined in, and after a few minutes of pandemonium, they stopped to listen.

Not a sound. No furtive movements in the brush. The creatures, whatever they were, had been successfully frightened off.

"I think we should go back to the house now, Leo," Alex said.

"Why? The animals are gone, and they didn't bother me after I walked away the first time I was here."

"*Why* didn't they, though?"

"I don't know. Maybe they weren't that hungry," Leo guessed.

"And what kind of food would they be after, Leo? In a place like this?"

"Let's not go there, Alex. I'm sure there's a perfectly reasonable explanation for all this."

"I am all ears."

"Maybe the house used to be a funeral parlor, I don't know," Leo said.

"With the morgue all the way out here?"

"There may have been more outbuildings back in the day between here and the house."

Alex had to admit that that could be a possibility.

"Come on. I still want to show you the garage."

Though the sun was still up, it had drawn closer to the horizon and very little light was filtering through the densely intertwined branches overhead. Though not troubling to Alex, Leo was worried that she wouldn't be able to fully take in how rundown the building was in this light. He was about to say as much when they heard a sound not usual for the middle of the woods.

Somebody was hammering up ahead.

They picked up their pace, and when they arrived at the site, Leo's jaw dropped.

The garage had been fully repaired.

While Leo was staring, who should walk out into the evening but Cooper Black, wearing overalls and a tool belt, with a hammer in his hand.

"Oh, no way," he muttered under his breath.

"What do you mean, hon?"

"That garage was falling down!"

"I guess he fixed it," Alex said.

"That was, believe me, at *least* a two person job with everything that needed to be done to this place." He stepped forward and into the garage, eyes up, inspecting Black's handiwork.

Black regarded him with ill-concealed amusement. If he hadn't been mute, Alex was quite convinced that he'd have been laughing out loud at her husband.

When Leo came back out, he was still just as confused. He turned to Cooper Black and said, exaggerating his lip movements, "Good job. It looks great."

Black sarcastically placed both hands over his heart and smiling, closed his eyes in mock ecstasy.

"Sawed-off little fuck," Alex muttered.

The caretaker walked back into the murk of the newly repaired garage, reemerging with his tool bag in his hand. He paid not the slightest bit of further attention to them as he departed down the path back to the house.

Once he was lost to view, Leo said, "It's all fixed. It looks like a whole new garage in there. You should have seen it, Alex, it was a mess. It should have fallen down long ago.

Everything in there was so rickety. And he fixes it, by himself, in one day?"

"He is strong, Leo. You've seen that for yourself."

"Strength is only part of it. There were long beams in there that had to be replaced, not to mention the roof joists. You need somebody to hold up one end while you screw in or nail in the other."

"Maybe he propped it on something. Jesus, this is weird," Alex said.

"What's weird—aside from the obvious?"

"That *I'm* being the voice of reason. I'm not used to it."

Leo laughed.

"Suffice it to say, Leo, that he found a way. The garage is repaired and we don't have to do it. I'd say that's just fine, wouldn't you?"

"Yeah, sure it is. I'd just love to know how he did it, that's all."

"Well, he's not about to tell you. Now where is that mumbling house you were talking about?"

"Over here." Alex followed Leo down the narrow path, and sure enough, as they neared the structure, the mumbling got louder.

"I was right," Alex said.

"What is it?"

"My dear city boy, this is a chicken coop."

"No!"

Alex nodded, grinning widely. Let's go take a closer look. It sounds like a big flock. This must be where they get the eggs for the house. Come on."

Out behind the coop there was a fenced-in outdoor run for the hens—about three dozen of them. At the moment, they were crowded together, eating something off the ground.

"What are they eating?" Leo asked.

"Probably scratch feed or maybe some carrot or turnip greens," Alex replied.

"Whatever it is, they sure seem excited about it," Leo said.

"Chickens are easily excited. My Gramma's chickens used to follow her around like puppies, begging for food. Of course, they always got some, which could be why they continued to do it. I remember one time when…" Alex's reminiscing was cut short by the look on Leo's face. "What?"

"Look what they're eating."

A few hens had eaten their fill and moved away, giving them a clear view of the dead bloated cat they had been recently consuming with such enthusiasm.

Alex turned and immediately vomited up her breakfast.

"No wonder those eggs tasted strange!" Alex exclaimed after wiping her mouth on the handkerchief Leo proffered. "It wasn't the meat at all."

"Are you all right?"

"I am now, but I may never eat another egg in my life."

"You and me both." Leo looked green around the gills himself. "Let's get back to the house. I've had all the exploring I can stand for one day."

By the time they emerged from the wooded path, it was deep twilight and evening mists were rising from the vast lawn around the house, lending it a lonely, forbidding aspect in which Baron von Frankenstein would have been perfectly at home.

They clomped wearily up the steps and put their backs into pushing the absurd front door open and then, again, to close it.

"I need to get to a bathroom right away," Leo said, and flew down the hallway to use the half-bath in the Billiard Room. He wouldn't admit it out loud, but the frieze in their bathroom gave him the creeps, too. He made it just in time to raise the seat and vomit into the toilet. He opened his eyes and looked down after it was over.

His vomitus was filled with bright red blood.

"Goddamned ulcer!" Leo shook his head. He couldn't believe it was making a comeback—and here, of all places. He decided against telling Alex that it was acting up unless it became too obvious to conceal. It had flared up before, years ago, and the problem resolved itself after he spent a couple of days on bland, easily digestible foods, so he wasn't worried. He flushed the toilet a couple of times and cleaned any splattered areas, sprayed some air freshener, then washed his face, rinsed his mouth, and feeling much better, went to find Alex.

She was stretched out on their bed with a cool face cloth on her head, still looking very pale. Leo sat down next to her on the edge of the bed.

"Still not feeling too good, huh?"

"I feel like I want to drink a gallon of water and throw up again just to clean my insides out. I've never, ever seen anything so appalling in my life. I hope to God we don't catch something—or don't already have something. Have you noticed anything unusual, heath-wise?" Alex wanted to know.

Yeah—just. "No, not really. How about you?"

"Maybe that's why I've been seeing things."

Leo smiled. "I'm no doctor, honey, but you were seeing things before we started working here. Remember the Mertzes? I don't think that has anything to do with the 'chicken feed.'"

"Oh. Right." She thought for a minute, then said, "You know, Leo, somebody fed them that dead cat on purpose, and has probably been feeding them roadkill right along."

"Why do you say that?"

"Think about it. The run was completely enclosed with chicken wire—even the top. The openings I saw weren't big enough to allow anything larger than the tiniest mouse through. And the excitement the chickens showed for that dead animal tells me that it wasn't the first time it was on the menu. I think that's what they get fed regularly."

"Oh, Alex, come on. That's pretty far out, don't you think?"

"How else did the cat get there if not tossed in by someone who walked through the chicken coop to do it?"

"Cooper Black?"

"Who else? And you know something else I noticed? His diet seems to be centered on those horrible eggs—he eats a ton of them."

"I wondered where all the eggs went when I made my breakfast. Seemed like we had a couple of dozen in there yesterday, and this morning there were only five left."

"I've noticed that they get replaced every afternoon, always maintaining a two dozen count. He drinks a lot of milk, too; a gallon a day, it looks like. That gets replaced every day, as well. I bet he's a lacto-ovo vegetarian."

"A what?"

"Somebody who consumes only eggs, dairy products, vegetables, nuts, grains, and so forth. No red meat. No meat of *any* kind. He seems to go through a lot of abalone, too, though, and I'm not sure how that would fit in that kind of a diet... you know, if seafood is allowed." She paused. "Or, if abalone is really what's in those packages."

"Just leave those packages alone, Alex. Whatever's in them, I don't want to know about it and neither do you. What I'm wondering is how he ever got employed by Theodora? She's all gung-ho for red meat eaters."

"I don't know. Odd, though, isn't it? Drastic change of subject Leo, but I think I'm going to close my eyes for a while. I still don't feel too great."

"Well, try not to think about... you know... anymore. I'm going to lie on the couch and read. I'm hoping that John Adams' life will take my mind off ours for a while. Sleep tight. I'll get you up in a couple of hours for supper, if you don't get up by yourself." He kissed her on the forehead, then headed for the Library, shutting the bedroom door quietly behind him.

Alex's stomach was actually in much better shape than she let on. She just wanted some alone time to think and...

She suddenly remembered the red leather bound book and her heart beat faster. She crept out of bed and retrieved the duffle bag from the closet. Once she had the book in her hand, she heard a soft noise behind her.

She stood and spun on her heel.

The bookcase was opening.

Chapter Seventy-Four

Alex watched the bookcase swing fully open, revealing a set of stairs that stepped downward into darkness. She considered the open passage for a moment and concluded that it was an invitation.

She tiptoed to the closed bedroom door and opened it the tiniest crack.

Leo was sound asleep already, with his open book resting on his chest. He'd probably stay asleep for at least an hour, maybe two.

Alex closed the door and, with book in hand, she picked her hoodie off the chair and stepped over the bookcase-to-who-knows-where threshold.

As her foot touched the third step, the bookcase closed behind her. She shrugged and continued downward.

Must be the back way to the basement. "Hello? Hello, Friends?" she called. *'Shadow People' to 'Friends.' What a difference a day makes.*

The air around her filled with whispers, susurrations and chilled breezes from unknown sources. Gone, however, were the shrieks, moans, and screams of before. Their relationship, if that's what it was, had evolved into one of cooperation, mutual respect, and as hard as it was to believe, a sort of friendship that went deeper than Alex's collective label for the entities in the basement.

That was if the Friends were even there at all… if Alex's mind wasn't orchestrating the entire thing. It could easily be the case, and that strong possibility frightened Alex more than anything else. *Stop thinking that way! You've made a commitment, now stick with it!* she admonished herself.

"Where does this passage lead?" she whispered, beginning her descent.

In answer, an image of a duck popped into her mind and interpreting it as a warning, she immediately lowered her head.

She heard an audience laughing.

"Try again, I guess," she muttered. "Where does this passage lead?"

Image of a baby chick.

The penny dropped. "Down?"

Audience applause.

"Thank you so much. I am well aware that it goes down," Alex said, chuckling. She found it fascinating that these beings seemed to have a sense of humor. "Let me try once more. What is our destination?"

Before they could send her an answer via one of her senses, she reached the foot of the stairs.

"Are we in the basement?"

Gardenia scent.

"Are you too weak and cold to speak with me?"

Scent of roses.

"All right. How about if we do this: How about only one of you moves through me several times to get warm enough to speak and remember—sort of a spokesman for the rest of you? I promise I'll give what warmth I can to the rest of you later on. Would that be okay for now? " Alex said, wondering if she was a complete lunatic who was merely standing in the dark talking to herself.

In response to her question, the face of her long dead, beloved little brother Siddie appeared in her mind, smiling and nodding. Alex gasped.

How could they possibly know about Siddie?

Maybe she *was* crazy.

Before Alex could comment further, the delegated Friend moved through her and drew away some warmth. It made three more circuits before Alex asked it to stop.

THAT IS MUCH BETTER THANK YOU it whispered. *YOU HAVE THE BOOK*

"Yes. I found it last night. I couldn't have done it without your help."

WE HELP YOU YOU HELP US YES

"Yes. I haven't even looked at the book yet. I was just going to when you opened the passage door for me."

LOOK NOW The urgent whisper spun and ricocheted off the surrounding stone walls, sounding like many voices instead of just one.

Alex opened the leather bound volume. The inside front cover was emblazoned with the words *Memento Mori* in Old English calligraphy. It was beautifully done and reminded her of the illuminated manuscripts she once saw at the Getty Museum in California. Alex marveled at the thought. California? Was she ever in California doing something as normal as visiting a museum? Or stopping at a café for a cup of coffee? Or going to the movies?

Normalcy seemed to be screening its phone calls these days.

She forced her wandering mind back to the book. *Memento Mori*. The term was not unknown to Alex but, at the moment, she couldn't summon up where she heard it or what it meant.

She turned to the first page.

She remembered.

The first page held a photograph of two men, dressed as laborers. They were sitting on the sofa in the Library, eyes closed. They looked like they were sleeping, but Alex knew better.

They were dead.

She flipped through her mental trivia file and recalled reading somewhere that *Memento Mori* books were popular during Victorian times. People would dress their departed loved one in fine clothes and put them in a chair or reclining on a sofa, or even posed with the rest of the family, and a photographic portrait would be taken. Few people owned cameras in that era, and photographs were prohibitively expensive, but funds were saved, begged or borrowed in order to have a photograph taken as a remembrance of the person who had died. Many times, this was the only photograph the family would ever have of that person—hence, *Memento Mori*— a remembrance of the dead.

Alex had never actually seen one until now, though she was pretty sure that this book had nothing to do with Victorian history. She gazed down at the faces of the two dead men.

They looked familiar. Now why was that?

She continued to flip through the book. There were no names beneath any of the photos, just the year in which the picture was taken. It began with 1978.

"My God. This book goes back thirty years," Alex whispered in awe. She refused to wonder if there were other extant volumes that predated this one.

The last page had no photo, but "2008" was inscribed in the same calligraphic hand beneath the blank area where the glued down black mounting corners marked the resting place for the final photo.

It didn't take the imagination of Walt Disney to figure out who was meant to complete this volume.

"But *why*?" she murmured. Alex turned over the last page and discovered a clear plastic zippered pouch which contained flat, neatly folded papers.

The contracts! Probably one for every person in this book… and two who weren't.

She was about to take them out and look them over when the voice at her elbow interrupted.

Come There is something you must do now

Alex didn't question. She re-zipped the flap, closed the book, and started walking. Her thoughts were traveling in so many different directions that they'd need a flight plan and a Sherpa Guide named Niblic to get back.

As it turned out, the passage the bedroom opened into was one of the side tunnels in the basement—one of the tunnels she had been initially herded away from the first time she met the Friends.

Stop here

On her right was a door.

OPEN IT TAKE WHAT IS INSIDE

Alex complied, then resumed walking.

TAKE THE NEXT PASSAGE ON YOUR LEFT AND CONTINUE TO MOVE FORWARD

She did, and after that, the Friend was quiet, though she knew it was still with her. Alex passed the time counting her steps, since she'd long ago, and for no special reason, measured the length of her stride. As a result, she could judge the distance she walked with remarkable accuracy.

They'd gone nearly a quarter mile when the Friend spoke again.

STOP HERE

There was another door on her right.

WE HAVE ARRIVED OPEN THE DOOR AND WALK

When Alex finally opened the stubborn swollen door, she was surprised to see light beyond it. The door opened onto a claustrophobia-inducing oubliette with a set of six concrete steps, topped with a patined copper open gridwork cover through which moonlight shone. She wasted no time climbing the stairs, pushing up the cover at the top and emerging... into the strangest tableau she'd ever seen.

Alex stood at the edge of a sea of tall, weedy grass, throughout which were scattered three-foot tall houses. It looked like a community for garden gnomes.

And they weren't just *any* little houses. These were miniature, finely detailed scale replicas of the main house, right down to the color. Many of them were the worse for being out in the weather, but even those that were falling down still bore an unmistakable resemblance to the main house.

The Black House.

But why are they here? Outside? If somebody built you a scale replica of your house, wouldn't you keep it inside?

As she stood there puzzling, she suddenly realized she was alone. The Friend hadn't left the basement with her, so she went back down to find it.

"Why didn't you come with me?"

I CANNOT

"Why?"

IRON REPELS WE CANNOT CROSS

"But the cover is made of copper."

The Friend pointed at the threshold, and Alex looked down to see the iron plate that ran across the top of it.

"Why have you brought me here? What are those houses doing out there? Why have you shown this to me?"

LOOK AGAIN came the whispered reply.

Alex stepped back out into the moonlight. The sky was clear with the moon waxing and slightly more than half full. Even someone without Alex's gift would have been able to see detail clearly. It was easy to determine which of the houses were the more recent additions, since there was less weather damage to them. She squatted down to examine the house closest to where she was standing.

It was truly remarkable the way the woodworker had captured every detail of the Black House in miniature. It would have made a marvelous doll house for some lucky child; but instead, the painstaking energies of a true craftsman were evidently found wanting and his work relegated to rot; forgotten, in this overgrown, neglected place.

Alex stood and circled the house in the tall grass to see if the detail was as precise from all sides, and discovered a tiny copper plaque at the rear of the replica, affixed beneath one of the second floor windows. She bent closer to read the inscription

Engraved in Old English, it simply read, "2006."

She stood up and stepped away, then walked through the strange area, counting the houses. Some were so ruined by the punishing New England weather that there was nothing more than small piles of old wood to mark where they once stood. Alex was amazed that even that much evidence was left after years and years outdoors. *They must have built them from high quality teak and water sealed the hell out of them.*

The copper plates didn't disintegrate, though, and where

the houses were no more, she found one in each pile of rubble.

Total house count: 30.

Alex's hand flew to her mouth once she realized what the Friend had shown her. She hurried to the newest looking house on the lot.

Its plaque read, "2008." She was about to turn away when she noticed something carved just below the roof peak.

Alex ran back to the basement. She needed answers and she needed them fast.

"Are those what I think they are?" she demanded once she was back in the cool darkness of the basement. "Those houses—they're grave markers, aren't they?"

Scent of lilies.

"Please, please warm yourself again. I need for you to speak to me."

The Friend moved through her rapidly four times, then told her what she had to do using the shovel she'd taken from the closet in the tunnel.

The graves were all shallow.

She didn't have to dig down very far.

Chapter Seventy-Five

Alex dug woodenly, her mind a blank. A medic would have said she was in shock, and she probably was, but she couldn't take the time to acknowledge it.

She couldn't think about the mortal danger she and Leo were obviously in. She couldn't think about the little maniac hiding upstairs. She couldn't even think about a way for them to escape, because Leo would never believe her and would balk at the very idea.

And that's if... and it was a big 'if'... all of this was even happening outside of what appeared to be her rapidly deteriorating mind.

All she could do was dig. It was all she could handle at the moment.

She used the battered leather briefcase that had been in the closet with the shovel to store the fruits of her labor—if you could call them that. She had also tucked the *Memento Mori* in there for safekeeping.

Just when she reached the point of such profound mental and physical exhaustion that she felt she couldn't lift another shovelful of earth, she realized that she was done. Each gravesite had been excavated—well, all but one—dealt with, then refilled.

She surveyed the area to see if it would look disturbed to anyone else, and had to work hard to quell her rising hysteria. *Disturbed?* Disturbed? *Hiring painters once a year, having them build their own grave markers, then killing them off and burying them in your back yard? No, there's nothing* disturbed *here!*

Alex shuddered, gathered up the briefcase and the shovel, turned her back on the stage of her *Danse Macabre*, and plodded back to the dark, cool sanctuary of the basement.

She hoped that Leo had passed the last couple of hours wrapped in the serenity of a deep and dreamless sleep.

Chapter Seventy-Six

After an hour of restless sleep, Leo awoke with a start when his book slipped off his chest and hit the floor. He sat up, retrieved the fallen volume and placed it on the coffee table. Now that he was awake, he didn't really feel like reading anymore, and went to check on Alex.

He opened the bedroom door as quietly as he could, and saw that the bed was empty, so he looked past the bed toward the bathroom.

"Alex? You okay?"

Nothing.

He strode across the room in two steps, fearing that she might have passed out in the bathroom; but when he got there, he found it empty of all but the threescore appalling faces lining the walls. *Damndest bathroom I ever saw that can be this crowded when there's no one in it.*

So where was Alex?

Leo walked back into the bedroom and pulled aside a curtain. It was full dark now. She couldn't be out walking. Christ, it was creepy enough walking around outside this joint during the day.

Leo made a quick circuit of the first floor and couldn't find her anywhere. That left the basement or the forbidden second floor.

He opened the door in the kitchen, shouted down the stairs, and received no reply there either.

He walked to the front door and tugged it open, thinking that Alex might be having a drink on the front steps.

But, no.

He closed the door and walked back down the hall. He stopped at the foot of the stairs that wound away up to the second floor, and looking at them, could only think of an old

Red Skelton routine:

"If I dood it, I get a whippin'…

"I dood it!"

Leo and Junior, the Mean Widdle Kid took the richly carpeted stairs two at a time.

Chapter Seventy-Seven

Alex stole back into the bedroom through the bookcase door, after the Friend told her how to open it again from her side of the room. All she had to do was remove the thick red candle from the sconce on the wall next to the bookcase.

But before she did that, she examined the threshold. Sure enough, there was another iron plate running across the top.

Alex was now more convinced than ever that she was suffering a complete mental meltdown and her lunatic mind had now taken control and was writing the script. Remove the candle from the sconce to open a secret passage? It was right out of *Young Frankenstein*. She supposed that, to close it, she'd have to "put the kendle beck!"

Wonder where Frau Blucher is Alex thought as she lifted the candle, then set it back in place.

The door swung shut.

Alex sighed and wrapped the ratty old briefcase which, heavy on its own, was now quite a bit heavier, in a couple of old sweatshirts, as she had been instructed. Once she hid the odd parcel under the bed, she stripped off her graveyard glad rags and stepped into the shower. The faces on the wall didn't even bother her anymore, she was so tired.

After today, she wondered if she'd ever feel clean again.

$\mathfrak{Chapter}$ $\mathfrak{Seventy}$-$\mathfrak{Eight}$

Leo wasn't sure quite what he'd expected to find at the top of the stairs, but this wasn't it.

There was nothing up there.

Not a carpet on the floor.

Not a stick of furniture or decoration of any kind.

Not a single light fixture.

Just silence and dust.

He tiptoed down the hall to the first of four doors and turned the knob. It wasn't locked and opened onto a moonlit bedroom that clearly had gone unused and uncared for for the better part of twenty years. The curtains and bedclothes hung in rotted tatters. What once must have been a costly oriental rug had lost its value to moths years ago. The bed itself—a sleigh bed, probably magnificent in its day—was riddled with woodworm and had partially collapsed. Every surface was an anchor for dust-laden cobwebs abandoned by an army of spiders a generation ago in search of more fertile hunting grounds.

Leo felt the hairs on the back of his neck rise, and backed quickly out of the lifeless room, shutting the door. Had he stepped in and looked a bit closer, he might have noticed the faded clown paintings staring out beneath the thick layer of grime.

Back in the hall, he stood, motionless. He had no idea what the consequences would be if he were discovered on the second floor, and wasn't anxious to find out.

Nothing stirred. He knew he should count himself lucky and get back downstairs immediately, and was about to do just that when he heard voices two doors down.

He crept close enough to hear.

"I thought you told me these builders were dolts! *She* is too smart by half!"

It was Ross Hamilton.

"Oh, stop worrying. She can't possibly figure it all out. And even if she does, Cooper will take care of it. This shouting is most unattractive, Ross."

Theodora's voice.

"Yes, father, really—they paint walls for a living. It doesn't exactly indicate a high IQ. As a matter of fact, it doesn't even indicate a normal IQ."

Fat, loudmouth Jane.

"They were poking around by the garage, so you know they've seen it," Ross said.

Leo assumed that "it" was the morgue.

"Oh, so what? Honestly, father, give it a rest, will you?" Jane bleated.

Candace hadn't put her two cents in yet, and Leo wondered if she was in the room. *Yes, probably playing pocket pool with Daddy.*

"Nevertheless, I think we should go have a chin wag with Cooper," Ross said.

Leo panicked. He didn't want to be caught when they left the room, so he ducked into the room next door just in time.

The Hamiltons headed down the hall in the opposite direction, still arguing. Leo heard another door slam, then silence reigned once more.

What the hell was going on here? They were supposed to be in Phoenix for the summer, weren't they? And it was obvious that no one had lived up here since Christ left Chicago. The second floor looked like a long-abandoned tenement building, unpainted walls, warped floor boards, and all.

Leo wondered briefly what Cooper Black's room was like.

He released the breath that he was unconsciously holding and gazed around the room he'd chosen as a hiding place.

It was the first room Leo Renfield ever looked at that looked back at him.

Moonlight flooded in, illuminating the décor. There were eyes everywhere. Somebody had covered every square inch of the walls and the ceiling with realistically painted human eyes. They were all rendered in pairs in strips of faces between the nose and the forehead. The room looked like it was auditioning for an interrogation room in Hell, and would have been more than even Hieronymous Bosch could have handled. There were even eyes on the floor and on the inside of the door.

And they all looked hostile.

In the center of the room, beneath an enormous skylight, were a stool and a gleaming brass telescope the size of Mt. Palomar mounted on a hydraulic lift. Evidently the skylight opened to allow the viewing station to rise up through it and out into the night.

Leo need wonder no further. He'd found Cooper Black's room.

Over by the window, there was a child-sized heavily buttoned Morris chair and an end table upon which a tiny Tiffany lamp rested. It's low wattage bulb revealed a large martini centered on the coaster beneath it. As Leo drew closer, he could see the sweat on the glass. He bent and sniffed it.

Yep. Gin, all right, and recently poured. Black will be back for it soon. Wouldn't have pegged him for a Gibson man, though.

That was what Leo thought until it became clear that what was floating in the glass was not a large cocktail onion.

How he reached the first floor again without screaming would be a mystery for the ages.

Chapter Seventy-Nine

Cleaned up now, Alex looked quite a bit less like an escapee from the *Thriller* video. The fact that she'd had only one hour of sleep in the past twenty-four had caught up with her, though, and she hung her bathrobe over a chair, slid into bed, and snuggled under the comforter.

Just before she settled into sleep, she realized with the detachment of a lucid dreamer, why the faces in the *Memento Mori* looked familiar.

They were the same faces that were carved into the bathroom wall.

Chapter Eighty

Once Leo hit the first floor, he charged down the hall toward the Library.

He needed to think.

He needed a drink.

He needed to think with a drink.

Leo detoured to the kitchen and got the bottle of Johnny Walker Black out of the pantry. He knew he could just as well have left it on the tray in the Library with the rocks glasses, but somehow, taking it from the pantry—the place where they kept their celebratory Wild Turkey a lifetime ago at their house—made it seem more special. Or perhaps it felt as if he'd brought a touch of home with him.

Probably a little bit of both.

Alternatively, it could just be that old habits die hard.

With trembling hands, he filled the ice bucket, then, bottle in hand, ambled to the library to sip and ponder.

Leo poured himself a generous double and loaded it with ice. He picked up the siphon to add some fizz, then decided against it and put it down. Then he picked it up again. Then put it down. He repeated this several more times, and to anyone observing him, he would have called to mind an automaton in need of adjustment.

Finally, drink in hand, he drifted away from the table and settled into one of the leather Library chairs—a pleasant reminder of the evening he'd spent with Earle at his club. Leo closed his eyes, conscious of his heartbeat, willing it to slow down. He breathed deeply, searching for the happiest image his troubled mind could locate, and recalled a family cookout at Bantam Lake when he was just a kid.

Uncle Willie had just bought a twenty-foot speedboat and had trailered it to the lake to moor it; but once he had it in the water, he drove it across the lake and around the spit to dock it at the cottage Leo's clan had rented for the summer. He was so proud of that boat, named "Anunka" after an Egyptian princess, that he'd wanted to take everyone out for a spin.

There was quite a crowd, so it was probably the Fourth of July family picnic; Leo couldn't remember. The adults, as always in his family, went first when any activity was suggested, and all eight of them boarded the small craft. When Uncle Willy put the boat in reverse, it was so heavy that he backed it right underwater. At the time, Leo couldn't breathe he was laughing so hard, watching his relatives in their dresses and good pants and shoes, wading out of the lake. Even now, it made him chuckle and he instantly felt better. He opened his eyes and took a sip of his drink.

A funny story and great scotch. The only thing that could improve this moment would be if I knew where the hell Alex was.

He sat a while longer, remembering other good times he had at the lake that summer, then put his half-consumed drink on the coffee table and stood to visit the porcelain auditorium. He had concluded that Alex must be exploring the basement and put his worrying aside for the moment.

He didn't even notice Alex asleep on the bed when he passed through the bedroom.

Leo gazed at the faces as he took care of business. They looked different to him. Had their positions changed?

No, not possible.

Still…

Cut it out now! They're carved faces. They don't move! his father's voice screamed in his head. He could almost hear him taking off his belt—the silky sound the leather made snicking through of the loops on his pants. His father had taught him, very early in his life, that it was effeminate for boys to be fanciful and to banish all such flights of imagination from his mind. Throughout his childhood, the old man had made it his mission in life to beat him into the pragmatist that he had become. He flushed, zipped and turned toward the door.

Alex was standing there, looking tousled from her nap. "Hi. I thought I heard you."

"Alex, honey, where have you been? I searched everywhere for you!"

"I was asleep, Leo."

"I looked in here an hour ago, and you weren't here then."

"No. I wasn't here an hour ago."

"But how did you get back? You would have passed me, and I didn't see you. I wasn't upstairs for all that long," Leo said.

"Upstairs? Leo, you went upstairs?" Alex was incredulous. That was more like something she would do rather than Leo. "Oh, man! What's it like?" she asked, her eyes sparkling. She just loved a good secret.

They both sat down on the edge of the bed, and Leo filled her in.

"I want to go up there," Alex said.

"No, hon. I was lucky I didn't get caught. No telling what would happen if we did."

Alex was clearly disappointed, but had to concede Leo's point. "You're right—too risky. Damn. I'd love to see it."

"You wouldn't say that if you'd been up there. And where were you, anyway?"

"Basement and points south," Alex replied.

"I yelled for you and you didn't answer."

"I probably couldn't hear you. I was really far away from the house at one point."

"You couldn't have been. Though I grant you that the foundation must be gigantic for a house this large, the basement wouldn't extend beyond the house," Leo explained.

"This one does."

"Are you sure you didn't just get turned around and lost? Were you exploring those side tunnels? Could have happened then," said Leo the ever-sensible.

Alex decided not to fight it. What was the point? He'd never believe her and she couldn't bear to see that sad, pitying look she knew she'd get if she pressed the point. "Yeah, I guess that would explain it, all right."

"It doesn't explain how you got back here without my seeing you, though," Leo said.

"Oh, that's easy. There's a secret passage behind the bookcase."

Leo laughed out loud. "Now it's secret passages? You're joking, right?"

Without a word, Alex stood, stepped to the sconce, lifted the red candle and placed it on the dresser.

The bookcase opened into the room on hidden hinges.

Alex did a couple of dance steps, then flung both arms across her body in a circle, ending with them outstretched with both palms up, indicating the opening the way a ringmaster might present the dancing bears.

Leo's jaw dropped and he just sat there, staring.

"Well?"

"There really is a secret passage," he murmured.

"Apparently."

He came over to inspect. "Sorry I didn't believe you, hon," he said, his eyes glued to the dark opening.

"S'okay. It's pretty unbelievable. If you'd told me about this, I probably think you'd been watching too many horror movies, too."

This, of course, was not true. Alex would have believed him without question.

"Where does it go?" Leo asked as he searched the doorway for a mechanism of some kind.

"The basement."

"Really? But why?"

"Don't know. This opening is the end of the tunnel after the Wine Crypt."

"Was this house maybe the last stop on the Underground Railroad, or something?" Leo ventured.

Alex sighed. "I'm sure it was the last stop for a great many people."

"What?"

"Nothing."

"Show me where it goes. I'll get the flashlights."

"Tomorrow, Leo. I'll show you tomorrow, I promise."

"Okay." He turned his attention back to the open bookcase. "How do you close this?"

"Think *Young Frankenstein*," Alex said.

"*Young Frankenstein*? What does *Youn*... oh, I see. " Movie memory in gear, he replaced the candle in the wall sconce.

The bookcase swung silently shut once again.

"I wonder how many more of these there are in the house," Leo marveled.

"Funny, I'm doing my best *not* to wonder," Alex said.

"How did you find this one?"

Alex would have loved to answer him truthfully, but didn't want to give him any more reasons to commit her than he already had.

"Oh, I picked up the candle to smell it—to see if it was scented." Safe answer. He'd seen her do that a million times with colored candles when they were shopping.

"And is it?"

"Unfortunately, no."

"You said you were far away from the house at one point. How do you know?"

"It felt far away," Alex said.

"Well, like I said, the tunnels wouldn't go beyond the foundation, so they must wind around down there like a digestive tract. You probably weren't as far away from the house as you thought."

"Could be," Alex said. It was true that she hadn't been paying much attention to twists and turns in the tunnels. She was looking down so she wouldn't trip over anything and was concentrating on counting her steps, so it could have happened the way Leo said. She thought back. Could she see the house from where she was? She didn't think so, but by that time she was in such a state of shock that geography wasn't really a high priority, and she hadn't thought to look around to get her bearings.

"What if the owners built tunnels that would lead away from the house, Leo? Isn't that possible?"

"Sure it's possible. Were the tunnel walls and roof shored up with wooden beams?"

"No. All the tunnels look exactly the same—like they were cut out of solid rock. Could that be?"

"It would be an unthinkable expense to bring an auger down there to drill long tunnels back when this house was built. Hell, the bill would curl you hair and boil your brain even now, so I don't think that's too likely a scenario," Leo said. "Did this one tunnel take you all the way to where you came out, or did you have to take other connecting tunnels?"

"Other tunnels."

"So what did you find?"

"A graveyard."

"Oh."

"You don't seem too surprised," Alex said.

"I'm not. Back in the late 1700s it was a common practice, and legal, to bury your loved ones on your property. It's probably full of relatives of the original owners. Does anyone keep it up?"

"Keep it up?"

"You know—mow the grass, stuff like that."

"Not that I could see, no."

"So it's probably been forgotten, then."

"Oh, I think it gets remembered once a year or so," Alex said.

"Really? Why?"

"I'm afraid to tell you. You'll think I'm more nuts than you already do."

"I don't think you're nuts, Alex."

"But you don't believe the things I tell you."

"Well, you must admit, some of the things you've told me

are pretty far out there. But once…"

"…the pills kick in everything will be fine—I know."

"So tell me."

"Oh, what the hell. The graves didn't have normal gravestones or markers."

"So what did they have, then?"

"Three foot scale model black houses, just like this one," Alex said miserably, studying the carpet and waiting for the platitudes. When none came, she looked up.

Out of Leo's parchment white face stared two horror-filled eyes.

"Leo! What's wrong?"

"I wondered what it was for," Leo murmured.

"I thought those were your initials! So you did make one of them, then. Was this what you were building for that mysterious client of yours when you barricaded yourself in the workshop?"

"I can't tell you."

"So don't *tell* me. Blink once for 'yes' and twice for 'no'."

Leo blinked once.

"Glad that's cleared up," Alex said.

"How do you know they're grave markers, Alex? Maybe that isn't a cemetery back there."

She explained about the photo album and how it came to be in her possession, but left out the Friends for now. He'd *never* believe that.

"Let me see the book," Leo said.

Alex ducked under the bed and pulled out the peculiarly wrapped package.

"Why is it all tied up in your sweatshirts?"

Jesus, this was getting difficult. "I was concerned about dampness," she replied. Even to her ears, it was one lame-o excuse. She was absolutely floored when Leo bought it.

As she unwrapped the briefcase, he asked, "How did you know where it was?"

499

"What? The *Memento Mori*?"

A realization dawned in Leo's eyes. "What did you call it?"

"*Memento Mori*—remembrance of the dead. Victorians used to have pictures taken of their dead loved ones as a sort of souvenir."

"Wait a sec.'" Leo said. He opened the closet door and rummaged around. "Where the hell did I put that? Ah, here it is."

He handed Alex a folded scrap of paper.

"Read it, please. Out loud."

Alex read:

"WHERE SHALL I FIND YOU?

I know not why I write this

Nothing seems to sway

The world goes on

Alive and strong

Every bless-ed day

But now I do not hear them

Aside from tired sighs

Seeing is my one belief, but

Everything is lies

My days do not grow shorter

Even though I try

Not to scare the lady

Who'll help us say, "Good-bye"

She'll find *Memento Mori*

She'll do what must be done

To help us rest forevermore

Our battle will be won"

"Where did this come from? Did you write it? It looks like

your handwriting," Alex said.

"I transcribed it, then I forgot about it because it didn't make any sense to me. It was painted onto a mirror in the basement. When you mentioned *Memento Mori* I remembered it. This poem is about you, isn't it?"

"Looks like."

"Alex, what in blazes is going on here?"

"There's a lot I haven't told you, Leo, because I knew you wouldn't believe me. I couldn't stand it, so I kept most of it to myself."

"Tell me now, Alex, please," he said. "I'll believe you, I swear to God."

Alex took a deep breath and plunged forward, telling Leo all about the Friends and who she thought they were and how she'd managed to find the *Memento Mori*.

"But why are they still here? If they're dead, why can't they move on?" Leo asked.

"I don't know yet. I think it has to do with the contracts," Alex said.

"I think I might know why," Leo said. "Remember when we were here the first time—to sign the contract? There was a line in there that I jokingly questioned—it said something to the effect of agreeing to remain in the house until the work is completed."

"Are you saying that maybe they all died before the work was finished?"

Leo nodded. "Maybe they're trapped here."

"But Leo, contracts don't work like that! They're not enforceable beyond death."

"Maybe this one is."

"Have we just changed places?"

Leo snorted. "No. We've just joined forces, that's all. And about damned time, too. Finish your story."

Alex detailed her day in the graveyard and told Leo what now had to be done.

He listened carefully and when Alex was finished, said, "Whatever is going on in this house, I think we need to go with what you've said; though I don't know how you're going to get Cooper Black to submit to his part in what you've told me. But I have to say, there are a lot of things that make more sense now. Let's err on the side of caution."

"Thank you, Leo."

"Come on, let's take that briefcase into the Library and get a better look at all this stuff."

"Okay. Hey, do you smell something burning?" Alex sniffed the air.

Chapter Eighty-One

Alex stuffed the *Memento Mori* back into the briefcase with the other items, then hauled it up by the handles and dashed after Leo into the Library…

…where Cooper Black awaited them with a gun in his hand.

The Renfields stopped in their tracks.

Gesturing with the firearm, Black indicated that they were to sit on the sofa that was in front of the huge roaring fire he'd built in the walk-in fieldstone fireplace.

They sat. Alex glanced at Leo, who was the picture of terror.

She glared at Black's impassive face. "Put the damned fire out, you sonofabitch!"

"Oh, I don't think so," he replied.

Alex started with surprise.

"Oh, yes, I can speak and hear quite well," Black said. His voice, deep and cultured, belied his stumpy fairy tale appearance. He sounded like a Shakespearean actor.

"But…"

"I believe you both were told that I *don't* speak, not that I *can't*. As is the case with most people with rudimentary listening skills, the error in assumption was yours. Never confuse unwillingness with inability. As to the fire—I think I'll just leave it the way it is. It controls your Troglodyte of a husband. You I can handle nicely with my little friend here. Say, 'hello.'"

Alex snorted derisively. "You're far too short for that line."

"Nevertheless, I am armed and you are not."

"So what happens now? What was all this for?" Alex

demanded.

"What happens now? You both die," Black said, taking a tone that would be used to explain a simple concept to a mental defective.

"But why? We haven't done anything to you. Why kill us?"

"You have perpetrated no offense whatsoever as far as I am concerned. I do this on the behalf of another."

Alex was confused, and it showed.

Black sighed. "For someone with above average problem-solving skills, I'm truly amazed that you haven't put it all together for yourself by now. This house is a living entity—I'd have thought you'd have tumbled to that when you felt the walls and the floor get warm. And when did that happen?"

"We noticed it right after I smashed my nose against the wall."

"And therefore...?"

"That hinky furnace that Leo found... those copper pipes off all the sinks and tubs that led to it..."

"Quite so. The house's circulatory system. It runs on blood—and rather efficiently, I might add. This is also why there is nothing driven into the walls here—they will bleed if punctured. It was fortunate that you spewed so much blood on the wall gouge you made when you sustained your injury that it camouflaged the blood seeping from the wall itself. And when you washed your blood down the sink, it provided the house with enough energy to heal itself and stop its own hemorrhaging. By the time your husband got around to repairing the damage, it was not much more than a scratch compared to the initial gouge."

"There couldn't have been enough blood from my nose to run a whole house," Alex cried. Then she remembered Leo's description of the second floor. It evidently wasn't enough to run the whole house.

"It doesn't take much, believe me. And remember all the other nourishment you've provided," he said, nodding at Leo's bandaged hands. "But I'll explain, since you shouldn't go to your graves with unanswered queries.

"This house requires sixteen pints of blood per year to, for lack of a better term, 'survive.' The blood of two adult human beings. Since the average human being has slightly less than ten pints, with two deaths per year we are nearly two pints to the good. When the house is sated, the owners have nothing to fear from it. It's rather like a lion or a tiger in that regard. Once it has had the requisite nourishment, it becomes much less dangerous and will leave the occupants alone until the appointed time the following year. Of course, when females in the house menstruate, they must do it elsewhere. The house can revive early if too much blood goes down the drain. With all the bleeding you two have done since you arrived, the house is now ravenous for this year's final feeding."

"That's the reason for the morgue," Alex said.

"Precisely."

"You'll pour our blood down the drain. What about our flesh?"

"Ah, well, you already know the answer to that, I believe. I do so love the eggs here, don't you? And now that your visit here is coming to an abrupt end, I can stop my deliveries for a time, since our feathered friends will no longer have to eat, shall we say, 'leftovers.'"

"You mean roadkill," Alex said. "But the deliveryman brought abalone."

"Again you make an incorrect assumption. He brought a parcel *marked* 'Abalone.' With your insane attachment to animals and your unrelenting social consciousness, we knew you'd never touch anything that you thought contained an endangered species."

"What's with the animals that show up when the doorknob at your little house of horror gets rattled?"

"Ah, you are referring to the Protectors in the woods. They are the reason you were told not to stray off the paths. Had you ignored that advice, you wouldn't be sitting here now. Their diet is similar to that of the chickens—the only difference being that though they will eat dead food, they much prefer to chase down their prey and kill it themselves."

"So that's why there aren't any typical forest sounds. All the animals, birds and bugs are dead," Alex murmured. "We only saw a few crows since we came here, and one of them wasn't afraid of us at all." Alex was desperate to keep Black talking while her mind ran like a car downhill without brakes to figure a way out of this.

"Precisely. That is why I must feed them regularly. And as to the bird; you met 'Dickens,' a family pet that has lived here for many, many years and is canny enough to remain on the paths when he touches down and thereby avoids the Protectors. The others you saw with him will probably not fare so well."

Alex glanced at Leo. He looked bad. He was trembling violently and sour sweat that had nothing to do with the rapidly climbing temperature of the room poured off him; his shirt was already soaked through, and he had forgotten everything but the fire crackling ten feet in front of him. Alex sighed inwardly. Her poor Leo—and here she sat, unable to help him. It was frustrating to the point of madness, but it was clear that if they were to live through this, it fell to her to come up with an escape plan.

"I have another question," Alex said.

"Ask."

"Why haven't they passed over—the ones downstairs?"

"They didn't complete the work," Black answered simply.

Leo had guessed right. "I've never heard of a contract that was enforceable beyond death."

"With our contracts it isn't that particular clause that commits, but the signature." He saw that Alex wasn't putting it together. "Remember the ink? That lovely purple ink? Theodora does blend it herself. The formula is one tenth blue ink and nine tenths blood of the signer. Dr. Orbon always saves her a dram or two when he does the pre-employment physicals. But you'll like it in the basement—lots of company."

"What about the Mertzes and that outrageous garden?"

"What about them?"

"Did the house do that, too?"

"Certainly. Though you bled heavily in your residence, the

house creates and runs the entire town, so the house itself did receive your offering. You wished for a garden and neighbors. It was vital that you be kept happy so that you would remain until the house grew strong enough to keep you here, though I must admit that the garden was a study in overcompensation. As you have observed for yourself, I imagine, when the house is undernourished the town is run with a skeleton crew, if you will."

"The house heard us?"

"Yes, indeed. The only things its 'senses,' for want of a better word, can't penetrate are things which it did not create."

Now Alex understood why she had to wrap the briefcase in her old sweatshirts.

"So conversations in our truck…"

"Beyond hearing without an open window."

"And the bleeding in our house?"

"Provided energy for the creation of your garden and the Mertzes."

During all this palaver, Leo was waging an internal war to overcome his fear, though it was not evident to look at him. His murder-filled eyes made it clear that his dearest wish was to take Cooper Black apart slowly and with as much suffering as possible.

Black must have noticed it, because he leaned down, not taking his eyes off Alex, and set a piece of kindling aflame. He held it until it burned steadily, then waved it in Leo's face.

"How about a little fire, Scarecrow?" he sneered, co-opting Margaret Hamilton's famous line. Leo pushed back into the sofa as far as he could, but Black still advanced.

Lightning fast, Alex's martial arts training asserted itself and she kicked the burning kindling out of his waving left hand. It flew through the air and landed on the floor next to the heavy drapes, which caught fire almost instantly.

After such a brilliant move, Alex followed it with the rookie mistake of taking her eyes off the enemy to watch the flight of the burning stick; and the last thing she remembered was Black catching her hard across the temple with the butt of his pistol.

Chapter Eighty-Two

Black cleared his throat. "You will please hand me that briefcase." He didn't even seem at all fazed by the fact that the room was on fire.

"What about…"

"Once I slit your wife's throat and pour her blood down the drain, the house will take care of it," he replied dismissively.

Leo regarded Alex with a mixture of horror and deep regret. She needed his help and yet again, he sat immobile. *First I ignore her and she nearly bleeds to death, and I'm doing it again because I'm afraid of fire.* And now it looked as if he was going to die like his parents and siblings had. He and his wonderful Alex were going to burn to death, and it would be his fault.

Leo was about to drop into the abyss of self-pity for the last time in his life—

When…

"Snap the fuck out of it, you goddamned little bastard!" Leo's father's voice screamed in his head. "Ooooooooh, it's a fire! Oooooooh, I'm so scared I'm just about to piss myself! You damned well better grow a pair and take care of your responsibilities! What are you? A man or a goddamned fucking, shit-for-brains pantywaisted crybaby?"

Something inside Leo snapped. Distracted by his fury, he suddenly found strength from a long buried rebellious source. He reached across Alex's unconscious body, seized the worn briefcase, and held it against his chest, a huge paw of a hand on either side of it.

"I'll take that, if you please," Black said, backlit by the fireplace.

"You're good for nothing! You're nobody! Your head is in the clouds! You're a disgusting empty-headed little slime who'll never amount to a hill of beans!" his father bellowed again.

An uncontrollable hate-filled rage welled up in Leo. He roared like the lion he so resembled and fired the briefcase, as hard as he could, right at Cooper Black's chest.

Direct hit.

Black tumbled backward into the fireplace, briefcase and all, and was swallowed by the roaring flames.

He didn't make a sound.

The room was now engulfed, and the question now was, could Leo get them both out in time. He stoked his fury until it burned bright in his heart, fueling it with it memories of the years of beatings and berating he'd taken from his father; and with that as his shield and sword, he set about getting them both out of the inferno the Library had become.

Wide-eyed and panting as if he'd just run a marathon, he shot up from the sofa. If he didn't get moving, it was going to be over for both of them; and if the fire didn't get them, a stray bullet from the gun Black had taken with him probably would once it got hot enough.

Leo reached down and picked Alex up. Then he turned to the Canary wood Library door.

Too late.

The smoke was now too thick to move through and the doorway was in flames.

He had waited too long.

And now they were going to die for it.

Unless...

He carried Alex to the bedroom, kicking the door shut behind him. He put Alex down on the bed, ran over, lifted the red candle, then as the bookcase opened, gathered up Alex again and disappeared into the basement.

When his foot touched the third step, the bookcase panel swung shut behind him, stranding him in total darkness.

Leo moved as fast as he could down the stairs and into the tunnel, talking to Alex all the while, trying to rouse her. So intensely focused were his efforts that he didn't notice the whispering right away.

He put Alex down on the floor, and lightly patted her cheeks. It was then that he heard them… the Friends.

THIS WAY COME NOW a disembodied voice instructed.

Leo gathered Alex up once again, and following the voice, was off.

"Are you Alex's 'Friends?'" Leo asked.

YES WE ARE GRATEFUL TO YOU BOTH YOU HAVE FREED US FROM OUR IMPRISONMENT HERE YES WE WILL SEE YOU TO SAFETY BEFORE WE LEAVE THIS PLACE WE OWE YOU MUCH BUT WE NEED ONE THING MORE

"Name it."

The Friends told Leo what to do and where he could find the tool for it, which he picked up on the way, then continued his mad dash down the tunnel. He followed their directions, and sure enough, after what seemed like an eternity underground, he arrived at the little oubliette with the stairs.

This time, after Leo used the pry bar to lift and discard the iron threshold plate, the Friends accompanied Leo and Alex outside.

SHE IS COURAGEOUS YOUR LADY SHE TOOK ONE SMALL BONE FROM EACH OF OUR PITIFUL SHALLOW GRAVES SHE DID EVERYTHING NECESSARY TO FREE US WITHOUT A SINGLE THOUGHT OF HERSELF THEN YOU FORCED COOPER BLACK TO BURN BONES AND CONTRACTS WITH HIS OWN HAND. OUR ETERNAL GRATITUDE IS YOURS the spokesman Friend said, then added, *IT IS NICE TO BE WARM AGAIN*

Leo smiled. "You're welcome and I wish you a good journey."

BEFORE THE JOURNEY WE MUST KNOW IF SHE IS TO LIVE OR TO DIE IF SHE IS TO DIE WE WILL TAKE HER WITH US IF NOT WE WILL LEAVE WISHING YOU A LIFE LONG AND HAPPY

"She'll be fine, don't worry. She wouldn't want you to wait another minute in this horrible place on her account," Leo assured the apparition.

FAREWELL THEN

"Good-b…" Suddenly, Leo heard voices approaching. He picked Alex up off the ground and scurried behind a dense boxwood hedge.

"This is the second time this had happened in just three decades! I told you she was too damned smart. And now Cooper's dead, and the bitch and her husband have disappeared!" It was Ross Hamilton.

"Cooper is of no use at all to the house. He had a poor diet and anemic blood," Theodora said. "It was fine for car repairs, but the house is more complicated."

Leo peeked out through the leaves. All four of them were standing there at the edge of the graveyard. Leo was glad he'd closed the tunnel cover after him. He looked for the house and was surprised to see that it was about two thousand feet away.

"Well, Ross and Candace, I am sorry to say that the house still requires its meal. Jane and I, as you know, are ineligible, having stepped in once before. It is time for you both to do what you must."

As Leo watched, Ross and Candace Hamilton joined hands and walked to what was left of the burning house. Right in front of the blazing Library, they embraced passionately, then strolled into the fire.

Theodora smiled down at Jane. "I think it's nice that it gets a hot meal now and then, don't you, dear?"

"Yes, Mother," Jane replied, gazing at the rapidly dwindling structure. "The question is, is it going to get it in time?"

𝔆𝔥𝔞𝔭𝔱𝔢𝔯 𝔈𝔦𝔤𝔥𝔱𝔶-𝔗𝔥𝔯𝔢𝔢

Alex was still unconscious. Leo debated about staying hidden where they were until she revived, but then decided against it. If she was out this long, she probably needed a doctor right away.

He peeked through the hedge again. Theodora and her pig of a daughter were gone, so he hoisted Alex and headed for the garage as fast as he could move. He expected, at any minute, to feel a bullet in his back and was surprised when he didn't.

Their first concern is the house. But once they get that under control, God help us.

After what felt like an eternity of walking to Leo's laden arms, he arrived at the garage. The Caddy was unlocked and he laid Alex across the bench seat in the front. The back of the car still made his skin crawl and he wasn't about to put Alex in there alone. Once she was settled and secure, he rounded the hood, and found that Black's pedal extenders were still attached and would block Leo's getting behind the wheel. Not only that, but there were no keys in the ignition.

Okay. Stop. Think. Where would Cooper Black hide the keys?

He checked the more pedestrian spots—the glove box, the visor, under the driver's floor mat.

Nothing.

Leo stepped out of the car. There had to be tools around somewhere. Black would have done the maintenance work on the car right here, wouldn't he?

Sure enough, there was a miniature workbench hidden in the far corner of the garage, covered and invisible until you were right on top of it. Leo grabbed a ratchet set to remove the pedal extenders, as well as a ball peen hammer and a screwdriver and did his best to remember how his Frog Hollow friends had boosted cars growing up in Hartford.

Extenders gone and back behind the wheel, he adjusted the seat, said a quick prayer and knocked the ignition cap off with the ball peen hammer.

"Okay. Now what?"

Whispered instructions were supplied by the protective Friend that had followed them to the garage, staying behind until they were safely away.

Leo turned the screwdriver and the Caddy turned over with a roar. "Thank you, Friend," Leo called.

WE WILL MEET AGAIN BUT UNTIL THAT TIME GODSPEED

"Good-bye," Leo said, eyes glistening. He put the Caddy in gear and sped out of the woods, accompanied by a new worry.

I hope the hell I can find my way home.

He was maneuvering the huge car through all the switchbacks of the wooded trail when he suddenly found himself just above Judson Avenue. But how could that be? If that were true, he would have been able to see the Black House from home. Confused, he drove down their street.

Every single house was on fire.

He put the pedal to the floor and flew to their house. He left Alex in the Caddy while he started up his truck, then he transferred her to the passenger seat and belted her in. Leo evaluated the house and decided that the fire hadn't yet reached the proportion to keep him from rescuing Clara's wonderful vase; but then saw how mistaken he was when he opened the door and stepped onto the porch that ran between the kitchen and the shop.

"Damn! I'll miss that vase. Sorry, Clara," he muttered. The shop was ablaze, as well, and Leo's heart broke at the loss of all his tools and equipment.

As he drove his truck back up the street, he saw the burning Black House at the top of the hill.

We could have walked to work.

His cell phone busily melting back at their house, Leo stopped at the first phone booth outside of Woodhaven that he found and called Earle's emergency number, waking him out of a sound sleep. Ten minutes later, Leo was parked at Munson's office, awaiting the doctor, who arrived soon after. Leo carried his still unconscious wife through the lobby and placed her tenderly on an examining table. Earle took one look at her, and immediately summoned an ambulance. When it arrived and Alex was on board, Leo climbed in as well, after promising Earle he'd call him as soon as he could to let him know what was happening.

***

Alex awoke in a hospital bed. She'd sustained a mild concussion and the ER physician had admitted her overnight for observation.

"Leo?"

"Hi, honey. Glad you're back."

"What happened?"

"Where do you want me to start?"

"From where I got hit in the head. I remember up 'til then."

Leo recapped the end of their employment for her.

"At least we made it out of there alive," Alex sighed.

"That's about all we made it out of there with, I'm afraid," Leo sighed.

"What do you mean?"

"All that cash we were paid is probably ashes by now. I have a grand total of $2,000 of it in my wallet, and that probably won't even cover this hospital bill."

"So we start over, that's all," Alex said.

"Yeah, I guess we do," Leo said, patting her hand. *Start over with* what*? Not only is all the cash gone, but all my tools, too.*

"Did you call Dr. Munson yet?"

"Oh, gee, no I didn't! Better do that now," Leo said, picking up the phone.

The doctor was relieved to hear of Alex's prognosis and, before disconnecting, told Leo that he'd rescued the two sheet-wrapped bundles from the back of his truck in case it rained

515

and that they would be in the office for him.

Puzzled, Leo thanked him and replaced the receiver.

Chapter Eighty-Four

The next morning, Leo and Alex took the bus back to Dr. Munson's office, arriving there just in time to enjoy coffee and doughnuts with him. He was brought up to date on Alex's health and the fact that they were unemployed due to their employers' house burning down, but not much else. Who'd believe it?

"So what will you do now?" Earle asked.

"I think we'll be spending a couple of weeks with a friend of ours in Gloucester, to rest up and regroup," Alex said.

"That sounds like a fine idea. Perhaps you'll be able to give Jack a call while you're up there. I know he was sincere about that dinner he offered you, and he still feels terrible about that stunt we pulled, Alex."

"That's a good idea. We'll be sure to call him."

Earle stood. "That's fine! Oh, and don't forget your parcels." He opened his closet and carefully pulled them out.

"What in the world…" Alex said.

"They were in the back of the truck. Earle brought them in just in case it rained. Thank you for that, Earle," Leo said.

"You're welcome. What are they, if you don't mind an old man's curiosity?"

"I have no idea. Let's open them and find out."

Earle provided a pair of scissors, and Leo cut the twine and unwound the sheet. There was another sheet beneath it, upon which was written, "Thank you." Alex and Leo looked at each other, and when they looked back, the message had vanished.

The second sheet came away and there, spread in front of them, were the seven paintings that Theodora had consigned to the trash bin.

"I think we'll be able to pay that hospital bill now, Leo,"

Alex said.

"I think you'll be able to *buy* that hospital now," Earle said. Before they left, he gave Leo the name and number of an art appraiser he knew of who had a spotless reputation. The doctor also extracted a promise from both of them that he'd have first refusal on the Chagall.

The other bundle held Clara's vase.

Chapter Eighty-Five

After Alex got out of the hospital, the Renfields reconnected with Dr. Jack Henderson, as well as Clara and her new boyfriend she'd met on Yahoo Personals. Nobody was more surprised than Leo to discover that the guy Clara was so crazy about was none other than Manny Viviani. And with good reason—he treated her like a queen.

So here they all were, but not on Jack's dime. This was the Renfields' party, and Earle even drove up to Boston for the get-together. Manny chose a *ristorante* that he knew of in the North End called *Terramia*, touting it as the best Italian food in Boston; so they all met up there.

He wasn't wrong. Alex's *Ravioli Di Fichi Con Maile* was delicious beyond belief, and provided yet another reason to make the relocation move she and Leo were presently considering. It was going to take many visits to try everything on this wonderful menu.

After dinner, they'd adjourned to The Comedy Connection to catch the show. Jack made the reservations and had managed to snag them a ringside table.

"It feels weird to be back here again," Alex said. "I've never seen the place from this point of view before."

They chatted about the state of contemporary comedy until the lights dimmed, then they turned their attention to the stage. The first comic, or "opener" as he's known in the business, entered from the wings, in shadow, to mild applause.

But when the spotlight hit him, the crowd went wild.

It was Burlington, Massachusetts native, Steven Wright. Alex grinned. She loved the upscale comedy clubs for just these surprises with which they favored their audiences occasionally. The Comedy Connection was one of the longest running comedy clubs in the country, operating for more than twenty-five years. Lots of big name comics got their starts in this very club. Most of them didn't forget it, either, and stopped in from time to time when they happened to be in town.

But the surprise didn't end there. Steven looked down and winked at Alex, then turned back to the mike.

"And now, ladies and gentlemen, I'd like to introduce a celebrity in our audience who dropped out of the comedy spotlight a year ago, but is with us here tonight. Let's hear it for Alex Bluestone!"

Alex stood to thunderous applause and cheering. Blinded by the two spotlights shining in her eyes, she squinted, smiled and waved.

Leo watched Jack as he watched Alex. Oh, the man was still enamored, no question, but Leo wasn't worried. He knew that Jack would be content to admire her from afar, as always. Plus, Leo really liked the guy and wanted him for a friend.

"Could we get you to come up onstage and do a few minutes, Alex?" Steven asked.

Alex shook her head.

"Oh, go on Alex," Leo said.

"Yes, please," Jack urged.

Alex shrugged. "Okay, you asked for it," she called, and joined the thin comic with the wild hair to a standing ovation.

Amid the applause, Steven turned to Alex and, in his best Sally Fields, said, "They like me! They really like me!" She laughed until she cried.

While the applause died down, Alex looked at the ringside table and her dear friends—some old, some new—and her wonderful husband, all eager for her to do what she loved— make people laugh.

It was the happiest twenty minutes of her entire life.

Chapter Eighty-Six

"I don't know what the hell we're going to do if things don't pick up pretty soon. I'm gonna have to sell my tools just to keep food in our mouths—then where'll we be?" Thomas Pritchett said to his son. "It's a good thing this place is dirt cheap, or we sure wouldn't be eating much today."

"I know, Dad. But something will turn up, you'll see. It's not like we're not trying to find jobs."

The occupant of the next booth looked around the divider.

"Excuse me; did I hear you say you were looking for work?"

About the Author

Carson Buckingham knew from childhood that she wanted to be a writer, and began, at age six, by writing books of her own, hand-drawing covers, and selling them to any family member who would pay (usually a gum ball) for what she referred to as "classic literature." When she ran out of relatives, she came to the conclusion that there was no real money to be made in self-publishing, so she studied writing and read voraciously for the next eighteen years, while simultaneously collecting enough rejection slips to re-paper her living room... twice.

When her landlord chucked her out for, in his words, "making the apartment into one hell of a downer," she redoubled her efforts and collected four times the rejection slips in half the time, single-handedly causing the first paper shortage in U.S. history.

But she persevered, improved greatly over the years, and here we are.

Carson Buckingham has been a professional proofreader, editor, newspaper reporter, copywriter, technical writer, comedy writer, humorist, and fiction author. Besides writing, she loves to read and work in her vegetable garden. She lives in the United States in the state of Arizona.

www.ingramcontent.com/pod-product-compliance
Lightning Source LLC
Chambersburg PA
CBHW061024030726
47504CB00002B/246